The TWELVE DAYS *of* CHRISTMAS

Written by

SUSAN STOKES-CHAPMAN

A Collection of Short Stories in

TWELVE STAVES

LONDON:

Printed for Harvill:

An imprint of **VINTAGE BOOKS,**

One Embassy Gardens

MM.XXV

HARVILL

1 3 5 7 9 10 8 6 4 2

Harvill, an imprint of Vintage, is part of the
Penguin Random House group of companies

Vintage, Penguin Random House UK, One Embassy Gardens,
8 Viaduct Gardens, London SW11 7BW

penguin.co.uk/vintage
global.penguinrandomhouse.com

Penguin
Random House
UK

First published by Harvill in 2025

Typeset in 11.25/16.5pt Adobe Caslon Pro by Six Red Marbles UK, Thetford, Norfolk
Printed and bound in Great Britain by Clays Ltd, Elcograf S.p.A.

The authorised representative in the EEA is Penguin Random House Ireland,
Morrison Chambers, 32 Nassau Street, Dublin D02 YH68

A CIP catalogue record for this book is available from the British Library

ISBN 9781787304666

Penguin Random House is committed to a sustainable future
for our business, our readers and our planet. This book is made
from Forest Stewardship Council® certified paper.

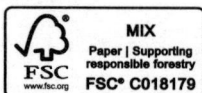

The
TWELVE DAYS
of
CHRISTMAS

Also by Susan Stokes-Chapman

Pandora

The Shadow Key

For Mum

O You merry, merry Souls,
Christmas is a coming,
We shall have flowing Bowls,
Dancing, piping, drumming.

Delicate Mince pies,
To feast every Virgin,
Capon and Goose likewise,
Brawn and a Dish of Sturgeon.

Then for your Christmas Box,
Sweet Plumb Cakes and Money,
Delicate Holland Smocks,
Kisses sweet as Honey.

Hey for the Christmas Ball,
Where we shall be jolly,
Jigging short and tall,
Kate, Dick, Ralph and *Molly.*

Then to the Hop we'll go.
Where we'll jig and caper,
Maidens all-a-row,
Will shall pay the Scraper.

Hodge shall dance with *Prue,*
Keeping Time with Kisses
We'll have a jovial Crew.
Of sweet smirking Misses.

ANON 'DICK MERRYMAN'
Round about our Coal Fire: OR, Christmas
Entertainments (1730)

STAVE I.

Of Fruits & Follies

A PARTRIDGE IN A PEAR TREE

It is typically considered that a tale such as this should end with a wedding rather than begin with one, but at this moment the residents of Merrywake were installed within the garlanded pews of Wakely Church, quiet witnesses to the marriage between the darling of the county of ——shire (and, indeed, of her honourable parents), the eldest Pépin daughter, to one Nicolas Toussaint.

Such a marriage had instilled somewhat mixed feelings in the congregation. That the gentleman was rich could not be disputed, nor the fact the couple appeared to be matched rather admirably in disposition, for Juliette was kind and Nicolas more than passing amiable; so too was the lady considered a veritable beauty and her smiling suitor extremely handsome. To many, these facts alone were enough to soothe any niggling doubts that might have lingered. Who, after all, could deny the happiness present on the young couple's faces as they stood before one another at the candlelit altar? Yet it could also not be denied that Seigneur Nicolas Toussaint was a Frenchman, a matter which roused much mistrust.

Of course, it was widely known the Pépins were of French extraction themselves, but that family had long been settled in Merrywake, where four out of the five daughters were brought into the world, all of them educated in the manner of English customs and so very well too that one scarce remembered to hold their lineage against them. Viscount Pépin himself stated publicly he had no sympathy for 'Little Boney' and his now-thwarted ambitions, and if it had not been for an old childhood injury in his left shoulder the viscount would have willingly fought under Wellington's helm. With no sons to call to military order, the Pépins were far removed from the conflicts which had so long reigned overseas.

Yet not all the residents of Merrywake could boast of such a remove. The twilight days of 1816 saw Wakely Church's pews possessed of vacant seats once belonging to sons and husbands, cousins and nephews, so too fathers and brothers, and though it was Christmas Day and a wedding at that (which should have occasioned utmost joy in the hearts of everyone in attendance), the sight of Toussaint sliding a gold ring onto his pretty wife's finger still felt rather raw to some.

For Miss Frances Partridge – sitting as far back in the

church as propriety would allow considering her position as lady's maid – she gave not one fig her mistress had fallen in love with a Frenchman, beyond what such a circumstance would mean for her future. Frances teased the skirts of her finest wool gown between cold-tipped fingers and kept her head assiduously bent, making sure as she always did not to raise her eyes in the event she might catch a certain someone's gaze. *That* was a hurt long buried, but as the happy couple proceeded down the aisle and Juliette (who understandably only had eyes for her new husband) did not look her way, Frances felt an overwhelming sense of loss.

How different matters would be if she had married. If fate had not so unhappily turned against her all those years before, then she would never have been forced into the position of abigail at all, and now, for her prospects to be once again in question, and so late in life, too ... She pressed the old locket which rested beneath her dress, felt the coolness of silver against the thin skin of her chest. Unbidden, the memory of a stolen kiss impinged upon her mind, and in a moment of uncharacteristic weakness Frances *did* raise her eyes to look to the man who had only moments ago performed the ceremony, but he had already departed the altar. Frustrated with herself for letting the memory thus affect her, Frances stood and followed the congregation outside just in time to see Juliette throw her bouquet of pink spray roses into the air, which fell into the waiting hands of Miss Prudence Brown, causing gasps of unladylike outrage from three of the four remaining Pépin daughters.

The girls pouted at the now giddy housemaid before sliding their eyes balefully to their eldest sister, who simply shook her head at them with affection. Smiling, happy, kind-hearted Juliette – how like her to treat her sisters' foibles in such a manner! It was this generous mark of character Frances would greatly miss. The week before, Juliette had asked if she might be prevailed upon to quit Merrywake and continue on with her as a companion, whereupon Frances might accustom herself to a more 'peaceful' way of living, but the idea of leaving the village in which she had spent her whole life was a most distressing thought, and Frances had declined the offer. Sixty-eight was far too great an age to be gallivanting across Europe. No, she would be better off staying where she was. To stay meant continuing her service to the other girls, and since none of them were yet in possession of marriage prospects of their own, Frances' position was secure for at least some years hence. But oh, what a disagreeable fate!

In truth, Juliette and Charlotte were the only daughters with whom Frances had no trouble – Juliette, due to her gentle nature and Charlotte, because she had no interest in being 'fussed over', much to the distress of the viscountess who had long bemoaned her third child's disregard for ladylike behaviour. But Maria, Louisa and Rosalie . . . Frances disguised her sigh with an over-bright smile as Toussaint helped his bride into the chaise, and raised her hand to wave. Well, those other Pépin girls were most wearisome.

She would not lose Juliette *quite* yet, at least, Frances reminded herself as the vehicle's wheels made their first rumbling turn, set in motion by Toussaint's own prize stallion. The chaise was only to take the couple back to Wakely Hall, for the viscount and viscountess had quite insisted upon their daughter staying with the family until Twelfth Day, whereafter the seigneur and new seigneuresse would finally begin their journey on to Paris.

Paris. A place so very far from dear quiet Merrywake. But the alternative, Frances thought, as Rosalie – crying in a most aggravating fashion for a girl approaching eighteen – was led away by her mother to their waiting carriage, the other Pépins following closely behind . . . perhaps she could yet change her mind.

'Miss Partridge?'

'Oh, Mrs Denby,' Frances said, turning to look into the red-cheeked face of Wakely's cook. 'Such a lovely service, did you not think?'

'Quite charming,' Bess Denby agreed, 'and how like Miss Juliette to think to invite the servants. We were all so happy to be asked.'

The pair looked after the departing chaise, its white ribbons fluttering in the breeze, and Frances forced a smile.

'Indeed, she has no airs or graces. But then, her parents are much the same – they treat us all with just as much civility and kindness as they do everyone.'

At that moment the Pépin carriage trundled by, led by the Wakely coachman and a pair of handsome dappled greys. Though the windows were shut against the creeping cold, the sound of Rosalie's crying could be clearly heard through the glass and Frances and Mrs Denby shared a knowing look.

'Such a singular girl, dear Juliette. So unlike her sisters. You shall miss her dreadfully.'

'And I will worry for her dreadfully, too. To go to Paris, so soon after . . .' Frances shook her head. 'But Seigneur Toussaint tells me the city has been occupied by our English soldiers. No harm will come to her, he rests assured.'

Not one second after the words left her mouth did Mrs Denby's eyes fill, and Frances bit her tongue.

'Forgive me,' she said, softening her voice. 'I had not meant to remind you of . . .'

The cook gave a smile that did not quite hide her pain, but patted her hand.

'I hoped I might beg a small favour of you,' said she as two of the servants' traps departed after the Pépin carriage. Mrs Denby's gaze drifted to another being boarded by some of the lower servants, all of whom were in fervent high spirits, especially Miss Brown who looked pleased as punch with her new rose bouquet.

'Of course,' replied Frances. 'How might I assist?'

The other woman hesitated. 'Well, we have so much to do already back up at the hall. I should ask one of *them* by rights –' and here she gestured to the lowers on the newly boarded trap – 'but being of local stock they've been allowed the afternoon to spend with their families on Christmas Day, and I did not want—'

'Mrs Denby,' Frances interrupted. 'Pray, take breath and try again.'

The cook glanced away to a point beyond Frances' shoulder and back once more.

''Tis just the viscount wishes for some pears to adorn the

garlands for the ball, and it's no secret that Reverend Soppe's orchard boasts the best ones this time of year.'

Something much like a sharp sliver of cold pierced her chest as she understood to where the cook's glance had gone: the small copse of trees behind the church.

'Oh no,' Frances found herself whispering. 'Surely there is *somebody* else you can ask?'

A look of regret crossed Mrs Denby's round face. 'To be sure, there is no one. Mrs Wilson refuses to spare the uppers on such a menial task, and *I* cannot for I've so much to do myself. Venison to prepare, syllabubs to make ... It would delay me even further. Since you have been given the whole day,' Mrs Denby finished, 'I thought you might be willing to assist.'

The sliver slid from the confines of Frances' chest right down into her stomach where it stuck like an icicle.

It would be churlish to refuse Mrs Denby. Frances had, after all, no plans. She had intended to return home by way of a pretty walk along the boundary wall of Wakely Hall (for the countryside was most affecting this time of year when the frost was newly settled on the foliage and glittering like tiny white crystals), then thought to spend the rest of the day reading at leisure within the small apartment set out for her use, blessedly some rooms removed from her tiresome charges. The Pépin girls would have no need of her today, she had been promised so by their mother, who fully understood Frances' preference for solitude this time of year. But of all the days for Mrs Denby to ask of Frances such a deplorable favour!

That woman was waiting patiently for her answer.

'I ...' Frances took a shuddering breath and quenched her pride. 'I shall ask the vicar directly.'

A look of relief crossed Mrs Denby's face.

'You have my gratitude, Miss Partridge, truly you do,' and though Frances had never confided in the cook of her past troubles, servant gossip at the time had undoubtedly acquainted her with at least *some* of the particulars, so it must be assumed her gratitude was genuine. As if to clarify the fact, the cook patted Frances' hand again and smiling said, ''Twill be fine, just you see.'

Frances wanted to counter such a reassuring comment with a doubtful one of her own but the fourth and final servants' trap had descended upon them, and with Mrs Wilson clearly impatient to be gone Frances chose to hold her tongue. Instead, she watched with an acute feeling of foreboding as the housekeeper made room for Mrs Denby on the bench, the trap sprang forwards on its wheels, and the echoing clop of horses' hooves transported the small party down Merrywake's frosted road towards the comforting familiarity of Wakely Hall.

For Witherington Soppe, the Christmas period was a time he considered to be a thoroughly miserable affair. He had not always found it so – as a youth (when he would gallivant about his ancestral home of Heysten Park without a care in the world), he rather enjoyed the pleasantries of the season and looked forward to it with keen optimism – but age and experience had garnered in him a sense of acute melancholy and aggravation that seemed to worsen year upon year, a most inconvenient state of mind for a vicar.

Was it not his *duty* to always keep his spirits cheerful, especially at this holiest of holy times? Did the Bible not say that a merry heart maketh a cheerful countenance? But alas, Witherington's heart was not merry, and had not been so these past fifty years.

Christmas Day was especially difficult. It was an unpleasant reminder of all he had lost, and to perform a wedding on that day as well was a particularly heavy blow. Still, Witherington thought, as he removed his vestments, the worst was over, and it relieved him greatly to escape as quickly as his old legs would carry him through the orchard and push the heavy door of the parsonage tightly closed, shutting out the crisp December chill.

His home was everything Witherington purported to be – dignified, neat, tidy – and though a trifle larger than he found entirely comfortable for a widowed gentleman of two-and-seventy, well, there was not much help for it. The parsonage had once belonged to a vicar who had, unlike himself and Eliza, been blessed with a family and made great use of its many rooms, rooms which Witherington decided some years ago to shut off. What need had he for a dining room when he barely received guests? What use for three bedrooms and two sitting rooms, when one of each would serve perfectly well? And with Mrs Jenkins to administer to the kitchen and other chambers necessary to domestic habituality, he had no need to venture forth into any one of them. The library was the only room in the parsonage that he put to good use, and it was there Witherington found himself heading, with every intention of seating himself by the fire with a treatise on how to cultivate winter roses until that lady brought him his supper tray.

It was a sizeable library, each shelf carefully organised by subject – *A Treatise Concerning Religious Affections* and *Olney Hymns* were nestled amongst other texts such as *The Parables of Our Lord and Saviour Jesus Christ*, Baskerville's *Book of Common Prayer*, and the *King James Bible* (from which he composed his sermons), where further shelves kept a far wider collection of titles pertaining to horticulture. Of course, one might become thoroughly sick of reading after a while, and when such an occasion occurred Witherington could be found putting his knowledge to the test by tending his garden and orchard, tasks to which he lost many an hour. It was often said that gardening was good for the soul, a perfect remedy for disappointment and loneliness; certainly, the task of pruning rose bushes and eradicating weeds from his turnip patch afforded him a feeling as near to pleasure as it were possible for him to muster. And when *that* feeling had dissipated, he would take himself off for a long walk with his sketchbook and endeavour to document the local flora and fauna of Merrywake, though always in the opposite direction to Wakely Hall.

Today, however, was not one of those days. Today, he would read. Mrs Jenkins had already lit the fire, setting the library most charmingly in warming shades to make up for the lack of morning sun streaming through the west-facing windows, and the sight of it gave him cause to endeavour a rare smile. Crossing the worn Persian rug, Witherington came to stand before one of the bookshelves; his prized copy of James Clarke's *A Cata-logue* was pushed aside in favour of a set of papers resting next to it and then, with something like a contented sigh, Wither-ington donned his spectacles and settled down in the armchair with *A Treatise on the Venereal Rose,* keen to spend the next few hours absorbed within its fascinating pages. Thus, too, he would have done, were it not for the jangle of the front doorbell which sounded that very instant.

Witherington lowered the treatise. Mrs Jenkins was not a live-in housekeeper – she came twice a day to ensure the typical domestic duties were carried out and that the vicar was well fed. Beyond this, he was very much left to his own devices and there-fore required to answer his own front door.

How aggravating! Who would think to call on him on Christmas Day, when it was supposed the people of Merry-wake would be happily ensconced in their own residences? Why bother the Reverend Soppe just at the point at which he was to distract himself from his unwanted memories? And it must be said that the last person Witherington expected to find on the other side of the door was the very subject of those memories herself.

'Good morning, vicar,' said the lady standing stoutly on the other side of the door, and it took Witherington one breathless moment to respond.

'Miss Partridge. How do you do.'

Neither spoke further, but each watched the other warily. Frances, who had taken such great pains these past years to never look at the man beyond a fleeting moment when circumstance necessitated it, perceived in him a great change up close – he was still uncommonly tall, but what had once been a lithe figure now appeared over-thin; his cheeks were hollowed, his skin pale, and though Reverend Soppe did not look ill per se, he had lost the gangly puppy-dog look of the young and exuberant man she remembered. In fact, the exuberance which Frances once took such delight in appeared to be all but vanished; the vicar of Merrywake's expression was as grey as his thinning hair.

Witherington, too, found Miss Partridge vastly changed, but in this he felt no great shock – he had often perceived the lady when she attended church, marked with something akin to regret (though he should never admit to such a thing) that she always chose to sit herself in one of the middle pews rather than in the permitted benches close to the Pépin brood. Still, she had never sat far enough away to prevent his marking that she had, in contrast to himself, developed over the years a fuller figure than the one she possessed at eighteen, and a decided roundness to her face. Only now that she was but an arm's length away from him could Witherington see her still-pretty curls were peppered silver, and when she addressed him so coldly as 'vicar' just then, that Miss Partridge had at some point acquired a tiny chip in one of her front teeth.

'Vicar,' said Frances again, hoping her nervousness did not betray itself in the wobble of her voice. 'Forgive my intrusion on such a day, but I come on an errand.'

'An errand?'

The reply was sharp, hostile, and in that moment her regret

at agreeing to the cook's request was profound. Still, he had no right, no right whatsoever, to speak to her in such a derogatory tone, not when it was *he* who had jilted *her*, and so Frances squared her shoulders and gave the best expression of scorned affront she could muster.

'On behalf of Mrs Denby. She has asked if you would be willing to spare some of your pears.'

'My pears.'

It was not a question. As the words left his mouth the reverend had raised a finger to his face, pulled a pair of wire-rimmed spectacles half an inch down the line of his crooked nose and peered at Frances over them. She spared the fleeting and frustratingly maudlin thought that Witherington never used to wear spectacles, before raising her chin in defiance.

'Of course, vicar, I would not have come myself except that Mrs Denby was required back at the hall and had no one else to spare to call on you.'

Silence. A muscle twitched in his sinewy jaw. Frances drew herself taller.

'They are for the viscount,' she said in tones most biting. 'He has expressed an ardent wish to use the pears in his festive decorations. I am sure you could spare *some* for his lordship?'

At the mention of that man the reverend's face softened, and so it should for Viscount Pépin was a gentleman Witherington held in highest esteem. Was it not Viscount Pépin who – being such a kind soul – secured the living at Merrywake for him and, later, offered succour when Witherington's son came early, without passing breath? Was it not Viscount Pépin who, later still, dealt with the unfortunate particulars of Eliza's death and engaged the services of Mrs Jenkins so to ensure he would be well taken care of in his old age?

And so it was that Witherington found himself grunting and nodding his head.

'I suppose I can spare a few.' He jerked his head in the vague direction of the orchard just beyond the parsonage's garden gate. 'Help yourself to them.'

Frances opened her mouth to thank him, when all of a sudden she had a mortifying thought.

'Oh dear.'

The reverend threw her a look that raised his thinning eyebrows upward on his wrinkled brow.

'What is it?'

'Mrs Denby . . .' Frances felt herself colour and was thankful she wore a high collar. 'She did not provide a basket with which to collect them. I don't suppose . . .'

The vicar's lined face shuttered. With another grunt he bade her wait and turned, disappearing back into the dim confines of the parsonage. Frances watched him go with a bite of her lip and wondered if he celebrated Christmas at all for no foliage hung within, no candles warmed that darkened hallway. Was he lonely, without Eliza Granville to keep him company, the woman who so long ago had been her friend, and the means of destroying all her prior hopes?

Presently Witherington returned, a wicker basket in his hand.

'Here,' he said, proffering it to her at arm's length. It held within it snatches of dust and small pieces of worn leather that looked to be flakings from book spines.

He always had liked his books.

'That should serve.' The vicar hesitated, moved awkwardly from foot to foot. 'There's a ladder near the woodshed.' He looked her up and down then, and Frances was conscious how dowdy she was, how short and squat. 'You'll be needing it, I should think.'

And with that Reverend Witherington Soppe shut the door quite firmly in Miss Frances Partridge's affronted face.

Insufferable conceit! Unless he had forgotten (and Frances was sure he had not), Witherington knew perfectly well how much her height bothered her, and to say such a thing without allowing any opportunity to offer up a rejoinder was most infuriating. She had not even the satisfaction of thanking him to shew she was better mannered. For, really, at their ripe age, neither one had a right to be so childish, no matter how much hurt had passed between them.

With a huff Frances stomped round the back of the parsonage where the woodshed nestled between the privy and a lopsided gate which opened out onto the fields south of Wakely Hall. Here was where the vicar walked sometimes – Frances had occasioned to see him (mercifully unobserved) striding long-legged across the pastures that made up Old Mr Hodge's farmland, making, no doubt, for Wakely Forest. How often had they trysted between those towering poplars, so sure of themselves and each other before all had come to ruin? Well, Frances thought as she hefted the icy-runged ladder under one arm and returned the way she had come, clearly the vicar was not tortured by such memories for if he were he would not have spoken to her in so unfeeling a manner.

Frances plodded across the grass, the heels of her leather boots tapping hard upon the hoarfrost. The ladder was bulky; the wicker basket swung against the cold wood with an oddly hollow *smack* and she was perceivably out of breath by the time she returned to the orchard, whereupon she stared consideringly up at the trees.

It took some minutes for Frances to settle on which to divest of their fruit. Mrs Denby did not state how many pears Viscount Pépin required, but by Frances' calculations the garlands he wished decorated would be located within the ballroom, dining room and drawing room, the grand staircase too, of course ... surely no more than three pears per garland were needed, and no more than two garlands per room. That meant she might deprive six of Reverend Soppe's trees evenly whilst still leaving some for his own enjoyment.

Not, Frances sniffed, that he deserved it.

Settling the basket beneath the first pear tree, she propped the ladder against the trunk. It did not occur to Frances in that moment that this was foolhardy of her, that the ladder might slip or that the rungs themselves would be slippery beneath the soles of her boots. Up she went, wicker basket hanging from the crook of one arm, and began to pick the pears from their branches.

Oh, but it was difficult to proportion her weight correctly whilst the basket hung from the crook of her elbow and she reached for each pear one-handed! More than once the ladder wobbled precariously, and despite the cold Frances soon found herself perspiring. It might, perhaps, have made the task easier if she had left the basket on the ground and thrown the pears down into it, but this would serve only to damage them and what good would they be then? The viscount would not wish for spoilt fruit upon his garlands, and so Frances persevered; terribly slowly and with the greatest of care.

Straight-backed, Witherington watched all this from the sitting room he had not shut off from the rest of the parsonage. It was the only one of the two that faced the orchard, and he often – during the balmy months of summer – sat by the open window and admired the lush canopy of leaves his fruit trees afforded, listened calmly to the rustle of them when a sweet-smelling breeze chanced to pass through their branches. He enjoyed too the way the sunlight dappled between those glossy leaves, like joyful dancing lights . . . but his pear trees held no foliage in December. The pears Witherington grew were a winter variety of French origin (a gift from the ever-generous Monsieur de Fortgibu) and he liked them for their sweet, melting flavour. He liked too the look of them – their green skin was often touched with a very appetising ruby red, made all the more obvious against the dull leafless branches. And without those leaves, the stark winter sunshine shone unobstructed. Witherington could see from Miss Partridge's profile that she was squinting as she reached up to pluck another pear from its stem.

He shifted at the window. The woman had succeeded in divesting four trees of his prized pears. Why did she not take from just one and have the matter done with? Why make things so difficult for herself? Well, Witherington thought with a grim expression on his face, Frances had always been stubborn. Once a thought entered her head, there was as much chance of her changing her mind about it as a hound would loose its fatal grip on a fox's neck. Oh, but whatever was she doing *now*? At this rate she would lose her footing and fall. Of all the ninny-hammered things to do. Did she not see it was too high?

And so it was in that moment that Frances had committed herself to plucking from a tall and lofty branch one particularly handsome-looking pear. So large, so stout, so lushly green and rosy! Would it not look perfect in the ballroom, crowning a garland on the mantle? But alas, the sun was in her eyes, she was too short, could not *quite* find purchase, and her foot was beginning to slip . . .

'Miss Partridge!'

Too late. The ladder wobbled precariously on the hoarfrost and with a curious skip in her stomach Frances felt herself fall. Crying out, she reached for one of the lower branches of the tree as the ladder clattered to the ground and the wicker basket swung against the trunk, causing her to release it from her grasp. There came below a rather loud *oomph* accompanied by that oddly hollow *smack* and Frances – hanging from the branch with both hands, little booted feet kicking nothing but air – found strength enough to twist her head in the direction whence she heard the sounds.

Below, staring up at her with narrowed eyes, was none other than Witherington Soppe himself, the basket of pears in his arms.

'What a fool you are,' he exclaimed. 'Do you have no sense at all?'

'Well, I declare!' Frances managed, directing her attention now to the branch from which she desperately dangled. 'Would you really prefer to scold me instead of offering your assistance?'

'If you had not acted so foolhardily you would not have need of it.'

Frances gritted her teeth, gripped the tree branch a little harder. *Intolerable man.*

'If you please, Mr Soppe! Now is not the moment to be indelicate. I require your help – I fear I cannot hold on much longer.'

To this there came no answer. Instead, Frances heard him place the wicker basket on the ground, the clatter of the ladder being set upright.

'There,' said he. 'To your left. Can you . . .?'

She twisted to see. The ladder was close – all she need do was swing. But Frances Partridge was not a lithe creature; the very act of it would be most inelegant. Swing she did, however, her limbs all ascrabble, and soon succeeded in bringing the toe of her foot to a frosty rung.

'Almost there,' Witherington murmured, and by heaven was that a *laugh* she heard in his voice? And *then* – making her quite jump for the shock of it – she felt a hand at her waist, steadying her.

'Oh!' she gasped, clutching the ladder tight. 'Mr Soppe, if you please . . .'

Frances had no notion what it was she was pleading for, but the hand he had placed on her waist was instantly removed, and the lady felt some small flutter of regret.

Compose yourself, she thought as she at last found her way to the safety of terra firma and turned, blushing, to face her rescuer. He stood now at an appropriate distance, no trace of humour in his countenance at all.

'Thank you,' said Frances, for there really was nothing else to say, and in reply the vicar cleared his throat.

'You are welcome.'

By the tone of his voice, it did not much sound to Frances that he meant it, and feeling most slighted she pointedly wiped her hands on her dirt-scuffed coat and sniffed.

'A gentleman might have offered to hold the ladder for me in the first place instead of simply telling me where it was and letting me struggle by myself.'

Mr Soppe's eyes narrowed. He had since removed his spectacles, and now that the glass no longer obscured his eyes Frances was reminded how, once, they shone with pleasure when he looked on her, rather than with annoyance as they did now.

In truth, Witherington was not annoyed. That is not to say he did not feel some semblance of the emotion, having had his day disturbed in such a manner, but no, he felt unaccountably moved. How his heart had jumped when he saw Miss Partridge begin to flounder! How he had run as fast as his old legs could carry him, in fear she would be harmed! And how guilty he felt about all of it, for the lady was quite right. A gentleman – no indeed, a man of God – *would* have offered his assistance from the start, but the moment he looked upon that beloved face all his wounded pride reared its ugly head, the hurt from long ago as fresh then as it had been fifty years afore. Yet despite all this, and the relief he felt upon seeing Miss Partridge safely aground, Witherington could not bring himself to apologise. Instead, he said in tones most grudging:

'I will assist you now, if you still require it.'

It took all of Frances' will not to shew her surprise, or her gratitude, for it must be said she had been rather frightened up in that tree.

'Why thank you, vicar. I'd be much obliged.'

Mr Soppe's face soured, but he turned to the basket (which rested now beside the tree trunk) willingly enough.

'How many more do you require?'

'Just four. Three from that tree over there, and . . .'

She trailed off, looking at the lovely big pear that had cost her the loss of her dignity. Reverend Soppe followed her gaze.

'Oh, very well,' he said. 'Allow me.'

Frances held the ladder for him as he – with rather more vigour than might be expected for a man of his advancing years – climbed up and plucked down the pear with ease, and when he handed it to her their fingertips brushed together for the barest of moments. Her breath caught, she turned away, and gestured to the sixth and final tree.

'That one, now, vicar.'

She did not think she said these words in a manner he might

construe in a bad light, yet Witherington Soppe turned on her then with such venom that Frances took a step back in shock.

'Oh, for pity's sake,' he snapped, blue eyes ablaze with an emotion she could not name. 'Stop calling me "vicar"!'

Frances blinked at him rather owlishly.

'But you *are* a vicar. How else might I address you?'

Witherington shook his head, that old hurt overpowering his guilt.

'Come now, do you not think I hear your scorn? It positively drips from you. Good morning, vicar. Of course, vicar. Why thank you, *vicar*! I know how much you *despise* addressing me as such, when once you might have called me "my lord".'

Miss Partridge stared. 'Whatever do you mean?'

'Oh, do not pretend with me,' he returned, quite unable to keep the anger from his voice. 'I know you, Fan, know you better than you realise. I always have.'

At the sound of her old pet name Miss Partridge drew herself up.

'Upon my soul I do *not* pretend, nor do you know me at all if you can speak such nonsense.'

Witherington shook his head. How easily those long years disappeared in the face of wounds which had never truly healed.

'Do you dare stand in front of me and declare yourself ignorant?'

To this the lady raised herself further, as tall as she might hope to achieve considering her squat stature, and Witherington would have laughed at how sweet she looked if his temper had not been so ripe.

'Ignorant?' she was exclaiming, an indignant flush pinking her delightfully round cheeks. He watched her clutch the pear he had just retrieved between her fingers, and the fleeting thought occurred that if she were to grip it any harder it would bruise.

'Ignorant, yes,' he exclaimed in return. 'Perhaps over time your conscience has found a way to justify your betrayal, but I cannot fathom how such cruelty could be dismissed so readily.'

Witherington felt his heart hammering in his chest, the bitter relief of finally expressing the words he could not bring himself to utter all those years ago no real relief at all. In the silence that followed he expected Miss Partridge to turn away from him with a curt dismissal, to abandon him as she had before, but instead she stared with an expression of deep shock on her face; to his disbelief her breath hitched and her soft brown eyes filled with tears.

'My,' Miss Partridge whispered, 'you have a nerve to speak of betrayal and cruelty when you yourself have such mastery of them.'

He did not expect that. His forehead furrowed.

'Madam?'

Miss Partridge took a step forwards so that they were mere inches apart. Witherington smelt the distracting fragrance of lavender upon her spencer.

'I should have known,' she said bitterly. 'Like father, like son, all Heystens are the same, and I scold myself daily for not having realised it sooner.'

Whatever Witherington had expected her to say, it was not this.

'What on earth do you mean?' he exclaimed.

'Oh,' she cried, turning her face. 'You, now, pretend ignorance!'

'But I do. I cannot—'

'I saw you,' Frances declared. 'You and Eliza, kissing under the poplars fifty Christmases ago, in the very place you asked for *my* hand!' She took a shuddering breath at the memory. 'How could you? How could she? You both betrayed me, and I cannot forgive it.'

Nor could she forget it. Eliza Granville, the girl who she thought to be her friend, had stolen the man she loved. What a fool Frances had been, to confide in her. But she had been young and so very sure of Witherington that she felt no qualms at telling her friend of their plans to marry. It did not occur to Frances that Eliza might have been jealous. She thought her fellow maid would be happy for her. How very wrong Frances had been.

As Frances tortured herself with the memory, Mr Soppe set his jaw.

'A pretty tale,' said he, 'but you had already chosen to end our engagement when you discovered my father had disinherited me.'

Frances stared. 'I beg your pardon?'

'You may beg!' Mr Soppe cried. 'Just like I begged my father to understand that your lack of fortune had no bearing on my love. But it seems money meant more to you than I did, given that when you found out he had cut me off you felt it in your heart to do the same.'

Now, Frances could scarce take breath.

'How can you *say* such a thing?'

'Because it is the truth. You never loved me, Frances. It was all a lie.'

'Was it?'

With a little sob Frances pulled at her neck with her free hand (for the other still clutched the pear), tugged the lace of her collar down to expose the chain there and began to wrench it from the confines of her stays. Mr Soppe watched her in confusion until she brought forth a silver locket engraved with filigree swirls.

'If I never loved you, why should I keep this, all these years?'

She heard his breath catch. He stepped forwards, took the little oval in his hands and opened it – within one side there nestled a lock of dark blonde hair, within the other a small portrait of a man, the very mirror of the one who looked down upon it, if not for the passing of five decades. All three he had given her, and she had treasured them, always.

'I do not understand,' he whispered. 'Why keep this, when . . .'

Frances shook her head. 'I kept it because I loved you. I always loved you, even though you betrayed me so cruelly. I swear, I did not know about your disinheritance until Viscount Pépin announced the living which allowed you and Eliza to marry.'

There was silence as he took this in. A sharp breeze cut around the orchard but neither one of them appeared to feel it, wrapt up as they were in their own confused memories.

'I did not betray you,' the reverend said. 'At least . . . not in the way that you think.' He sighed, raised his gaze to hers. 'Eliza came upon me in the forest. I was waiting for you as I did every week, but you had not come.'

'I'd been waylaid!' cried Frances. 'The previous night the viscountess, she . . . she had fallen ill, and I was needed. I begged Eliza to tell you, that I would come as fast as I could, but when I arrived there you both were, in each other's arms. I could not bear it. I ran back to Wakely. I wanted to be as far from you as possible.'

It was Mr Soppe's turn to stare.

'I thought you already knew of the disinheritance.'

'*How?*'

'I do not know. I do not know! You had not come, Eliza said you had changed your mind, and I assumed the worst.' An expression of pain crossed his face. 'Pity me, Fan. I was distraught at the thought of losing you, and when Eliza offered comfort . . . It was a foolish kiss, a moment of madness, that was all. But I did not expect her to go to *her* father, nor for him to demand a marriage between us. She claimed more happened than it actually did, and he threatened to tell the whole village. It was a matter of honour. I had no choice.' He shook his head. 'What a shock it was to all of them, when they realised no money would come from the union. How angry was Eliza, what further injury, to find she must take the less fashionable name of my mother. Believe me, Fan, our years together were not happy.' Witherington shook his head. 'I have been in misery since the moment we wed, and all the years after.'

With shaking hands Miss Partridge took the locket from his

fingers and closed the clasp, tucked it once more down the collar of her dress.

'How was I to know you had not already intended her as your bride?' she whispered. 'You did not even write, did not explain.'

'I could not,' Witherington said. 'I was so hurt, so angry.' He frowned. 'You could have written to me too, you know.'

'I could not,' Miss Partridge whispered, 'for the very same reasons. But I never stopped loving you, Withers, never.'

'Nor I you.'

She sucked in her breath, dared to meet his searching gaze. 'Really?'

Witherington smiled then, a true smile that brightened his grey features and made him once more look young.

'You have aged, Frances, but your eyes are as beautiful as I ever found them. Like chestnuts, they are, I always thought it.'

Those eyes filled with tears. Witherington gently took her round face between his hands.

'Fan, my own darling Fan. You *will* marry me now, won't you?'

'Oh, Withers,' Frances said on a choke of laughter, finally daring to believe her good fortune. 'What complete and utter fools we have been. All these wasted years!'

'Then let us waste no more of them,' the reverend replied, his usually subdued voice tumultuous, but quite powerless to stop it from being so he gathered her in his arms and held her tight, the stout and rosy pear pressed firmly between them.

STAVE II.

The Christmas Box
Two Turtle Doves

'S'not fair.'

'Fair?'

'Fair!' repeated Lowdie Lucas, who hissed the word from between her teeth, but not so quietly that the other servants could not hear her. ''Tis not one bit fair at all that we should be working our fingers to the bone when the little misses upstairs have Christmastime off.'

'Off from what?' came her companion's rejoinder in tones proportionate to wry amusement. 'Sewing? Idle chitter chatter? Playing the pianoforte monstrously ill?'

'Exactly!'

Katherine Allen lowered the gravy pan she was scouring, and

levelled the girl next to her with a look that Lowdie (had she been paying attention), would have studiously ignored.

'And what would you be doing otherwise?' said Katherine. 'You would be bored witless without your chores. It's not as if there is much to entertain the likes of us around here anyway, not with our families so far distant. We can hardly traipse about the countryside all day in the cold and there's nothing to do upstairs in our room, is there, beyond darning our linen.'

This perfectly reasonable point did not seem to have an effect on Lowdie. The girl merely sniffed, and applied herself with half-hearted enthusiasm to the soiled breakfast plates in the Belfast sink.

'I should be happy enough sleeping for the next two weeks,' Lowdie countered. 'No getting up at dawn, no fires to light or benches to scrub.' In a defiant manner she jutted her dimpled chin in the direction of Mrs Denby, who at that precise moment was preparing a goose for that evening's dinner, its downy white feathers fluttering in the air like errant snowflakes. 'No listening to *her* bark out orders. Right bee in her bonnet, that one,' Lowdie muttered. 'She's getting as grumpy as Old Hag Mulligrub.'

Katherine attempted to hide a smile but duly failed. Mrs Wilson – the recipient of such an uncharitable nickname – was not in earshot (upstairs, she supposed, giving one of the uppers an earful on account of some imagined indiscretion). Still, it was not fair to Mrs Denby for her to smile so, and therefore Katherine wiped it clean from her face, transforming it instead to a mildly scolding downward turn of the mouth.

'Be kind,' Katherine said, lowering her voice. 'You know perfectly well why she is in bad spirits.'

Lowdie pulled a face.

'But it is Christmas.'

'Precisely.'

'But, Kate—'

'Lowdie, hush. Consider your own words – it *is* Christmas, and it does you no good to be peevish. This is the natural order of things. We have it far better here than most others in service.'

'*Hmph!*' came the uncharitable reply, but no word further was declared, and so Katherine resumed her scouring.

The pair fell into silence, though it could not be said to be a companionable one. Lowdie had been working for the Pépin household just shy of a twelvemonth, but had struggled in that time to form any meaningful attachments to her fellow servants. It was in Katherine that the younger maid confided (or, rather, complained) for they shared a bedroom, but if truth were to be told Katherine – like the others – found Lowdie Lucas rather trying. She glanced at her; the scullery maid had upon her round face a rather comical look of deep vexation as she attempted to prise a globule of dried scrambled egg off a pretty china plate of periwinkle pattern, becoming increasingly ham-handed as the seconds drew on, and Katherine grimaced. The periwinkle service was a favourite of the viscountess, and she would be very upset if there was yet another casualty. Lowdie had broken one of the bowls from its set not two months before, and been scolded something terrible by Mrs Wilson . . . but it seemed the girl did not care. Indeed, much of what the housekeeper said to Lowdie (in fact, what *most* people said to her) went in one ear and out the other.

Lowdie grunted as the egg scrap detached itself from the porcelain. Katherine let out a relieved sigh.

Unfortunately, that was the way of it with Lowdie – always the first to complain, always the first to make trouble, never caring what she did or said to upset a person. In Katherine's opinion Mrs Wilson had the right view of her: churlish and ungrateful were the words she used in one of her more rigorous scoldings. The only reason Lowdie had not been dismissed was because her work was adequate, and (more notably), Viscountess Pépin would not hear of it, though heaven (and the lady herself, of course) only knew why.

Lowdie placed now the plate on the rack, and sank her arms back into the soap suds to wash another, a grumble upon her chapped lips.

Churlish. Ungrateful. One might not have thought such disobliging things of a girl in possession of such a lovely name – Lowdie (so she proudly told Katherine the first evening she arrived at Wakely Hall) was a pet form of Loveday, and Katherine had thought it so unusual, so singularly pretty. Alas, the moniker did not suit the girl at all; 'Loveday' matched her neither in looks nor in character, for Lowdie was a plain little thing with a habit of sulking over the silliest consequence.

Such as not having Christmastime off.

Katherine wiped the gravy pan clean of excess sand and

ground oyster shells, and picked up another, wiping her perspiring forehead with the sleeve of her elbow as she did, then set to work once more.

There was something to be said for Lowdie's chagrin – Christmas at the Pépin household was always so fearfully tiring. Every year the hall became home to guests as early as the Feast of St Nicholas, with many staying on until Twelfth Day, and so with one full month of entertaining to be had the servants at Wakely Hall were hard-pressed to find a moment alone to themselves, for there were almost triple the number of sheets to launder and chamber pots to empty . . . and, of course, a continuous tower of plates to clean and pots to scour. By rights – as kitchen maid – Katherine should not have been helping Lowdie at all, but with so much to do and not enough time to do it in, there was simply no help for it.

Katherine glanced again at Mrs Denby, absently pressing the hard grit beneath her fingernails. No one, it seemed, worked as tirelessly as she did. So many dishes to prepare, with only Katherine to assist her, nor would the cook hear of Mrs Wilson hiring in more help. *Absolutely not!* said she vehemently when the notion had been broached earlier that month; no one but she could be trusted to broil a haddock or roast a potato or steam a plum pudding. And to be perfectly fair to the woman, her dishes were never anything less than complete perfection. Mrs Denby was always kind enough to ensure the servants were served a sumptuous feast in keeping with their stations, and there were *always* leftovers to be had, no matter how many guests there might be in attendance at the hall.

Still. Mrs Denby *had* been barking out orders in tones decidedly unlike her usually cheerful chatter, and Katherine knew that it could not be accounted for simply by the taxing busyness of the season. The cook was slathering the now featherless waterfowl with butter, its pink-pimpled skin slick and glistening in the candlelight, but she was almost *violent* in her ministrations, causing Katherine to frown. Did Mrs Denby think particularly of her missing son in that moment? Or was she simply applying more effort to the task as a means to distract herself from thinking about him at all?

It was difficult *not* to think of Phillip Denby at this time of year. Katherine remembered him to be a shy, quiet boy, always so happy (or so they all thought) playing his tin whistle by the fire. Even Mrs Wilson had doted on him, she who doted on no one. What a shock it had been when, at barely sixteen, Phillip chose to take the king's shilling. He had already spent five Christmases away from Merrywake, and then, two years ago . . .

Well, there could be no further thought to be spared on the matter, for next to Katherine there was an almighty clatter, a sharp intake of breath. All of a sudden a rush of soapy water sloshed over the sink, drenching Lowdie's apron and Katherine's pattens with suds, turning the flagstone floor into a rather large and filthy puddle.

'Oh, lawds!' Lowdie spat, looking down at her soiled garments as if they themselves were at fault.

'What happened?' cried Katherine, shaking her feet in an effort to rid herself of drips. 'Not another periwinkle?'

In answer Lowdie sucked her finger, where blood had

bloomed at its tip and was running down to her knuckle in a single crimson thread.

'There was a chip,' she said meekly, and it should be noted that Lowdie Lucas had never been heard to speak in so meek a manner before. 'I did not *mean* to drop it.'

'Is it broken?'

Both maids spun about as fast as a wink. Lowdie's heart dropped to the pit of her stomach, for there she was, Old Hag Mulligrub herself, standing hard as brass with those bony arms of hers folded tight across her chest.

Mrs Wilson was a rather terrifying creature. Ask any of Wakely Hall's servants and they would affirm that the housekeeper was a woman of most stern and unsympathetic nature with a tongue as sharp as knives, a tongue which she turned on Lowdie with as much force as a redcoat at arms.

'I hope for your sake that it is *not* broken, as the value of it shall be docked from your pay.'

The housekeeper stepped forwards then in a manner greatly intimidating. Lowdie tried not to flinch, sticking fast as tar to Katherine who stood equally still at her side.

'Such a plate would cost at least six months of your salary, I am quite certain.'

Six months?

Well! This seemed hardly fair, to be punished so severely for a mere accident. It was not *she* who caused the chip in the porcelain that cut her finger and caused her to drop the plate. Lowdie would bet her finest mobcap on the culprit being none other than Miss Louisa who was considered to be the clumsiest chit in all of

Merrywake. Such a truth was common knowledge – did not the second to youngest Pépin daughter spill her soup all down the front of Lord Heysten's waistcoat on Thursday last? She should know, too; it was Lowdie who was tasked to clean said waistcoat, and no amount of white vinegar would serve to rescue it.

Such were Lowdie's thoughts at that particular moment, and so her prior meekness dissipated (the pain which caused it being presently discounted in favour of embracing her ire), and ignoring the growing clutch of Wakely Hall's servants which had begun to form behind the housekeeper she drew herself up as tall as she might be prevailed upon to manage.

'You would dock me six months' pay, all for a piece of flimsy china?'

Mrs Wilson blinked. Her pockmarked face shone.

'You would be best served to mind that tongue of yours, my girl,' came the answer, smooth as cream. 'Your last mistress might have suffered it but here at Wakely things are done differently.'

'So they must be, if maids are punished for dropping plates. 'Tis not as if her ladyship can't afford another to replace it.'

Katherine sucked in her breath. Such mode of talking would surely lose Lowdie her place. At the very least such impudence should be punished with a cuff of the ear, but the housekeeper stood unmoving. Still, if Lowdie were not afraid of Mrs Wilson Katherine *was*, and so too the rest of the servants – Prudence Brown was positively cowering behind Ralph Hornby, and even her dear Nash (usually such a strong-willed man) was wincing into his neckcloth.

'Well, Miss Lucas,' was, finally, the icy response. 'You are to go now up to your room. For your insolent tongue you shall receive no dinner or supper, and as for the plate . . . I shall speak to the viscountess and make the point, once again, how unsuitable you are to hold a position in this household.'

The implication was clear – immediate dismissal – and the breath Katherine sucked in had stoppered her throat. Please, she thought of the girl standing stiff-backed next to her, please do not make this worse for yourself, and to her relief Lowdie did not, though her face had turned a rather unsavoury colour of puce. Instead she tugged at her wet apron and, having untied the strings, proceeded to throw it on the floor (oh, Katherine *tsked* inwardly, right in the puddle!), then stomped from the scullery, pushing past the servants hovering in the kitchen with her snub nose upturned.

The silence that followed was loud enough to break glass. Katherine swallowed, shifted wetly in her pattens, and seeing the way her feet sloshed in the puddle Mrs Wilson raised one thinning eyebrow.

'Get that cleaned up,' she snapped. 'You are a bad influence on that girl, Miss Allen, for you allow her too much leave to let her mouth run.' Mrs Wilson paused then, gave her a brusque look up and down, narrowed her eyes at the grit that still dusted Katherine's red fingertips. 'Those pans should have been finished over an hour ago. Make haste,' she added, clapping her thin hands so hard her palms must have stung. ''Tis bad enough I have one lazy maid in this household. I won't stand for two.'

It was all Katherine could do not to cry out in affront. Such censure was hardly just – she worked mighty hard; had she not helped Lowdie with the dishes on top of her own role in assisting Mrs Denby? Over the housekeeper's shoulder Katherine met Nash's gaze. His blue eyes held in them an expression of both sympathy and annoyance, for he never did like it when his sweetheart was scolded, especially at the expense of Lowdie Lucas.

'Yes, Mrs Wilson.'

The housekeeper sniffed, turned a haughty head. The movement was carried out in so speedy a fashion that Wakely's servants had no chance to disperse, and seeing them crowded so tight together in the doorway of the scullery necessitated Mrs Wilson to clap her hands sharply again.

'Get back to work, all of you. There shall be no dilly-dallying. The Busgroves arrive this evening and we have no time to waste.'

Mrs Wilson then departed. It was only when the door of the housekeeper's room shut with a pronounced *thump* that the servants' hall seemed able once more to breathe, and the sounds of discordant hustle and bustle returned to fill the air.

Almost immediately, Nash was at Katherine's side.

'For the love of God, Kate,' he murmured, crouching to help her clean the flagstones. He picked up Lowdie's discarded apron and proceeded to use it to mop the floor. 'I do wish you would not draw attention to yourself.'

'Why, Richard Marmery,' Katherine replied, sucking in her breath. 'You know I do no such thing.'

'But you do,' said Nash, wringing out the apron into the bucket Katherine had pulled from under the workbench. 'I know for some unfathomable reason you feel sorry for Lowdie, but the more you allow her to take advantage of your kindness the more you shall find yourself on the receiving end of Wilson's bite.'

Katherine blew a stray strand of hair away from her face. Gently Nash tucked it back into her mobcap, and the sweetness of the gesture caused her lips to twist.

'Would you have me be as unfeeling as the rest of you? I am kind to Lowdie because no one else is.'

Nash gave her a peevish look. 'I am not unkind, nor am I unfeeling. But you know as well as I do – as well as the rest of us – that Lowdie is extremely *un*likeable. She makes things so damn difficult. You know she made poor Prudence cry the other week, all because she took objection to the way the girl breathed! It was not Prue's fault she had a blazing cold and Wilson refused to let her spend the day in bed.'

Katherine *did* know. Prudence had been maudlin the rest of the day, and it irritated Mrs Wilson so much that she reprimanded her for (as the housekeeper put it) having the face of a whipped dog, which made Prudence cry once more for that was the second animal she had been likened to in the space of six hours. What had set her off in the first place was Lowdie scolding her for (as *she* put it) sounding like a winded donkey. Which – to Katherine's shame – had actually made her laugh.

'Nash,' she said tiredly, standing up, bucket in hand. 'I know how you feel. How you *all* feel. But my conscience simply will not allow me to treat her poorly.'

'Yet you find her as vexing as the rest of us.'

'So I do. But since we share a bedroom I would much rather keep the peace than make myself uncomfortable. Besides,' said

Katherine, dipping her hands into the sink to search for the plate that was the cause of the whole sorry business. 'You would not love me if I was not kind.'

At this Nash blinked, then let out a low chuckle.

'I suppose I have no argument to that,' he said softly. 'But please be careful. If Wilson dismisses you too, you shall have to go to Heysten Park, and I truly do not think my heart could stand it.'

It was a lovely thing to say – Katherine had always felt so safe in Nash's affections when he shewed them in so warm a manner, and she was about to turn to him and say so when her fingers brushed against ... Her heart sank, and from the basin Katherine brought forth one half of what used to be an expensive periwinkle plate.

She and Nash stared down at it and he grinned.

'Well,' he said, a little laugh catching in his throat. 'It looks like my warning is no longer of purpose. Lowdie Lucas has no hope in hell's chance of keeping her position now.'

'Nash, you are beastly. It was an accident – whatever you think of Lowdie, she did not break it deliberately. To lose her position because of it is most unfair. What a witch Mrs Wilson is!'

If her words were not enough to make Nash pause and reconsider his own, then the mode of Katherine's declaration was, and so the footman moved closer, snaked his hand about his lover's waist.

'Oh, come now,' said he, planting a tender kiss behind her ear. 'I *am* sorry, I suppose, for Lowdie, that she should lose her place for such a trifling thing. You're right, Wilson *is* an old rusty guts, but Kate, you know I only care for your well-being. I would be quite lost without you, and it is to *our* future we must think, not hers. You know I'm saving every penny I can so we can marry. Please, do not jeopardise what could soon be ours.'

Katherine in that moment felt perfectly wretched. She desperately wanted to take comfort in Nash's words but the injustice of it all prevented her from doing so. She had a mind to go directly to Viscountess Pépin herself since she had always been such a sympathetic voice to Lowdie's indiscretions. But such an action would surely ensure her own downfall for Mrs Wilson would be the first to hear of it, and Katherine had no wish to find herself too without a position, especially at Christmastime. The only other house of consequence in the immediate vicinity was Heysten Park, and oh, such stories she had heard! The old lord had been renowned for treating his servants abominably ill; improper dalliances with house-maids, offensively poor pay, only one day of rest for the whole twelvemonth ... Katherine had no notion of how the current lord ran the estate but she had no wish to find out, nor allow Lowdie to be subjected to such a fate as being forced to do the same. How could she allow the housekeeper's threat of dismissal to go unquestioned?

It would seem in that moment that Katherine's anguish had been heard from up-high, for not one moment later the trilling of excitable chatter wended its way through the servants' corridor, and into the kitchen swept the viscountess herself, followed by three of her five daughters – Miss Maria, Miss Louisa and Miss Rosalie – each carrying two large baskets laden with boxes wrapt in crisp brown paper. Immediately Nash removed his arms from Katherine's waist, all of Wakely's servants dipped a curtsey or bent in a bow, and with a bright smile Viscountess Pépin waved them up.

'Good afternoon to you all!'

'Good afternoon,' came the chorus of replies, making the viscountess beam all the more. With a flourish of her pretty skirts (such a vibrant shot of teal satin amid the drab earthen colours of the kitchen), she looked at her servants and said:

'I wanted to visit you here to tell you personally just how much the viscount and I and our daughters – not to mention all our esteemed guests – appreciate how hard you have been working.' She nodded at her words, fair curls bobbing merrily either side of her ears. 'From the wonderful food you have provided for us, to the lighting of fires and the making of beds, to the preparation of our baths and the cleaning of Wakely's vast rooms, your efforts have all been noted and appreciated. This season's festivities would not have been possible without you.'

There were murmurs of gratitude about the servants' hall. The Misses Maria, Louisa and Rosalie all smiled and nodded in agreement with their mother, who spread her hands in a kindly gesture just as Mrs Wilson slipped discreetly back into the room, and Katherine could not help but narrow her eyes at the housekeeper.

How dare she, Katherine thought. *How dare she!*

'You have been so very patient with us,' Viscountess Pépin continued. 'I am fully aware that these past days have not been easy, nor will the next week be as our annual Twelfth Night Ball draws near, and so I wish to say just how much we all value each and every one of you.' The viscountess looked then to her daughters who raised their laden baskets. 'To express our thanks – as is tradition the day after Christmas – we present you all with a festive box. Each item within has been chosen in the hope they will be of use to you ... and this time we included a more personal token of our esteem, each individual to its owner.'

Katherine and Nash shared a surprised look.

Every year the viscountess delivered a gift box to her servants. It was a mark of her goodness, a perfect example of just how different the estates of Wakely Hall and Heysten Park were – at Wakely, servants were paid well and never received an unkind word or look or gesture from their master or mistresses. Their rooms were amply furnished and never cold. They were given two free days a month. And Christmas was always, always, marked with a small box of gifts. Katherine knew what to expect – she would receive a sweet plum cake (for she baked them), a small jar of honey from the viscount's hives, a beeswax candle, a shiny sixpence, and a brand-new smock. Nash would receive the same, except in place of a Holland he would have a linen necktie. These little items always touched Katherine's heart and she never expected nor wanted more. So, for Viscountess Pépin to include something else? Well, 'twas a most unprecedented and delightful surprise.

'Please,' said the viscountess now. 'We shall call out your names one by one.'

And thus, she did. First came Mrs Wilson, then Mrs Denby; next Viscount Pépin's valet, Ralph. As the rest of the servants collected their gifts, Katherine tried to ignore the spiteful thought that the housekeeper did not deserve a box at all, and was still mulling over her peevishness when Viscountess Pépin called out Lowdie's name. The viscountess looked about her in confusion when the scullery maid did not step forwards.

'Where is Loveday Lucas?'

Katherine curled her toes inside her damp stockings. Her pulse quickened. It was as if a spark of fire had set ablaze in her chest. It was as if, too, Nash could sense it, for he put upon Katherine such a look of warning! But it was too late – she could not help herself – and Katherine cleared her throat.

'Mrs Wilson sent Lowdie to her room, my lady.' Then, quite deliberately, she added, 'Without dinner or supper.'

Katherine sensed rather than saw the furious look directed at her from the vicinity of the housekeeper's stiff-backed stance on the other side of the servants' hall; it was to the viscountess that Katherine directed her gaze, who blinked back at her in shock.

'Without dinner or supper?' she echoed, then turned to address Mrs Wilson. 'Why has Loveday been sent to her room?'

Mrs Wilson (and in that moment Katherine thought her quite the Old Hag Mulligrub Lowdie always called her), pursed her prune-like lips.

'In disgrace, my lady. She broke one of the blue china plates.'

Viscountess Pépin's shoulders dropped.

'Oh dear,' said she with a sad shake of her finely curled head. 'Not another one of my periwinkles?'

'Just so, my lady. And Miss Lucas shewed not one bit of remorse, either.' Mrs Wilson cleared her throat. 'If you would

43

be so kind as to spare me a moment, I should like to discuss her behaviour with you.'

'I see.' The viscountess returned Lowdie's box to Miss Maria's basket. 'Very well, Mrs Wilson. But first,' she said, face brightening, 'we must finish distributing the boxes. Prudence Brown?'

And as Prudence came eagerly forwards Katherine heard Nash breathe a heavy sigh of disappointment, saw quite clearly this time the angry look Mrs Wilson sent her way. But when it was Katherine's turn to accept her own Christmas box she held her head high and bestowed upon Viscountess Pépin an expression of pleading, and by the manner in which that lady's fair brows drew together, Katherine felt assured her mistress had understood the message she had attempted to impart.

It was in those moments of gift-giving that Loveday Lucas lay upon her bed. It would appear at first if one were to regard the scullery maid in such repose that she did not care one bit she had been sent to her room with no prospect of either dinner or supper (for here, at least, her wish of a little time off had been granted) but the truth of it was rather different. Lowdie *did* care that she had been sent to her room with no prospect of either dinner or supper, for deep down in the pit of her (rather peckish) belly, it upset her greatly that she should be subject to such unfair punishment.

It was just a plate, Lowdie thought, and an ugly plate to boot.

That she had perhaps deserved it to a degree on account of her quarrelsome tongue was a thought that impinged furtively upon her mind, and Lowdie sucked the cut on her finger as she stared at the whitewashed ceiling. Katherine had hung a sprig of holly from one of the beams to incite some festive spirit, but at that very moment Lowdie felt none. She knew perfectly well her behaviour caused discord between her and her fellow servants, but so often Lowdie found herself unable to curb it. *This* was what came from growing up in a houseful of boys with no mother to protect her from their teasing; *this* was what came of never playing with dolls or tea-sets and possessing not one single friend of the female sex. This was what came of reaching the grand old age of twenty with as much freedom as one could shake a bonnet at, then being forced to curtail oneself in a place so far away from all she had ever cared for.

She missed her pa, and she especially missed her brothers, but with each of them lost to the battlefield and as a consequence her father to the bottle ... well, there had been no other choice but to come here. How would Old Hag Mulligrub feel if she had lost all those she loved so very dearly? How would *she* feel, to be so lonely and so very misunderstood? Lowdie was sure Mrs Wilson would not be so boorish if she knew of her history, but it was something she had never divulged – not to the housekeeper, nor to anyone.

The sun – which had already been weak in its efforts to shine that day – gradually disappeared from the room. The sprig of holly became a mere shadow against the now-black beam. Below, the faint bustle of evening chores in the servants' hall sounded in muffled resonance, and ignoring the rumble in her stomach, she felt herself begin to drift off to sleep. It was just as Lowdie had

45

turned to a position that felt most comfortable to instil slumber that there came a soft tap upon the oak door, and without waiting for any call to invite entry, it swung wide open.

If it were Kate, she would have come into the room without preamble, and certainly would not have bothered herself to knock, so it was with surprise that Lowdie peeked blearily at the silhouette now standing at the threshold.

'Who is that?'

''Tis Mol.'

'Oh,' Lowdie huffed, and though her tone might to Molly Hart be construed as churlish, it was in fact one of relief that it was not Mrs Wilson who stood at the door. But before she might say anything further, Molly took breath.

'The mistress has sent for you.'

Like a shot, up Lowdie sat.

'Lawds! You do not mean it?'

Oh, but this was a disaster. Mrs Wilson had always threatened Lowdie with dismissal, but she never truly thought that Viscountess Pépin would allow it – she had always struck Lowdie as being too soft, too *nice*, and it had made Lowdie (she grudgingly admitted to herself) complacent. Was it not the viscountess, after all, who had offered her the position here at Wakely Hall to begin with?

''Fraid I do,' said Molly then. 'And by heaven, Lowdie, does Mrs W look fit to burst her top with glee.'

The other maid's expression could not be marked from where Lowdie sat tight-chested on the bed, but she could well imagine it – Molly's cheeks would be flushed in barely concealed excitement. Perhaps, even, with a little gloating. Wakely Hall's longest-standing housemaid was, one must own, that sort of girl.

'You coming then?'

And so, with such a profound feeling of sickness in her stomach, which had quite replaced the feeling of hunger that had been there afore, Lowdie followed Molly Hart down the poky stairwell of the servants' quarters. Presently she found herself outside the viscountess' sitting room, and with a small smirk Molly tapped her knuckles upon the door; a soft 'Come in' followed, and within seconds Lowdie found herself alone with Viscountess Pépin, who watched her with an air of what could only be described as profound disappointment.

'Loveday,' said she. 'Please be seated.'

Such a request felt strange – there was the viscountess, seated in all her finery behind a fancily carved wooden desk on which lay a shiny gold inkwell and a box prettily wrapt in brown paper and gingham ribbon, asking a servant dressed in stained skirts to sit on what looked to be a chair altogether too expensive for the likes of Lowdie Lucas – but said girl did as she was told and sat, nervously clasping her sore finger.

'Well, then, Loveday. What are we to do?'

It was all Lowdie could do not to wince. The disappointment in the viscountess' voice was even more pronounced than the disappointment of her expression, and for the first time since arriving at Wakely Hall Lowdie became conscious of the most peculiar feeling that she did not wish to leave it. Such a feeling precipitated a need to defend herself, and so it was that

Lowdie found words spilling forth from her mouth in an abominable rush.

'M'lady, I did not mean to break the plate! There was a chip in it, you see, and my finger caught –' here she held up her finger and the fine red cut that could be seen upon it – 'and I know I was rude to Mrs Wilson, but she really is *very* unkind, not just to me but to *everybody*, and I—'

Viscountess Pépin had raised a hand. Lowdie caught her tongue.

'Are you unhappy here, Loveday?'

'M'lady?'

''Tis not a difficult question. Are you unhappy?'

It was a question Lowdie had often mulled over in the darkness of night when Wakely Hall was asleep and Kate's soft snores kept her lively mind company.

'I've not been happy, I must own it. But to say I am *un*happy would mayhap be a little too far.'

'I see.' The viscountess paused. Her elegant fingers tapped the point of her chin. 'I had hoped you might find your way to finding contentment here at Wakely.'

'Contentment' was also a word too far to describe Lowdie's feelings regarding her position at Wakely Hall. While Loveday Lucas felt regret at the loss of her family and her freedom, and as much as she missed the steady familiarity of her old life, she did not miss the harsh words which her father's drinking provoked, nor the fear that his bitterness might find itself wielded not by his tongue but by his fist. He had driven their charwoman away with his erratic behaviour. He lost work, too, though that had not been his fault – why come to a lowly button maker when the new factories produced hundreds of them by the day? The wars had taken far more from Lowdie than the lives of her brothers, and so with her siblings gone and no money to support them, what else could Lowdie do but advertise? When the letter from the viscountess arrived, such an overpowering feeling of relief had overcome her . . . Until, of course, upon arriving at Wakely, Lowdie discovered a weariness of a different making.

She supposed the viscountess thought she was doing Lowdie a kindness in offering her the position of scullery maid, but it could not be said that such a grand lady should have any notion of the kind of work a scullery maid might actually undertake. How would a viscountess know what it was to wake at the crack of dawn and draw water from the yard pump, stamping her feet to keep warm in the bitter chill of winter air, only then to lug the bucket inside and spend endless time heating it at the range? Could Lowdie truly be supposed to find herself grateful? To be sure she was no stranger to hard work – she had kept house for her father as soon as she had been old enough to do so – but their small cottage was nothing compared to a grand estate such as this. How might she express these thoughts to Viscountess Pépin? Kate might think Lowdie had no care of what she said to a person, but when that person was a viscountess, well, she knew well enough not to insult the hand which fed her, and so all she could venture was:

'It's not that I am ungrateful, m'lady. But life at Wakely is so different to what I'm used. I . . .' Lowdie ducked her head. 'I confess, I have struggled to adjust.'

Viscountess Pépin frowned. 'It is of Mrs Wilson's frequent opinion that you have not even tried. She claims you are insolent. That you care little for your workfellows and make no effort to hold them close. That you encourage discord belowstairs. I believe you said some choice words recently to Miss Brown?'

Lowdie sniffed. Perhaps she had been a little unkind to Prudence, but the maid really *had* sounded like a winded donkey! *Exactly* like the one her father used to own before he sold it for a bottle of brandy. Well, she would apologise, for she had not meant to upset her, though there had been no need for Mrs Wilson to tattle. Lowdie felt then such a spurt of resentment for the housekeeper, she found it quite impossible not to raise her voice.

'Has Mrs Wilson complained of the quality of my work?'

The viscountess' large eyes widened slightly at Lowdie's accusatory tone.

'No,' she said after a moment. 'Mrs Wilson has even been prevailed upon to confess your work is more than adequate, but despite this she is most adamant that you are to be dismissed. However,' Viscountess Pépin added, 'while I consider dismissing anyone at this time of year a great cruelty, I do not wish to force you to stay somewhere you do not wish to be. Would you prefer to leave, Loveday?'

Such relief and gratitude did she feel that at this, Lowdie was mortified to find her vision blurred by tears.

'No, m'lady,' she whispered. 'I . . . I don't want to go home.'

Not to that cold and lonely cottage. Not to her bottle-bound father.

The viscountess sat back in her elegant seat of blue brocade and heaved a sigh.

'Your mother was the kindest woman I have ever known. I always felt so at peace when she was near. Martha delivered all my children but Juliette and Rosalie, and saved my life twice – once with Charlotte and before that, with my little Edmond. I cared for her very much. For her to die in childbirth herself . . .' She trailed off and shook her head. 'It grieved me dreadfully to hear of the deaths of your brothers in the wars. And then to discover your father's condition . . .' Viscountess Pépin shook her head again. 'Why else would I have offered you a home here at Wakely? I could not let Martha Lucas' daughter struggle when she had given mine life.'

And now Lowdie could not stop her tears from falling, no matter how hard she tried. The viscountess gently pressed a handkerchief into her hand and Lowdie took it, whereupon her ladyship waited patiently for her to dry her face.

'I have not told Mrs Wilson this,' she continued. 'I felt it best you did not have preferential treatment, especially as you had no experience in a household such as this. I would prefer not to confess that the reference I provided for you was false, that there exists no such person as Lady Foly. But if you truly wish to stay, you must endeavour to deserve my falsehood.'

It took a moment for Lowdie to once again find her voice, and when she did it was on the verge of breaking.

'They do not like me, m'lady.'

The viscountess blinked. 'Whatever do you mean, Loveday?'

'The other servants.'

Viscountess Pépin hesitated. 'Is this, perhaps, because you have not given them leave to?'

Lowdie found herself lifting her shoulders in a half-hearted shrug, which did not quite answer the question. But then she confessed to something she had dared not put into words before:

'I am unlikeable.'

'Oh, dear me, my child,' returned the viscountess without taking breath, 'I doubt that. *I* like you. Katherine Allen likes you.'

Lowdie wiped her nose on her sleeve in an unladylike fashion. 'She does?'

'Why yes! She was most concerned for you earlier, so I do rather think it would behove you to not be quite so keen on shutting people out. I suspect, Loveday, that beneath your rather prickly exterior, there is a young lady who is just as kind and exceedingly likeable as your mother was.'

It was a little too much for Lowdie's heart to bear. She burst forth into tears once again, and as she clutched her ladyship's handkerchief to her face Viscountess Pépin awkwardly cleared her throat.

'As for the periwinkle,' she announced, 'they were a gift from the viscount. I had seen the set in a window display in London some years ago, and liked them so much that when Louisa was born he ordered them for me as a present. It is one of the reasons why I treasure the periwinkle set so highly – the set is my way of commemorating both my daughter and Martha Lucas. Louisa, you see, was the last child your mother delivered of me.'

Lowdie gulped and lowered the handkerchief.

'I did not know, m'lady, upon my word. I truly am so very sorry.'

The viscountess sighed. 'Well, there is nothing to be done about the broken pieces now. But please, Loveday,' she added, her voice softening once again, 'do be more careful. That set, as you now know, carries a great deal of meaning for both of us.'

For Lowdie Lucas to feel overcome with emotion was a very rare thing indeed, and so – quite incapable was she now of forming a suitable answer – she merely offered one tearful nod of her head.

'I shall tell Mrs Wilson you are to stay,' were Viscountess Pépin's next words, 'and that she should see a vast improvement in your behaviour henceforward. I shall also ensure you have something to eat this evening – I will not have my servants starved. No, no,' she added as Lowdie attempted to return the rather sodden handkerchief, 'keep it. But enough tears. This is cause to be happy, is it not?'

'Yes, m'lady,' whispered Lowdie, still overcome. 'Thank you, m'lady.'

'Very good.' There was a brief pause in which the viscountess bit her lower lip. 'Loveday, I assume you heard that Miss Partridge, my abigail, is to be married?'

Lowdie dabbed at her eyes. 'Yes, m'lady.'

'This means,' Viscountess Pépin continued, 'that I shall soon be without a lady's maid. I shall need to hire out for another, but I thought, perhaps, that one day *you* might suit the role. You have some way to go before I can offer you the position, but may I presume you might be interested a few years from now?'

Lowdie stared. *Lady's maid?* Well, now, there was a mighty thing. Would not her ma be proud? And while Lowdie's silence in the face of such an offer might have indicated she was not receptive to the notion, the opposite was clearly writ upon the maid's blushing face, and so the viscountess simply smiled and pushed the wrapt box across the desk.

'This is for you,' she said, and it took a moment for Lowdie to gather her surprise.

'For me?'

Viscountess Pépin proffered a nod. 'It is tradition on the second day of Christmastide that all Wakely Hall's servants receive a gift box. This is yours, and there is one gift in particular I should like you to be mindful of.'

'M'lady?'

The viscountess softly tapped her fingers together.

'They come in pairs, and often appear when one finds oneself at a standstill in one's life. They offer peace, love and friendship, if you chuse to open your heart. Remember, Loveday, that no matter how far we think we have strayed from our path, one can always be guided back to what matters most. We can start again. Your mother reminded me of that, when I was feeling particularly maudlin. It was she who gave them to me when Edmond died, and I should like you to have them now.'

It was then she stood, prompting Lowdie – rather awkwardly – to do the same.

'Merry Christmas,' the viscountess said, and clasping the box and handkerchief to her breast Lowdie found she could barely contain the flutterings of her heart.

'Merry Christmas, your ladyship.'

Katherine was troubled when Molly told her that Viscountess Pépin had called the scullery maid to her sitting room. All through dinner she sat silently nursing her plate of capon and parsnips, hoping against hope that the viscountess had interpreted her pleading look and not dismissed Lowdie. Later, Nash had attempted to raise her spirits with a dalliance in the larder, but Katherine had not the patience to bear his honeyed kisses and in a huff he left her to compose riddles in his new journal, whereupon *she* was left to apply herself to her evening chores in the most distracted of tempers. It was in the cold store that Mrs Wilson found her, precariously pushing the syllabubs she had prepared onto one of the topmost shelves, and when the housekeeper said her name it was all Katherine could do not to drop them.

'Mrs Wilson.'

Katherine chewed her inner cheek. Her bravado from earlier had quite vanished, and while she did not regret her actions Katherine did regret the potential result of them. What punishment was Old Hag Mulligrub going to inflict for her impudence?

'I hope, missy,' said the housekeeper in scathing tones, 'you are proud of yourself,' to which Katherine dared say nothing. 'Since it is, apparently, the season of festive cheer and forgiveness I shall not take matters further, but in future you will keep your nose and tongue out of household business or you'll find yourself on the doorstep, do you understand?'

Of course, Mrs Denby would put up a mighty great fight if the housekeeper dared even try to turn her only kitchen maid out, but Mrs Wilson was a force to be reckoned with nonetheless and Katherine had no wish to risk dismissal and so, swallowing hard, she uttered a very quiet and contrite 'Yes'.

Mrs Wilson clasped her hands to her front. 'That's better. Keep a civil tongue in one's head, Katherine Allen. Remember that.'

'Yes, Mrs Wilson.'

'Good.'

'Mrs Wilson?'

The housekeeper, who had already made to leave, turned in the doorway of the cold store. In the shadowed light her small-pox scars shewed particularly deep.

'Will . . . Will Lowdie be dismissed?'

Mrs Wilson glowered.

'It appears that her ladyship has decided to ignore my advice.' The housekeeper paused. 'Miss Lucas is a very lucky girl. How long she continues to be so, remains to be seen.' And with one last disparaging look, Mrs Wilson vacated the threshold.

So profound was Katherine's relief that she did not hesitate to make a hasty retreat to her bedroom as soon as she was able, whereupon she found Lowdie sitting cross-legged on her bed, an empty plate and the contents of her Christmas box dotted about her on the coverlet.

'Oh, you've eaten. I am glad,' she exclaimed with a broad smile. 'And you have your box! What did you get?' But in that moment of crossing the room she heard the distinct sound of a forlorn sniff, and Katherine's smile fell swift as flight from her face.

'Lowdie! Why are you weeping? Mrs Wilson says you are not to be dismissed after all, so surely there can be no cause for tears?'

When all Lowdie could manage was a hiccoughed sob in reply – and that into a rather limp-looking handkerchief – Katherine sat down heavily on the scullery maid's bed. 'Oh, Lowdie, please do say.'

Another hiccough came forth, and it was some moments before Lowdie could compose herself enough to answer.

'The viscountess,' she whispered, 'was awful kind. She told me such nice things.'

'Well,' Katherine replied, 'she is *always* kind and says nice things. And so generous, too,' she added, gesturing to the box upon the bed. 'Tell me, what special gift did she give you? We all got the same, except for one particular thing that – so the viscountess said – was unique to us.' Lowdie did not answer. Indeed, she was not even looking at her, and impatiently Katherine shifted on the coverlet. 'I got some silk ribbons for my hair, *you* know how unruly it is, Nash got a writing journal, and Prue was given a little vase for the bouquet she caught yesterday.' Still, Lowdie did not speak. Katherine frowned. 'Well? What about you?'

Finally Lowdie raised her eyes, but the words that came out of her mouth were not ones which Katherine expected to hear.

'Do you think I'm unlikeable?'

'Un . . . likeable?'

Oh dear. Such a question to be asked! Had she not earlier

that day confessed to herself she found Lowdie Lucas somewhat trying? Had not Nash declared Lowdie to be that very word? But how to answer?

The struggle must have shewn upon Katherine's face, for Lowdie turned hers and uttered a desolate groan.

'I do not mean to be. But Pa always used to tell me that it did no good to be weak. *Don't let anyone walk over you*, he said. *Weakness kills*, he said. It was what killed Ma, and I must believe it for she died having me.'

It was the first glimpse of Lowdie's former life Katherine had ever been allowed; it felt as though she had uncovered a closely guarded secret, and Katherine was conscious then of feeling humbled that Lowdie should share that secret with her.

'No matter what your pa said,' Katherine replied gently, 'there is a difference between being weak and being nice. You do not have to fight us tooth and nail. When you first came here, we were all ready to be your friend, but Lowdie ... you made it so difficult.'

'I know I did.' Lowdie lowered the handkerchief. 'Kate?'

'Yes?'

'I'm afraid.'

'Why?'

'Because even if I were to be nicer, I do not think anyone would wish to be friends with me now. I've been too disagreeable to suppose it would be possible.'

Katherine hesitated. 'Perhaps, at first. But in time ...'

Lowdie's lip twisted, and she turned a little so that Katherine was able to glimpse something nestled within the folds of her new Holland smock. It was to this Lowdie reached, and she placed – to her surprise – two small birds side by side between them.

'Turtle doves,' said Lowdie, to which Katherine frowned.

'Turtle doves?'

'You asked what the viscountess gave me.'

At Lowdie's nod Katherine reached out to take them. Now she held them in her palm, she saw that the doves were made of finely embroidered grey wool, and they were the prettiest little pin brooches Katherine had seen. But why should Viscountess Pépin give such a gift to Lowdie? As if sensing her unspoken question, Lowdie sighed long and low.

'She told me my ma gave them to her.'

Katherine looked at her, confused. 'Your ma?'

Lowdie nodded. 'She was her midwife, long ago.'

'Well, that certainly explains things,' said Katherine, and Lowdie smiled a little, soft and sad.

'The viscountess told me that doves offered friendship, if I chose to open my heart. I think her ladyship meant for me to give one of the doves to somebody, but if no one wishes to be my friend they are useless. I have no one.'

These words were said in so forlorn a manner that Katherine felt a tiny pull of sadness in her chest. Very gently, Katherine reached for Lowdie's hand and pressed the little brooches so they sat snugly between their palms.

'Tush, Lowdie Lucas. You have me.'

'I do?'

'Of course you do. You might make me despair whenever you

59

dare open your mouth … but Lowdie,' Katherine said with a giggle, 'I'm not altogether sure what I'd do without you now.'

'Oh, Kate!' said Lowdie, eyes shining. 'Do you really mean it?'

And Katherine *did* mean it, she truly did. Nash and the other servants might dislike the scullery maid … with fair reason, too … but Lowdie was not a bad sort at all – it was clear now that she had a pure heart beneath that rough exterior and ribald tongue, and as Lowdie – positively beaming from ear to ear – pinned one of the little embroidered doves to Katherine's breast, Katherine was quite determined that before the end of Twelfth Night they would all know it.

STAVE III.

Faith, Hope & Charity
THREE FRENCH HENS

It was no secret that Monsieur Benoît de Fortgibu had a penchant for plum pudding. To be sure, the promise of one on his arrival to Merrywake had undoubtedly swayed his decision to attend the wedding of his oldest friend's daughter, and though the Frenchman considered English dishes somewhat lacking in the nuanced flavours and presentation so typical of French cuisine, a plum pudding was quite a different matter altogether.

Benoît had been first introduced to that most delectable dessert near thirty years afore, when – on a visit to London – he collided with Viscount Pépin in the doorway of Fortnum & Mason, where, upon recommendation, he had intended to purchase one of their famous Scotched Eggs. So delighted was each gentleman to find they were fellow Frenchmen that they agreed to prolong their encounter in an adjacent restaurant, within which the monsieur sampled his very first plum pudding and vowed that no Scotched Egg would ever be equal to it.

One might think Benoît de Fortgibu would be thoroughly sick of plum puddings by now (he had already ingested five of them having arrived in Merrywake the day before Christmas Eve, and with ten more to come, the monsieur was sure he would be rather portly by Twelfth Day), but how could he resist the mouth-watering taste of rich currants and orange zest, the warming sluice of sweet brandy? Such joy those puddings afforded him, though such excesses made him a deplorable glutton. But oh, what agreeable sin! He really was quite incapable of refusing them, especially considering he would not likely have the pleasure of another for at least a twelvemonth.

Benoît's smile of pleasure dwindled and he shivered into the collar of his greatcoat. Plum puddings were a rarity in his home country. Before arriving at Wakely Hall it had been quite some time since the monsieur had had the good fortune of encountering one. In fact, it had been six years ago, when he had been stationed in Paris.

So infrequent was it to find an English pudding in France – Bonaparte's Continental System had made the transport of British goods damnably difficult – the monsieur had parted with a full week's pay to ensure its procurement for his Christmas dinner. Perhaps such an act was selfish (for it was the only pudding to be found in the city, so he was assured, and he knew perfectly well that others might be more deserving), but if one were to doubt Benoît's generosity of spirit then they would be gravely mistaken, for despite the rarity of such a find he still agreed to share it.

At the memory, the Frenchman frowned. If he had known Émile would turn out the way he had, perhaps he would never have shared his pudding at all. Benoît always thought the boy kind, gracious, compassionate. Certainly, on the two occasions they had met, Émile demonstrated these attributes admirably. How betrayed Benoît felt, then, when he first read *La Paix Conquise*, and how mistaken in his own judgement! To find that the poet had become so cruel, so inimical towards his fellow men ... it disturbed him greatly. It was clear the wars had not affected Émile as they had Benoît. If they had, the boy would never have written such an antagonistic poem.

Car l'empereur l'a dit: Toi, tes fils, vous mourrez. 'For the emperor has spoken: You and your sons will die.'

He shook his head. Such a cavalier attitude to death. So senseless, so naïve. For Benoît, serving under Napoleon had been a matter of necessity – the monsieur was part of the *Ancien Régime* and his allegiance was then, and always would be, to the king. To debase himself and his principles so deeply for the sake of that Corsican Fiend was still a source of great shame to Benoît, and would be to his dying day.

How would he ever forget the horrors of battle, the thousands of innocents dead at his command? He had not, so Benoît keenly felt, deserved the rank of colonel, and it was a relief, when Bonaparte was at last defeated, to renounce it. Indeed, with the emperor now safely banished to the South Atlantic, Benoît might settle happily in his beloved France, knowing sanity had once more returned. After the festive period was finished the monsieur looked forward to escorting Seigneur and Seigneuresse Toussaint to Paris, where he would then continue his journey the four-and-seventy miles south-west to Orléans, a home he had not returned to these past thirteen years.

Oh, how Benoît had missed it, and his little set of apartments overlooking the Loire. If only Sophie had lived to share his twilight years with him – he would never forget the day a letter had arrived at his tent in Russia, informing him of her death. Typhus, her sister said. How strange, when only that morning the first of his soldiers fell to the same disease. No, Sophie would not be waiting for him in Orléans. She had left him quite alone.

At his feet, then, there came a sprightly *cluck*.

Well, Benoît thought, smiling again, he would not be *quite* alone – he had his darlings to keep him company. The monsieur looked down at said darlings with affection, waddling along on their little leather leads. No care had *they* for the chill air; not that their clawed toes might be cold upon the hoarfrost, or their pin-bright eyes should sting from the icy breeze, for they were creatures familiar in constitution to the great and wild outdoors.

If they had belonged to anyone other than Monsieur de Fortgibu, there would have been much surprise to be had; but just as it was no secret that the Frenchman had a penchant for plum pudding, it was also no secret that the monsieur's greatest pleasure was keeping chickens as pets, even during those fateful wars (it was a wicked luxury to always have an egg for breakfast in his tent, but Benoît was quite convinced his life had been prolonged from the habit of doing so). In fact, his hens were his pride and joy, and he treated them as he would have treated his own children, if he and Sophie had ever the good fortune to produce them.

'*Alors*, Espoir,' said now the monsieur. 'Is this not the most splendid weather for December?'

The bird turned its black head at the sound of his master's voice; Benoît grinned.

'You do not answer, but I see you agree. Look how you prance, my *petit* Houdan!'

Espoir's wings stretched in reply, and satisfied, the monsieur turned his attention to his La Flèche.

'And what of you, little Foi? What say you?'

But it was not the brown hen which answered but the white, in a series of charming little trills.

'Ah, Charité, my little angel. 'Tis a glorious winter's day, *n'est-ce pas?*'

And so it was. Benoît was at that moment taking a turn about the pretty walk alongside the boundary wall of Wakely Hall, where he took great delight in the frost which had settled on the foliage, glittering away in the sunlight like minuscule diamonds. He took delight too in the way the clouds made sumptuous pillows in the blue sky, the smell of ice in the air, the song of four blackbirds perched high in the towering trees. After experiencing so many atrocities during his deployment, the monsieur made it a course of habit to find delight in everything wherever and whenever he could.

After all, life – one must concur – was to be enjoyed, not suffered.

Determined, then, to not think upon recent years and to commit himself to this more positive frame of mind, Benoît walked down the country lane abutting the estate, his three hens waddling on their leads, until he reached a small gateway. This gateway presented him with a choice: turn left and complete the circle that would take him back to the entranceway of Wakely Hall, or turn right down the lane that passed through an iron gate and into the woodland, thence out onto the fields adjoining Hodge Farm, and, well, it being such a glorious winter's day, he chose the latter. It was, considering his resolve to be cheery, the correct choice; three of Fernand Pépin's five daughters had begun to stretch the monsieur's usually long patience, and if being absent from the hall a trifle longer than planned ensured his continued good spirits into teatime, then it was all for the better.

'Come, my little beaks,' chivvied Benoît as they reached the gate. 'Through you go.'

One by one he guided his hens through the narrow gap, lifting their leather leads high above the iron bars so he might squeeze through himself without entanglement. Alas, the Frenchman's fingers being not as nimble as they used to be, one of the leads slipped through them.

'Foi! Come back here this instant!'

The brown hen ignored the plea – off went the La Flèche into the trees, and with a grumble Benoît gave pursuit.

Out of all his hens, Foi was the most precocious. And fast,

too, Benoît thought as she diverted from the frosted path into Wakely Forest, Charité and Espoir trundling behind with little excitable trills. Once or twice he had to wait for them to catch up with him, and so Benoît began to grow concerned when, after ten minutes of wandering, he had yet to find his third feathered pet. But then, just as the Frenchman feared Foi had become lost, he heard a single loud *cluck*.

Benoît stopped. Such a sound was not typical of Foi. Hens clucked, of course, but the manner in which Foi had done so indicated there was cause for alarm. Afeared for her safety (for Benoît did so adore his hens), he followed the direction from which the sound came until he found himself in a small clearing.

It was a charming sight – the trees sparkled in the sunlight, and with the sky being so very blue the snow was lent a similar hue. The sun cast shafts of hazy light through the bare branches, illuminating a half-frozen stream which emitted a gentle bubbling sound and, in any other circumstance, Benoît might have been drawn to rest a while beside it. But no such rest could be had, for there was his little Foi lingering on the stream's icy bank looking down upon – *Mon Dieu!* – what looked to be the body of a little girl.

What the Frenchman felt in that moment could not be described, but his heart pounded hard in his chest as a memory assaulted him – still so painful, still so raw, after all these years – and swallowing the lump that had formed in his throat, he beckoned Foi to return to him.

Foi did as she was bidden, and with trembling hands Benoît tied the leads of all three hens to a nearby holly tree. Unused to being tethered, they lifted their tiny heads and each began to emit little nervous chatters.

'Hush now,' he murmured, and experiencing then a terrible sense of dread Benoît approached the stream cautiously. He knew not if the child were alive, but when he found himself some three yards away Benoît whispered hopefully, *'Mademoiselle?'*

There came no answer. Benoît wondered what to do. He certainly could not leave her.

Not after what happened in Krasny.

Cautiously (for he was not as lithe as he once had been) Benoît inched his way down the bank. The earth was hard and cold where the water had not reached, but further down, the sluggish current lapped at the muddy verge. Though he was intent on keeping his footing, Benoît fearfully glanced at the child – the icy water did not touch her, be praised, but her cheeks were pale and streaked with dirt. Even her dark hair held within its strands the crusted dusting of ice. The poor, poor thing. Had she been in Wakely Forest all night?

Soon Benoît reached her. Afraid to touch her in that moment, he watched the girl in the hope that he might detect the rise and fall of her little chest. Then he did detect it, and relief flooded the Frenchman like a balm.

'Mademoiselle?' he whispered again. 'Can you hear me?'

When no response came, as gently as Benoît dared, he reached out to touch the little girl's forehead. It was freezing, which did so frighten him that Benoît gripped the child's shoulder and shook it hard.

'*Petite*, wake up. You must wake!'

Perhaps it was the force of his shake that woke her, or the desperation in his voice, but the girl's eyes shot open. Benoît's profound relief was immediately dashed however as the poor child emitted a terrified squeal and scrambled to her feet in a desperate attempt to flee.

'Oh, please,' Benoît cried, trying to hold her still. 'Please do not run!'

But the child could not run, for he saw now that her ankle was trapped between the sinewy branches of a tree, its roots submerged in the hoarfrosted bank of the stream. Down the girl fell, and crying pitifully she scraped at the earth in a bid to escape him. A tattered shawl fell from her shoulders, and in that moment he found himself not in the pleasant peaceful county of ——shire, but back in the harsh frost-bitten fields of Krasny, looking into the petrified eyes of a girl dressed in rags. He had pleaded with her to retreat to the safety of the village, reached out to her in desperation – to shoo her away, to take her onto his horse, he knew not – only to watch in horror as a cannonball blew her little legs from under her. She had taken minutes to die, in which all Benoît could do was hold her tiny hand until the light faded from her button eyes, her whimpers drowned out by the sounds of battle that continued on around them. The memory was so chilling that, quite unable to stop himself, the Frenchman uttered a hollow cry, and the sound was enough for *this* girl to squeal again and redouble her efforts to escape.

'*Mademoiselle! Arrêt!*'

His French appeared to shock the child – she stopped her

struggles and stared at Benoît in alarm. Hoping to alleviate her panic, he released his grip on her shoulder.

'Forgive me,' he said. 'I did not mean to alarm you. But I saw you here and oh, what a fright you did give me! I thought for a moment you were dead.'

The comment seemed to calm the child somewhat, for she wiped her runny nose and ducked her head, awkwardly wringing her skirts, whereupon a great feeling of pity and tenderness swept over Benoît.

'Come now,' he said gently. 'Will you permit me to release your ankle from its trap? It must be hurting you dreadfully. I shall not harm you,' he added, when the girl stiffened. 'You have my word of honour, *petite*, I assure you.'

She raised her gaze to his. Of course, the poor child could not know for certain that Benoît would not harm her, but she must have seen something in the old man's kindly eyes, or heard the sincerity in his tone, or perhaps saw his fine manner of dress, which convinced her to very slowly nod.

Gently, Benoît began to move the branches of the trunk. It took a minute or two, for they were fiddly and did not bend easily, but soon the little girl's ankle was free.

'Can you stand, *mademoiselle*?'

The girl tested her weight on the foot which had been trapped, and though she winced she offered another tiny nod.

Just like the child in Krasny, this girl appeared to be no more than eight years of age. She wore a dress most unsuitable for the season, being thin and of paisley fare. Her boots were scuffed with mud, her pale cheeks and bare arms patterned with dirt, and her dark hair was a veritable rat's nest. As she wrapped the dirty rose shawl she wore tighter about her shoulders, Benoît saw on closer inspection it appeared once to have been fine, having clearly been a pretty shade of pale pink. Little satin roselets were sewn into the shawl's tattered hem.

This shocked him. Benoît had assumed the girl was a vagrant, a pauper child with no home to call her own, which of course was bad enough though not, regretfully, unusual. But for a child of quality to be out in such treacherous conditions was exceedingly strange indeed.

'My dear girl,' said the monsieur, wonderingly. 'Where is your family?'

There came no answer.

''Tis a very cold day to be outside,' he tried carefully. 'Do you have nowhere to go?'

At this she gave a small shake of the head.

What to do, what to do!

Well, what to do before anything else, Benoît realised, was return to the safety of the forest floor, and so the Frenchman said:

'Come, little one. Let us climb free.'

This feat too, took some minutes, for though the child was sprightly enough, Benoît was not – his old knees had stiffened, and therefore he was slow. It crossed his mind as he scrambled up the bank that the little girl would run from him the first moment she reached the clearing, and he was in no fit state to stop her.

Run she did not, though – she waited for him patiently, and when he reached the top of the bank she even held out her hand to assist.

'*Merci, petite. Merci!*'

And so there they both were – standing in a charming sunlit woodland clearing looking thoroughly bedraggled, and the irony of it was not lost on Benoît. He would have laughed, if he had not been so anxious that by doing so he might frighten her off. She may have helped him up the bank, but she was still watching him warily. For a moment he was quite at a loss what to say to her, until – the child having licked her lips – a thought occurred.

'Are you hungry?'

From his coat pocket Benoît removed a small and rather misshapen napkin-wrapt bundle. Of course, one could easily and rightly guess what said napkin might contain; inside it was the last slice of his daily plum pudding, which he had intended to save for a mid-walk refreshment, and Benoît smiled what he hoped was a kindly smile.

'Some plum pudding for you, *ma chérie*. And though in our little escapade it has become a trifle squashed, I assure you it will still taste delicious. Here,' he added, spying a large rock at the clearing's verge which would serve perfectly well on which to place his offering, 'I shall leave it here . . . just so . . . and you may help yourself. I shall not take one step closer.'

The little girl regarded the plum pudding, unsure. But in an instant her hunger overrode any doubts she might have had at taking it, and so she proceeded to limp towards the rock. In all of three mouthfuls the slice was gone, and Benoît could not help smiling at the look of delight on the child's face.

'See, *petite*, was that not nice?'

The child managed another small nod, but still she said nothing. Was the poor thing mute? Benoît wondered. Well, what a terrible thing if so. But then, he reasoned, she had voice enough to cry when he woke her. Perhaps she was still afraid of him and needed drawing out. With a flourish of his hand the monsieur took a deep and formal bow, ignoring the painful creak in his knees.

'My name, *mademoiselle*, is Benoît de Fortgibu. And these are my feathered friends.' Here he gestured to Foi, Espoir and Charité still tethered to the holly tree, and her gaze fell to the three hens in doe-eyed wonderment. 'We are newly arrived in Merrywake as guests of Viscount and Viscountess Pépin. Do you know the Pépins, *chérie*?'

Of course she did not – she could not possibly – but that was by the by.

'They are a delightful family,' continued the monsieur, quite determined to continue this conversational mode of discourse, 'most kind and most generous. The viscountess especially would be extremely distressed to find one such as yourself all alone, especially at Christmastime.'

The little girl looked away. The Frenchman's heart gave a sharp tug.

'Please, *petite*, do tell me why you are all alone? Where is your family?' And this time the child looked to the old man, moving her mouth in a whisper. 'Forgive me,' said Benoît, 'but you must raise your voice, for my hearing is not what it was.' Here he hesitated. 'Cannon fire, you see. In Russia. Perforated eardrum. Do you understand?'

At this the little girl cocked her head, and took a small step forwards.

'What are your chickens called?'

Such relief the monsieur felt at hearing the child speak! And oh, what a forlorn and quiet little voice it was too. It made his heart reach out to her all the more.

'Why,' said he in reply, 'how rude of me – I introduced myself and not them! *Tsk tsk*, such ill manners shall not do. I will rectify them immediately.'

Benoît crossed the clearing and untethered his hens, raising their leads to urge them forwards one by one.

'Here is Espoir. Handsome, *n'est-ce pas*? But then, he knows it too. See how he preens?'

And he *was* preening. Glad to be released from the holly tree, Espoir was at that moment ferreting about with his beak in his black feathers, ruffling the tiny white flecks scattered within.

'Do not judge him though,' continued Benoît, pressing a knowing finger to his nose. 'He is the sweetest, most docile breed. Very friendly. You may pet him, if you like – he is rather partial to a little chuck under the chin.'

The monsieur was not sure if the little girl would oblige, but after a moment's hesitation she approached. Benoît tried not to notice how red her fingers were as she bent to caress Espoir's sleek feathers, and when she did the fowl tilted his head with a spirited *cluck*.

'There, see, he likes you,' Benoît declared, to which the little girl smiled in reply, and what a lovely smile she had; it lit up her sweet cherub face so beautifully one might forget it was covered with dirt. A veritable doll would she be, if someone only took to the care of her. 'I assumed,' he continued, 'that Espoir was a girl, like the others when I bought him. An oversight by the young lad when he sorted them at market, I'm sure. I thought I'd have more eggs for breakfast, so when my little Houdan turned out to be *un mâle* it was quite the shock.'

The child stood up straighter then, pressed her little hands once more into her filthy skirts.

'What's *her* name?' she asked, nodding at the white hen which lingered close to her master's leg.

Benoît beamed. 'That is my little Charité. She is partial to the attention of children for she does so like to be cuddled. Though she is, it must be said, a little shy.'

He had chosen his words with care. Not that it was a false-hood, for Charité could be shy around strangers, but the monsieur wanted to ascertain the depth of the *child's* shyness and see if he might be able to draw her out further, for he had decided then and there that she should be brought back to Wakely Hall. Conscience, and yes, guilt, would not allow him to abandon her. Glorious winter's day that it was, the light would soon draw in and the cold turn bitter and sharp in the night air. But would the girl's shyness, her caution (for Benoît perceived no fear in her at that present moment), allow him to escort her to safety and warmth? He was about to broach the subject, when the little doll asked:

'Why are her legs blue?'

Benoît blinked, and had to recall himself before answering.

'Because, *ma chérie*, she is a Bresse. Such markings are typical of the breed. She is quite striking, is she not? Isn't her red comb pretty?'

The little girl nodded, but turned her head.

'I like this one.'

It was to the last of his hens she was referring, who at present was pecking at the shrivelled shell of an acorn nestled in the hoarfrost.

'Ah,' Benoît said knowingly, 'my lovely brown La Flèche. 'Tis her tail you like, *oui?*' and the child nodded again. 'Peacock plumage. Particularly handsome when the sun shines on it. All those splendid rainbows! Oh, yes, my little Foi is a beauty indeed.'

The child looked thoughtful.

'Please, sir, what does Foi mean?' she asked, looking at him with such innocent interest that the Frenchman's kind heart gave another little turn in his chest.

'Why, *mademoiselle*, it means Faith.'

Her small face coloured as if the answer pleased her, which in turn pleased him.

'Espoir means Hope,' he said next, 'and Charité . . . can you guess?'

The little girl's eyebrows drew together in thought. 'Charity,' came the answer, and Benoît clapped his hands in pleasure.

'*Mais oui!* Splendid, little one, splendid.'

The question of course was not a difficult one with the word being so similar in sound to its English counterpart, but nonetheless Benoît sensed that here was a little girl of education; he was convinced now she must have originally come from respectable stock. Where else might she have come into possession of a shawl of pale pink embroidered with tiny satin roselets? Where else might she have inherited the pleasing way in which she spoke? This was no farmer's daughter, no milkmaid. But who was she?

There really could be no other call for it – the child simply *must* return to Wakely Hall with him, and he could only hope the Pépins would discover the child's identity in due course.

'I wonder, *ma chérie*,' said he, 'did you enjoy your plum pudding?'

The delighted smile which had crossed the girl's face in consequence to Benoît's praise wavered. Almost fearful again, she gave a small nod.

'Well, then, you must come along to the house and we can ask Mrs Denby for a plum pudding of your own.' Immediately she began to shake her head, but Benoît would not be dissuaded from his duty. 'Oh do, *mademoiselle*! You would not be disappointed, of that I can assure.' He assumed a thoughtful expression. 'If plum puddings are not to your taste, I am sure another culinary delight could be found. Mrs Denby is quite famous around these parts for her roast goose dinners. Besides,' he added, as the little girl's eyes grew large and hungersome, 'it will be warm at Wakely Hall. A bed can be found for you there, somewhere comfortable to shield you from this horrible cold.'

It was at that moment there came an icy breeze that wove its way through the leafless trees, sending a shudder through the

Frenchman on the very spot where he stood; the child clutched at her threadbare shawl, and even the three hens trilled at the change in the air. Benoît raised his nose to the sky, then looked down at the child in all seriousness.

'There will be more snow tonight,' he said, more firmly than he had spoken to her before, for he was keen to press his point. 'Come, *chérie*. Surely you do not wish to spend the night outside, again, alone?'

If Benoît de Fortgibu had harboured any doubts that the child had *not* spent more than one night sleeping in the wilds of Merrywake, these doubts were quashed in that very instant, for the girl's pale eyes shone then with tears.

'Very good,' the monsieur said with a smile. It was one of relief, but to the girl he hoped it portrayed only sincerity and warmth. 'Perhaps you might wish to walk Foi for me? She can be a boisterous little chick when she wishes, but with you, *petite*, I believe she will be quite at ease. Besides,' he added with a small laugh to lighten the mood once more, 'three hens can be an awful handful. You would be doing me a great service.'

Shyly the child held out her hand, and Benoît placed Foi's little red lead into her dirty palm.

'Shall we?'

And so off they went. Their progress was slow for the poor girl had sprained her ankle, but Benoît patiently guided her from the clearing – back through the woodland, onto the path, up towards the iron gate. Once more he lifted his arm and the leads of Espoir and Charité to allow easy passage through the narrow gap, and a little way behind him the child did the same. What a fast learner she was, the Frenchman thought as he turned left to complete the circle that would take him and his new companion back to the entranceway of Wakely Hall. Such quick wits, such gentle manners!

Whoever could have abandoned her?

They walked in silence at first, for this was a thought that deeply troubled him; the ghost of the Krasny girl would not leave him, and so too his memories of Émile. How *could* such a sweet innocent boy grow up to become the man he so evidently became? The Frenchman pictured the child Émile in that moment – rosy-cheeked with eyes aglow at the taste of rich currants and orange zest, a smile of pure pleasure upon his cherubic face. How similar the little girl at his side had looked, and Benoît found himself compelled to speak of the comparison.

'You will not be the first *enfant* I have converted to the joys of plum pudding,' he murmured as the girl limped beside him down the woodland lane. 'I once met a boy in my home city of Orléans. I was visiting the boarding school there.' Here Benoît paused and managed a small conspiratorial smile. 'I delivered a lecture on the intelligence of chickens, would you believe, and he was seated at my table. The school knew of my love of plum pudding and was kind enough to procure one for me. But, as with yourself, I shared my pudding with young Émile. He had never encountered one before and was most perplexed by it, but I urged him to try a slice and to my delight he found it just as pleasing as I did. Now you have tasted some for yourself, I am sure you would agree.'

She did not answer, but the monsieur did not expect her to. His only intention at that moment was to keep the girl safely with him and not scare the poor dear away the nearer they reached the hall.

'Six years ago,' he continued, his smile fading once again, 'I encountered the fellow again. A man of nineteen and by then a promising poet. Two years later his *La Paix Conquise* was so admired it even won the praise of Napoleon. Old Boney told me so himself.'

Benoît swallowed.

It was the same Russian campaign, some days before they reached Krasny. While the snow had not yet started to fall in earnest the cold was impenetrable; the troops set up their white tents for the night as an icy wind shot sharply about the camp, the French flags billowed up a frenzy, and while the soldiers shivered about their meagre fires Napoleon sat wrapt in sumptuous furs within his palatial shelter, a glass of Chambertin wine in one hand, Émile's latest work in the other.

'That young Deschamps,' said Bonaparte to Benoît, whom he had called so as to issue orders but since – in his liquor – had diverted the conversation elsewhere. 'He understands what I am about. He recognises the inferiority of England, the spirit of France. See how the poet calls me King? *He* knows what it is to be a *true* Frenchman!'

Being one of the emperor's colonels, the monsieur could do nothing but agree, although in truth he had been bitterly disappointed – *non*, angry – that Émile should have been so seduced by a man who had been the cause of so much needless bloodshed, a man who came into power not through the will of God but an act of rebellion.

Nos armes font les rois. 'Our weapons make kings.'

With a cough Benoît caught himself, only to find the girl staring up at him with button eyes so very like the Krasny child's that he found himself quite unable to meet her inquisitive gaze.

'Well,' Benoît concluded, flustered, 'I digress,' to which Charité clucked loudly as if she agreed with him. 'The point I wish to make is that we came upon one another in a shop in Paris, where Émile attempted to purchase the very pudding I had put by myself.' The monsieur sighed wistfully at the memory. It was two years before Émile had written the poem, a time when Benoît still thought him honourable. 'What a funny thing it was,' he mused. 'Émile told me he had never forgotten my generosity, and seeing the pudding on the counter had roused in him that one special memory of Christmas in Orléans.'

'What did you do?' asked the girl.

'Why, *ma chérie*, I shared it with him again. Most pleased was Émile, too, I can tell you. What a merry pair we made that December afternoon. How affable he was.'

Affable. Yet the young man Benoît thought he knew could not be reconciled with the poet. Did Émile feel guilt at the terrible words he had written? Did he recognise their savagery, their needless viciousness, now that the bloodshed was over?

Foi clucked, tugged on her lead, distracting him. The girl allowed the leather a little slack. As if in pleasure the brown hen shook her peacock tail feathers and scarpered forwards to join Espoir and Charité, who were at that moment sauntering some

81

paces ahead, Benoît having already allowed them free rein of their leads.

'Espoir,' the monsieur scolded. 'You pull, *mon garçon*.' He tweaked the cockerel's green tether; the little Houdan uttered a tiny cluck in response but then heeded nicely, stepping into line.

Up ahead, Wakely Hall came into view. It was a grand-looking house, with a classical portico of pillars at its entrance. It was fortunate enough to face west, overlooking a sweeping lawn to a large ornate pond, and beyond, reaching fields and the vastness of the forest whence they had just come. Oh, Wakely, Benoît smiled. He had spent many a happy visit under that roof, thanks to the generous hospitality of Fernand Pépin. His own town house in Orléans could not begin to compare with the freedom he so often felt there. How he enjoyed reading his novels in the pillared orangery, how he delighted in meandering about the grounds, walking his three darlings down the yew tree avenue situated at the side of the house, and it was at that moment the unlikely pair reached the gate that opened out onto that avenue. Benoît held it open for the child to step through, but she lingered at the threshold, suddenly unsure. He could see the apprehension in her pale face, marked with pity how her blue eyes darted this way and that.

'Come, *petite*. You will be quite all right. Have faith.'

Her gaze snapped to his, then, and something in her expression changed. The monsieur could not decipher what it was he saw there, but whatever it was the child felt it was enough to assuage her fears for through she limped, little Foi at her toes.

'There now. Mrs Denby shall provide you with a meal of roast goose, as promised,' he told her, taking now her hand, which sat so small and cold in his.

'And plum pudding?' came the plaintive answer, which made the monsieur shout a laugh.

'*Mais oui!* Of course, of course.' He grinned down at her. 'So you did like it! I am so very pleased.'

When they arrived at the kitchen door the smell of fresh mince pies assailed the monsieur's nostrils, and Benoît beheld Mrs Denby removing a fresh batch of them from the stove. Particularly irked did she look too, for the second-youngest Pépin daughter was at that moment attempting to claim a pie for her own.

'No, Miss Louisa,' scolded the cook, attempting to swipe her away. 'You shall burn your fingers.'

'But they smell so delightful,' pouted the girl, a declaration with which Monsieur de Fortgibu could not disagree.

'*Mais oui,*' said he then, guiding the child and his hens inside before shutting the door behind them, 'most delightful, Mrs Denby. Once they have cooled, might we beg a pie or two?'

The cook, Miss Louisa and Katherine Allen (who held another tray of the delectable treats), all turned, at which their mouths dropped as they beheld the monsieur and the little girl at his side.

'Good heaven,' remarked Mrs Denby, recovering herself by placing the tray down upon the table. 'Who is this? The poor mite. She looks fit to faint.'

'Mrs Denby,' said the monsieur with a small bow. 'If you

cannot spare a mince pie at present, could I prevail upon you for another of your excellent dishes? I have promised this little girl a meal of roast goose and one of my plum puddings. Would you be so good as to oblige?'

There was a moment's hesitation (for this was an unexpected request), but soon – amid the whispers and stares of Wakely's servants – the child was ushered in to sit before the fire, a cup of warm cinnamon milk placed in her tiny hands, while the kitchen maid hurried herself to prepare a plate of leftovers and one of the monsieur's puddings. As the little girl sipped from her cup, Benoît took Miss Louisa and Mrs Denby aside.

'I found her all alone in the forest,' he murmured. 'Her ankle is sprained. You must understand, *madame*, I could not leave her there.'

'But she cannot stay *here*,' the cook whispered, tweaking her apron as the two hens standing between them pecked at the raw pastry stuck to it. 'Where can we keep her? I believe the guest rooms upstairs are all taken or soon to be, and the servants, well . . . I cannot ask them to vacate their beds on account of a foundling.'

'A foundling?' came Miss Louisa's high-pitched response. Wide-eyed, she turned to stare at the child. The monsieur's sigh – if she had bothered to mark it – held within it a hint of impatience.

'I do not think her a foundling,' said he. 'Look at the shawl she wears, the quiet manner in which she conducts herself. And if you were to hear her speak, you could not think her to be of low stock.' Benoît grew pensive at the thought. 'We must discover where she belongs. Miss Pépin, if you would fetch your parents, I shall explain it all to them.'

Miss Louisa readily agreed and – giving a soulful look at the steaming mince pies on the table – retreated into the servants' corridor and out of sight. The cook watched her go with a dubious expression.

'Oh, monsieur. I do hope they come quickly. If Mrs W finds the child here – and eating our leftovers at that – she will have much to say about it, you can be sure.'

''Tis Christmas,' said the Frenchman, patting Mrs Denby's hand. 'Surely she cannot be so uncharitable at such a time?'

At this the cook looked troubled, but unable to keep himself from his charge Benoît was already approaching the little girl and did not see Mrs Denby's expression.

'There now,' he said, releasing Espoir and Charité from their leads (who proceeded to scuttle off across the flagstones and almost collided with a snub-nosed scullery maid – *Oh, lawds, you bothersome chickees!*), 'you shall be kept safe and warm here, just as I told you. But might I beg something in return?'

The child blinked up at him. Her eyes were watery, though from the warmth of the kitchen or emotion, he could not be sure. Still, Benoît was gratified to receive a nod from her, and with a gentle smile he put his hands upon his knees.

'Tell me, *petite*. What is your name?'

She ducked her head and did not answer. Foi – still attached to her little red lead – proceeded to settle herself at the child's feet where she began to preen her glorious brown feathers with happy little trills.

Benoît sighed. If the girl did not wish to divulge her name, he would not force the issue, nor could he, for in that moment the kitchen maid returned with a warm plate of roast goose and vegetables, and a steaming plum pudding. The child's face alit with pleasure, and Benoît was struck again how similarly Émile had regarded *his* pudding, all those years ago.

Émile, Benoît thought, as the little girl greedily ate her supper. Surely the boy he once knew had not completely disappeared? It was perfectly possible, now the wars were over, that the poet *did* feel remorse for the poem he had penned; he had been young, after all, when he wrote it, and did not everybody make mistakes?

Certainly, Benoît had made plenty of his own. The memory of the Krasny girl would always haunt him, so too the memories of all the atrocities he had committed during those awful years under Napoleon's rule.

Perhaps, Monsieur de Fortgibu thought, he would meet Émile again. If he did, there was a chance his faith in the poet would be renewed, and as the Frenchman watched the lost girl joyfully savouring her plum pudding, he found a sense of hope rising within him for whatever the future had to bring.

STAVE IV.

Mistletoe Gambol
Four Colly Birds

As Monsieur de Fortgibu predicted, more snow *had* fallen, and to such a degree that the four servants who had volunteered to collect the foliage to decorate Wakely Hall were required to bundle themselves up in an array of scarves and cloaks to accommodate it.

Indeed, four inches of snow had descended from the winter sky at a gentle yet steady pace from the hour of twilight, and while the countryside of Merrywake looked glorious in the stark morning sunshine (for the fields were a twinkling blanket of white and the trees wore their sparkling boughs with aplomb) the terrain was troublesome to navigate. Only a half-hour had passed since leaving Wakely, but already the quartet had been obliged to manoeuvre down a slippery ha-ha and a frozen river-bank, no mean feat for the member of the party who had been prevailed upon to push the wheelbarrow. Still, the path was clear enough now they had found their bearings, and, as the servants crunched towards Wakely Forest, the housemaid Prudence Brown turned to her companions and made a point of expressing her admiration for the snowy poplar trees in the distance.

'How affecting they look,' she sighed wistfully. 'Pretty as a painting! And see there – does it not look like they wear little pom-poms?'

Ralph Hornby, Viscount Pépin's valet, squinted at the poplars from beneath his leather cap. Upon seeing said pom-poms his dark eyes lit with pleasure, and puffing up his chest he exclaimed:

'That's mistletoe! Shall we add some sprigs to the collection? I'm sure it would go down splendidly back at the hall. Imagine all those *tons* gambolling about the night of the ball, seeking out some dark nook with a Pépin sister! And I'm sure we can slip a sprig belowstairs – seems a shame to let *them* have all the fun.'

'Oh yes,' breathed Molly Hart, who looked up at Ralph with admiration. 'What fun we could *all* have if given half the chance!'

Ralph laughed, Molly preened. Prudence gave another little sigh.

'You know Mrs Wilson will not let us have mistletoe in the house,' she said. 'She'd throw it on the fire.'

Molly – as if affronted by such a suggestion – swung the empty basket she was carrying like a mallet.

'I'm sure we could find a little cranny in the pantry. Mrs Wilson never goes in there, does she? Mrs Denby won't allow it.'

'She'd find it anyway, I'm sure,' came the desolate reply, 'and into the fire it would undoubtedly go.'

'That, my dear Mol,' said Ralph, flinging a long arm about her slight shoulders, 'is because old bracket-face has never been kissed, and wishes no one else to have the pleasure. I'd wager my shiny new sixpence on it. And what a tragedy that is, to have never experienced the wildly exhilarating feeling of a good kiss!'

Such a declaration succeeded in making both Molly and Prudence giggle, but William Moss – who had paused from his task of pushing the cumbersome wheelbarrow through the white slew without assistance (a fact perceived by him most pointedly) – narrowed his eyes at Ralph's back.

'Not everyone kisses their way about Merrywake like you do, Hornby, and it will serve you to remember we are in impressionable company.'

With a long whistle Ralph released Prudence's shoulders and spun about to address him.

'What ho, Will! Such prudishness. I would have you know I only kiss ladies who wish to be kissed.'

At this Molly looked at Ralph with an expression that gave no doubt as to *her* wishes, but his attentions were firmly planted on William, a smirk playing about his handsome face which William answered with a deep frown.

'But do they realise you have no mind to kiss them honestly?' he countered. 'I dare say you have no inclination of setting your cap at anyone, despite all your flirtations. I'd be wary if I were you, Mol.'

Ralph rolled his eyes and Molly, with a faint air of injury, tugged at the lace of her Christmas box shawl. Prudence – with an uncertain look upon her face – pushed ahead towards Wakely Forest and those delightful pom-pommed poplars. William, however, watched the ambling trio crunch through the snow ahead of him, and shook his dark head.

Ralph Hornby had held the position of valet for some years before William arrived at Wakely Hall. The son of a butcher, William had no taste for the cruel barbarism of that trade, and as soon as circumstance allowed him the opportunity he left his home town to forge his own way in the world. That is to say, William prevailed upon the Pépins for a position, and Mrs Wilson's speedy acceptance of his application (*Wakely is in dire need of an under-gardener*) made him rather more sympathetic to her, and therefore less willing to hear invectives of the kind Ralph Hornby chose to impart.

That, and William really did disapprove of the valet's cavalier treatment of Wakely Hall's maids.

It had always been so. William observed early after his arrival at the hall that many of Wakely's serving women were half in love with Ralph, and in truth this knowledge was most vexing for William. It was not that he himself wished for the attentions of the fairer sex; no, it was more that he found the valet's behaviour so disagreeable. Having grown up with three younger sisters, he knew how he would feel if *their* hearts were toyed with in so rakish a manner. That, and the fact that he—

His thoughts were interrupted by a tinkling, feminine laugh. William looked up. Ahead, Ralph had linked arms with both Prudence and Molly, chattering blithely away. Oh, yes, he was a charmer, that one. William raised his head to the sky, and in doing so marked the mistletoe suspended from the branches of those ever-nearing poplar trees.

What, he wondered, did a kiss even feel like? *Was* it wildly exhilarating, as Ralph claimed? William tried to imagine such a circumstance: the closeness of two bodies pressed against each other, the shared experience of warm breath upon one's lips. Were lips soft to the touch when kissing? Or were they hardened in passion? William's imagination was not ripe for the task.

He had seen his parents kiss, of course. So too his sister on her betrothal to the local blacksmith. But such kisses were always so polite, devoid of the desire he had imagined romantic kisses to hold. And did kisses differ between those shared by male and female, as opposed to those shared between—

William shook his head. These were thoughts he must not think.

Somewhere, a blackbird sang. He raised his head to find it, eventually spying the colly perched on a holly branch on the outskirts of Wakely Forest. William called for the others to stop.

'We can start here,' he said when they joined him.

From the wheelbarrow he pulled out a pair of long-handled shears and passed them to Ralph, who looked at them with a faint expression of disgust.

'What's the matter?' William asked. 'Too much like hard work for you?'

'Of course not,' replied Ralph, with a tone of affront. 'But I am here for advisory purposes only.'

'Advisory purposes?'

Ralph raised his chiselled chin. 'Usually it is Mr Cobb who collects the foliage, so I suppose you can be forgiven for not knowing my role in this endeavour, but I never *pick* the stuff. The viscount has trusted me to oversee the placement of the Christmas garlands for years now and never once have I been required to get my hands dirty. Tell him, Mol. *You* know what's what around here.'

'It's true,' said Molly with a toss of her dark head. 'Ralph's talents are far more suited to the application of decoration than to outside work. Valets are above such things.'

To this William stared, keeping his countenance as neutral as he was able to under the circumstances. Mr Cobb, Wakely's gardener, currently indisposed with a cold, had not disclosed this information to him when he collected the wheelbarrow from the gatekeeper's cottage earlier that morning, but if he had William was sure he would have had some choice words to say about the matter. As upper servants, Molly's and Ralph's tasks were nothing to those of the lowers such as him and Prudence, but until that moment William had not fully comprehended the hierarchy which existed between them, and it left an unpleasant taste in his mouth. Suppressing a deep sigh, he placed the shears against the sharp leaves of the holly bush, then removed a pair of clippers from the woollen confines of his double-breasted work coat and handed them to Prudence.

'There's some decent-looking firs a little way in. Cut a few sprigs, won't you? The stems aren't very thick lower down, 'twill be easy enough,' and as Prudence nodded (thankfully) readily enough, William turned to the upper housemaid. 'See if you can't seek out some pine cones. Enough to fill that basket. If you can bear to get your hands dirty, that is.'

His tone had been deliberately derogatory, and William was satisfied to see that Molly marked it. However, the housemaid simply glanced pointedly at Ralph and said in a manner that set William's teeth on edge:

'I'd rather stay here and help Ralph advise. Prudence can scavenge for pine cones, can't you, Prue?'

William ground his teeth.

'I won't argue with Hornby, if that is the way of things, but you volunteered to come along, and if it wasn't to help us then I can only assume it was to shirk your duties back at the house. I wonder what Mrs Wilson might say to that when I tell her all you did was stand about making cow-eyes at the valet?'

At this, Molly paled and turned imploringly to said valet, whose mouth twisted in a wry grin.

'Better do as he says, Mol.'

She blinked, clearly not expecting such a reply; and nor, it must be said, had William, who stared at Ralph with no little surprise. Prudence, who had been watching the exchange with a nervous expression upon her face, tugged at Molly's arm.

'Come on, Mol,' she said. 'Our job will be far more fun together, and the faster we do it the faster we'll be home.'

'Easy for you to say,' sniped the housemaid. 'You don't have a mansionful of beds to make when you get back.'

'No, but I do have chamber pots to empty. Out of your chores and mine, I know which I prefer . . .'

93

And with that Prudence tugged at Molly's arm once more, to which the upper housemaid reluctantly consented to being pulled into the depths of Wakely Forest, leaving William and Ralph quite alone, except for the blackbird which still perched unperturbed upon the frosted holly branch.

Aside from a few instances where Ralph had been obliged to convey a request from Mrs Wilson or, on occasion, the viscount himself, the valet had never been alone with William before, for their circles at Wakely Hall were very different. As Mr Cobb's assistant it was rare for William to cross paths with Ralph Hornby at all beyond their sharing a table at mealtimes. Ralph was a man of comfort and order; William was a man of outdoor pursuits, and he took his duties very seriously. Mr Cobb had been kind to him since he arrived in Merrywake three years ago, and with this being the first time the gardener had relinquished a task typically undertaken by him, William was determined not to let the gardener down.

'Well, then,' said he awkwardly to the valet, brandishing the long-handled shears. 'Do you want to advise me which to cut?'

Ralph, who had been standing with his arms crossed over his chest assessing the holly bush with a look of contemplation on his handsome face (and he really *was* handsome, Will thought, with his shock of coal-black hair that fell so attractively across his fine forehead), came to stand next to him. The valet did not appear to notice the faint blush that had bloomed upon William's cheeks, instead reaching out his arm to point at a branch heavily laden with spiked leaves.

'This one. Lots of foliage.'

With care William clipped the suggested branch, deposited it in the wheelbarrow.

'And that one too,' said Ralph, pointing. 'Nice bend to it. The one above has a good shape as well. The trick is,' the valet added, 'to consider how the branches might rest on a mantelpiece. Those have just the right amount of curvature.'

William cut the branches as bidden. He supposed, he thought grudgingly, that the branches *did* have a pleasing shape – if it had been left purely up to him, William would have simply cut some of the lower branches and had done with it. It was as he was depositing these branches too into the wheelbarrow that Ralph pressed his arm.

'And there,' he said, gesturing to one higher up, 'that one still has its berries. Viscount Pépin likes a little shot of red in his garlands.'

It took a moment for William to answer, for Ralph's hand on his arm had distracted him; the valet's touch was gentle in a way William had not expected (although, as the viscount's dresser, one must suppose Ralph had to be gentle), and it made him more nervous than he already was. Swallowing hard, he took a stronger grip on the shears.

'Very good.'

William raised the shears, and as he did, above them, the blackbird offered a few notes of song which made him pause.

He liked blackbirds. Any bird, in point of fact; indeed, any animal. His father once called him too soft for harbouring such 'feminine fancies', but of all the positions Mrs Wilson could have offered him, gardener's assistant was the one best suited to his constitution; after the brutality of the family butcher's, it was a relief to work within the beautiful grounds of Wakely Hall every day, to hear the soothing sound of birdsong and witness new life in spring – such joy William experienced when he first found a nest of wood mice within the rose border, the chirrup of chicks in the yew trees! It was as if, when he came to Wakely, he could finally become a little more himself.

'I'm surprised,' murmured William as he cut the branch, 'that there are still berries left. The birds should have eaten them by now. Here ...' and he plucked one, offered it up to the colly. 'This belongs to you, really.'

The blackbird cocked its head. Like Ralph, its colouring was coal. A male then.

'Ah, don't be a cork-brain, Will. It won't come—'

But it did. Down the bird flew onto his gloved hand, and took the berry in its beak. It looked at William then with such keenness, as if to thank him, before flitting away at speed into the forest.

Ralph let out a low whistle.

'*Well, well*, you're a dark horse, aren't you? Quite literally charming the birds from the trees,' and the teasing way the valet said the words made William colour. 'Don't be embarrassed,' he laughed, nudging his arm again which made William's blush worse. 'Wait until I tell the ladies. They'll all be cock-a-whoop when they hear. Women like a gentle soul, and you're not a bad-looking fellow ... Not bad at all.'

William pushed past him, the branch still in his other hand, and put it in the wheelbarrow with the others.

'I don't want attention from any lady,' he muttered.

'You don't?'

His back was turned and so he could not see the valet's face, but William could hear plain the surprise in Ralph's voice.

'I ... I don't have time for it.'

There came then a heavy pause. A snow-crunched step behind him.

'You don't have *time*? Ain't that a fine excuse. I'm sure if you wanted a lady love enough, you'd make time. Shew any of them that little trick of yours and they'd flock to you.' William said nothing. Ralph rounded the wheelbarrow to look at him. 'In fact, let's step into the village on our next afternoon off. We can go to the Crown. What a good-looking pair we'll make. Two black-haired devils, ready to shew Merrywake's girls a little bit of heaven!'

William's insides churned, both with mortification and that other feeling, the one he had taken great pains to bury deep but was presently failing to control.

'Why must it always be about women with you, Hornby?' William snapped, wishing now he had not sent Molly and Prudence into Wakely Forest, and his tone pulled Ralph up short.

'Why must *you* be so churlish? Life is too short to be churlish.'

'I'm not churlish.'

'But you are,' insisted Ralph, 'especially with me. I mean ...' and here the valet moved to stand directly in front of William so he was forced to look at him. 'What was all that with Mol earlier? *I'd be wary if I were you*,' he mimicked with a raising of his black brows. ''Tis only harmless flirting, and that's all I'm suggesting we do, really. It's just a bit of fun.'

'To you, perhaps,' countered William. 'But . . .'

'But what?'

'But . . .'

Oh, but William could not find the words! And what could he say, really? Because William *was* churlish to Ralph – from the moment he'd met the charming valet and discovered not only his predilection for flirting and the cavalier way in which he did it, but William's consequent feelings about the matter, he made a point of being so. To be churlish towards Ralph Hornby was the only way in which William knew how to hide the truth, to deny the deadly fact that would, if anyone were to discover it, be the means to see him hang:

Backgammon player. Indorser. Sodomite.

His father had called him all of these, and worse.

Ralph was watching him. The teasing expression was no longer there, replaced instead with a thoughtful one which left William frightened. Had the valet, in that moment, guessed? But no, surely not, and somehow William mustered the strength to shrug.

'I simply do not consider playing with the hearts of ladies entertaining. Let us finish with the holly,' he added, brisk. 'A few more branches should do it, I think?' and with that William turned his attention back to the bush.

To his relief the valet said nothing further but turned to the task at hand; soon they had relieved the holly of four more branches and were following the sound of chatter through the winding path of Wakely Forest.

'Is it true,' came Prudence's voice, 'that Miss Juliette—'

'Seigneuresse Toussaint,' came Molly's haughty correction.

'Yes, *Seg-nur* . . .' Prudence struggled over the word before discarding it. 'Well, is it true she has taken charge of the little girl?'

''Tis true. I had to make up the cot bed in the old schoolroom, and what a fuss the seigneuresse made over her! Treated her like a doll, she did. Queer little thing, but the Pépins have quite taken to her and that silly old Frenchman let the child sleep with one of his hens last night. Can you imagine?'

As William and Ralph emerged from the trees, Prudence was adding a twig of fir to the small pile at her feet. Wide-eyed she exclaimed she had never heard the like, to which Molly agreed vigorously, but before they could continue the conversation Ralph cleared his throat.

'How do, ladies? Let's see what you've conjured up.'

Presently the holly branches in William's wheelbarrow were joined by a healthy collection of pine cones and fir stems, at which Ralph announced there would be quite enough for Viscount Pépin's festive garlands.

'Are you sure?' Molly asked, eyeing the wheelbarrow dubiously. 'I'm *sure* something is missing . . .'

'I'll fetch the rest from the garden,' Will replied, keen now to return to Wakely Hall, where he might seclude himself away from temptation. 'It's only rosemary, bay and box we need now.'

'It isn't,' replied Molly coyly. 'What about the mistletoe?'

'Oh yes, of course! Come on, Will,' cajoled Ralph, watching him with a look that William could not – nor wished to – fathom. 'It can't do much harm.'

'But Mrs Wilson . . .' began Prudence in worried tones, and in response Molly rolled her fine blue eyes.

'Don't be such a prude, Prue.'

''Tis just a lark,' rejoined Ralph, and William sighed.

'Do as you must then. But be quick about it.'

'Well . . .' Molly looked between the other three. '*I* cannot reach, and Prudence certainly can't.'

Ralph frowned. 'And I *did* say I'm only here to advise.'

William sighed again, more heavily this time. 'Fine, then. Prudence, give me those clippers.'

Still looking monstrously worried she did as bidden, and William began to shimmy up the tree.

It was just as well, he thought, really. The further away from Ralph Hornby he was, the better. And the higher up he went to reach the mistletoe, the calmer William felt; the cold air grew sharper and he breathed it in deep, and soon he was far enough up the poplar to see the extensive fields surrounding Wakely Hall, Hodge Farm up on the hill, and the cluster of buildings further down that made up the village of Merrywake. It was a truly beautiful sight, and what peace William felt, to know this was his home, that this idyllic life should be his. But what loneliness, too, that he was destined to live it alone.

Birdsong trilled at his ear; William twisted to see.

Two blackbirds sat watching him, and though there was no way to be sure, he was almost positive one was the same colly he had fed not a half-hour before. Both birds were coal black with bright orange beaks and a striking yellow ring about their eyes, and sitting so close together, too, wing touching silken wing. 'Twas unusual, William thought, to see two males together, and he smiled wistfully.

At least they *will not be lonely.*

'Make haste!' shouted Molly.

'Be careful!' called Prudence.

With a huff William turned to the nearest cluster of mistletoe, and snipped off two sprigs. It was all he dared take and as he inched his way back down, Ralph began to sing:

> *The Misletoe hangs from an oaken beam,*
> *The Ivy creeps up the outer wall;*
> *The Bays our broken casements screen,*
> *The Holly-bush graces the hall.*

Molly clapped and cheered, and called for another to which Ralph obliged, taking a surprised Prudence in his arms to dance her about the snowy forest:

> *It happen'd, that some sport to shew*
> *The ceiling held a Misletoe.*
> *A magic bough, and well design'd*
> *To prove the coyest Maiden, kind.*

'Ralph,' cried Prudence as the valet spun her about with great muster. 'You go too fast!'

'How else am I supposed to turn your head?' came the humorous reply. 'But remember, Prue, there is no mirth without mischief!'

Ralph had drawn the maid close to his chest (Molly Hart looked vexed indeed), and at that moment William, seeing it all with clenched jaw, reached terra firma. The blush upon Prudence's face was furious with Ralph's arms about her waist, and over her bonneted head he met William's gaze. There was something about the valet's expression that hinted at a challenge, but there was no chance for William to consider it for there was then a crunch in the undergrowth, the shrill *yap yap* of a dog.

All four of Wakely's servants turned.

Come from the direction of Old Hodge Farm was there standing the young Mr Hodge, his black-and-white terrier at his side, and he was staring at Prudence and Ralph with a mien most stunned.

'Mr Hodge!' Prudence gasped, shrugging out of the valet's arms as if she had been burnt. 'I didn't . . . you must not . . .'

In that moment, William understood. There was, it seemed, an understanding between Prudence Brown and Nathaniel Hodge – the housemaid appeared on the verge of tears and the farmer was staring hard now at the forest floor, a muscle in his freckled jaw working furiously.

'Have you seen a lamb wandering about in the forest?' mumbled he. 'One of mine escaped its pen this morning.'

Mr Hodge's tone was flat, quite devoid of emotion. In fact, the farmer's entire countenance appeared now as if he did not care at all, but William knew better; he knew well what it felt to have one's heart irrevocably bruised.

"Fraid not, Hodge,' came Ralph's droll answer. He had not relinquished his hold on Prudence's hand despite her fervent pulls. 'No little lambs about Wakely Forest except sweet Prue here.'

The farmer blinked. The terrier barked. And then, silent as you please, the young man nodded, retreated the way he had come, his canine companion trotting loyally behind.

'Mr Hodge . . .'

Prudence's call was plaintive, her eyes wet, but the young man did not turn, and as Ralph met his gaze once again all William could do was shake his head and bestow upon him a look of great admonition.

It was a divided group who returned to Wakely Hall.

For William, the journey was achieved in a silence punctuated only by Prudence Brown's hiccoughed sniffles and the rumbled lurchings of his wheelbarrow through the snow. If he trusted himself to keep his countenance William might have offered the poor maid some words of comfort, but the truth of it was he did not trust himself at all, so angry was he with Ralph Hornby, and all he could do was proffer her his creased handkerchief.

Oh, how rotten that man had been! It was clear Prudence was upset, but all the valet did was shrug his shoulders and declare that a little jealousy hurt no one.

"Twill do young Hodge good,' said he with a laugh. 'Perhaps now, Prue, he might shoot his aim,' to which Molly Hart had agreed, professing the whole sorry business a veritable lark, and possessively linked arms with the valet. To William's surprise he had shrugged her off, whereupon Molly glared and trudged out of the forest behind him, with Prudence and William trailing further behind in even lower spirits.

William watched the back of Ralph's dark head, and not for the first time questioned why he should find himself so drawn to him. He was evidently not a nice fellow; despite his uncommonly good looks Ralph possessed no redeemable qualities for he was a tease, a flirt, a selfish unfeeling cad. What, William thought, would the valet do if he was to discover his secret? He felt sure Ralph would either disclose the truth to the whole household, or find some way to torture him with it. No indeed, it would be best for William to pull his head from the clouds and never think of Ralph Hornby at all.

It was in this melancholy frame of mind that William continued his ungainly plod across the fields, until at length the small party reached the gravel drive of Wakely Hall, whereupon another party of equal number stood at the bottom steps of the house, clearly having returned from a morning walk. William spied Viscount Pépin, one of his daughters, Seigneur Toussaint, and a very tall and finely dressed gentleman whom he did not recognise.

'Ah ha!' called the viscount, waving the servants over with a broad and welcoming grin. 'Are these my garlands, Hornby?'

The viscount – Willam knew from experience – was a fine and jolly gentleman with easy, unaffected manners. Of middling height, never to be seen with his hair askew or his shoes unpolished (though Ralph surely had something to do with that), he might give the impression of a man who prided himself most conceitedly on his appearance, but Viscount Pépin held no airs or graces. He was beloved at Wakely Hall for his unfailing kindness, generosity of spirit, and his conscientious respect for those who served him. Often the viscount had stopped William in his tasks to discuss at length the state of the gardens and his beehives, or the merit of growing pineapples, and though he found some measure of enjoyment in such discussions, William was always somewhat relieved when Viscountess Pépin interrupted them to remind her husband that his gardeners did not have the time to indulge in idle chatter.

'Yes, my lord,' replied Ralph with a formal bow. 'The finest specimens have been selected for you, as always.'

The viscount approached the wheelbarrow, eyes alight beneath the rim of his hat.

'So they have, Hornby, so they have! They shall make a wonderful display together with Reverend Soppe's pears and Cobb's additions from the ornamental garden. How is he, Moss? Any better?'

'Middling, my lord. Still keeps to his bed, I'm afraid.'

'Well,' came the cheerful reply, 'you are doing a fine job in his absence.'

'I do my best, my lord.'

'Just so, just so,' enthused Viscount Pépin, looking very much as if he meant to offer more praise, but then his eye caught on the sprigs of mistletoe. 'Ah, but what have we here? We did not have *these* last year,' and he plucked one sprig from the wheelbarrow to hold up so his three companions should see.

'Mistletoe,' exclaimed Miss Pépin. 'Oh, what fun!' to which the seigneur frowned.

'Fun, Maria?'

'Why yes, brother,' she said, looking to him, blonde curls bobbing in the icy breeze. 'And I dare say our guests will find it most amusing.' Here her pretty face fell into a frown. 'But I would hang it, Mr Hornby, somewhere not quite so easily found. I do not think *Maman* would be best pleased if our guests spent the entirety of the ball beneath it, no matter how much fun it might be!'

At these words Seigneur Toussaint looked confused.

'Forgive me,' said he, 'but I do not understand the significance. Why would one linger beneath a sprig of mistletoe?'

The party laughed, and William, not entirely sure what to do with himself since they had not been dismissed, knew neither how to act nor where to look in the face of a conversation above his station.

'Why, Nicolas,' said Miss Maria, eyes round with shock. 'Ladies and gentlemen *kiss* beneath it!'

'Oh,' came the bemused reply. 'I thought mistletoe was merely a symbol of prosperity and long life.'

The finely dressed man standing next to him chuckled and heartily slapped a gloved hand upon Nicolas Toussaint's shoulder.

'Ah, *mon ami*, you've lived such a sheltered existence!' (His voice – William thought – was exceedingly pompous.) 'Kissing under mistletoe is a long-held tradition here. It's deemed bad luck not to follow through.'

'Well, I find that highly irregular. What if the lady – or gentleman, for that matter – does not want to be kissed?'

Viscount Pépin chortled. 'My dear boy, it is not as if couples find themselves beneath it by accident.'

'But if they do?'

The other man, the pompous one, shrugged.

'Then the kiss is taken.'

Seigneur Toussaint gave him then a look which William could not define, but if he were to guess, it was distinctly disapproving, as if his behaviour was commonplace. Not seeing the look Miss Maria, smiling, linked her brother-in-law's arm.

'Dear Nicolas, you're such a goody-goody. However does Juliette manage you?'

'Maria,' came the weary reply. 'I am sure my Juliette should think the same as I. Where is the romance? Love is not a game. Do you not agree, my lord?'

This last was addressed to Viscount Pépin, but he was not given the opportunity to answer for the other gentleman exclaimed with a laugh:

'What a way of putting it, Toussaint. I daresay kissing beneath the mistletoe is an exceedingly pleasant experience for both parties, game or otherwise.'

'Oh, Morley!' exclaimed Miss Maria, her cheeks colouring a distinct shade of pink. 'You are incorrigible.'

'I am not incorrigible at all, my dear Miss Pépin. I merely speak the truth.'

There was much chortling then, all in fine jest, but because William had not been sure of where to direct his eyes his gaze had turned to those of his fellow servants, and it was at this moment that a flush of pink had crept too upon Molly Hart's cheeks. Indeed, she was looking at the man named Morley in so direct a manner (and was that gentleman not returning her oh-so-shameless look?) that William felt obliged to clear his throat.

'If you'd be excusing us, your lordship,' said he to Viscount Pépin, 'we'd best be getting along.'

'But of course, my good man,' replied the viscount with a broad smile. 'The sooner the garlands are put up the better. Hornby, would you mind awfully if you saw to it this instant? I am impatient to see the house dressed for our celebrations. You know the days preceding Twelfth Night are my favourite time of the year.' Here Viscount Pépin frowned. ''Tis Cobb who assists you usually, is it not? Well, why don't you have Moss here help instead, since the dear chap is still so out of sorts?'

The bottom of William's stomach dropped to the toes of his boots. Mr Cobb had not mentioned that he would have to assist *inside* the house as well as out! And though it made sense for William to apply himself to this task too under the circumstances, it was most disagreeable, for had he not only a half-hour afore resolved never to even *think* of Ralph Hornby? How might such a thing be achieved *now*? But the valet was already bowing his dark head.

'Of course, my lord,' said he, with a small and rather pleased-looking smile on his face which William did not like. 'We shall attend to the matter this instant, shan't we, Mr Moss?'

Rather dejectedly, William took himself to the ornamental gardens where he collected the rosemary, box and bay leaves to accompany the holly, fir and pine cones, then returned to the house. Ralph – who in the meantime had commandeered the wheelbarrow and arranged the foliage into neat piles on the chequerboard-tiled floor of the vast entrance hall – was waiting for him, a basket of pears at his feet.

'Could you have taken any longer?' he drawled, rolling up his sleeves to display his lean forearms. 'We don't have all day, Will. I've yet to iron his lordship's inexpressibles for this evening, and he still hasn't decided which of his waistcoats to wear so I must iron *all* of them.'

Ignoring him, William deposited the tin bucket he carried next to one particularly large pile of foliage that had balanced upon its top a scrap of paper on which was written the word BALLROOM.

'And what are those for?' asked William, tone over-sharp as he pointed to the basket of pears, and Ralph sniffed.

'Touchy, aren't we? Still angry, I suppose,' but when William did not answer the valet shrugged. 'The pears,' he said, 'are to crown the displays.' Ralph squatted down then to sift through the Reverend Witherington Soppe's bounty. 'Miss Partridge collected them on Christmas Day. Three pears per garland I think she proposed, and I am inclined to agree. Oh, but this one is bruised. Clumsy biddy.'

William looked down at the offending fruit in Ralph's hand. It was a handsome pear, lushly green and rosy, but undeniably there *was* a bruise set within a small indentation in the flesh, as if the old woman had gipped it a little too hard.

''Tis not the end of the world. The pear can easily be displayed bruise-side back. The viscount will never know.'

'Hmm,' Ralph frowned, but after a moment of contemplation he placed the damaged pear back into the basket. 'Well, we can hardly replace it now at such short notice.'

He stood, stretched out his arm towards him, and William, breath catching, took an involuntary step backwards.

'Oh, for pity's sake,' cried Ralph, and William was surprised to see something akin to hurt cross his face. 'You'd think I'd struck poor Prue the way you're carrying on. Look,' he said, 'just give me that bucket and fill the wheelbarrow with that pile there.' He prodded his toe at the foliage labelled BALLROOM. 'All you have to do is put the garlands where I tell you to, and if my presence bothers you that much, I'll stand six safe paces away. How does that sound?'

William did not answer, he merely glowered, but Ralph seemed to accept this for an answer and turned on his heel towards the ballroom, bucket and basket in hand. William stared after him with a peculiar feeling in his belly.

Ridiculous, that he should feel guilt at acting so childishly! But how could Ralph possibly understand his feelings? *Still angry, I suppose.* William heaved the fresh-smelling pile of foliage back into the wheelbarrow. Though more than an hour had passed since the incident with Prudence and Mr Hodge in the forest, he *did* still feel angry.

Angry, and damnably anxious.

So often had William imagined an opportunity to share some time alone with Ralph Hornby. How many times had he watched him at the dinner table flirting so confidently with the housemaids, while William sat quietly at the far end and wondered what it would be like to have the valet look at *him* with such affection or touch his arm in a manner so familiar? As vexed at Ralph as he was, the attraction William felt for him was hard to suppress, and now he must pass an hour or more alone with him hanging garlands. No wonder he acted as he had.

'Come along, Will,' Ralph called from where he lingered in the doorway of the ballroom. 'The faster you go, the sooner it will be done.'

The valet had already cleared the mantelpiece by the time William joined him. Setting the wheelbarrow down, he waited for Ralph to offer his first instruction.

'That long curved one,' said he, pointing to a holly branch on the top of the pile, and diligently William removed it from the wheelbarrow. 'Lay it there, on the right.'

A large mirror hung upon the mantel. As he set the holly branch upon it, William glanced up. Ralph was watching him, and it struck William yet again how very good-looking the valet was. Sleek black hair, pale skin, smooth jaw, straight nose, pink lips. William swallowed, glanced at his own reflection. He too had black hair, but in comparison to the prim and proper valet, he was a swarthy specimen with unruly curls that never sat well on his head, and a nose that crooked too far left. It never used to be so, but William's father did have such an awful temper . . .

'Good,' Ralph said softly, still looking at him in the mirror. 'If you place another branch on the opposite end, now. Get the one with that nice bend at the base.'

Suddenly, despite the size of the ballroom and the fact that no fire had been lit in the grate, William became rather hot. He could distinctly feel a patch of heat within the dip of his back, and with a little *huff* he tore his grey eyes away from the valet's seductive brown.

Was Ralph mocking him? Or was William simply losing his mind to strange fancies?

'This one?' he asked, somewhat breathless.

Ralph hesitated.

'Yes, that's it.'

William did as he was bidden; Ralph pointed next to a twig of fir, a sprig of box, and when the mantel was finally dressed, they both between them added the last flourishes of pine cones, rosemary and bay. Finally, Ralph reached for the large pear and nestled it directly in the middle, bruise-side back.

'The crown,' he murmured. 'What do you reckon, Will? Not bad for your first go,' and despite the fluttering in his throat at Ralph standing so close (six safe paces away, indeed) William offered up a hesitant smile.

'I think it nice.'

'Nice?' came the affronted reply. 'Come on now. It's far better than *nice*.'

'Very well,' conceded William. 'Beautiful.'

Ralph turned his head to look at him.

'Yes,' he said softly. 'I think so too.'

William's breath caught as their gazes met. What, he thought, was Ralph about? They had been speaking of the garland, but in that moment the meaning became unclear, and suddenly frightened, William turned away.

'Let us do the rest,' said he, pressing the pulse at his throat. 'The faster you go, the sooner it will be done, isn't that what you said?'

Ralph frowned but agreed readily enough, and the two men busied themselves with the other garlands until the ballroom, dining room, drawing room, and grand staircase had all been dressed. With one final flourish Ralph placed a sprig of mistletoe directly beneath the stairs, and in celebration sprang into song:

> *The Misletoe's berries are fair and white,*
> *The Ivy's of gloomy sable hue ;*
> *Red as blood the Laurel's affect our sight,*
> *And the Holly's the same with prickles too!*

'Join in, Will. You know the words.'

But William, simply relieved the whole matter was done with and in no fit mood for song, deposited the empty bucket and basket in the wheelbarrow, and made to remove it from the entrance hall before Mrs Wilson should commit herself to a fit.

'Where are you going?'

Turning, William saw that Ralph was standing at the baize door leading belowstairs, one hand holding it open.

'I just . . .'

'No,' said the valet with a shake of his head. 'We're not quite done.'

'Oh.'

Confused, William followed Ralph down the narrow corridor and into the kitchen. The smell of roasted meat flooded his nostrils, and he tried not to salivate as he watched Mrs Denby baste a capon, fresh and crisp and golden from the stove. Ralph appeared oblivious; with a strange sort of smile upon his face, he beckoned William to the pantry with a crook of his finger.

William hesitated. He did not wish to confine himself within a cramped store cupboard with Ralph Hornby. He was not sure his wits could manage it. But Ralph beckoned again, and worried that the other servants would wonder what they were about (for Lowdie Lucas was already looking at him, a question on her round face), William rushed across the flagstones whereupon the valet disappeared into the pantry.

'What are we doing in here?' he whispered as the door shut behind him, and with a flourish Ralph pulled the second sprig of mistletoe from his pocket.

'Had you forgotten?' said he, his voice resonant in the small space. 'Mol *did* say we should put some in the pantry where old Wilson won't find it.'

William watched as the valet proceeded to hook the sprig of mistletoe to a small bolt protruding from the low ceiling.

'Any excuse, I suppose,' William muttered, ashamed he should feel even an ounce of jealousy, 'to get Molly alone for a kiss.'

'What?'

Ralph, having his back to him thought William, must not

have heard, and so he grumbled, 'Nothing,' to which the valet *tsked*.

'Not nothing. I heard you perfectly.'

He turned to look at William, and the stare he gave him was grave.

'I have no interest whatsoever in Molly Hart.'

'Of course you do not,' sniped William. 'You have no interest in anyone. The way you flirt with all the maids,' he continued, 'just goes to shew how insincere you are. The stories I've heard—'

'Stories are all they are,' said Ralph firmly. 'Has it never occurred to you that all my flirtations are merely a front?'

'A front?'

'Yes. For how I truly feel.'

Ralph stepped closer. William's heart clenched in abject panic.

What is he about?

'I would like to leave.'

'Really?' Ralph rested his hand upon William's arm. 'There is mistletoe above us. Don't you know what that means?' And without so much as a warning Ralph drew William to him and planted a kiss upon his trembling lips.

It was everything William wanted it to be, and more. The kiss was gentle at first, but the meeting of soft lips soon hardened into a passion William had never once dared to imagine. The two men pressed against each other in the cramped pantry, and though the door could open at any moment, whereupon it would all be over for them both, two words turned cartwheels in William's giddy mind: *wildly exhilarating, wildly exhilarating, wildly exhilarating!* But, alas, the kiss was over all too quickly. Dazed, William opened his eyes to find Ralph staring at him.

'Why did you do that?'

'Because I wanted to.'

'Why?' William whispered. 'Because you have found me out and wanted to tease me?'

Ralph's fine eyes widened in surprise. 'I wanted to kiss you because I recognised in you someone like myself.'

William stared.

Someone like myself.

He understood what the valet meant to say, but his words, William knew, could not be trusted and with difficulty he swallowed.

'You lie. You are not a nice man, Ralph Hornby. You are not a gentleman. Aside from all those girls you flirt with, what you did to Prue, to Mr Hodge ...'

Ralph sighed. 'Perhaps it *was* a mite harsh. But you shall soon realise that what I did was a way to seeing the pair betrothed. Just you watch. What you do not understand about me, William Moss, is there is a reason behind everything I do.'

'And I wonder if your reason now is to play a cruel joke.' William's voice caught. 'They hang men like me.'

'Like us,' Ralph said softly.

William shook his head.

'I do not believe you.'

Again the valet sighed. 'Have I kissed a chit or two in my time? Of course I have. I had to *know*, you see. And then, when I realised –' here Ralph shook his head – 'the safest course seemed to continue as I always had. That way, I thought, no one would suspect.'

He took William's hands, rough to the valet's soft.

'I always wondered if you shared my . . .' Ralph licked his lips. 'The way I caught you watching me in the servants' hall when you thought I wasn't looking. The way you avoided my gaze whenever I sought you out in the gardens after Wilson or the viscount gave me instruction. But I wasn't sure until earlier today when you blushed so delightfully in the forest. And then I had to test it, with Prudence, with Mol. You looked so jealous, so charmingly angry! In the ballroom just now . . . Was I imagining it? Did you not feel the warmth between us?'

William took an unsteady breath. The valet smelt distractingly of fir.

'You are toying with me. I know you are.'

Ralph hesitated. Released him. In that moment – despite it all – William felt bereft.

'I know it must look that way,' he murmured. 'But please. Why can't you give me a chance?'

William hesitated. How could he? But then Ralph looked at him in such a heartfelt manner that he found it in himself to smile, which made the valet smile in turn.

'A chance, Will,' he said softly. 'I do not expect you to trust me right away – I've been beastly, I admit it. But why don't we go down to the Crown on our next afternoon off as I suggested? No devilment, no little bit of heaven. Unless, of course,' he added, his voice seductive, low, 'it is between you and me.'

William did not know how to respond. He wanted to – oh, how he wanted to – but for so long he had watched Ralph Hornby flirt unscrupulously; would William just be another of the valet's conquests? Or, worse . . . *was* this a cruel and deathly game?

Ralph let out a breath then, leaned in to hover his lips near William's ear:

Nor black nor ensanguined red for me :
The Misletoe only is my delight :
For pure as love all its berries be,
And to kissing my Will's sweet lips invite.

William leant away.

'Those aren't the words,' he whispered, and Ralph chuckled low in his throat.

'Ah,' he whispered back. 'You *do* know them then.'

Both men stared at each other for what felt like an endless moment, until, at last, William dared relent.

'All right,' he said, cautious. 'I shall go with you to the Crown. To get to know one another better. At least . . . at least at first.'

'That is all I ask.' In the confines of the pantry, Ralph's eyes shone. 'Believe me, Will, I know what it is we risk. But I would brave it all, if I knew you felt the same as I. How lonely I have been!'

And as Ralph held him close William thought of a pair of blackbirds singing together, high in the poplar trees of Wakely Forest, beneath bouncing pom-poms of blooming mistletoe.

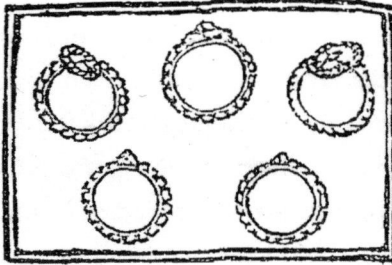

STAVE V.

A Most Unsuitable Suitor
FIVE GOLD RINGS

Ambrosia Pépin, third Viscountess Wakely, had always been an optimistic woman. She was one of those singular creatures who saw the best in every body and every thing, even when others did not. Indeed, Ambrosia prided herself on such a quality, and for many a year such virtuousness of heart had held her in good stead – it was often remarked upon that she was a generous hostess and the kindest of mistresses, as well as a doting mother and loving wife. It seemed to Ambrosia that, by always shewing such encouraging fortitude of mind, fortune might continue to smile down upon her, and so it was with this outlook on life that she hoped her greatest wish should eventually be realised ... to see each of her five daughters happily married.

Of course, she had already achieved a splendid match for her eldest, though for some time Ambrosia had worried the happy event would never take place at all. Such a pronounced delay had been a surprise to everybody, for Juliette Pépin was blessed so truly that there had been no shortage of suitors. Aside from her many accomplishments and beauty (a trait which should Ambrosia have been of a vain inclination she might have attributed to herself), Juliette was, above all things, kind, and had been the darling of the county from the moment the Pépins entered it. Everywhere Juliette went she was admired and loved, always making time for each of Merrywake's residents whether they were lowly milkmaids or one of the proud (and often obnoxious) family of Busgrove Bank. The moment she entered society, Juliette received countless gentlemen vying for her hand. However, she was of a particularly discerning temperament, and by the time Juliette was nearing the age of two-and-twenty she had not only refused the offers of four eligible men, but almost shied off from the marriage mart altogether, for not one of the *haut ton* appeared to please her. In fact, during the last London season she had flatly refused to attend a single ball. Little had Ambrosia known (for Juliette possessed a quiet and private mind), that her heart was already engaged elsewhere.

It was her friend Nicolas Toussaint who had engaged it, and what a relief when he finally announced his intentions and she accepted them! The seigneur was already well known to the family – Nicolas' father Louis (named after the French King) had been a childhood friend of Fernand's, and at his request the son had frequented Wakely Hall for the last four summers after

Louis' death. Thus, a true and wholesome romance blossomed and grew between him and Juliette, away from the ballrooms of London and the assemblies of Bath. Out of all the gentlemen who had attempted to court her, only Nicolas could make Juliette blush so rosily and smile so widely, and in turn only Juliette could evoke a laugh so delighted in Nicolas and produce in him so fierce an affection, that their love of each other could not be doubted by anyone who saw them together. And so, having one daughter finally married, Ambrosia hoped that equally successful matches might be made for the rest of her brood. Unfortunately, Ambrosia could not fathom a way to achieve it, for each of her four remaining daughters posed a rather difficult problem.

The viscountess sighed from where she stood at the window of Wakely Hall's drawing room, and turned her fine head so she might look upon the girls in question.

Maria, her second child, a spritely maiden of one-and-twenty, had a particular love of balls and any sort of frivolity, which often made her the talk of the season . . . but not in a way that could be construed in an encouraging light. Maria – being vivacious and pretty – was no less popular than her elder sister but she was a lively creature, lacking Juliette's tact. More than once had it been necessary for Ambrosia to call for the carriage after Maria let her tongue run to the point of insult, thereby reducing her marriage prospects to such a degree that she was still unwed after her fourth year out.

Her third daughter, Charlotte, was at that very moment ensconced on the sopha nose-deep in a copy of – Ambrosia squinted at the spine and frowned in displeasure – *A New Account of Some Parts of Guinea, and the Slave-Trade.* Charlotte was, it might be inferred from such an observation, rather too inclined to turn her mind to matters of which no lady should have any notion, and held no interest in marriage whatsoever. Charlotte had stated quite earnestly only that very morning at breakfast that she thought it no problem at all for her to remain unmarried since all men were 'louts and coves', and so she had no intention of subjecting herself to one of them, thank you very much.

This then left her youngest girls, Louisa and Rosalie, who, though sweet and biddable at nineteen and seventeen years of age, possessed a deficiency of aptitude in any of the expected ladylike pursuits. It was not that either girl had stinted in her efforts (nor had their governess, who had tried very hard to teach them), but neither girl could sing or play the pianoforte, displayed no proficiency in any language but English (which was rather a sore point with the viscount), and their embroidery was exceedingly poor. In such circumstances one might hope that Louisa and Rosalie should make up for their shortcomings by being, at the very least, handsome like Charlotte was, but it appeared that nature saw fit to allow the girls to fall short in that department too. Most would be inclined to describe them as plain, which Ambrosia supposed was better than being considered completely ill-favoured, and at least they could be depended upon to be well behaved at social events.

If all that were not enough, each of the girls (Charlotte aside), had set her eyes upon the only man in the world whom Ambrosia could *not* bring herself to see the best in:

Sir Robert Grey, Duke of Morley.

No worse a scoundrel could be found in all of England, Ambrosia was quite sure.

To begin with, Nicolas' friend – whom he met during the course of his education at Cambridge – had not aroused in Ambrosia any particular suspicion, but then rumours started to circulate about town last season of the duke's scandalous relations with a Covent Garden actress, and Ambrosia herself had been witness to a rather imprudent flirtation at the Pump Room in Bath. All that aside, he carried a particular air of arrogance and self-satisfaction Ambrosia did not like, and in consequence she had not wished to have the Duke of Morley stay at Wakely. However, as Nicolas' best man she could hardly refuse, and so the viscountess was forced to hold her tongue. Unfortunately, the moment the cad stepped across Wakely Hall's threshold Maria, Louisa and Rosalie lost all sense of decorum and had been making doe-eyes at him ever since.

Ambrosia confided in Fernand her concerns, but he merely replied that the girls were being silly (*Ah, jeune amour!*) and he felt sure that a man of Sir Robert's station would not insult the family of his friend's wife, nor his friend, by behaving in a rakish manner towards any member of the household. She was not to trouble Nicolas or Juliette about the matter. To which Ambrosia had dutifully agreed.

But oh, how she wished to speak with them! If Nicolas knew her fears, Ambrosia felt sure he would consider them and act accordingly. As he was by way of marriage now the brother of her other daughters, it was up to Nicolas to take matters up with the duke if he were to shew any signs of acting improperly. If the viscountess had been blessed with a son, she could have trusted him to take the matter subtly in hand.

Ambrosia turned back to face the window. There had been much hope of a son in those early years. Ambrosia often wondered what little Edmond might have been like had he lived. He would surely have possessed a good and generous nature like his father, and perhaps would have looked like him too; pleasing to observe, with a regal standing and warm brown eyes. Not the poor bloodied thing that Martha Lucas had so gently wrapt in a linen shawl and placed in Ambrosia's shaking arms for her to mourn . . .

She looked out onto Wakely's lawns and the long line of yew trees which led down to the ice-capped pond at the far end. Edmond's monument lay in the middle, a stone urn on which was carved a dove, his tiny body long committed to the earth beneath, never to grow a day older, never to inherit Wakely Hall and its lands. How wretched she had been when she lost him. Him, and all that might have been. But – as Martha told her gently – one might begin again, and at length she did, the pain of Edmond's loss fading day by day in the wake of her five healthy daughters, for whom Ambrosia wished nothing but happiness and husbands. But what good was that when she could not secure suitable matches to make such wishes a reality?

'*Maman,*' ventured Louisa from where she lay supine on the sopha, her fingers dipped lazily into a bowl of gold and silver sugared almonds. 'Is Lord Heysten coming to the ball next week? I should so like to apologise for being so clumsy. He did not stay long enough for me to speak with him.'

'He has been invited,' replied her mother, turning away from the window. 'Of course, whether he should see his way to attending I cannot tell you, not after the scene you caused last week.'

The mention of his lordship succeeded in distracting Ambrosia somewhat, for the whole palaver had been deeply embarrassing. Lord Charles Heysten had been most put out when Louisa had, in a moment of enthusiasm whilst conversing with Lady Falshaw's daughter, flung her arm down upon her periwinkle bowl which resulted in Mrs Denby's excellent hazelnut and parsnip soup slopping onto the gentleman's new embroidered waistcoat. The incident had quite ruined the evening, for Lord Heysten left early, leaving said waistcoat in the care of Martha's daughter, Loveday (Ambrosia smiled a moment). The waistcoat was cleaned as well as could be, and had since been returned to Heysten Park, but the damage was done and what a shame it was too – the note of apology Ambrosia included was ignored, and she had not heard from his lordship since.

Which in truth really was rather ungracious of him.

In the corner where she sat embroidering a handkerchief for Juliette's trousseau, Maria uttered a little *huff*.

'I cannot see why you should wish him here,' said she, pulling a piece of fine gold thread through the muslin to add a tiny flick to the arm of her sister's initial. 'I have never met a man so boorish.'

'Dearest,' scolded Ambrosia, 'Lord Heysten is not boorish. He is merely a man of reserve and good sense. I daresay it was very gracious of him to accommodate your ill-mannered questions. Your father and I were deeply mortified you carried on so.'

Maria rested her embroidery. 'All I did was suggest he build some ornamental gardens in the grounds of Heysten Park, like the Chinese Pavilions in Vauxhall or the Rotunda in Ranelagh. Think of the parties he could have! He would be the catch of the county if only he allowed it. To be sure, the depth of his pocketbook certainly makes up for his lack of good looks.'

'Maria . . .'

'*Well!*' Ambrosia's second daughter sniffed at her mother's warning tone as Louisa tittered into her almonds. 'I only speak the truth. He would be far more appealing if he put his money to some entertaining use. He does not even squander it, just sits on it like a mother hen. I tell you, *Maman*, 'tis a waste. Heysten Park has been going to rack and ruin for years – now the old Lord Heysten is dead, the new one should really do something about it.'

'Sir Robert,' mused Rosalie dreamily, 'says that if Heysten Park were his, he would install a lake in the grounds and build a Grecian temple on its bank, with roses growing up its pillars.' Ambrosia's youngest sighed wistfully. 'Can you think of anything more romantic? It would make a fine backdrop for a wedding ceremony . . . do you not think, *Maman?*'

Ambrosia frowned. The question had been leading, and there could be no doubt as to why Rosalie should ask such a thing. But before she could answer there came a groan from the figure upon the windowseat.

'For goodness' sake, Rosalie,' said Charlotte, turning a page of her Snelgrave. 'Do you truly have no ambition in life other than to marry?'

Rosalie, who sat cross-legged on the floor playing with the family cat, sent her sister a despairing look.

'Just because you have no desire for a life of matrimony does not mean the rest of us are at fault for wanting it.'

Charlotte regarded her sister balefully.

'Do you honestly wish to be shackled to a man who would think of you merely as a chattel, a body to produce offspring year after year, and afterward have not one single word to say to you beyond *Good morning* and *Goodnight*?'

'Oh,' cried Rosalie, 'Sir Robert would not treat a lady in such a way, I am quite sure.'

'Then you are a bigger simpleton than I thought.'

'Charlotte,' scolded Ambrosia, 'do not be cruel,' to which the young lady rolled her eyes, and Rosalie bestowed upon her mother a smile.

Ambrosia did not like that smile, however – it was altogether too bright, too blithe, and caused in her a profound sense of unease. What, pray, had the Duke of Morley been saying to her youngest child that should put such thoughts into her innocent head?

'I think Sir Robert would make a fine husband,' said Louisa in wistful tones.

'He's unquestionably rich enough,' added Maria, needle bobbing. 'There can be no supposing *he* is stingy with his pocketbook. He could keep me in silks and satins for years. Have you not seen, after all, how finely he dresses?'

'I have,' breathed Rosalie, still with that silly smile upon her lips. 'I have never known a man so handsome. Indeed, I think him quite the handsomest man in the county!'

'*I* think you a silly little fool.'

To this Rosalie stuck out her tongue at Charlotte and chucked Mr Palamedes under his ginger chin. Louisa thoughtfully crunched on an almond. Maria continued to sew. Ambrosia, who wished to warn her daughters of the grievous disadvantages of their suit but could not – at that present moment – find the words or the vigour for such a task, turned instead to Charlotte.

'Do you not think, dearest, that you are being a little too harsh in your opinions? Not all gentlemen are as you describe. Your father is not.'

Charlotte lowered her book, and looked upon her mother with what could only be described as an air of sympathy.

'But so many are. I concede that *Père* is an exception, a rarity among men. But even so –' and here Charlotte looked about the room at her sisters, her point as clear as crystal from the way she lingered upon each of them – 'five of us. Six if . . .' She trailed off, little Edmond an unspoken memory. 'You were very lucky, *Maman*,' said Charlotte softly. 'But still, I should hate to be producing so often, with scarce time to breathe between one child and the next, and that's even if I *survived* the birthings. Would you not have preferred to see the world? To make some change in it for the better?'

Ambrosia opened her mouth to speak, but Maria – who had uttered a most unladylike snort – intervened.

'I do not think marriage can be so onerous as you make it out to be, sister. Look at Juliette and Nicolas! What a fine pairing *they* make, and they were friends first before they embarked upon a match. And while I do not suppose I could make a match as superior as theirs in terms of affection –' and at this she gave a rather pointed sniff in the direction of her other sisters – 'I intend to marry *very* well indeed.'

'Though you might be pretty, Maria,' muttered Louisa, scowling into her golds and silvers, 'you are hardly fit to be the wife of a duke.'

It was a rather uncharitable thing for her to say, but Ambrosia did concede that owing to Maria's often unladylike behaviour the statement was correct. At Louisa's comment, however, Maria merely shrugged, laid aside the handkerchief and pushed her needle into the arm of her chair.

'I am the eldest out of all of you. Sir Robert almost certainly thinks of *you*, Louisa, as a child.'

'At least *I* am well behaved at social gatherings.'

'*You* are an inelegant brat. Consider what happened at dinner last week.'

'*Maman!*' cried Louisa in affront. 'Can you believe—'

'No wonder Lord Heysten has not come back to Wakely,' continued Maria, ignoring her sister's ire with an upward turn of her pert nose. 'Who would wish to be seated beside such a clumsy creature as you?'

'Girls!' interjected Ambrosia. 'I will not have you lashing out at each other. 'Tis Christmas, a time for us to be merry. I shall not—'

'I do not see why either one of you should marry Sir Robert when it was *I* who caught Juliette's bouquet.'

Such a declaration succeeded in silencing all three ladies, and in surprise Ambrosia, Maria and Louisa turned to face a pouting Rosalie.

'At least I would have, if Miss Brown had not got in my way. Truly, *Maman*,' said her youngest, 'I should think it most unfair if Maria or Louisa were to get engaged before I did. The bouquet was meant for me. *Fate* put the bouquet in my path, *fate* shall see to it that I am the sister to marry next, and I am certain *fate* has deemed me to be the next Duchess of Morley!'

At this Ambrosia was quite unable to summon a response. It was Charlotte who interceded – having for some minutes neglected her book to witness the ridiculousness of the conversation – and she proceeded to huff and roll her eyes.

'Oh, for pity's sake, Rosalie, listen to yourself. However can you be so cork-brained? If such a thing as fate existed, then logic dictates that fate does not work in *almosts*. 'Twas Miss Brown, not you, who caught Juliette's flowers. You truly are a fool, sister, and no man wants a silly wife. Especially not a duke.'

'No man wants a wife who reads all day either,' came the tart reply.

'Just as well I have no wish to take a husband then, isn't it?'

'Girls,' groaned Ambrosia, pressing a finger to her left temple, where the beginnings of an ache had started to pulse. 'Please. It has been a tiring few days, and I am in no mood for your bickering.'

Louisa – who through all her faults was at least sensitive to her mother's moods – held out the bowl of almonds. 'Oh, *Maman*. Sit. We are sorry, are we not?'

The girls looked between themselves, and in due course nodded. With a small sigh of relief Ambrosia crossed the room and took a silver-coated nut between forefinger and thumb.

'I shall sit, but at my desk. I will pen a letter, I think.'

Maria's fair brows shot up. 'To whom?'

'Lord Heysten,' Ambrosia replied, seating herself, and said nothing more.

The girls did not venture another word either, and for this the viscountess was glad for her head had begun then to pound in earnest. Still, such alarming talk – most especially on Rosalie's part – about securing the hand of Sir Robert Grey, and Louisa's mention of Lord Heysten, had presented in Ambrosia a spark of an idea.

Under no circumstances at all was she willing to entertain the likes of the Duke of Morley as a prospective son-in-law. Unfortunately, while he remained under her roof Sir Robert was a threat, and with no other men of age or fortune currently in the vicinity of Merrywake (the Busgrove heir did *not* count!), there was no means of distraction for her daughters. Of course, there would be many gentlemen in attendance on the night of the ball, but how many of them would be suitable matches? So many sons of her and Viscount Pépin's acquaintances were already spoken for, or too young, or too old. However, did not Lord Heysten recently mention a renewed acquaintance with his much younger cousins, the Sharpes?

Ambrosia removed a crisp piece of paper from her desk drawer, nib of her swan feather quill poised before the inkwell, but for a long moment she hesitated.

The Sharpes were a fine family (so he said), and possessed more than one eligible bachelor. They would make a welcome addition to the Twelfth Night Ball . . . if only he could be prevailed upon to agree to invite them to stay with him, as he had implied he might. Yet Ambrosia felt most acutely that the incident with Louisa and the soup, not to mention Maria's impropriety, had soured the relationship between Lord Heysten and the Pépins, for what other excuse could he have for not responding to her perfectly amiable letter?

Throughout Ambrosia's troubled musings the fire crackled comfortingly in the grate. Louisa munched her sugared almonds. Maria's needle flew. Charlotte turned another page of her Snelgrave and Rosalie played with the cat on the rug.

Well, until his lordship confirmed that a rift now existed between them, there could surely be no harm in extending the olive branch once again. With a frown of concentration Viscountess Pépin dipped the quill:

My dear Lord Heysten,

I trust this letter finds you well, and in better spirits than when I saw you here at Wakely. Again, I wish to express my sincerest apologies for what occurred at dinner Thursday last, and those of my daughters – Maria, who is mortified to have caused offence with her insensitive comments, and Louisa, who is sorry to have damaged your fine waistcoat. I trust you are satisfied with our attempts at repairing the damage, but if you are not, I am of course more than happy to send payment for its replacement. You need only communicate your wishes, and I shall see to it directly.

Ambrosia paused. It *was* vexing that he had not replied to her first note. She had been earnest in her regrets, and it was ungentlemanlike to have ignored it, especially when she thought she had been making such good progress.

The fact of the matter was, she had spent weeks attempting to garner favour with Lord Heysten. His father, Archibald, who had finally passed from this world in the summer, had been much like his own father: cold, cruel and calculating. It was Theophilus Heysten who had disowned his firstborn, Witherington, after he made what Theophilus deemed a disastrous match, and proceeded to transfer his riches to Archibald, the second son, who made no effort to repair the breach. Theophilus had shunned the Pépins for providing Witherington with a living after he was disinherited. After Archibald's death, when the fortune and estate of Heysten Park passed to his son, Charles, it had been the hope of everyone that he might take after his reverend uncle. Indeed, the newest Lord Heysten had spent many years travelling the Americas, having declared some years before his wish to have nothing whatsoever to do with his father. So, when he was forced to return home to take on his inheritance, Ambrosia thought it a perfect opportunity to connect the families again.

And why should they not have helped Witherington? Ambrosia still felt guilt for the part she had played in Mr Soppe and Miss Partridge's separation. If she had not fallen into premature labour with Edmond, Frances would not have been late for their meeting and Eliza Granville would never— Ambrosia shook her head, placed the silver nut she still held on her tongue and began to suck. Frances had only been a housemaid then, so happy and innocent in the throes of young love, though the match was vastly imprudent. But despite the pronounced differences in station Ambrosia believed Witherington to be much in love too, and she had expected their engagement to be announced at any moment. But then ... Well. Elevating Frances to the more reputable position of lady's maid and companion had been the only way Ambrosia could dampen the claws of scandalous gossip in case they should find their way beyond the walls of Wakely Hall, and Fernand – being such good friends with the original Heysten heir – had done what he could. Still (and here Ambrosia smiled into the crunch of her almond), true love won out in the end. Frances and Witherington were to be married, and Viscount and Viscountess Pépin could not be happier at such an unexpected development.

But, to the point in hand. Charles Heysten had dined with the Pépins five times since his return to Merrywake and had been, if not enthusiastic about repairing the rift between the families, accommodating enough. But then – Maria having already dampened the mood with her flighty suggestions – the matter of the waistcoat occurred, and it seemed all Ambrosia's attempts to heal the breach were in danger of failing. With another frown, she reapplied her quill:

You must of course have discovered by now that your uncle has announced his plans to marry since we last met, with the happy event occurring the morning of our Twelfth Night Ball.

The wedding is to take place under special licence at Wakely Church, conducted by a parson from the next village, and the viscount and I will be hosting an intimate reception here at the hall. I would not presume to advise on your actions in that quarter, but I do hope you still might be prevailed upon to attend our Christmastime festivities in the evening. The invitation is of course extended to your cousins, the Sharpes, as they would be <u>most</u> welcome to join our festivities if they have – or intend to – come to Merrywake.

'Oh, no! Please say *she* is not coming?'

Ambrosia – realising she was reciting her letter out loud as she was often wont to do – lifted her quill from the page.

'What was that, dearest?'

'Cordelia,' said Rosalie, the blue ribbon with which she was teasing Mr Palamedes now quite still.

'Cordelia?'

'Yes, *Maman*, Cordelia. She is the youngest Sharpe cousin.'

'Oh! You have met the cousins already, then?'

'Only her,' replied Rosalie with a grimace, 'and such an abominable creature she is too. Cordelia was positively beastly to Louisa in Bath, was she not?'

At this Ambrosia frowned. 'Louisa? *Was* Miss Sharpe beastly to you?'

'Well,' Louisa said quietly, bashful. 'Only a little.'

'That's not true,' interjected Maria. 'She was needlessly vicious at Lady Warwick's Midsummer Soirée, and I let her know it.'

'Dear heaven. Whatever did she do?'

Ambrosia watched Louisa with concern, who would not meet her mother's gaze.

'Honestly, *Maman*, it was nothing of consequence,' but then Louisa swung her legs about on the sopha to sit upright, and in doing so the almond bowl tipped over and a stream of gold and silver sugared pebbles scattered onto the Axminster rug. There was much commotion in that moment, as all the girls and their mother attempted to return the almonds to the bowl, with Mr Palamedes making the feat all the more difficult for thinking the whole thing a mighty fine game, and it was some minutes before Ambrosia could return to the matter at hand.

'Come now, dearest. What did Cordelia Sharpe *do*?' and finally Louisa huffed.

'She trod on my skirts and tore my gown.'

'Oh,' Ambrosia replied, not a little confounded. 'Was that all?'

'No, that was *not* all,' retorted Maria. 'The little vixen insisted it was Louisa's fault for not paying attention, because she was – and I quote – "overindulging at the buffet table", and that if Louisa had not been so gluttonous she might have minded her feet.'

'*And*,' interjected Rosalie, 'she said so in front of all the young men, including Mr Grose.'

'Mr Grose? That fine young man you met in London last season?'

It was Maria rather than Louisa who nodded.

'Cordelia said that Louisa's only chance of finding a husband was if he were willing to bankrupt himself at Fortnum's to feed her. Everybody laughed, *everybody*, and to make matters worse . . . Mr Grose laughed along with them and removed himself from her dance card.'

Louisa, then, sullenly pushed the refilled bowl of sugar almonds away from her, and Ambrosia felt her chest grow hot with indignation.

The gentleman in question had been – so Ambrosia recalled – more than passing amiable towards Louisa earlier that year, and the viscountess had hoped something might come of the connection. Alas, Louisa had not mentioned Mr Grose once since the summer.

And now she knew why.

If only she had been there! The night of Lady Warwick's Midsummer Soirée Ambrosia had been ill with a frightful headache. Usually she attended all social gatherings – often to keep a careful watch on Maria – but that evening the viscountess could not face the hot fug of an assembly room in July, and with Juliette and Charlotte choosing to stay behind to keep their mother company, her other daughters had been left in the care of the viscount.

'Where was your father during all of this?' she asked faintly.

Maria shrugged. 'Discussing pineapples with investors, I assume. Remember, *Maman*, it was in Bath he settled on the idea? I don't think we saw him all evening, and since we left for Merrywake early the next day he was unlikely to hear of it from the gossipmongers.'

Ambrosia tightened her grip on the quill. Oh, Fernand!

He was not a selfish man by any means, but so often he failed to see that which was before his very eyes, wrapt up as he was in the care of others or of his own pursuits. The realisation that he had been oblivious to his daughter's suffering was upsetting to her, and upon seeing Ambrosia's troubled expression Maria tossed her head.

'Do not worry, *Maman*. Cordelia soon had the smirk wiped off her face.'

The viscountess regarded her daughter warily.

'What did you do?'

Maria grinned wickedly. 'Let us just say her fine muslin gown is no longer white, but a lovely shade of claret.'

'I see ...' As the girls laughed, Ambrosia turned back to her letter with a deeply puckered brow. What to do? She could not extend an invitation to the brothers and not to the sister. Certainly, questions would be asked, not least by Lord Heysten himself. But to have such an odious creature as a guest at Wakely Hall was a distressing notion. And what of the brothers? Were they of similar constitutions? But, considered the viscountess, there could be only one way to discover the truth of it. What other option had she? No, invite the Sharpes she must, including their dreadful sister ... and let the girl see where her insults took her then!

At that moment there was a knock upon the drawing room door, and Ambrosia's eldest daughter entered the room.

'Good afternoon, girls,' greeted Juliette, lilac skirts swishing gracefully about her satin-pumped feet as she crossed the rug and placed a dainty kiss upon the viscountess' cheek. 'Good afternoon, *Maman*. Do you know, I think I am quite worn out?'

Maria – with a rather too-knowing look in her eyes – smiled widely. 'I can imagine.'

'Maria,' said Ambrosia in as stern a manner as she could muster. 'I hope you *cannot* imagine! Such thoughts are vastly unsuitable for a girl of your age.'

'Of *any* age,' chimed in Charlotte, barely raising her head from her book, and both Louisa and Rosalie giggled. Juliette, patient as she always was, merely gave them all a faintly admonishing look.

'That has nothing to do with it,' she said warmly, but the blush that had appeared on her round face might be taken to indicate otherwise. 'I am speaking, of course, of our little house guest.' Juliette's colour faded a fraction. 'Do you know, *Maman*, she is a clever creature. Monsieur Benoît has been teaching her chess and she has beaten me at the game twice in the last hour. The girl is clearly educated, but refuses to reveal where she is from. I fear someone must have scared the poor thing to such a degree that she is disinclined to tell.'

Ambrosia shook her head. 'It is all so strange. A child of quality must surely be known to be missing.'

'Exactly,' said Juliette, sitting herself beside Louisa on the sopha. 'But every time I ask anything about her past she grows pale and silent, and I feel monstrous cruel for pushing her. Oh, hello, my ginger prince. How fare you?'

Mr Palamedes, who, like everybody, adored Juliette, had approached her as soon as she sat, and was now padding his paws on the cushion of her lap, a sure prelude to his settling down upon it.

'Perhaps,' mused Rosalie, 'she escaped a dastardly guardian who planned to marry her off to some wealthy old relation.'

At this Charlotte sent her youngest sister a withering look. 'You read far too many ludicrous novels.'

'No matter her background,' cut in Maria, standing to proffer the embroidered handkerchief to Juliette who sighed in admiration at her sister's immaculate stitching, 'the child cannot hail from Merrywake – a notice of her disappearance would have circulated by now if she did. Why don't you ask Lord Heysten in your letter, *Maman*?' she suggested. 'Did he not mention he donated to some charities in London? Perhaps he might know something.'

Now that *was* a good idea! Sometimes Maria could be perfectly sensible if she wished it.

'I shall do so at once, my darling,' said Ambrosia, raising her quill once more and dipping it into the inkwell. 'But, how to word it . . .'

> *On a different and more delicate matter, I hope you might be willing to assist in a circumstance most troubling. Ordinarily I would not ask such a thing of someone who is such a recent acquaintance, but I remember you spoke of your charitable connections in London when you dined with us lately, and I wondered if you might have heard any word – through them – of a missing child?*
>
> *Two days ago, our good friend Monsieur de Fortgibu happened upon a little girl in Wakely Forest. She was malnourished and possessed the appearance of a vagrant, but her speech is eloquent, and she had on her person a garment that seemed more suited to a child of good breeding. The item*

is a pink shawl with satin roses sewn into the fabric. Her age is thought to be that of either seven or eight. She will not tell us her name. Beyond this, not one of us here at Wakely can garner from her much more information than that. If you can be of any help to us in this matter, we should all be extremely grateful. She appears to be a dear sweet child, and I sincerely wish to discover where she has come from, and how we might be best positioned to help her.

On all counts I have outlined in this letter, I soon hope to receive a response and wish to be

Sir,

Your most obliged and humble servant
Viscountess Ambrosia Pépin

'I think that will do very nicely,' said Juliette, for once again Ambrosia had spoken aloud to the room, and looking down at the letter the viscountess nodded. The missive *would* do, and she would instruct the footman, Mr Marmery, to arrange for its immediate delivery. For now, however, the task must wait as her stomach then proclaimed itself in a singular fashion, prompting Ambrosia to look upon the clock on the mantel and announce that it was time for them all to dress for dinner.

Wakely Hall had, from the Feast of St Nicholas, received a steady stream of guests. The dining room (which looked particularly festive with the addition of a pear-crowned garland adorning the fireplace), was near fit to bursting, and the company which the Pépins now hosted about the table was of wide and varied stock. There was Sir Gregory Warwick and Sir Victor Marshchild together with their vastly elegant wives; the (most unsuitable) Duke of Morley; the (most pompous) Earl of Starling; the esteemed family of Busgrove; the widow Lady Falshaw, whose daughter, Lucy, was a shy little thing but had found a doting friend in Louisa. Seated too at the table was Monsieur de Fortgibu; the dancing master Mr Thorpe and his wife, Cecily (who had once been Wakely's governess); and directly opposite them the Reverend Soppe, seated beside (of course), Miss Partridge.

As one must imagine by now, Wakely Hall's dining room was exceedingly large, and so it is perhaps easy to see why those belowstairs should find Christmastime a trying period in the Pépins' social calendar.

The conversation flowed freely for such an eclectic mix of guests and Ambrosia — despite the headache that had not yet ceased — kept a pleasant smile upon her face and touched her wine glass to her lips. Poaching was discussed over dishes of roasted pheasant and goose; the recent election of Sir Victor as the local magistrate conferred about amidst the fish course; Napoleon's exile became the topic of choice across platters of salmagundy; the abolition of slavery deliberated over bowls of cauliflower soup (a conversation to which Charlotte's attention, so Ambrosia noted with displeasure, was markedly keen); and as the jellies and plum puddings were brought in (much to Monsieur de Fortgibu's delight) the conversation shifted to that of the upcoming nuptials of the Reverend and the Pépin daughters' former abigail.

However, during such particulars, a loud and fluttering laugh could be heard from the opposite end of the table. Turning her face in its direction, Ambrosia frowned to see Rosalie making rather foolish eyes at the Duke of Morley.

The viscountess watched as he leant to say something close to her daughter's ear, whereupon Rosalie gave forth another fluttering laugh, Sir Robert laughed heartily in turn, and Ambrosia swallowed a mouthful of wine. As a guest of the Pépins, it was natural that the duke should be attentive in his considerations to Rosalie; indeed, to all her daughters and herself. However, on closer inspection was his hand not a little *too* near to Rosalie's, and did he not look at her with an expression bordering on the inappropriate? Whatever did they laugh about, for goodness' sake? Dear Rosalie did not have the wit to amuse a man of his intelligence, nor could she possibly understand the nuances of an educated man's humour. Impossible to ask, too, what with Ambrosia ensconced at the other end of the long dining table, and there was still time to pass yet before the gentlemen would withdraw to the parlour and the women to the drawing room. Ambrosia smiled and did her best to converse pleasantly with the rest of the party, trying to ignore her growing misgivings and the painful ache at her temples.

The viscountess passed a glance at her other daughters. Charlotte of course gave not one fig that Rosalie had commandeered all of the duke's attention, but Maria and Louisa were clearly put out. Though Maria was seated at the middle of the table and had been prevailed upon to converse with the earl, she still managed to send piercing looks downwind to her youngest sister, and as for Louisa, who sat directly opposite Rosalie and Sir Robert ... Well, Louisa's glares of chagrin could not be missed. Even Miss Falshaw who sat next to her appeared conscious of it, for the girl could scarce look up from her plate and her cheeks were a decided shade of pink. Desperately Ambrosia took another sip of her wine. Oh, how dreadful this was! Surely the other guests would begin to question why her daughters were behaving with such little decorum? Over the rim of her glass the viscountess attempted to meet the gaze of her husband, but he was deep in conversation with Mr Busgrove – no doubt about his recent investment in those troublesome pineapples – and was therefore quite insensible to this horrid state of affairs. Ambrosia pursed her lips. If her husband remained oblivious to the tribulations of his daughters, it was simply up to her to deal with the matter. In fact, she would ensure that tomorrow and thereafter, until the Duke of Morley left Wakely Hall, her daughters would be seated as far away from the rogue as possible.

At long last, the moment to depart the table arrived. As soon as the ladies were gathered in the drawing room and Lady Warwick had seated herself at the pianoforte to play a minuet, Ambrosia wasted not one moment in pulling her daughter aside.

'Whatever were you speaking of to the duke?' she whispered, and a great blush spread upon Rosalie's chest, up her neck, and blossomed in her cheeks.

'Why, his grace was telling me of his excursions on the Grand Tour,' her youngest exclaimed. 'Did you know Sir Robert is a painter? His tutor instructed him in the style of the great portrait artists of Holland.' At this Rosalie bestowed upon her mother a delighted smile. 'Oh, *Maman*! He said I was just as beautiful as any of their sitters, and that perhaps he might paint *me* one day, and looked at me with such sincerity that I feel sure fate *is* taking its course despite what Charlotte said, and that he shall offer for me before the Christmas season is out.'

Well, let it be said that it took some restraint on Ambrosia's part not to fall into a fit of hysterics then and there. Such anger did she feel in that moment! Not on her daughter's part, for a girl of such impressionable mind cannot be blamed for thinking such idealistic thoughts, but for the Duke of Morley that he should, firstly, lie so blatantly (for as has already been ascertained Rosalie could not ever be called beautiful), and secondly, allow Rosalie to develop the impression that he felt more for her than he truly did. Men such as he often played with young girls' hearts and had no care as to the damage they might cause. Well, Sir Robert Grey, Duke of Morley, would certainly not play with Rosalie, nor any one of her daughters. Ambrosia would see to it.

Determined, she guided Rosalie into the shadowed corner of an alcove, blessedly unnoticed by the other ladies who looked on in rapt admiration as Lady Warwick's fingers danced skilfully over the piano keys.

'Dearest,' said the viscountess now, in as calm a voice as she could muster. 'I believe that you must be on your guard. The duke will not – despite his ardent flattery – be looking to you as a partner.'

'But *Maman*—'

'You are far too young, first of all. The differences in your age would make the match improper. You are barely out the schoolroom. You know nothing of the world.'

'I do not care about that!'

'But I do,' the viscountess pressed, 'and so will he, I can assure you. Based on his standing in society Sir Robert will want to take a more experienced woman as his duchess and, perhaps more importantly, one possessing a fortune greater than we can allow for you.'

Rosalie gave a breathless laugh. 'Oh, he is rich enough without my dowry and can scarce have need of it. And in regards to experience, well, I can learn, can I not? I shall be a good wife to him, *Maman*, I can assure you of it.'

Heavens! Ambrosia had hoped to dissuade her gently, but it was abundantly clear that poor Rosalie was blinded by naïveté and infatuation. It seemed there was no way to avoid it – she would have to break her sweet daughter's heart herself.

'Let me be clear, Rosalie,' Ambrosia said, in a tone so unlike the one she normally employed with her daughters that her youngest's eyes went positively round. 'You will not marry the Duke of Morley. I forbid it.'

'Oh, but *Maman*! I do not understand. *Why?*'

Rosalie's voice had risen; Ambrosia glanced at the other ladies. Miss Falshaw had turned her head and was nudging Louisa with her elbow, who twisted in her seat with furrowed brow.

'Because, Rosalie,' whispered the viscountess, 'I do not believe the duke to be an honourable man.'

'Nicolas would not be friends with someone *dis*honourable.'

Ambrosia hesitated at this. 'It is possible that Nicolas has been mistaken in his choice of friend.'

'What proof have you?'

'There has been talk, Rosalie. An actress in London. Some rather questionable behaviour in Bath—'

Rosalie turned up her pert little nose. 'I do not believe it. Have you not warned us, *Maman*, of judging a person based on the gossipmongering of the *ton*?'

Ambrosia *had* warned her daughters of such a thing, for society could be vicious, and though the viscountess was deeply troubled she still felt a measure of pride that her dear girl would endeavour to think the best of the duke. Unfortunately, she had witnessed firsthand that – for once – the *haut ton* were completely correct in their remarks.

'I myself observed Sir Robert in a dalliance.'

Rosalie stilled. Despite the dimness of the alcove, Ambrosia saw her daughter's expression pale.

'When?'

'This summer, dearest, in Bath. I saw him in close proximity to a lady in the Pump Room. 'Twas crowded, I do admit, so such closeness might ordinarily be overlooked. But I regret to say that the placement of his hands and hers were quite suspect. I did not see the lady clearly for her back was to me, but she was blonde, tall, with a lovely tortoiseshell comb in her hair. She appeared most enraptured by the duke, and he by her. I believe they shared a kiss.'

Tears sprang to Rosalie's eyes.

'No, *Maman.* 'Tis not true!'

'Oh, dearest,' Ambrosia said gently. 'Why would I lie?'

'To hurt me!' cried Rosalie, whose voice no longer held within it a whisper but a shriek that caused Lady Warwick to stumble over a trill.

Ambrosia tried to take her hand, but Rosalie would not allow it.

'Darling, I would never hurt you.'

But is that not just the thing Ambrosia had set out to do, so that she might warn Rosalie away?

'I do not understand it,' said poor Rosalie, who had succeeded now in drawing the attention of the whole room. The ladies stood, expressions of deep concern upon their faces. '*Père* would not be so cruel!'

'Whatever is the matter, Miss Rosalie?' asked Frances Partridge.

'Why does the girl cry so?' queried Lucinda Busgrove, and in answer to both Rosalie covered her tear-streaked face with her hands and ran from the room. Louisa attempted to follow, but Ambrosia shook her head.

'Let her go. Rosalie will wish for a moment alone, of that I am sure.'

'*Maman?*'

'Just a little misunderstanding, my dear.'

'Indeed,' interjected Lady Marshchild, 'so it must be, for none of us here would ever say *you* were cruel, viscountess!'

Ambrosia inclined her head, and with a smile upon her face

which she did not feel, chivvied her guests and daughters back into their seats, whereupon – after encouraging Lady Warwick to delight the company with a piece by Beethoven – she set forth to venture after her youngest child.

So determined was she to comfort Rosalie, she almost tripped over Mr Palamedes in the entrance hall. He jumped, the ginger hairs of his back rose, his tale bushed, and Ambrosia knelt to reassure him. Mollified, the cat sauntered off towards the stairwell with a purr, and if it had not been for this Ambrosia might have missed the movement from the shadows. A hushed gasp caused her to pause, for it was evident that someone hid beneath the canopy of the grand staircase. Rising, Ambrosia peered into the semi-darkness.

'Who is that?' she called, and the sharp scent of fresh pine from the garlanded banister assaulted her nostrils at the turn of her head. 'Rosalie, is that you?'

There was a pause, then the reluctant drag of a foot, and to Ambrosia's surprise the person who should emerge was not Rosalie at all, but the housemaid Molly Hart.

'Molly!' exclaimed Ambrosia. 'Why do you linger beneath the stairs?'

'I ... my lady ... forgive me, I—'

The manner of this stuttered declaration prompted Ambrosia to approach, and in doing so the viscountess observed three things: one, that an upper portion of Miss Hart's garment was askew; two, that beneath the staircase there hung what appeared to be a small sprig of mistletoe; and three, that the maid was not alone, and the man with whom she kept illicit company was none other than the Duke of Morley himself.

If only Rosalie could witness this! Here, before Ambrosia's very eyes, was proof that Sir Robert was indeed an abominable rogue, and the very person she needed to prove it to had fled.

'Molly,' Ambrosia bit out. 'Go to your room. Immediately.'

Molly Hart – who was usually such a confident and spirited girl – felt no compunction to disobey. The maid skittered from beneath the dark confines of the stairs and made a hasty retreat to the green baize door directly behind them, leaving the duke and viscountess alone together in the entrance hall.

As the duke emerged from beneath the stairs, Ambrosia took his measure. It was no wonder that Rosalie, Louisa and Maria were so taken with him – dressed exquisitely, he was remarkably tall with dark hair that shone silkily in the candlelight; *this* was a man whom nature had favourably blessed. But such dashing good looks would not have the least effect on Viscountess Pépin, of that one could be certain.

'What, your grace, is the meaning of this?' asked she. 'Do you have no shame?'

For the Duke of Morley's part, he appeared not the least bit shamed at all.

'You come into my home,' continued Ambrosia, 'and abuse the hospitality of myself, my husband, and my son-in-law, whom you claim to be your friend, by contriving a dalliance with one of my servants, then have the gall to stand there as if you have done nothing wrong?'

'Madam,' came the drawled reply, 'it is hardly as if I were attempting a dalliance with one of your esteemed daughters.'

'But not through want of trying,' she returned. 'I know you have been whispering indecencies into Rosalie's ears, and I've no doubt you have done similarly with Maria and Louisa. Regardless of the fact, a maid's honour is no different to that of a lady of noble birth.'

Sir Robert barked then an obstinate laugh.

'Is that so? I rather think differently.'

Ambrosia stared. *The cad!* If anything were to make her angrier than she already was, it was this.

'No woman,' she replied tightly, 'no matter her station, deserves to be abused.'

'I can assure you, viscountess, I was not abusing ... Molly, was it?' the duke shrugged, smiled. 'I can assure you, the girl was willing. In fact—'

'Be that as it may,' Ambrosia cut in, in tones most scathing, 'I will not stand for such indecent behaviour in my home.'

She waited for a stark reply, and was relieved that one did not come. Instead, Sir Robert merely stared at her languidly, and in turn she narrowed her eyes.

'Because it is Christmas,' Ambrosia said, 'and because I neither wish to cause a scene that should embarrass my husband, nor upset the seigneur and in turn my eldest daughter, I shall not instruct your removal from this house. But mark my words, your grace, if I see you near any one of my daughters again, or my servants, I will not hesitate to change my mind.'

The Duke of Morley's lip curled, but he inclined his head and deeply bowed.

'Have no fear, madam. Your daughters – and your maids – shall be perfectly safe from me. I see now not one of them is worth my effort or aggravation.'

And with that the rogue turned on his heel and strode across the hall, blithely humming a festive melody underneath his breath, leaving Ambrosia staring after him aghast, clenching her fists, Mr Palamedes circling her feet with a sonorous purr.

STAVE VI.

The Humbled Heart

SIX GEESE A LAYING

It was a long-held tradition that every thirtieth of December, six golden eggs were hidden about the interior of Wakely Hall.

The notion – it can be of no surprise – was concocted by Viscount Pépin. Already there had been a game of Hoop and Hide, Cards and Dice, and a rather hectic hour of Bullet Pudding, whereupon Miss Louisa forfeited in her endeavour and made a dreadful mess of flour on the parquet floor of the tea room. Indeed, games such as these were a festive staple for the family and guests of Wakely, but a mighty inconvenience for Mrs Esther Wilson and her servants who were required to tidy up after them. Such Christmas traditions held no joy for the housekeeper and were (in Esther's opinion) a ridiculous waste of one's time.

With a huff, she placed the goose eggs into the basket, not stopping to admire how fine a job Mr Hornby had made of the gold paintwork, for such niceties were below the housekeeper's attentions, especially today, when Esther found herself particularly vexed. Ordinarily she would have instructed Miss Hart to hide the eggs, but the maid was currently forbidden from venturing upstairs unaccompanied, and since Esther could not spare one of the other maids on account of the household being so very busy, it fell upon her to complete the task herself.

What a revelation, to find that Molly Hart had been discovered in a dalliance with the Duke of Morley! These past two years the girl had been prone to flirtations – despite rigorous scoldings on the subject – but never had the housemaid shewn herself to act upon them. Miss Hart never used to act in so forward a manner, and what facilitated this change Esther could not say, but to risk her virtue and position, for a man of such superior rank who could offer her nothing, was most foolish. If it had been any other of her girls she would have ordered their dismissal immediately, but as Miss Hart was her longest-standing housemaid, Esther was loath to put the suggestion to Viscountess Pépin. Even if she *had* demanded Miss Hart's dismissal, Esther knew she would have been overruled, for the viscountess was altogether too soft-hearted when it came to her servants. Take, for instance, Loveday Lucas. Never in all her years of service had Esther encountered such a wilful, disobliging creature. She glanced at the scullery maid at work on the other side of the servants' hall. It must be said that the girl's behaviour was improved these past few days. Esther noticed faults like a hawk and never missed mistakes that any of her servants made; but had Miss Lucas not polished all the saucepans admirably? What of the stove, which she blackened beautifully the other day without a single word of complaint? And had Esther not seen Miss Lucas attempting to cheer Miss Brown (whose recent fits of melancholy had set the housekeeper's teeth on edge), where before the girls had avoided one another? Even Mr Marmery seemed a little more inclined to smile at the scullery maid, though this was no doubt due to the interference of one Miss Allen; she and Miss Lucas were, it seemed, quite as thick as thieves. Esther was still irked that the kitchen maid had undermined her on the day of the Christmas boxes. *Friendship*, the Viscountess Pépin said. *Katherine had only acted in friendship.*

Esther scowled. She preferred to keep all aspects of her life professional, preferred to dedicate herself to the running of Wakely Hall and its servants and nothing more. Order was important – in a life of service there was no room for friendship or emotional entanglements of any kind. They clouded judgement. They made one weak.

'Mrs Wilson? Is everything all right?'

Bess Denby was watching her over a half-plucked goose.

'Why should it not be?'

The cook raised her sparse brows. 'Well, you looked ever so displeased just now. If I can help with anything at all—'

'You can help, Mrs Denby, by minding the preparations for this evening's dinner rather than minding me.'

At Esther's sharp retort the other woman's face shuttered, and for one brief moment the housekeeper felt a small flicker of regret. Of all Wakely Hall's servants, Mrs Denby could always be relied upon to perform her duties well. Even at this time of year, when the cook found such merriment so very difficult. Her comment had been uncharitable, Esther knew, but instead of offering an apology she turned to Miss Allen who at that moment was removing butter from a cow-shaped mould.

'Where is Marmery?' she snapped. 'I cannot hide the eggs without the riddles to go with them.'

Miss Allen hesitated and fiddled with a small brooch upon her collar. Esther was just about to scold her for wearing an item that so clearly was not suitable for kitchen work when the footman, better known to the other servants as the more dashingly monikered 'Nash' on account of his rather idealistic notion of becoming a Romantic Poet (a notion of utter nonsense, so thought Esther), appeared at the doorway of the dry larder, brandishing in his hand six slips of paper.

'Here I am.'

Esther frowned at him. Such writerly endeavours – though the housekeeper could not fathom why – were encouraged by the Pépins, particularly at Christmastime. *His* festive box had contained a fine leatherbound journal, which he waved about in so insufferable a manner at the dinner table later that same evening, Esther had been prevailed upon to confiscate it until the next morning. Now, with a self-satisfied grin, Mr Marmery held out the papers on which were written his riddles and proclaimed:

'I'm mighty proud of them, Mrs Wilson. Pray, would you like to hear one?'

'No, I would not,' replied Esther, taking the slips unceremoniously from him and dropping them in the basket without a glance. 'I have no time for such nonsense. I just hope for your sake the riddles can be understood. Last year Miss Maria puzzled over them for hours and *no one* won the crown. I dare say it ruined the Christmas festivities.'

The footman's grin slipped. He stood up straighter in his buckled pumps.

'I can assure you, Mrs Wilson, they are most clever but not in the least bit difficult. My writing has vastly improved this past twelvemonth.'

He glanced at Miss Allen, who sent him an encouraging smile over a line of eight buttery cows, prettily displayed on a pewter dish. Esther sniffed.

'Well, let us hope Viscount Pépin agrees with you. And,' she added in a sharper tone, 'speaking of the viscount . . . Hornby – are you not supposed to be pressing his lordship's breeches?'

The viscount's valet was, at that precise moment, lingering at the kitchen door, conversing in low tones with Mr Moss, whose swarthy cheeks were flushed as if he were hot.

Which was perfectly impossible since the snow had not let up since daybreak.

'Yes, Mrs Wilson,' came the grudging reply.

'Then get to it and stop letting the cold air in.' Esther paused, sent his companion a withering look. 'I thought better of you,

Moss. 'Tis not like you to shirk your duties, and you've no time to either what with Cobb still sick.'

It came to her attention then that the other servants had dwindled in their own duties to watch this exchange, and with a purse of her lips Esther clicked her fingers.

'Back to work, all of you,' ordered she, and like sheep at the famer's whistle they scattered. The housekeeper watched them recommence their tasks with a vigilant scowl.

The servants of Wakely Hall did not like Mrs Esther Wilson. The housekeeper *knew* they did not like her, but was their liking of her so very necessary? Their obedience was far more important – and though Esther was perhaps a trifle harsh and sharp-mouthed at times, she was above all things just and judicious, a statement which (she was sure) could not be doubted. No, indeed, the housekeeper of Wakely Hall did not require her servants to *like* her, and Esther was by now quite used to solitude; most evenings she sat alone in her neat and tidy housekeeper's room with a pot of tea and her Bible, and thought herself vastly contented . . .

But in truth, deep down, Esther was not content at all.

She should be, she thought as she climbed the servants' stairs and pushed open the green baize door leading into the grand entrance hall. She had everything she could ever require in life – a comfortable and lucrative position in a prestigious household, where she wanted for nothing. But oh, how lonely she often was, and how frustrating to have her good advice ignored by the viscountess over and over again! Were her years of loyal service not enough to garner respect? 'Twas true much had changed since her time at Heysten Park where rules were so often broken and servants forced to suffer the—

Esther stopped. Frowned.

Mistletoe. Beneath the stairs.

Well! thought the housekeeper, tugging it free of its hook. What would Mr Hornby say (who was undoubtedly the culprit of such a folly, for was it not he who festooned Wakely with its winter foliage?) if he knew that Miss Hart had found herself in an indelicate position because he had acted so imprudently?

Esther tossed the offending plant into the basket, and closed her eyes briefly in an effort to calm herself before crossing the entrance hall to the ballroom, where she placed the first golden goose egg and riddle on the windowsill, then concealed it behind its red velvet curtain. The next she hid in the library, where she found Miss Charlotte seated within her favourite reading nook immersed in a book . . . until the lumbering curly-haired Busgrove boy emerged from the east wing to sidle forth and disturb her.

'My dear Miss Pépin,' Esther heard him simper. 'I wondered if—' upon which she promptly closed the door.

Private conversations were not for the ears of housekeepers.

Esther adjusted the eggs in the basket. Whoever found a golden egg could only keep it if they solved the accompanying riddle. The player who solved the most riddles was rewarded with a crown made from fir and bay leaves collected from the garden and announced King or Queen for the evening. It was a game that Miss Maria often won – each year her gloating could be heard down in the servants' hall – except for last year, of course, and Esther hoped for everybody's sakes that Mr Marmery's writing *had* improved, else they would never hear the end of it.

The housekeeper crossed the entrance hall again, her heels clipping on the polished chequerboard-tiles. The third egg and riddle she was to place in the billiard room, but it was with much chagrin that Esther found it inhabited by Miss Juliette's new husband Nicolas Toussaint, and more particularly (the housekeeper pursed her lips in displeasure) the Duke of Morley.

'Forgive me for disturbing, seigneur.' She paused, pointed. 'Your grace.'

'Not at all, Mrs Wilson,' smiled Mr Toussaint, rising from his inspection of the ivories, assessing, so it must be assumed, his next shot. 'Can I be of assistance?'

'Not at all, sir,' replied Esther. She clasped her hands tightly about the handle of her basket. 'I am simply come to distribute an egg.'

The seigneur blinked. 'An egg?'

'For this evening.'

'Ah,' exclaimed the Duke of Morley then, who turned his cue to hold it like a staff. 'Is this the treasure hunt Miss Maria has been wittering on about for days? How droll.'

Esther regarded the man. He appeared everything that was charming – smiling, jovial – but the housekeeper knew far better. How distressed Viscountess Pépin had been when she spoke with Esther that morning!

A scoundrel! A blackguard! He has no regard for any female. Be on your guard, Mrs Wilson – mind your girls, as I shall mind mine.

But of course, it was not Esther's place to speak her true thoughts, and so she merely said:

'Yes, your grace.'

Sir Robert leant on his cue, his gaze roving over Esther's face. She knew perfectly well what the man stared at so brazenly, and it took all of her effort not to press her hand against the dents embedded in her face.

'Would you wish us to vacate the room, Mrs Wilson?' he asked, as if he was not being monstrously rude. 'For but a moment or two, while you conceal your precious cargo? I give you my honour we shall not look for it afterwards.'

The duke licked his lower lip and then – very deliberately – winked at her. Esther's stomach tightened. Honour, indeed. Men like him deserved to be horsewhipped and set to the dogs. She pinned on him an insincere smile.

'That would be most kind.'

'Splendid,' Sir Robert said. 'Come, Toussaint. I'm certain a reprieve would help you in any case. You have hardly potted a ball this half-hour.'

The gentlemen departed, and it was with relief that Esther released her breath as the heavy oak door shut behind them.

Her ladyship was quite correct in her estimations. Scoundrel! Blackguard! He must surely know that Viscountess Pépin had informed the housekeeper of his attempted liaison with one of her maids. The duke had mocked her just then, that was clear.

In a state of ill-temper Esther secreted the egg and riddle beneath the billiard table. As she relinquished the room once more to the gentlemen, she pointedly ignored the Duke of

Morley's conceited bow, and left the vicinity of the lower rooms as fast as her feet might carry her.

Upstairs was where she decided to hide the final eggs – three up, three down (the neat order of the distribution pleased the housekeeper exceedingly) – but the hiding places must not compromise any of the family or guest bedrooms. Esther, then, was required to be a little more inventive in her choices, and at the top of the grand staircase she paused to consider them. The portrait gallery would do for one egg; there was a hidden alcove near the old schoolroom which would be suitable for another; and as for the last . . . Esther frowned for a long moment before the answer revealed itself. Yes, indeed! On the second-floor landing there was a figurine of a cherub set in gold. If she were to conceal the egg in the crook of the angel's arm which held the harp . . .

Quite satisfied with this solution, the housekeeper set forth towards the portrait gallery. There was a pleasing picture of the Pépin family, painted when the girls still gambolled about Wakely Hall in their pretty lace-capped shifts, and presently Esther found herself beneath the portrait, concealed the egg and riddle behind the vase of white and red cyclamen displayed on a mahogany pedestal in front of it, then turned into the corridor that led on to the schoolroom.

'Oh! *Oh!*' cried Esther, holding tight to her basket, for what should be waiting for her around the corner but a brown-feathered hen. 'Oh,' cried the housekeeper once more, as the bird pecked at her skirts. 'Begone, foul fowl. Begone!'

Such a commotion did she so make, that the door to the

schoolroom – already partially open – opened further, and out stepped Miss Juliette, as was.

'Mrs Wilson! I am awfully sorry,' apologised the new Seigneuresse Toussaint, taking the hen into her arms, which flapped its wings and uttered a loud and almighty *cluck*. 'Forgive me. We were so invested in our game of chess we did not notice Foi had escaped. Is that not so, dear?'

Juliette Toussaint half-turned, and Esther observed the small child who lingered on the schoolroom's threshold with wide and startled eyes.

She was a thin little thing but at least, the housekeeper noted, now clean. Esther had been disturbed to discover that the Pépins had taken in such a filthy wraith, for heaven knew where the child had come from and what diseases she might bring into the house. It had been very wrong of Monsieur de Fortgibu to bring the girl back to Wakely (even if she did have a sprained ankle), and Esther was most profuse in her objections to Viscountess Pépin, but once again her sage advice was ignored.

'*Madame*,' said Esther, in as respectful a tone as she could muster. 'It would be of great assistance to us belowstairs if the monsieur restricted his birds. 'Tis unclean to have chickens run amok. Only yesterday one of my maids was prevailed upon to clean their droppings from the rug outside the viscount's study.'

Juliette Toussaint inclined her fair head. 'Of course, Mrs Wilson. I shall make sure Monsieur Benoît is aware, and in the meantime keep little Foi here confined. It shall not happen again.'

But it *would* happen again Esther wished to declare, looking down at the brown hen in the young woman's arms with deep disapproval, for the monsieur refused to leave his feathered pets outside where they belonged, and they could not be relied upon to defecate in the tray of dirt which had been placed in the Frenchman's quarters for such a purpose. She dreaded to think what state the Persian rug there would look like by Twelfth Day, and a little meanly Esther hoped Mr Palamedes might make a meal of them.

During this exchange the little girl had been staring at her, and Esther met her rather too-direct gaze. For one brief moment she felt a spark of recognition (why did the child's expression look so familiar?), but then the brown hen clucked once more, the housekeeper blinked, and the notion was gone the instant it appeared.

'Thank you, seigneuresse. My maids and I would be very grateful.'

Esther dipped her knees, and with a sweetly apologetic smile the eldest Pépin daughter retreated to the schoolroom, where the child took the hen in her arms, and the door gently shut behind them.

The housekeeper sighed. It was a truth that could not be in any measure denied, that members of the aristocratic class had no notion of the realities which allowed them to live such blesséd lives. Miss Juliette need not clean chicken excrement from the rugs on which they trod, nor empty the chamber pots *they* used to relieve themselves. Her mother, the viscountess, need not feel shame and defeat when *her* orders were undermined, nor suffer the gloating that came thereafter as a consequence. No indeed, the family Pépin and those of their ilk had not one idea of the realities of running a household. What, mused Esther, would any of them do without a capable housekeeper to take care of their every need and whim? Oh, Esther thought, as she deposited the fifth egg and riddle within the shadowed alcove next to the schoolroom door, what would she give to witness any one of the Pépins experience a single ounce of the problems she had contended with over the years! What satisfaction would she thus have!

Esther shifted the basket, made her way across to the other side of the house – through the portrait gallery, thence through the passageway and up another flight of stairs. So lost was she in her thoughts that she found herself at the rosewood glass-paned cabinet which contained the golden cherub in no time at all, and it was just as she was reaching into the basket to remove the sixth and final egg that she heard a distant but great and wretched sob.

Her hand paused. Esther turned her head. The second-floor landing was situated just within the divide which separated the rest of the hall from the corridor of family bedrooms, but not so close to them that placing the last egg there should be an invasion of their privacy. Still, that pitiful-sounding sob must have been extremely loud for Esther to hear it, which was concerning indeed.

Silence fell, and after hesitating a moment she turned once more to the task at hand. But when she again attempted to touch the last golden goose egg, a series of muffled cries erupted down the corridor, and unable now to ignore them Esther followed the heartbreaking sounds until she found herself standing in front of the youngest Pépin daughter's chamber.

'Miss Rosalie? 'Tis Mrs Wilson. Might I come in?'

There came an almighty sniff. Esther pressed her ear against the wood.

'Miss Rosalie?'

For one drawn-out second the housekeeper did not think the girl would answer, but then, on the tail of a hiccough, there came an unsteady 'Yes'.

Esther opened the bedroom door. The room was steeped in shadow, for Miss Rosalie had neglected to open the curtains. It smelt stale and stuffy. Her bed (in which the girl was sitting up), Esther was wholly unsurprised to see resembled a blackbird's nest – the sheets were scrunched up about her scrawny legs, and the coverlet of plum damask lay in a crumpled heap upon the floor, and as for Miss Rosalie herself . . . Well, it would be kindest for one to simply say that she did not look at her best.

'Mrs Wilson,' the girl hiccoughed, raising a shaking hand to her unruly hair which stuck to her head in greasy clumps. 'If *Maman* wishes me downstairs, please do tell her I am taken ill.'

Esther shut the bedroom door, laid her basket on the rug.

'I am very sorry to hear that, Miss Rosalie. You appeared perfectly well yesterday, and you have not – so I am aware – been outside and caught a chill.'

Miss Rosalie, in her childlike manner, tucked her knees beneath her chin (which had, so Esther could plainly see, an angry pimple on its tip).

'I *was* perfectly well, Mrs Wilson, until last night when *Maman* contrived to be so cruel.'

'Cruel?'

Here Esther frowned, since for all Viscountess Pépin's faults, the housekeeper could not say she was a *cruel* woman.

'*Maman*,' came the grave reply, 'forbids me to marry the duke.'

The words were barely out of the girl's mouth before she collapsed into sobs once again, and covered her face with shaking hands.

Esther pursed her lips. She had certainly never cried quite so much as Miss Rosalie did now, and *she* had suffered far worse. But diligently the housekeeper held her tongue, approached the bed, and took the liberty to sit down upon it and place a hand on the poor girl's shoulder to console her with an awkward pat.

'There, there, miss.'

Miss Rosalie did not appear to hear her, so wrapt up was she in crying, but presently the girl pressed her weeping nose into the sleeve of her nightgown, and looked up at Esther with wet red-rimmed eyes.

'I love him, Mrs Wilson,' she said soulfully. 'He is everything I could wish for in a husband – rich, handsome, amusing! He has been most attentive to me, and my parents should be nothing but pleased I have attained such an advantageous match, but *Maman* says the duke is not an honourable man. That she saw him in a dalliance with another young lady in Bath. How can that possibly be true?'

Ah. So Viscountess Pépin had not revealed to her daughter

that the Duke of Morley had also been caught in a liaison with one of the housemaids. How then, thought Esther, was she to proceed?

She could commiserate, of course, and say something neutral to cheer the girl without committing to a lie. But that, then, would be the wrong thing to do. Certainly, it would gall Esther to make the girl think her mother were in the wrong, when she knew full well the viscountess was correct, and Esther would never encourage Miss Rosalie to pursue the duke now she knew the man to be an unmitigated rake. However, her position in the Pépin household – though Esther was not always contented in it – was not one she dared risk by stating outright her true feelings on the matter. No, a more tactful approach would be more fitting.

'It is an upsetting situation, Miss Rosalie, I do concede.' Esther hesitated. 'I can only declare that your mother is not a woman who would say a thing and not have just cause. The Duke of Morley is a gentleman much older than you, after all, and it is not unusual for a man of fortune and position to not be as wholly, ah, innocent, as yourself.'

Miss Rosalie's expression darkened.

'I am not quite so innocent as you suppose, Mrs Wilson. Thanks be to Mrs Radcliffe's novels, I am under no illusions as to the shadier side of a man's desires.' (At this declaration Esther blinked.) 'But Sir Robert is not like that, I am sure of it. Why would fate throw him in my direction if I were not destined to marry him? I almost caught Juliette's wedding bouquet, you know, and would have if I had not stepped on my skirts. Miss Brown caught it instead, but the roses were *meant* for me, and considering how the duke has gone out of his way to be so solicitous towards me since he arrived . . .'

Miss Rosalie went on for such a time, Esther was prevailed upon to suppress an almighty sigh. Dear oh dear, the girl had truly taken up a fancy and run wild with it. No, no, such lofty notions would not do at all. With an inward wince she remembered her thoughts of not an hour before – *what would she give to witness any of the Pépins experience a single ounce of the problems she had contended with over the years! What satisfaction would she thus have!*

Well, while the context of this situation might not be quite what she meant, the similarities were striking, and not one bit of satisfaction on her part was to be had on account of it. But perhaps, mused Esther, as the youngest Pépin daughter came to the end of her fanciful tirade, in that vein, she should attempt another tack.

'Miss Rosalie—'

Esther swallowed. Oh, but 'twas hard. The housekeeper took a deep breath and tried again.

'Miss Rosalie,' said she, with more strength than before. 'Many years ago, I knew a girl much like yourself – young, romantic, impulsive. She thought herself in love with a man above her station in both fortune and rank. He . . . he made her believe he cared for her.'

The youngest Pépin daughter stared through spiky eyelashes, and before Esther lost her nerve, she cleared her throat.

'He promised to elevate her. To marry her. She believed him, only to find that when he had satisfied himself, he had lied. He never intended to marry the girl at all.'

The pit of Esther's stomach twisted. It had been many years since she had thought on such unpleasant memories, and remembering them – even in such basic terms – left her feeling quite unwell.

'If the girl had been older,' the housekeeper continued, 'if she had been wiser, had known more of the world, and more gentlemen within it, perhaps she might not have been taken with such foolish fancies. But alas, in her innocence she became too far entangled, and it almost led to her ruin.'

Miss Rosalie brought the bedsheet up to her mouth. 'What happened?' she whispered into it, and Esther hesitated. This was a memory she did not wish to relive, for it led to others that made her bitter, still, even now.

'The girl became with child, and the gentleman refused to make arrangements for their care. 'Twas only the actions of another man which saved her from complete ruination. He married her, and though the union gave her safety and respectability, she did not love him. And to make matters worse, the child died before it came to term, and so the girl led a rather unhappy existence thereafter until her husband died . . .' Esther trailed off. Attempted a smile. She squeezed Miss Rosalie's shoulder before reclaiming her own hand and clasping it tightly in the other. 'What I am trying to tell you, miss, is that though the duke has appeared outwardly to treat you with every courtesy and respect, you cannot know quite for sure of his character when it appears there is already doubt shed upon it. You must be absolutely convinced of Sir Robert, and if there is *any* doubt on your part, no matter how small, you must be mindful of it. If you are not . . .'

Esther's unsaid words were clear, and Miss Rosalie now stared at her rumpled bedsheets. Her tears had ceased, but her nose still shone, her cheeks were blotched red, and the little spot on her chin glowed furiously.

'And please do forgive me for saying so,' added the house-keeper, 'but you are still very young. To rush into anything at this point would be unwise.'

Deeply wistful, the youngest Pépin daughter sighed. 'But the wedding bouquet . . .'

'Was simply a wedding bouquet,' said Esther firmly. 'Nothing more. Now come, Miss Rosalie. You cannot stay in your room until Twelfth Night, or punish your mother by acting in such a maudlin manner. She meant only to put you on your guard, and if she is proven wrong about the duke's past conduct then no harm has been done. If Sir Robert is sincere in his attentions, they shall not wane after one London season. You need only wait a few months, need you not?'

For a long moment, Esther was not sure if her machinations had been successful. But soon enough Miss Rosalie sniffed heartily and sat up straight, pinning a small smile upon her dry lips.

'Thank you, Mrs Wilson.'

'You are welcome, Miss Rosalie. Now then . . .' Esther hesitated. 'Shall I send for a maid? Since Miss Partridge is no longer your abigail Miss Hart has acted in her place, but I'm afraid she is unavailable at present. I can, however, arrange for another of the maids to attend you.'

'That would be nice.'

'Very good.'

Esther rose then from the bed, and crossed Miss Rosalie's bedroom to reclaim the basket on the floor.

'What's in the basket?'

'Golden eggs, Miss Rosalie. For tonight's festivities.'

'Oh.' The girl's face fell. 'The treasure hunt. I forgot.' Her shoulders slumped. 'I *never* win the crown. 'Tis most unfair. Maria always gets a head start on me and she gloats dreadfully when she wins.'

'Well, miss,' said the housekeeper. 'I have yet to hide one egg . . . I can help you, if you like, if you promise not to tell.'

'Oh, Mrs Wilson! Truly?'

Miss Rosalie's face was in that moment lit up like a candelabrum.

'Of course.' Esther returned to the bed, deposited the basket upon it. 'Mark, Miss Rosalie, that I shall hide the egg on the landing, by the gold cherub. But here is the riddle, if you wish to solve it now.'

Esther removed the slip of paper on which was written Mr Marmery's conundrum, and together housekeeper and Pépin daughter leant in to read it:

As to my age, if you had never heard,
You'd think me ancient by my hoary beard ;
Yet my existence will so short appear,
I never yet was known to live a year,
Unless in climates far from Briton's shore,
Where I have lived for ages heretofore.
At my approach I make the stoutest yield,
And cause whole armies to quit the field.

The footman had done rather well; the riddle *was* clever, Esther did concede, and though the housekeeper could not consider herself an intellect, she surely possessed a great deal of logic and saw plain the answer. Miss Rosalie, however, looked perplexed.

'What could it be, Mrs Wilson? I cannot conceive of it.'

'Why, Miss Rosalie,' said Esther, with more patience than she felt. 'The answer is *Frost.*'

The girl stared down at the riddle a moment before her face cleared.

'Frost. Yes, of course,' she said with a nod, but in a tone that suggested to Esther the girl did not understand at all. But then Miss Rosalie raised her head and smiled at the older woman, and in that moment the housekeeper realised it hardly mattered. She had succeeded in comforting the girl, and had even (with luck) averted disaster.

'You know, Mrs Wilson,' said Rosalie now, as the housekeeper crossed the room once again to the bedroom door. 'You aren't anywhere near as heartless as all the maids say you are.'

Esther stopped. The shot of hurt she felt was most unexpected, but she managed to keep her expression a blank as she turned to face the girl.

'Is that so, Miss Rosalie?'

'Yes, indeed,' returned she, as if her words had not been so affecting. 'I've heard them often speak of you when they did not know I was about. Only the other day I overheard two of the girls when they were making up my bed.'

'And what is it they said?'

'Oh,' Miss Rosalie breathed, screwing her brows in recollection. 'Something about a plate being broken. I cannot recall the exact wording, only that they called you hard and unkind, and heartless, as I said. But they are wrong, Mrs Wilson.' The youngest Pépin daughter smiled widely, and in all genuine innocence. 'I am glad to find you are perfectly lovely after all.'

Perfectly lovely. The words made her wince, and to hide it Esther forced a smile.

She wondered which of the maids had spoken thus. Any one of the uppers could have witnessed the incident with Lowdie Lucas and the periwinkle plate. Still, it did not matter. Not really. As has already been marked, Esther did not require her servants to *like* her.

Did she?

'Good day, Miss Rosalie,' Esther said, curt. 'I hope you enjoy the treasure hunt.' And as the housekeeper shut the bedroom door behind her, she was mortified to find that she wanted to cry.

Esther had not meant to fall in love with Theophilus Heysten, but then, no woman ever *means* to fall in love. Often it comes upon one in unexpected ways, and Esther – beyond her sheltered childhood in which the only man she had ever known was her father – had not sought the attentions of the opposite sex. The opposite sex, however, wasted no time in seeking hers, and so overwhelmed was she (being then so very young and new to service), it never once occurred to her that a man of Lord Heysten's position could not truly mean to go through with his promises. Looking back, Esther could see how very foolish she was to have supposed such a thing possible, but at the time she had lost all sense of reason.

To discover she was with child had been a great shock, which twisted into shame and regret when she learnt that the gentleman had no wish to acknowledge either her or the baby. Heysten Park's butler, Thomas Wilson – who had not ceased in his own attentions from the very moment Esther commenced her engagement as a housemaid – had given her the means to avoid ruination and keep her place at Heysten, but he soon revealed himself to be a cruel, hot-blooded man with a fist like granite on the occasions he chose to employ it, which – after the loss of her child, a poor scrap of a boy that slipped out of her so small and silent one Christmas morning – he did to great effect. It was to Esther's profound relief that Thomas died of smallpox three years later, leaving her only with bitter memories and ugly scars.

In the housekeeper's room just off the servants' hall, Esther sat ruminating in her armchair by the crackling fire, Mr

Palamedes – perhaps the only creature at Wakely Hall who the housekeeper suspected found her company even remotely tolerable – lying in feline stupor at her feet. The flames crackled and fizzed where they held within their blaze the sprig of mistletoe Esther had removed from beneath the grand staircase, and she looked at its charred remnants with displeasure.

The Romans considered the plant symbolic of peace, of understanding (so the old Lord Heysten once revealed as he kissed her passionately beneath it). Symbolic of love. Esther scoffed. *Love.* Such a simple word, but one that held the power to cause so much pain and make those thwarted by it hard. Unkind.

Heartless.

Esther was not heartless. She never raised a hand to her charges and her punishments served to teach a lesson. Yes, Esther consented, she was an exacting woman, but it was the *role* of a housekeeper to run a strict household, was it not? Three rules, she had, and all perfectly reasonable:

—*Keep a civil tongue in one's head.*

—*Act with propriety and decorum.*

—*Work to the high standards expected within a country manor.*

These rules were no different than any to be found in an estate of quality, and Esther was convinced they did not make her heartless, yet that was what the maids thought of her.

Miss Rosalie said so.

At her feet the ginger cat stretched. The housekeeper sighed.

Esther had served as housekeeper for over thirty years – she arrived on the doorstep of Wakely Hall barely two weeks out of widow's weeds, determined to start afresh and leave the unhappiness of Heysten Park behind her, and this Esther thought she had done. Life trickled along like the rain that slid down Wakely's gutters, and servants came and went, as so often they might in a grand household such as this. The Pépins had no butler, not after Mr John Denby passed on; Esther was perfectly capable of running such a sizeable house entirely by herself, and disinclined to suffer the company of another butler who might wish to undermine her as Thomas so often had. Viscount Pépin graciously agreed when the matter was put to him, and it can be confidently said that Wakely Hall had not once suffered under her guiding hand. She had, Esther knew, done her best. Strict, yes, but always fair.

So why did she feel so distressed by Miss Rosalie's words?

A knock upon the door made Mr Palamedes jump.

'Come in,' Esther said tiredly and half-turned in her seat, expecting to see Mrs Denby who often at the hour of five brought the housekeeper a pot of tea, but the person at the door was not the cook at all but Miss Lucas, carrying a tray which she placed now on the small table beside Esther's chair. A plate holding a mince pie was set upon it, together with the expected teapot and teacup but also a glass, the pale steaming contents of which she did not recognise. The housekeeper raised a thin eyebrow.

'Where is Mrs Denby?'

The maid hesitated. 'She asked if I would come in her stead, ma'am.'

Esther frowned at both Miss Lucas' hesitation and her words. The cook, then, must have taken her uncharitable comment earlier far more to heart than the housekeeper had realised.

'And what is this?' she asked, gesturing at the glass, and the reply that came was guarded.

'Warm cinnamon milk, Mrs Wilson. Mrs Denby is trying something new. She . . . she thought you might like it.'

Esther swallowed.

So, the cook would not bring the tea things herself, but was still sweet-natured enough to send the housekeeper a glass of cinnamon milk, just because she thought the housekeeper would like it, and now Esther felt perfectly wretched.

'I see.'

There was a pronounced pause in which neither one of them looked at the other. Then the scullery maid hastily dipped her knees, but not before Esther saw the expression on her round face – Lowdie Lucas looked deeply uncomfortable and clearly wished to be gone.

Heartless. She was *not* heartless, and Esther would prove it.

'Wait.'

The maid paused, stiffened with apprehension, and the house-keeper took a nervous breath.

'Thank you, Loveday. You have come along swimmingly these past few days. I am very pleased.'

At this stilted declaration the girl's eyes widened in surprise, and that small measure produced in Esther the realisation that she had never once called Miss Lucas, or any of the servants, by their Christian names. It occurred to her too in that moment that Esther had never once said please or thank you for anything, nor acknowledged – as Viscountess Pépin so often did – the good work they all had done.

When, precisely, Esther thought in astonishment, had she become like this?

'You . . . you're welcome, Mrs Wilson,' said Miss Lucas.

The maid's voice was somewhat breathless in her shock, and Esther looked away so the girl might not see the flush that bloomed upon her scarred cheek.

'Would you send for Mrs Denby?' she asked then, with a somewhat brusquer tone to disguise her discomfort. 'I should like to speak with her.'

'Yes'm,' said Miss Lucas, and when the maid disappeared Esther picked distractedly at the warm crumbling pastry of her mince pie. Mr Palamedes – intrigued by the prospect of a treat – jumped onto her lap, and with deep resonant purrs began to knead her skirts. Esther scratched the feline behind his silky orange ear.

The fire crackled and spat. The mistletoe was now barely perceivable, a burnt sprig, its leaves ash, and Esther stared at it in a melancholy stupor until her door opened. Mr Palamedes (having given up his mission to procure the mince pie) vacated her lap and slipped through the door into the servants' corridor, just as Bess Denby shut it behind her.

'You wanted to see me, Mrs Wilson?'

The cook's voice was reserved. Esther's guilt swelled.

'Yes. Will you take a seat?'

She gestured to the small armchair opposite hers, so rarely sat in that its cushions were still as hard as the day Viscountess Pépin had it installed. Mrs Denby knew this, too, for she looked at the housekeeper with surprise before doing as she was asked, teasing the cotton of her apron which had upon it spots of brown sauce and a stray goose feather.

The two women looked at each other and Esther, in that moment, did not know what to say. The silence ran on, until Mrs Denby dared to break it.

'Dinner is prepared,' she declared, as if she thought herself to be under interrogation and was required to defend herself. 'Goose with an onion sauce and boiled mashed potatoes, and Kate has made a mighty fine job of the syllabubs. I—'

'Bess,' said the housekeeper quietly, and the use of her first name made Mrs Denby stop and stare. 'I want you to know I never intend to be so . . . ill-tempered. With you, or any of the servants.'

Still Mrs Denby stared. Esther cleared her throat.

'I spoke with Miss Rosalie earlier. She told me some of the maids had been complaining of me.'

At this the cook shook her head. 'Harmless chitter chatter, Mrs Wilson. Such young girls, they like speak harshly of me too when I scold them for getting in my way. I would think nothing of it.'

Esther smiled, though it was bitter – she could feel it was by the pull of her lips, how tight it was across her pock-marked skin.

'They called me hard and unkind. Heartless. I knew I was hard, for I always have been. How could I not be, after all I endured at Heysten Park? But Bess, I never thought myself unkind, nor heartless. Especially not heartless.' Esther shut her eyes briefly, then opened them once more as the fire crackled and spat. 'I have only ever endeavoured to run this household fairly. And as I *do* run it, I am required to be severe on those who do not work well. But unkind? Heartless? I confess, Miss Rosalie's words shamed me greatly. I am sorry,' the housekeeper added when Mrs Denby made to interrupt, 'that I was so unfeeling to you earlier. I understand that Christmastime is especially painful for you, what with Phillip being . . .' Esther trailed off, unable to finish. 'It has never affected your work, and I was wrong to imply otherwise.'

Bess Denby blinked, then blinked again. In the firelight Esther thought she saw a sheen of tears in the cook's eyes (for the mention of her son invariably did serve to have such an effect) but then she turned her head and the housekeeper could not be entirely sure.

'When you first came to Wakely,' murmured Mrs Denby, 'you were already, shall I say, of poor spirit. Having come from Heysten Park it can be of no surprise — no woman of service who came from there ever was contented. But in time they thawed. All of them, except you. John and I came to the conclusion that there was a good reason for that, and we left well alone. My Phillip seemed to be the only one of us that could ever make you smile.' Still with her face to the firelight, the cook shook her head. 'He was good at that, wasn't he? Making people smile.'

'That he was,' Esther said softly. 'That he was.'

It was true that young Phillip Denby could draw her out. Perhaps it was because he was so young, so quiet and well-behaved. Or, perhaps, she saw in the bonny lad an echo of the boy her own son might have grown to be, if he had lived. Often Esther wondered what had become of Bess and John's boy. Had he died well? Or was he still about in the world, and simply had no desire to come home?

At such an unwelcome thought Esther shifted on her chair so it creaked in its springs, and Mrs Denby turned back to face her, eyes now quite dry.

'The maids ... as I said, they are young. They do not understand enough of life to realise what it can do to a person. Let them never know the hardships so many of our class suffer under.' The cook watched the housekeeper in the shifting firelight. ''Tis true you irked me somewhat this morning, but I do not think you heartless. I simply think you a bitter woman, Esther Wilson, and you take that bitterness out on others. Which I must say, is a mighty shame.'

If the housekeeper had dared, she might have met the cook's gaze in that moment. But Esther did not dare. Instead she reached for the glass of cinnamon milk on the tea tray, and took a sip.

It was warm, comforting, and the spice gave it a rich and indulgent flavour. If one were to bow to a cliché, the milk *tasted* of Christmas, and Esther could not help but smile.

''Tis lovely.'

Mrs Denby inclined her head.

'But ...'

'But?'

'Might I make a suggestion?'

The other woman's fair eyebrows rose, for one thing Esther

had never done – for all of her long years at Wakely – was question the merit of Mrs Denby's cooking.

Esther placed the milk down, and went to the tiny cupboard on the other side of the room. From within she brought out a bottle (her own Christmas box gift) and two glasses, depositing the latter on the small table between them and pulling the cork of the former.

'Brandy,' said she, 'just a tiny drop,' and poured a tiny dribble into the glass. Esther brought it to her lips to taste, and with a smile handed the glass across the table to Mrs Denby, who consented to take it.

'Oh yes,' breathed the cook, licking her lips. 'Yes, you are quite right.'

Between them, the cinnamon milk was soon drunk, after which Esther poured more brandy into the two empty glasses, and the cook and the housekeeper – now looking so much more at ease in each other's company – clinked their drinks and drank.

Esther rarely imbibed. It was a treat she reserved only for Christmas, but always alone, and for the very first time the housekeeper wondered why she had not thought to invite Mrs Denby before this. The cook appeared to read her thoughts, for she settled deeper into the armchair and said, 'This is nice,' to which Esther nodded her agreement.

One glass turned to two, and at length, above stairs, there came a cry of indignation. It sounded very much to Esther's ears like Miss Maria, and in the warm fug instilled within her by the brandy, she wondered absently how Miss Rosalie did with the treasure hunt, and who might win the crown. But then Mrs Denby cleared her throat, quite distracting the housekeeper.

'Is that mistletoe?' the cook asked, squinting at the charred remains in the fire, to which Esther shrugged and took another sip from her glass.

'Not any more.'

Mrs Denby leant back into the armchair.

'Just as well, I suppose,' she said softly. 'After what you told us this morning of the duke . . . Poor Mol. It was Molly, wasn't it? Silly girl. Still, men like that always get their comeuppance. Sooner or later.'

'I am inclined to disagree,' murmured Esther, thinking of Theophilus Heysten, and though neither she nor Mrs Denby had explicitly stated that that man had anything to do with Esther's past, the cook clearly understood he had.

'Lord Heysten died alone, hated by everyone who knew him,' she said, watching Esther across the lip of her glass. 'If that is not penance for his sins, I do not know what is. Whatever he did to you, however you lived before you came to Wakely . . . you must not let this bitterness rule you.'

The brandy sat hot in Esther's stomach, and at Mrs Denby's words she wondered again when, precisely, had she become like this?

There was no definitive moment, not one event where the change occurred. Indeed, it had happened gradually, but there could be no denying that it all started with Lord Heysten. But as God was her witness, thought Esther – it would finish today. If it did not, she would risk becoming just like him.

Hard, unkind and heartless.

Esther looked at Mrs Denby, gripped firm her glass. And though she felt somewhat foxed and her vision was blurred, the housekeeper of Wakely Hall had never seen more clearly in her life.

STAVE VII.

First Impressions
SEVEN SWANS A SWIMMING

On the upper road that led from Heysten Park to Wakely Hall, a rider pushed hard his horse. The stallion was of Arabian stock, a breed known for its hot-blooded nature, a state in which its owner Charles Heysten was in at that very moment, for he had found himself experiencing a fit of agitation most pronounced.

His lordship had already been tired both in body and mind when – in a mood particularly dark – he had hastened a return from London and arrived in Merrywake at dawn that morning, in need of some respite and a chance to consider his next move, for his findings in that drear city (or lack thereof) had not been to his liking. Taking to his bed Charles had tossed and turned, in such a perturbed fettle he had been unable to sleep, and so decided to read the correspondence which had piled up upon the dresser in his absence.

Amongst a missive from his second cousin, Bertram, advising him that he and his siblings had started their journey south; another from Cordelia (Charles had tossed that one aside with barely a second glance); one from his new banker, Mr Busgrove; and a packet from a Mr Repton who enclosed some rather enterprising plans to redesign the park's gardens, there were two notes from Viscountess Pépin. He had sighed at the first and pinched the corners of his aching eyes, for he did not give one single fig about his waistcoat and he bare remembered what the other Pépin girl had said to him that night, so distracted was he by his own troubles. Charles knew only that the viscountess' daughters had given him the perfect opportunity to leave early so he could mull over his concerns in peace, and in doing so he had decided that he could not wait for word from his solicitor any longer and must venture to London himself. Yawning, Charles had reached for the second note, and beyond feeling some mild gentlemanly guilt at having caused Viscountess Pépin distress at not replying to her first (his being in London, at least, gave him a perfectly acceptable excuse), and surprise that his estranged elderly uncle had affianced himself so suddenly, he was about to discard the note entirely when his tired gaze landed upon the fourth paragraph ... and then, well, Charles could not look away.

He read it twice, thrice, a fourth and fifth time, but there was no mistaking the words. At first he felt relief, but then, when the unlikeliness of the situation hit him, that relief was replaced by doubt, and thence the aforementioned agitation, and so without waiting for his valet Charles stumbled into the clothes he had discarded only two hours before, headed to the stables, and gave the poor stable boy the fright of his life.

Now, at a little past eight in the morning on New Year's Eve, Lord Charles Heysten rode as fast as Samson could convey him the six-mile distance to Wakely Hall.

What turbulent thoughts flew about his head as he galloped down the turnpike road! First, that Faith should have by some means or other ventured to Merrywake, alone, was most perplexing and distressing. The village was at *least* a day's journey from the capital. How on earth had a child of only seven managed it? Mrs Doncaster did advise that some money had been stolen. Did Faith pay her way to ——shire? But, according to the viscountess, she was discovered in Wakely Forest in so grievous a state that it hardly seemed possible.

Lord Heysten gritted his teeth, pushed Samson harder through the snow. Of course, it was perfectly likely that the child Viscountess Pépin spoke of might not be Faith at all, but all his instincts screamed otherwise.

Perhaps it was because Faith was now, to him, more like a daughter, so long ago had their attachment been formed. Truth be told, Charles never much enjoyed the company of children, nor had he any wish to bring another Heysten into the world even if his injury had not prevented him from doing so, but Faith – being so sweet and gentle of temperament, so very *unlike* her father – had softened his heart. Charles saw in his care of her a kind of redemption, a way to right the wrongs of all the other Heystens before him. Now that it was in his power to do so he meant to treat Faith as she had always deserved to be treated, to give her the life she had been so cruelly denied. Had he not been toiling hard these past months to ensure Heysten Park was ready for her? So it must be said that when, two weeks ago, Charles found Faith had disappeared from Mrs Doncaster's Academy for Temperate Young Ladies, his lordship was distraught.

No words can describe the torture he experienced when he received that terrible missive from the academy's matriarch. Without a moment to spare he employed a runner to scour the city streets, instructed his solicitor to send out enquiries to all the London orphanages and workhouses, and Charles himself visited the more questionable venues which might have had occasion to chance their luck with a younger charge.

Such things were known to happen.

But to think, a surge of desperate hope filling his chest as Samson's hooves thundered upon the hoarfrost, if this child *was* Faith ... Well, what other little girl could possess a pink shawl embroidered with tiny satin roses, a shawl he had given to her himself? The child must be her, *she must be*, and with such an assurance possessing his mind, Charles pressed the Arabian on.

It was just as his lordship was breaching the crest of the first of Old Mr Hodge's fields, that Charlotte Pépin decided to take a turn about the garden. She was in a sour mood, for breakfast had been a trying episode – aside from there being some pronounced bitterness at the table due to none of the sisters winning the crown at last night's treasure hunt, Rosalie had not ceased sniffling on account of the Duke of Morley. Indeed, he appeared to have become bored of Rosalie's company, a shun which also extended to Maria and Louisa, meaning all three of her sisters had taken it upon themselves to blame each other for Sir Robert's change of heart. Charlotte was thankful, at least, that the Pépins – on account of wanting a little privacy with so many guests in the house – took their breakfast away from the others; it allowed her sisters to quarrel outside of company, and also meant Charlotte need not exert herself to be sociable.

The truth of it was, Charlotte preferred above all things to be left alone. Perhaps this was a singular preference for a woman of only twenty who was blessed to belong to a family of good birth and fortune, to whom ample opportunities were afforded ... except the opportunities afforded were not of Charlotte's preference. What need she for embroidery or music or the frivolities of balls and the suffocating words of Fordyce's Sermons so regularly pressed upon her by Mrs Busgrove? Of course, a woman such as she (who had spent most of her visit at Wakely trying and failing to pair Charlotte with her buffoon of a son – how on earth *he* won the crown last night could not be fathomed) had such a walnut of a brain Charlotte supposed that lady could not help it. But oh, how it pained her to know that esteemed works such as those of Mrs Wollstonecraft were regularly shunned by the women to whom her *Vindication* was directed? It pained Charlotte too that her sisters did not share in the consideration that women were meant for far more than being wives and mothers, the chattels of men. Even Juliette – who Charlotte felt had more sense than the others – wanted nothing more than to become these things, though at least her eldest sister admitted she wished to see more of the world beyond the confines of Merrywake, something she would soon achieve once she left England for France.

Charlotte sighed, the cold air pooling at her mouth, the crisp scent of frost tingling her nostrils, and navigated the first of the yew trees that stood in a long line either side of Wakely's vast lawns. It was her intention – despite the snow – to sit by the pond at the end of them, for it was a place she often went to feel at peace, a place where she could contemplate the world and all that might be achieved in it if she had the means to do so.

The truth of it was, Miss Charlotte Pépin wished to make a difference in the world, to use her position and what small amount of money she had for good. Take, for instance, the atrocities of the slave trade. She thought of the book she was reading by Snelgrave, the horrors it recounted. How could one condone treating other human beings so ill? It was unpardonable. And then there was the mistreatment of children in those wretched establishments she had read about in the weekly papers, the limitations imposed on women that Mrs Wollstonecraft expounded. Now, *there* was a female who had used her voice to great effect. But could Charlotte Pépin – third daughter of a viscount – say or do anything about any of it? Mrs Wollstonecraft had only been the daughter of a farmer which gave her some element of freedom, but Charlotte's exalted position in life was nothing more than a cage – she had no other recourse but to glimpse through the bars into a wider, freer world.

If she could only use her status to do even some small decent thing.

A soft whomping sound interrupted her musings, and Charlotte turned her head. With a sinking sensation she thought it might be that buffle-headed Nigel Busgrove, ready to descend once again upon her much-needed solitude, but instead Charlotte smiled. At the far end of the pond there was a swan, stretching its snowy wings.

'Good morning,' she called softly. 'Where is your mate?'

The great bird merely regarded her, its beaded eyes unfathomable. Was this the male or the female? The male was larger, she knew, but swans were sizeable birds no matter the gender, and at such a distance Charlotte could not tell which it was.

She liked the swans. Every year, they would bring their cygnets to the pond where they could raise them safely away from poachers, for though Merrywake was a peaceable place, such wretched pastimes were still prevalent. Did not the Earl of Starling complain of his nye of pheasants being decidedly thinner than usual the other night at dinner? Charlotte hoped that the swan's mate had not fallen prey to a poacher's gun. If it had, there would be no more cygnets to watch for in the summer, since swans were known to mate for life. Earlier that year Charlotte had had the privilege of seeing five of their cygnets raised to adulthood; seven of the creatures bobbing about safely on the pond, keeping the spirit of little Edmond company. Her gaze drifted to where his monument rose from the middle of the frozen body of water, the stone urn reaching high in the grey sky. She could see from where she sat the finely carved dove, the revered symbol of innocence, purity and sacrifice.

Sacrifice.

It was a word that held particular meaning for Charlotte. Dear little Edmond, the brother she would never know. She had asked one day, holding on to her father's hand, why there was a pillar in the middle of the pond. And so the viscount told her; how *Maman* had brought a little boy into the world, only to lose him soon after. And though it was uncharitable to think such thoughts, for it was Edmond in the end who was the ultimate sacrifice, had not her mother sacrificed herself, too? Her father's imparted knowledge made Charlotte realise how her mother had done the same on five other occasions; sacrificed herself again and again, over and over, becoming weaker and weaker, each and every time.

And for what, really? If Edmond had lived, he would have travelled the world, done and become anything he wanted. But her mother, her sisters, Charlotte herself . . . their lot in life was simply to breed and live under the helm of their husbands. Sometimes, Charlotte envied Wakely's maids – they had purpose, every day. But girls such as she . . . They were meant to be reined in, to be owned, to be passed from one man to another, just to ultimately sit behind their embroidery and fans and surviving children, all without a voice or a penny to their name. If Charlotte were to marry, the money first controlled by her father would then be controlled by her husband.

Oh, if only she had been born a boy!

Ah. There was the other swan, ambling across the lawn towards her. Smaller, too, which meant (Charlotte twisted on the cold stone lip of the pond) the swan swimming in the pond was the cob. But, frowning, Charlotte considered it more closely. The swan had not moved its position, was not swimming at all, in fact. Was there something wrong? As if in answer the magnificent creature made another *whomp whomp whomp* of its wings, together with a sound that cut harshly through its beating feathers.

It was a sound she had never heard before, something between a rattle and a sharp-pitched cry, and as the disturbing noise erupted from the swan's bright beak its elegant neck bobbed and stretched erratically. Charlotte leant forwards, squinted. Dear heaven, the swan was stuck!

The swan's mate – nearer now, and looking very threatening – honked at her, and in alarm Charlotte stood. She rushed further down the line of the pond so she might take a closer look (which made the male swan flap its wings more wildly) and gasped. Oh yes, the cob *was* stuck! The water had completely frozen over; the swan's legs trapped beneath the ice!

Charlotte spun about, a moan of distress on her lips. The pen stared at her with beady black eyes, cocking her head as if to say, *Well? What will you do about it?*

What indeed? Where, thought Charlotte, was the gardener, Mr Cobb, or his assistant, Mr Moss? Where was *anyone* for that matter? But the frosted lawns of Wakely Hall were empty, the servants' quarters situated on the other side of the house, and she could perceive no figure at the windows at whom to gesture for help. No, there was no one, and if she were to run back to the house now the poor swan would suffer further still.

The bird made another desperate noise, and thus it was decided: Charlotte did not need a man to help her. She would rescue the Cygnus herself.

It mattered not that it was the last day of December, and the temperature was below freezing. It mattered not that she wore nothing more than a walking dress (though it was warm serviceable wool), a pelisse of thick suede, kid gloves and leather boots, all of which would be ruined if they touched water. What need had she for such fripperies when an innocent creature needed help? And so, approaching the swan cautiously, Charlotte swung her leg over the lip of the pond.

She suspected her weight might break the ice and was therefore prepared for it. So when the ice did *not* break, she felt both surprise and a surge of confidence. Still, Charlotte was not (or so she considered herself) a stupid creature, and instead of tiptoeing across the ice she committed to distributing her weight more evenly by crawling on her hands and knees towards the straining swan. And oh, what an almighty racket it was making! On her approach the creature had begun to actually *hiss* at her, of all things – surely it should realise she was only trying to help? Unperturbed, however, for the third daughter of Viscount and Viscountess Pépin was a stubborn woman indeed, Charlotte continued her careful crawl.

It was as she was prostrate in so unladylike a position, her body pointed in the direction of Old Mr Hodge's lower field, that Charles Heysten galloped into view.

At first his lordship did not see Miss Pépin, for he was in the process of reining the Arabian in. He had just spotted the ha-ha, and was turning his head this way and that to ascertain how to gain entrance to Wakely's grounds from the rear, but as he did so he took in the singular sight – a young woman, on all fours in the middle of a frozen pond, derrière upright to the sky . . . crawling towards a swan!

Did the chit not realise how dangerous swans were? Worry tightened Charles' throat and he dug his heels into Samson's flanks, pushing the stallion onwards into Wakely Forest, taking the very same path as Monsieur de Fortgibu had some four days afore. In frustration he navigated those little gates, but Charles was a superior horseman and soon found an opportunity to jump the low boundary wall that separated Wakely Hall's lawns from the path, at exactly the same moment as there came a sharp and alarming *crack*.

Stranded in the middle of the pond, Charlotte froze. Her stomach leapt; her heart pounded. The swan hissed noisily; its mate flapped her wings. And just as Charlotte was contemplating the manner of her next course of action the treacherous ice broke beneath her knees, and into the water she went.

Charlotte gasped as a thousand icy needles shot up and down her body, and though she knew the pond could not be so deep that she could not stand up in it, the shock of the moment, together with the weight of her clothes pulling her down, made her quite forget it, and so she flailed in the water, unable even to scream. She could neither see nor hear except the pulsing of blood in her ears and the thunderous flash of white beating wings; no thought entered her mind, no measure of feeling beyond the notion that she could not breathe. It was only when she felt a strong pair of arms about her waist that Charlotte was brought back to herself, and she became conscious that a sturdy figure held her firm and was forcing her legs to straighten, so her feet should find purchase on the bottom of the pond.

'*What the devil did you think you were doing?*'

The voice which uttered these words was hard and unforgiving. A blunt voice belonging to a man that Louisa – so Charlotte remembered – had only the other day categorised as boorish.

'Lord Heysten,' said she, waspish. 'Unhand me this instant.'

'Unhand you?' came the biting reply, spinning her about in the water, his large hands pressing into the shoulders of her sopping wet pelisse. 'I shall not. It seems to me you are in need of severe *handling*!'

Charlotte stared at the man in front of her. If it were not for the way he kept her pinioned she would have raised her arm and struck him, the brute!

'For pity's sake,' he continued, dark eyes hard and glaring, 'don't you realise a swan's wing can break a man's arm? Think what it might have done to you, you fool of a woman!'

At this, she struggled in his embrace, sending the cold water surging between them.

'How dare you,' snapped Charlotte, quite unable to control her ire, but Lord Heysten merely raised his eyebrows.

'How dare I?' he snapped back in turn. 'I dare well enough, when you would risk yourself in such a manner! And you did not answer my question – what, Miss Pépin, did you think you were doing?'

'I, sir, was rescuing the swan. What else do you suppose I was doing?'

Her reply succeeded for one brief moment to stymie him, but almost in the same moment he sucked in his breath and released her.

'You mean that swan?'

'Of course, *that* swan!' Charlotte retorted. 'Why would I try to rescue the other one when it was safely on land? I—'

She had turned her head to look, and found herself unable to finish, for said swan was no longer in the pond. In point of fact, it was now standing beside its mate, and both birds were staring up at them from the frosted lawn, watching the pair of them in such a manner as might be taken for disgust. With a mixture of relief and chagrin Charlotte pinched her lips together and turned back to Lord Heysten.

'Well. *Clearly* the breaking of the ice and you barging in to manhandle me as you did, enabled the bird to get away.'

'Manhandle you?' His lordship ran a hand through his wet hair, exposing a lined forehead. 'You and I have a very different way of looking at things—'

'So it seems—'

'But I would much rather discuss this on dry land, would you not? It's damned cold in here, and I have no wish to lose my limbs from frostbite.'

It was in that moment that Charlotte realised she was shivering, and with chattering teeth she pushed past him and waded through the freezing water for the lip of the pond. She sensed rather than saw his attempt to assist her.

'I do *not* need your help!'

Charles narrowed his eyes but dropped his arms, and though he shook dreadfully in his waterlogged hessians and felt exceedingly vexed, he watched Miss Pépin's inelegant attempts at heaving herself out of the water with something bordering on admiration and a touch of reluctant amusement.

He had of course met stubborn women in his time. Had Clarissa not been of a similar disposition? Thinking of that woman his jaw clenched (for he had not thought about the countess for some time), and once Miss Pépin had extricated herself from the pond Charles in turn did the same, committing himself to standing a respectable distance away from Viscount Pépin's wilful daughter.

The larger swan, observing their return to land from an equally respectful distance, grunted, then emitted one single *hiss* for good measure. Miss Pépin sent the bird a sour look, and proceeded to mutter something under her breath.

'What was that?'

'Nothing,' she snapped.

'It did not sound like nothing.'

At this Miss Pépin tossed her head, which might have given her look of contempt a little more credibility were it not for the fact that some of her dark hair had fallen from its pins and stuck lank and wet about her face.

'I called it ungrateful.'

'Ah! You know, then, what ungrateful means?'

Charlotte Pépin scowled.

'If I were in need of rescuing, Lord Heysten, I might accede to the service you rendered me. But I can assure you it was *not* needed. I was perfectly able to right myself.'

'Balderdash. You were struggling in the water and panic had overtaken you, that much was clear. What I cannot fathom is why you should have thought a swan needed rescuing at all. I understood from my previous visits here that you were the clever one. Swans are more than capable of breaking any ice that forms around them. It would have set itself free when it was ready to. If you had read Bewick's *History of Birds* you would have known that.'

She glared at him. 'Mercy me, you really *are* boorish!'

Charles blinked. It was not an insult unfamiliar to him; he had been called such and worse often enough, and cared not one single damn about the fact. But somehow, from Miss Pépin's lips, the insult stung. He had done her a service, had he not, yet *this* was her response?

'You should be mindful, my lady,' Charles said darkly, 'of how you address others. Do your parents know how free your tongue is?'

'Indeed they do. I am reminded of my shortcomings daily.'

Miss Pépin let out her breath then, and something in the manner of her reply made Charles contemplate her with new interest.

He understood well what it was to be frowned upon by a parent. His mother – having died in childbirth – he could not account for, but his father . . . Had it not been for Archibald's cruelty, his harsh words and even harsher punishments, Charles might not have left Heysten Park and spent so many years away from home. He doubted, of course, that Miss Pépin suffered as he had once done, but all the same he recognised in her a kindred spirit, and as she turned her head to pick up her sodden skirts Charles caught a glimpse of passion in her expression that made him quite forget the cold he felt.

She was not beautiful, not beautiful like Clarissa had been, but then, no woman was. Yet even soaking wet Miss Pépin was handsome, with a striking pair of brown eyes that had a spark of gold in them, like crystallised honey. But then the moment was gone; Miss Pépin had swept past him, elegant head held high. Charles let her go only ten steps before he turned on his heel and called her name. She stopped, spun about.

'What?'

Her answer came like a shot. Charles liked her spirit, and in that moment could not help being just a little bit wicked.

'Aren't you forgetting something?'

She raised her eyebrows. 'I do not believe so.'

'*I* believe so. I believe you have forgotten to thank me. You may think you did not need my help, but I helped you all the same.'

That scowl again. The smouldering glint of honey. But the woman was sensible enough not to ignore propriety entirely and so she dipped into a condescending (albeit very wet) curtsey and said:

'*Thank you*, Lord Heysten.'

When she raised herself, she gave him what Charles supposed was the haughtiest look she could muster.

'You can see yourself to the house, I presume?'

With that she turned on her heel and crunched wetly across the snowy lawns without a backwards glance.

Charles took a calming breath, squeezed his cold and sodden cuffs, vaguely conscious of the fact that due to yet another Pépin sister, his garments had been ruined once again. He watched said sister, a small figure now, striding with purpose around the side of Wakely Hall, and shook his head. His horse, waiting some paces away, shook its head impatiently in turn.

'All right, Samson. All right.'

It was only as Charles was gathering the Arabian's reins that the two swans – which he had forgotten were there at all – gave a flurry of loud and almighty honks.

'Oh really?' he replied. 'Is that all you have to say for yourselves?'

And when the larger of the two merely stretched and flapped its snowy wings, Charles could not help but grin.

It was almost an hour later – having been obliged to change into a spare set of clothes belonging to the viscount (whose stature, thankfully, was not dissimilar to his own), and then proffered a warming glass of cognac – when he was finally able to demand to see the little girl presently under the Pépins' care. Upon being advised the child would be sent for, Charles found himself being shewn by the viscountess to her husband's study where they were to wait.

He had expected to find only Viscount Pépin behind that study door, and so it was a surprise to see – lounging on a sopha beside the roaring fire, book in hand and ginger cat on lap – Charlotte Pépin. She appeared quite recovered from their escapade in the pond; the only indication of it was that her hair now fell loose about her shoulders in a mass of dark waves. Her eyebrows shot up high when she saw him enter in the wake of her mother, and sticking a finger between the pages of her book she slowly closed it.

'Charlotte, my dear,' said the viscountess when she saw her. 'What do you do here? Surely you would be more comfortable in the library?'

The young woman hesitated. Her eyes darkened.

'Mr Busgrove,' was all she said.

'Ah,' came the knowing reply. 'Be that as it may, I do not think—'

'There is no need for Miss Pépin to leave,' interjected Charles. 'If the child is indeed my Faith, then I have much to reveal in regards to her. Your daughter might as well hear what I have to say.'

At this the viscountess looked confused, but she inclined her head nonetheless.

'Very well,' said she, and in that moment seemed to notice the disarray of her daughter's unruly tresses. 'Heavens, Charlotte, why did you not have one of the maids dress your hair?'

Miss Pépin merely sighed, reopened her book, and the viscountess shook her head in response. It was clear, then, she had no notion of their early-morning exploits, and for that, Charles was thankful.

'Lord Heysten,' said Viscount Pépin now, rising from his desk to shake his hand. 'I trust my garments are adequate?'

'Most adequate, I thank you. And please, do forgive me for the borrowing of them,' said Charles. 'In my haste to get here I fell from my horse into the river running through Wakely Forest.'

He did not dare look at Miss Pépin, who had gone quite still on the sopha but otherwise shewed no indication she acknowledged his falsehood.

'Is that so?' exclaimed the viscount. 'And here was I thinking you to be an expert horseman.'

Charles allowed a hollow laugh. Viscount Pépin laughed in turn, but it was clear there was a question in it, and when no further comment was forthcoming, the elder man indicated the chair opposite and bid his guest be seated.

The customary pleasantries were exchanged, but when these had been exhausted no further conversation was had. Indeed, Charles found himself too agitated to speak in any case. Aside from finding Miss Charlotte Pépin far too distracting to look at (all that glorious hair!), Charles could not stem his nerves about the child who would soon join them. His heart told him the girl *must* be Faith, but his head told him she could not possibly be so. As the minutes crept by a hard knot of anticipation formed in the pit of Charles' stomach, and when there came the distinct sound of footsteps approaching, he felt positively nauseous.

A knock came upon the door and when the viscount bade entry, an elderly gentleman crossed the threshold. Holding fast his hand, with – most bizarrely – a brown hen following on a red leather lead, was none other than the child Charles had feared lost to him for ever.

'Charles!' she cried, half-running, half-limping across the room into his waiting arms.

'Oh, Faith,' he said, holding her close, his relief profound. She was thinner than when he had last seen her (he could feel how slight she was in his embrace) but aside from a bandage wrapt tight about her ankle she looked otherwise unharmed. Still, despite his joy at seeing her safe Charles felt an anger rise within him, and it was all he could do not to shake her.

'Faith! What were you thinking, running away as you did? Do you not realise how frantic I was? Did you not stop to consider what might have happened to you? What *did* happen to you?'

His words were spoken perhaps a little more harshly than he meant, causing the tears already filling the child's eyes to fall, sending watery roads down her pale cheeks.

'I hated it there,' said she in a voice that wobbled. 'I wanted to be with you.'

'And I told you that until I made Heysten habitable again, it was better you stayed where you were.'

'But—'

'I cannot understand why you would risk yourself in such a way! You could have been harmed!'

Charles glanced at the old man who had accompanied her.

'You are Monsieur de Fortgibu, I assume? The viscountess said it was you who discovered her. You have my sincere gratitude.'

The Frenchman smiled warmly. 'It was my pleasure. Certainly, I could not leave ... Faith – *oui*? – out in the perishing cold.' He paused, gave a tiny bow. ''Tis a pleasure to finally know your name, *mademoiselle*. Now I understand why you took so fondly to my little Foi.'

These words succeeded in drying Faith's eyes; her face brightened instantly as she looked to the brown hen which lingered at the elderly man's feet, and the absurd thought passed in Charles' head as to how many fowl one could feasibly be expected to suffer in a day.

'Faith,' said Charles gently now, turning her so she would look at him again. 'What happened? By what means did you leave London? How did you come to be in Wakely Forest, all alone?'

'I ...' Faith rubbed at her little nose and ducked her head. 'There's a stagecoach that stops at the Golden Cross. So I took it.'

'With Mrs Doncaster's money?'

'I was going to return it,' she said soulfully. 'Or, at least –' and here she bit her lip – 'you would have.'

Charles frowned at this. 'Such assumptions are not becoming, Faith.'

The girl looked between him, Monsieur de Fortgibu and the Pépins. 'I know. But I meant no harm, Charles. I just wanted to come home for Christmas. I wanted to be with you.'

'But Heysten is not ready. How often must I say it?'

His frustration, his relief, too, was such that Charles could not contain his temper. Oh, the tenacious will of children! Whatever was he to do with her? It was as Charles was pinching the bridge of his nose that Monsieur de Fortgibu leant down to rest his hands on his knees.

'So you took a stagecoach. Then what happened, *chérie?*'

Faith's expression grew lively. 'Well, it was a jolly ride out of London! I rode at first with a nice old couple who were very attentive, because they were worried I travelled alone, but I told them I'd been sent for by my father and was meeting my new governess at the staging inn outside of ——. They got off after an hour or two, and then another couple came on who didn't say much, and then a kindly gentleman got on at one of the turn-pikes who gave me peppermint sticks, and then . . .'

Faith trailed off. Charles removed his fingers from his nose. 'And then?'

'I . . .' Faith's eyes filled with tears again. 'I ran out of money. I didn't realise how far Merrywake was. I didn't realise the coach would have to stop for the night.'

'Oh,' breathed Viscountess Pépin. 'You poor dear.'

The girl swallowed hard. The tears fell.

'I asked one of the stable boys how far I was from Merry-wake,' she said miserably. 'He pointed me in its direction and . . . I walked.'

'How long for?'

Faith sniffed. 'I'm not sure,' she whispered. 'Some days, at least.'

Charles sucked in his breath. 'Twas a wonder she had not frozen to death. A wonder too, he thought, his blood running quite cold, she was not abducted or worse.

'*Chérie,*' said the monsieur gently. 'Why did you not tell us any of this? Why did you keep so silent?'

'Because,' came the reply, in so small a voice it made Charles'

207

stomach twist. 'I was afraid. I knew Charles would be angry with me, and I was just so relieved to be somewhere safe and warm and with nice people . . .' Faith looked at him then imploringly. '*Are* you angry, Charles?'

It was all Charles could do to contain himself in that moment. Angry? Yes, by Jove, he was angry! At Faith for being so foolish, at Mrs Doncaster for not taking greater care, and himself for not seeing just how unhappy Faith had been. But when he looked into her tearful face all Charles could do was gather the child once more into his arms.

'You are safe now,' he whispered. 'That is all that matters.'

Against his shoulder Faith nodded.

'Please don't make me go back to Mrs Doncaster. I do not think I could bear it.'

Charles sighed, pushed her from him again and regarded her. By rights he *should* march her straight back to London. But how could he now, when it was clear Mrs Doncaster had been so careless? Besides, if Faith was able to escape once she would surely find a way to do so again, and if Charles were to send her back she would never trust him again. All his hard work at earning that trust these past seven years would have been for nought. No, he could not risk returning her to London. But what, Charles then thought, of Heysten Park? The house was in no fit state for a child to inhabit. *He* might be prevailed to suffer it, but not a little girl. It was a messy business indeed, but in that moment Charles could not fathom a solution and so he simply said:

'Very well.'

Faith threw her arms about his neck.

'Oh, *thank you*,' she cried, and when she released him Charles saw her tears had been replaced with an expression of joy which humbled him exceedingly. 'Can I finish my chess game, before we leave for Heysten? Monsieur Benoît is teaching me, and I am convinced I shall have him beaten in three moves.'

Charles blinked at her, then laughed. This was one of the things he loved about Faith – she always managed to turn a melancholy situation upside down. Monsieur de Fortgibu laughed too, but raised his silvery eyebrows in question.

'I am happy to continue, *chérie*, if Lord Heysten would permit?'

'By all means,' came the reply, and she pressed a kiss upon Charles' cheek. Then – Faith taking the brown hen by its lead in one hand, and the Frenchman's hand in the other – the pair left the study, shutting the door quietly behind them.

Feeling somewhat drained, Charles rose to stand. When he turned, it was to find the three Pépins watching him.

'I think, Lord Heysten,' Viscount Pépin said, 'that now would be the time to explain yourself,' to which Charles nodded.

'Yes,' Charles acceded, 'I rather think it is,' and proceeded to take the seat he had been sitting in before.

'As you are aware,' he began, 'my father and I were not on friendly terms. As soon as I was able I took my leave of him, and have spent these past fifteen years in America. There have been times, however, when I returned. My father, you see, had many debts, and at risk of losing Heysten Park entirely to his creditors

I was required – having since amassed a fortune of my own – to pay them. It was on one of these visits that I became aware that one of his maids was with child.'

'Ah.' Viscount Pépin's expression was one of pity. 'I see, Lord Heysten, where this is going.'

Charles inclined his head. 'So you might,' he said. 'Faith is the child of my father, and by relation, my half-sister.'

There was silence as the three Pépins absorbed this news.

'The maid begged for my help. My father had no notion of her condition, but it was providence, I suppose, that I came back to Heysten Park when I did, for she had only just begun to shew and a pregnant maidservant was hardly something my father could ignore. She would have been thrown out with nothing but the clothes on her back. I made arrangements, installed her in a boarding house in the city, and there she delivered the child. Unfortunately she did not survive the birth, and I was left with the baby.'

The viscountess shook her head.

'Poor, poor thing.'

'As you can imagine I had no recourse, no means to care for her. Instead, I found her a place at Mrs Doncaster's Academy for Temperate Young Ladies, where, until recently, she has spent her formative years.'

Charlotte Pépin looked to her mother.

'Did not Juliette say the child was educated? But pray, Lord Heysten, surely you could have done more for her? To spend one's childhood entirely without family is needlessly cruel.'

With a stab of guilt Charles turned his head. Miss Pépin's

gaze was deep and contemplative, as if she were cataloguing more than his unpleasant account.

'I had not yet inherited Heysten Park, and my business endeavours were, as I said, abroad. I could do no better for her than I did.'

'What kind of business endeavours,' asked the viscount, 'would keep you so long overseas?'

It was a question that Charles had hoped to avoid, for the answer shamed him greatly; there was, however, no other thing for it but to answer, and honestly.

'I owned a plantation.'

'A plantation?'

A look of disgust had appeared upon Charlotte Pépin's handsome features, and suddenly Charles realised he did not wish her to think ill of him, wished ardently to tell her his business endeavours were not what she assumed them to be at all, but then her father cleared his throat.

'Pray, Lord Heysten, continue.'

Charles turned his attention back to the viscount.

'I wrote to Faith every week. Saw her whenever I could. Then, when my father died and the estate passed on to me, I was finally able to put my affairs in place and return to England. I planned to remove Faith from Mrs Doncaster's entirely, but with Heysten being in such a state of disrepair . . .'

Due to Archibald Heysten's debts, the estate had been severely neglected. In truth, it was falling down about Charles' shoulders; damp had invaded the plaster, the wainscoting was riddled with woodworm, the floorboards rotting, the wallpaper peeling away.

There was much work to be done to restore his inheritance and make it habitable once again.

'So,' said Viscount Pépin, clasping his hands upon the rosewood desk. 'You decided to leave Faith in Mrs Doncaster's care?'

'Until,' replied Charles, 'such a time as I was able to provide for her properly. She was well taken care of in London. Her education was in hand, and I considered it the best place for her. But then, earlier this month, I received word she had disappeared. Now I must think of what is best for Faith. Heysten Park is not safe for a child.'

At this, Miss Pépin cleared her throat.

'Wakely Hall is.'

Charles and her parents turned to stare.

'Faith is clearly content here,' Miss Pépin said. 'She would be comfortable, and well cared for in our company. Close enough to Heysten Park that you, Lord Heysten, might see her every day if you truly wish it.'

The manner in which Miss Pépin said the word 'truly' rather grated, as if she did not believe his intentions sincere, but the viscount and viscountess had not marked it; they were too busy exchanging pointed glances in which a silent conversation had clearly taken place, and Viscount Pépin's eyebrows now rose with a smile.

'I think that a splendid idea, Charlotte! I declare, Lord Heysten,' said he, 'if you have no objection, Viscountess Pépin and I surely do not. The house will be quite empty without my dear Juliette. It would be nothing at all if Faith were to fill the void – she would be most welcome.'

Grateful, Charles inclined his head.

'While this would solve *some* of my problems, I still must think of Faith's education. Now that she has quit Mrs Doncaster's—'

Again, Miss Pépin cut in.

'*I* could teach her just as well here, I'm sure.'

At this Charles looked at her in astonishment. Such a suggestion was, surely, impossible. Daughters of viscounts did not do such things, and it appeared her mother thought so too for she shook her head vehemently.

'My dear,' reproached Viscountess Pépin. 'You are *not* a governess!'

'There is nothing wrong with being a governess,' came the arch reply, and again Charles marked the remarkable honeyed shine in her eyes that appeared to shew itself when deeply vexed. 'I am exceedingly well read, as you know, and I would enjoy teaching Faith immensely.'

'Charlotte—'

'*Maman*,' Miss Pépin said, in a tone that implied she was used to being undermined. 'Pray, let me do something useful for once. I am not some doll to be kept confined. I have a mind, let me apply it! *Père*,' she added, turning to the viscount, 'please. It can hardly do either one of us harm. There are no decent schools for girls about these parts, and what use was my having such a thorough education if I am not allowed to use it? I want for employment, and Faith is in need of schooling. It makes perfect sense.'

An affectionate smile was playing about Viscount Pépin's lips.

'Fernand,' began his wife warningly, but the viscount took her hand and patted it.

'My dear,' said he to his daughter, 'while *I* have no objection, it is to Lord Heysten you must implore, for the choice is entirely his.' He looked to Charles. 'Charlotte is the cleverest of my daughters and little Faith would not be at a disadvantage by any means. It would not be for ever, and we could certainly employ the help of Mrs Thorpe, who once was governess to *all* my daughters, if Charlotte found the task a struggle.' (Here, Miss Pépin pursed her lips in affront.) 'But why do you not take a day or two to consider?'

'Thank you, viscount. And to you, Miss Pépin, for your offer. Certainly, I would at least – for the time being – consent to Faith's staying here for the sake of necessity.'

'It would be our pleasure.'

Weary again now, Charles stood.

'If you'll permit, I beg my leave to return to Heysten Park. I've been travelling all night and have yet to sleep, and fear I shall fatigue if I stay much longer.'

Viscount Pépin inclined his head. 'Of course. But please, will you not stay here with us for what is left of Christmastide? My conscience would not permit me to allow you to stay at Heysten Park if it is indeed in such a sorry state. No, once you have refreshed yourself return here. A hearty meal will be waiting for you, and pleasant company.'

'My lord, I could not possibly impose upon your hospitality more than I have.'

'Nonsense,' intervened Viscountess Pépin. 'You *must* stay with us here at Wakely. It makes sense, after all, since Faith will be with us too. But what of your cousins? Had you invited them as you said you might?'

'I *had* invited them, my lady, but never fear – I have already arranged to have my cousins installed in the Crown Lodge.'

The viscountess appeared to hesitate, as if some thought troubled her, but then the lady's face cleared and she said, 'No, that will not do. They must come and stay at Wakely as well. Word can be left at the Crown that they should continue on their journey here.'

Such generosity was above and beyond what Charles could have expected, and immensely gratified he accepted with a bow.

'Thank you. Thank you all. Would you be good enough to tell Faith what has been decided?'

'Of course,' replied Viscountess Pépin. 'She is such a dear, sweet child.'

With one more word of thanks Charles bowed, first to her, then her husband, and lastly to Miss Charlotte Pépin, who merely watched him with eyes that – in that moment – were filled with abject dislike.

Some hours later, when the last beams of afternoon light had left the sky, turning it a rich shade of wintered navy, Charlotte sat on the windowseat in her bedroom contemplating that morning's events and the man to whom those events were connected.

Lord Charles Heysten. A decidedly arrogant man who – despite his shew of bravado in 'rescuing' her this morning – had treated Charlotte as if she were a mere simpleton. Did he not tell her she was in need of handling? Did he not call her a fool of a woman?

Charlotte grimaced. Mayhap she *had* been foolish in her attempt to help the swan; she owned that she acted in the heat of the moment, but that did not mean she was without sense. Why, she would act the same way again if it came to it. Lord Charles Heysten had no right to judge her for her honourable actions.

In any case, his lordship could not be deemed an honourable man. Oh yes, he might have arranged his sister's care, but to offload her to an educational institute where he knew she would grow up without family or friends, well, such an act was abominable. No wonder poor Faith had found herself in such a despicable situation – if he had just taken charge of the child as he should have from the start . . . And what, precisely, prevented him from doing so?

I owned a plantation.

That the words were in the past tense barely registered with Charlotte. That he had any part in the slave trade at all was, to her, the mark of a man who held the demands of his pocketbook above the demands of moral decency. No indeed, Lord Charles Heysten was precisely the kind of man whom she had every reason to despise.

Charlotte looked down at the book open before her.

When we purchase the Negroes, we couple the sturdy Men together with Irons.

She sucked in her breath and turned her face to the window, whereupon a movement outside caught her eye. On the snowy lawn below were the two swans, and Charlotte watched them in the dusk-light as they meandered between the yew trees. The male appeared in no way compromised after his confinement in the ice – the cob flapped its great wings and stretched its long neck without issue. *Could* a swan break a man's arm? She supposed it might, but Lord Heysten's words vexed her greatly:

I understood from my previous visits here that you were the clever one . . . If you had read Bewick's History of Birds *you would have known that.*

Charlotte snapped her copy of Snelgrave shut and dropped it on the plush velvet of the windowseat. Brutish man! But then she thought it would not do; though she did not seek his admiration Charlotte did seek his permission to teach his sister, and if Lord Heysten truly thought her a simpleton, who knew next to nothing about the capabilities of swans . . .

She rose and ventured downstairs to the library, where she searched the shelves for an author by the name of Bewick, and once she had found him proceeded to educate herself on, first, the nature of the Mute Swan, and then other birds which were detailed therein – the Red-Legged Partridge, the Turtle Dove, the Cock, Blackbird and Tame Goose – and it was thus occupied that Charlotte was unfavourably discovered.

'Ah, Miss Pépin! There you are!'

These words – so simperingly delivered – were received with not one ounce of pleasure by their recipient, who shut her eyes briefly in despair.

'Mr Busgrove,' said she, planting on her face an insincere

smile and turning to greet said gentleman, who stood before her – red-cheeked and sweating, clearly in his altitudes – with a wide-toothed smile of his own. 'You startled me.'

'Did I?' came the reply, and Charlotte could indeed smell sherry on his breath. 'Forgive me, Miss Pépin, I had not meant to. But so absorbed were you in your books, and so affecting did you look with your hair loose about your shoulders, I did not wish to disturb you by making undue noise.'

To this sickening declaration, Charlotte gritted her teeth. 'And yet,' she said sourly, 'I am disturbed.'

Nigel Busgrove, only son of the esteemed family of Busgrove Bank and therefore a man prone to thinking himself vastly superior in terms of status and affluence, gave an insincere chuckle and inclined his head. His blonde curls lay crisp against his crown by way of too much pomade, which he patted now upon his rise.

'So you are, so you are – forgive me again, but I sincerely wished to speak with you. I thought we might discuss last night's riddles together.'

Charlotte did her utmost not to sigh. She should have known that coming to the library (usually, for her, a place of refuge) was an unwise decision, but in her haste to ensure she was not wrong-footed by Charles Heysten again she had clean forgot that Mr Busgrove might discover her there. Perhaps she would not mind his company if he were not so transparent in his attempts at securing Charlotte's affections, and she could barely keep her countenance whenever he sought her company. Indeed, she remained amazed that he had won last night's treasure hunt, since he had always appeared to be such an addle-pate.

'I'm afraid,' Charlotte said, clutching Thomas Bewick's *History of British Birds* to her chest like a shield, 'that our discussion will have to wait. My . . . my father is in need of me.'

'No, no, he is not,' replied Mr Busgrove, pale eyes alight with some emotion Charlotte suspected was gleeful satisfaction, 'for I just left him discussing his investment of pineapples with my father, and they shall not wish to be disturbed, I am sure.'

Drat. Charlotte bit her lip, willed herself to think of something to say which might rescue her. But then there came the sound of footsteps on parquet, and suddenly Charles Heysten presented himself at the library door.

'Miss Pépin,' said he, with a formal bow.

'Lord Heysten.'

His lordship looked much improved from that morning. Before, he had looked tired and haggard, the suggestion of a beard apparent on his over-pale skin, his salt-and-pepper hair an unruly mess. Now, however, he was shaved and combed, dressed formally in his own attire of sober colours unlike the flamboyant style of her unwanted companion, and Charlotte found herself conflicted at the sight of him. In some measure she was relieved to no longer be alone with Mr Busgrove, but in another, her consternation that it should be *him* to interrupt them was great indeed. Seeing the pained expression on her face, his lordship looked between Charlotte and the man at her side.

'I apologise,' said he, with care. 'I am interrupting.' Lord Heysten turned to regard the inelegant Mr Busgrove and raised his dark brows. 'And you are, sir? I do not believe we have been introduced . . .'

Mr Busgrove beamed, hurried to shake Lord Heysten's hand.

'I am Nigel Busgrove, your lordship! You have recently undertaken the services of my father at Busgrove Bank, and I simply cannot *tell* you how thrilled we are you chose to trust us with your accounts. An honour, Lord Heysten, a true honour!'

Mr Busgrove was still heartily shaking his lordship's hand, and Charlotte found a little satisfaction in seeing Lord Heysten's strained smile.

'Of course,' he said, taking back his hand which he then surreptitiously wiped upon the hem of his tail coat. 'It made the most sense, under the circumstances.'

'So it did, my lord!' Mr Busgrove puffed out his chest which strained at the buttons of his mustard yellow waistcoat. 'We never could understand why your father insisted on using a London branch when we were so close at hand. Such shameless expense, all because the bank serves the royal family! Oh, it has a sense of history and patronage, to be sure, but Busgrove Bank has a sterling reputation of its own which will grow year on year.'

'Quite.'

'But the error has been rectified, so it has, and you will find we are much more affable and convenient.'

Lord Heysten's jaw clenched. 'Indeed.'

'In fact—'

'Busgrove?'

The younger man paused. 'Yes, Lord Heysten?'

'Absent yourself, won't you my good fellow? I have need to speak with Miss Pépin. Alone.'

Charlotte pressed her lips. Mr Busgrove blinked heartily.

'Oh.' He looked between her and Lord Heysten. '*Oh*,' he said again, and in that moment looked quite dejected; his fleshy cheeks reddened further, his lower lip fell so that Charlotte could detect the glisten of spittle upon it. 'Yes,' Mr Busgrove muttered, 'yes. I am much obliged to you. I . . .' And it was with such bumbling mutterings that Nigel Busgrove shuffled himself away.

Charlotte pressed her fingertips hard against the book. She did not like Mr Busgrove's '*Oh*' and its implied meaning, for it was clear the buffoon suspected a prior attachment between her and Lord Heysten which was really most degrading. Even if she were receptive to the notion of marriage, Charlotte would never stoop to consider the suit of a man such as *he*!

'Really, Miss Pépin,' said that gentleman in mocking tones. 'Must I always be put upon to rescue you?'

Charlotte lifted her chin, produced a pointed sniff, and raised an arching eyebrow in disdain.

'As with this morning, you quite mistook the matter. I was in no need of rescuing. I am *more* than capable of taking care of myself.'

'Are you quite sure? A swan and a Busgrove – rather formidable foes, I do concede.'

Lord Heysten wore such a look of amusement that it vexed her greatly. Seeing it, his lordship adopted a serious expression and stepped forwards.

'Come now, Miss Pépin. I think we got off on the wrong foot. Pray, might we begin again? I am sure we can be civil to one another at the very least, though I would prefer it if we could be a little more amiable than mere civility if you are to teach my Faith.'

This appeal made Charlotte pause, for his lordship suggested she *could* teach Faith, and the words were spoken with such earnestness ... but almost immediately she was assaulted with the memory of that ghastly line from Snelgrave and could not contain her disgust when she replied:

'I have no objection to maintaining a civil discourse with you if I am indeed permitted to have a hand in your sister's education. But beyond that I do not see a need to forward the connection further, not when your character is so clearly written.'

'Miss Pépin?'

'Any man who could have a part in the suffering of a human being is not worth my favourable attention.'

Charles regarded the young woman standing so proudly before him. It was rare a woman should hold his interest, but if the lady had spirit he invariably found himself drawn. Clarissa had been a mistake, a mistake that cost him more than his pride – her husband had made sure of that. The long barrel of a pistol. A lucky near-miss. That mistake of over a decade ago meant that, now, at five-and-forty, he had little to offer a woman beyond a crumbling estate and his affections if she should manage to engage them, and so for many years marriage had been the furthest thing from his mind.

Until, that is, he encountered a stubborn hotheaded miss trying to rescue a damn swan from a frozen pond.

'I think, Miss Pépin,' Charles said, 'you are suffering under a misapprehension.'

'Oh?'

'I saw your disgust when I revealed earlier that I owned a plantation. You think me a fiend.'

'Do you claim not to be?' Miss Pépin returned, widening those fine honeyed eyes. 'I do not see how you could be otherwise. Slavery in any capacity is disgraceful.'

'I quite agree.'

Miss Pépin stared. Charles drew a breath.

'The cotton plantation in question belonged to my father. He had purchased it in his youth, after he inherited Heysten Park from *his* father. Theophilus did not squander his fortune as Archibald later did – the plantation was the first of many ill-advised investments my father made, and it took some persuading for him to sign it over to me but his debts, being what they were, made the decision inevitable; in order for him to secure Heysten Park, I had to secure the plantation and take over the running of it.'

Miss Pépin narrowed her eyes.

'I see.'

'No, I do not think you do. Let me explain further.'

And so Charles did – he divulged to her his abhorrence of the terrible conditions Archibald Heysten's slaves suffered, how far the plantation's fortunes had dwindled without proper and humane guidance.

'I hired a more compassionate overseer, improved living quarters for the workers, and in time the plantation began once more to turn a profit. I confess that I was conscious of how my own fortunes were being made over the years because of it, but the earnings were necessary to pay for Faith's education and settle my father's other debts. Then, finally, when he died and Heysten Park returned to me, I was legally able to free the men and women, and sell the land.'

There was silence as Miss Pépin considered this. At length she said once more, 'I see,' and Charles replied, 'Do you?'

She hesitated, and he was gratified to mark that while she still clearly felt some conflict within herself the harsh expression she wore had softened, and that small victory was enough . . . for now.

He gestured to the book in her arms, which she had clasped tightly to her chest throughout their conversation.

'What were you reading before Busgrove interrupted you?'

A blush bloomed across her handsome face, and Charles smiled when she reluctantly admitted to the book's title.

'So you know, now,' he said, teasing, 'that swans *can* break ice if they so wish it?'

Miss Pépin's jaw clenched, her lovely eyes flashed, and it was all Charles could do not to take her in his arms and kiss her there and then.

'Forgive me, Miss Pépin,' he said in gentler tones. 'I do not mean to tease, but I confess you make it rather easy.'

Charlotte – feeling conflicted and not a little embarrassed – returned Bewick's volume to the shelf.

'You are not alone,' she replied, grudging. 'My sisters share your view and contrive to tease me almost daily. *Maman* especially does not approve of my reading habits and I admit I do not tolerate being spoken down to. It makes me somewhat irritable.'

'Yes,' Lord Heysten replied with a nod, 'I discovered that much this morning. And you must forgive the harsh way in which I addressed you then. I was not quite myself, and seeing you so close to harm made me even less so. I shall endeavour not to tease you again.'

Charlotte blinked. This admittance of error was quite unexpected, and though she could not quite bring herself to say he was forgiven, Charlotte did go as far as to accept that perhaps her first impressions of him were erroneous, and so she inclined her head.

At that moment the gong for dinner sounded, and Lord Charles Heysten dipped into a bow.

'Miss Pépin,' said he, 'will you allow me to escort you? I would be interested to hear about all the reading habits your mother finds so detestable. I do, after all, need to be quite sure you are teaching Faith something most enlightening.'

'Oh, never fear, my lord – I have every intention of enlightening her in ways she will find useful. Including how *not* to rescue swans from frozen ponds.'

And feeling rather pleased with her answer, Charlotte consented to take his arm.

STAVE VIII.

A Thread Unfinished
Eight Maids a Milking

The first day of a new year held no respite for a farmer. For Nathaniel – the son of Old Mr Hodge of Hodge Farm – his day started as it always did: at the hour of five he would rise from his bed (too short, really, to fit his lanky frame), turn to the small washstand at the window and splash water on his face, then the ruddy hair of his armpits. If nature necessitated it Nathaniel would use the chamber pot, after which he felt about in the dark for his garments which had, the previous night, been folded with military precision across the back of a simple oak chair that held the pitted scars of woodworm. No candle would be lit, even though in the winter months no daylight would illuminate the tiny room, for Nathaniel had become accustomed to the morning routine that took less than ten minutes altogether to complete; he could traverse the crooked confines of the farmhouse with sightless ease, and find himself outside in the yard long before the residents of Merrywake had stirred. No indeed, that it was the first of January, the very first day of a brand-new year, was of no consequence to Nathaniel Hodge, nor to his livestock – the cows still needed feeding, their straw changed and pens cleaned, so too the pigs and sheep before releasing the latter out into the fields . . . and all this must be accomplished by breakfast.

For only one man, the magnitude of these tasks might appear to be somewhat overwhelming, but Nathaniel was used to hard work and bitter weather, knew too the workings of the farm intimately since his father had begun coaching him almost as soon as he had outgrown his swaddling clothes, and therefore had no qualms about doing these tasks all by himself.

They were no hardship. Nathaniel enjoyed the uninterrupted stillness of a world not yet woken; those hours of early quiet he looked forward to each and every day. If one were to survey the young man as he closed the farmhouse door behind him, one would not fathom that, once, Nathaniel had resented this life which had been mapped out for him before he even left his mother's womb. Once, he ran away to escape it in an attempt to forge his own path . . . But alas, seventeen was too young an age to truly understand that the passing up of a scythe in favour of a blunderbuss was not a more favourable choice, and for four years Nathaniel lived through too many mornings that held in them not the promise of calm, but chaos. Too many times had he woken to the sound of cannon fire and the screams of wounded soldiers, too often had he seen the sun rise over battlefields filled with the corpses of cavalry and horses. Too long had he craved the peace of Hodge Farm and the company of a father who would not forgive him for leaving. Nathaniel had never been more thankful than to receive the bullet that shattered his femur and allowed him to return home. And though he would for ever walk with a limp, at least he *had* come home.

So many others had not.

Nathaniel made slow but steady progress across the yard towards the cowshed, his old black-and-white terrier, Buck, trotting at his heels. Nathaniel did not hum under his breath as some men are wont to, nor mutter absently the way his father had been prone. In truth, Nathaniel was naturally a man predisposed to silence, especially during this brief spell of morning contemplation in which he could reflect on the events of the previous day before he became distracted by those of the current one. That morning, however, Nathaniel Hodge was in an uncharacteristically preoccupied frame of mind.

If little Buck could speak, he might ask his master what it was that had set about this melancholia, but even if the dog could utter such a question Nathaniel would not have been able to answer it, for to even speak the name of the person responsible in the quiet space of his own mind was tantamount to torture.

Prudence Brown.

Sweet, innocent, Miss Prudence Brown.

At least, until four days ago, Nathaniel had *thought* her innocent. But now? Well, now, he was deeply wounded to discover that the girl he had been besotted with these past three years was not innocent at all.

Nathaniel opened the door of the cowshed. Inside, the scent of hay and sweetly pungent dung assailed his nostrils, the warmth of bovine bodies filled the barn; the cows watched him, some lowed in greeting, and as one of his favourites – a stocky Ayrshire by the name of Duchess – poked her brown-and-white head between the bars of her pen, Nathaniel took bitter comfort by reaching out to scritch her behind her silky ear. Duchess leant into Nathaniel's hand, and for a moment he let her grunt in pleasure.

It was Miss Brown who had named the cow. Nathaniel remembered the day well. He had been home from the Peninsula mere months and had not yet become master of himself; cannon fire and cries still filled his ears at night, dead soldiers and their steeds his vision. Summer marched into autumn, each night the same terrible dreams. By October Nathaniel did not think he could bear it, but then the calving season commenced and soon the miracle of new life began to erase the ending of others; those dear wibble-legged calves kept him pleasurably distracted, and so too did the presence of a sweet-faced girl who – on her days off – would pass the farm on her afternoon walk.

Prudence Brown, only sixteen, all innocence and friendliness – a breath of fresh air to a drowning man of two-and-twenty. She did not look at his limp and scorn it as the village girls did. She did not seem to mind that he was a gangly fellow with hair the colour of copper and a nose twisted from the butt of a musket, or care that he said very little, for she could run her tongue well enough for the both of them. Neither did Miss Brown turn her nose up at the smell of dung, or the unappealing look of pig-slops, and nor did she – upon arriving to the farm at the very moment a little calf slipped wetly from its mother onto the hay – flinch at the sight of it.

'I've always thought cows so pretty,' she had told him, and such a generous comment it was, for the newly birthed calf that lay so weak and bloody on the ground most assuredly could not be described as pretty in that moment. But the sincerity of her softly spoken words were enough to prompt in Nathaniel a feeling of profound admiration and delight, and so he said shyly:

'You can name her, if you like.'

Miss Brown's freckled face had lit up. She chose the name Duchess, and though Nathaniel thought the name a little too grand for an Ayrshire cow, he accepted it readily enough and vowed then and there to one day make Prudence Brown his wife.

Still, Nathaniel Hodge, for all his awkwardness and insecurities, was a considerate man. He did not wish to pressure a girl of sixteen into matrimony. The wife of a farmer was not an easy life – he knew that well enough, for his mother had despised it until her untimely death – and, like he once had, Miss Brown might wish to chuse another path. And so he had bided his time these past three years, cultivated a tentative friendship, introduced her to his father before age and infirmity took him. He allowed Miss Brown the time to understand the changing seasons of his life, and at length Nathaniel had been sure he had engaged her affections well enough to give him hope that when he asked for her hand in marriage, she would be inclined to say yes.

But that was before he saw her in the embrace of Ralph Hornby.

It had been a shock. Nathaniel had not believed her the type of girl to have her head turned by someone as tawdry, someone so officious, as Wakely Hall's valet. Nathaniel – who generally felt no inclination to dislike anyone – had never much liked Ralph Hornby, for the man took the greatest pleasure in teasing him, had done so since the moment Nathaniel began delivering milk and other provisions to Wakely Hall in lieu of Old Mr Hodge after his death. Miss Brown would always shyly let Nathaniel in at the back door, where he would stand overwhelmed and awkward near the hearth in the crowded kitchen, a cup of Mrs Denby's excellent soup in his hand while the sharp-tongued housekeeper, Mrs Wilson, counted out his payment in one of the back rooms, and during these moments Mr Hornby would mock Nathaniel's ruddy hair or muddy clothes, and ask rather pointedly if he had a particular fondness for the scent of manure.

So, then, to see Miss Brown attached to the valet in such an intimate manner . . . Well, the pain that so often troubled his leg was nothing in comparison!

Duchess huffed contentedly; Nathaniel dropped his hand, turned away. Looking at the Ayrshire was in that moment a little too upsetting for him, and so he busied himself with his morning chores and for the most part successfully managed to remove Prudence Brown from his thoughts. By the time he returned to the kitchen and fed Buck his morning portion of barley meal and potatoes, Nathaniel had convinced himself that he could manage one whole day of not thinking about Miss Brown at all.

Such was his frame of mind as he sat at the table with his tin cup of beer and small bowl of porridge, and Nathaniel would possibly have continued thus if his oats had not slid from his spoon and dropped upon the tablecloth, the globule landing on the embroidered milkmaid which adorned it and the faded threads of her skirts.

It was a tapestry of memories, that tablecloth – his mother had endeavoured year on year to fill the once-white cotton with scenes from his childhood; young Nathaniel riding his first horse, his father Abraham cutting the cornfield, and herself, Hannah, sowing the seeds for next season's harvest. There too, brought to life in fine brown thread, was the first herd of Ayrshires the Hodges ever bred, the rolling fields with a picturesque view of Merrywake village, Buck as a puppy chasing a goose. And then, along the border, little milkmaids to represent the daughters she craved and lost. After the last loss Mrs Hodge had not the heart to finish, and so one maid remained incomplete. That eighth milkmaid possessed only a blue dress and featureless face – no limbs with which to express herself, no countenance that might resemble a Hodge child, and in the maid's lack of defining features Nathaniel had imagined upon her the sweet countenance of Prudence Brown.

Being so alone in life, Nathaniel took great comfort in Prudence-Maid (as he dubbed the figure). He would speak to her sometimes when he found himself in the kitchen, cooking lonely meals for himself and for Buck. He would tell her about his day, and how he hoped his parents were proud of him for everything he had achieved at Hodge Farm, all by himself.

Nathaniel would tell Prudence-Maid how sure he was that his mother would have approved of her, and how sorry he was that she had died before they had opportunity to meet.

Nathaniel had been eleven when a fever took Hannah Hodge. Abraham was quite at a loss without her; he came to depend upon his son's assistance about the farm to such a degree that it was no wonder Nathaniel wished to escape it the first moment he could. But now ... now Nathaniel was alone, for Old Mr Hodge did not live past the first year of his return, and all he had to keep him company was a black-and-white terrier and a half-finished milkmaid, embroidered into a faded cotton tablecloth.

And now there was porridge on her. With a sigh Nathaniel scooped the offending oats from her skirt and wet his thumb, whereupon he attempted to remove the mark that remained but alas, he made it worse. The maid's pale pink skirts now possessed a grimy watermark, and he would have to ask Mrs Jenkins to wash it when she next came to collect his laundry. Which was ...

Nathaniel frowned. Having been in such a state of inattention these past few days, he had quite lost track of the day and time, but now he counted on his fingers (he moved his mouth silently, little Buck watching him with twitching ears) and sucked in his breath.

Mrs Jenkins was due tomorrow – Thursday – which meant today was Wednesday, which also meant that he was due to deliver Mrs Denby's order no later than noon.

Oh, but he could do without going down to the manor house! The first week of January Nathaniel always reserved for cleaning his tools and undertaking repairs about the farm. By next week the snow should have melted, enabling him to spread the slurry, clear the ditches, and prepare the ground for planting some new trees along the north borders separating the Pépin estate from Heysten Park. Even if he had not been indisposed to face Prudence Brown (or Ralph Hornby), Nathaniel would have preferred to stay put. But Mrs Wilson (on behalf of the viscount) paid him well, and such handsome income was necessary if he were to continue to run Hodge Farm. No, there was nothing else for it, he simply *must* venture down to Wakely, despite the pain he might experience in fulfilling his duty, and so before an hour had lapsed Nathaniel Hodge had readied the cart with all that was required, his trusty terrier Buck waiting for him on the sprung seat with a lively wagging tail.

If Nathaniel Hodge had found himself in ill temper these past four days, it was nothing to the upset which Prudence Brown felt. Mrs Wilson had remarked on it often (though it must be said she had been somewhat kinder with her scoldings just lately), and as a consequence Prudence made all manner of silly mistakes; she had left a chamber pot outside Lady Warwick's rooms, spilt the coal scuttle upon the floor in the drawing room (which Monsieur de Fortgibu's chickens wasted no time in treading in, leaving little black claw marks on the hearth), and dropped a whole bucket of dirty water over some newly cleaned linen. Well, this had been a bit too much for Prudence, who had promptly fallen into a fit of hysterics, and it was Lowdie Lucas of all people who comforted her. *What has happened?* the scullery maid asked, whereupon Prudence tearfully told her.

'Oh lawds, Prue, all this fuss over a man?'

'You don't understand,' cried Prudence, to which Lowdie had rubbed her nose and shrugged.

'Don't you worry yourself over it. If Mr Hodge likes you well enough, he'll not hold a grudge for long.'

But Prudence, having returned to the house after that disastrous garland-gathering excursion and hidden herself in her room so she might burst into tears, knew that could not be true. Mr Hodge was a gentle man, a good man, a kind man, and though a man of such qualities might be able to forgive a girl for some things, flirting with another was an indiscretion particularly damaging to a courting couple.

And they *were* courting, or at least Prudence believed them to be. Had she not spent all her afternoons off these past three years walking by Hodge Farm and conversing with the farmer for hours? Had he not allowed her to accompany him when he fed the lambs or milked the cows? Had he not (and this was most telling) introduced her to his *father*? Prudence had been sad indeed when the old man passed, for despite his grumblings he had shewn her such ease and friendliness. She felt sure that if Mr Hodge were to ask her to marry him, Old Mr Hodge would not have objected.

Drying her eyes, she had looked at the flowers that Miss Juliette (*Segne— Seigneru—* oh, never mind!) had thrown, which she had caught. Beautiful pink spray roses they were, sitting in the glass vase Prudence received in her Christmas box, so fresh and lovely. Roses were, so Prudence knew, the flower of love, and if one were to believe the superstition that whoever caught a wedding bouquet should be next to marry ... Of course, Prudence was not so silly as to believe that – Miss Partridge, after all, would be next – but she had thought catching it meant *something*. A culmination of her courtship with Mr Hodge ... a profession of his love.

But all that had been ruined on account of her behaviour with that rogue Ralph Hornby.

Now, as Prudence tried to concentrate on darning Katherine Allen's apron, she thought of that day with guilt. She had not meant to allow the valet to take her in his arms, but it was so wonderful to have a break from her work, so glorious to be out on such a crisp snowy day, that Prudence had found herself not really thinking; she had allowed Mr Hornby to hold her close and she had laughed at his guile like a fool. It was not as if, Prudence considered, she had done anything wrong, exactly. He held her for mere seconds, and he had only *danced* with her, nothing more. But how could Nathaniel Hodge know that? How could she explain?

Prudence would never forget the look of shock on the farmer's face, the flash of pain that crossed his expression before he was able to hide it. She had hurt him, hurt him badly, and in doing so had hurt herself. And it was not as if she could contrive a moment to get away to Hodge Farm and tell him the truth of it – at Christmastime no servant could be easily spared. Instead, she would have to wait until Mr Hodge delivered Mrs Denby's food order on Wednesday.

Which was today.

She tied off a thread, reached next for Richard Marmery's cravat. He had asked if Prudence might embroider a little N for 'Nash' in the folds, which he thought might be particularly dashing and in keeping with what a Romantic Poet might wear, and in the spirit of the season she was happy to oblige. At that moment the footman was seated at the far end of the table in the servants' hall writing away in his new journal, and Prudence watched as Katherine passed by him with a tray of freshly baked mince pies – the kitchen maid ran a finger along the back of Nash's neck in a gesture of intimacy, and Prudence envied them in that moment, that they should have found love in such a place as this.

With a sigh she selected a burgundy spool from her sewing box.

She enjoyed sewing. It was one of the only tasks she enjoyed as a housemaid at Wakely Hall. Unlike the others (except Lowdie – so she recently had discovered during their unexpected conversations of late), Prudence did not enjoy her role in servitude. Having been raised by her grandmother, with only a little money to secure their comfort, Prudence's childhood had still been a happy one – the old lady had taught her all the domesticities required of a small household, including the art of embroidery at which Prudence had grown quite adept. She had been perfectly content to keep house for her grandmother until the occasion of her death, whereupon Prudence had had little recourse but to seek a role in service. As a Merrywake local, she did not have to go far, but it was with deep sadness that she left behind the cosy little cottage of her childhood and ever since,

Prudence had craved the freedom of a life outside the confines of Wakely Hall. The idea that Mr Hodge might offer her that life had become as precious to her as the glass vase upstairs in her room. That the dream should have shattered so cruelly was a tragedy beyond compare.

It was at that moment there came from outside an all-too-familiar sound. Prudence could never mistake those cartwheels on the flagstone yard, nor the heavy clump of Mr Hodge's shire horse. And then there was little Buck with his excitable yaps, for Mrs Denby was always sure to give him a bone of mutton.

'Aye up,' drawled Ralph, from where he stood at the tiny window by the dresser on which Mrs Denby had spread out the ingredients for the annual Twelfth Night Cake. 'Look who it is, Prue – Mr Carroty-Pate, come to grace us with his loping company.'

A heat rose up Prudence's neck, where it settled hot and stinging in the crest of her cheeks.

'You hush now, Ralph! You hush this instant!'

The valet turned, a small pout on his bow lips.

'Ah, come now, Prue – I meant no harm.'

'Nor did you the other day so you said, but look what harm it did anyway.'

At this Ralph raised a finger to his nose and winked. 'Just you wait, Miss Prudence. You may be pleasantly surprised.'

Prudence blinked at him, unsure of his meaning or how to respond, but then there was no chance to as Katherine opened the kitchen door to reveal Mr Hodge – her beloved Nathaniel – standing awkwardly on the threshold.

She tried to catch his gaze, but to her anguish the farmer again refused to meet her eyes. Instead, he made his quiet perfunctory greetings to Mrs Denby, but for the most part kept his attention focused in its entirety on the kitchen floor. There came then a commotion, not out of the ordinary for a noonday delivery; Nash unloaded the cart of baskets filled with dead geese and rabbits, fresh milk and eggs, and other commodities of the vegetable variety that Mrs Denby had ordered, and he proceeded to spread the bounty upon the table. Katherine presented Mr Hodge with a cup of soup from the pot heating on the range, Mrs Wilson appeared and wasted no time making a tally of the items received, and when the housekeeper retreated to her room to collect Mr Hodge's weekly pay, to Prudence's horror, Ralph sidled over to the farmer in a manner (to her eyes) particularly sly, long arms laced behind his back.

'How do, Hodge? Did you find that lamb of yours?'

Mr Hodge hesitated.

'Aye. Up on the boundary wall.'

'Well, that's a relief, isn't it? Can't have little lambs lost, not in this weather.' Ralph tilted his head. 'And how do *you* fare, this lovely New Year's Day?'

Prudence saw the farmer's chin clench.

'Well enough.'

'Only that?' came the glib reply. ''Tis a great shame, it being the time for festive cheer. Isn't that right, Prue?' Mr Hornby added, turning to her with a jesting expression on his handsome face which Prudence did not like. When she said nothing and neither did Mr Hodge, the valet turned back front.

'Of course, I suppose living up there on that breezy old hill all alone you can't but feel a little maudlin this time of year. It's company you be needing, something to cheer your spirits.'

'Ralph ...' Prudence tried, for she could see how uncomfortable Mr Hodge looked, but her fellow servant had no mind for her.

'You should come to the ball!' Ralph exclaimed. 'Everyone needs a bit of dancing. Prue likes a good dance, don't you, Prue?'

In that moment Prudence could have hit him. How could he be so inconsiderate? How could he be so shamelessly brazen? Ralph knew precisely what he was about – he was riling Mr Hodge, goading him for a reaction, and Prudence could see plain that one was forthcoming; she could tell by the pink in the farmer's cheeks, the tic in his strong jaw, the curling of his fingers into a fist, and it made her want to cry.

'Servants do not go to balls,' was what he said now. His voice was quiet, but there was a hardness to it, a tone filled with abject dislike.

'They go to this one,' the valet replied. 'The Twelfth Night Ball and servants' ball is one and the same, here. Something of a tradition where all the aristos and riff-raff come together for a night, and I pretend I didn't shine the viscount's shoes that morning. Lots of fun, plenty of dancing as I said.' To Prudence's horror the valet pushed Mr Hodge's shoulder in what might be deemed to be a friendly shove, to which the farmer's lips thinned into a dangerous line. 'Why,' exclaimed Ralph, 'you could dance with Prue! She's a trifle too short for me so we discovered in the woods, but for you . . . well, I think she'd fit in your arms rather admirably, don't you think? Of course, that limp of yours might make a jig a bit difficult, but—'

'Hornby.'

The valet turned, so too Prudence, to see Mrs Wilson standing behind them, a leather pouch in hand, and Prudence released a sigh of relief, for Mr Hodge's fist had started to rise and she was quite sure the farmer meant to strike Ralph had it not been for the timely interruption.

'I would prefer it if you didn't keep Mr Hodge chattering away when I'm sure he has his own business to attend to. Just as you do, I believe?'

Ralph smiled, all politeness.

'Indeed I do, Mrs Wilson.'

'Then get to it.'

The valet inclined his head in assent, turned away from Mr Hodge, and as he did so bestowed upon Prudence a wink. He looked jolly pleased with himself, she thought, as he disappeared into the servants' corridor, though she could not imagine why. All Ralph had done was succeed in irritating Mr Hodge further. Nothing was said to commend her kindly to his thoughts. If Mrs Wilson had not interrupted as she had . . .

The housekeeper was at that moment handing the leather pouch to the farmer, who weighed it in his hand, and then he was thanking her, he was turning, and *oh!* he was leaving, she realised. Mr Hodge was leaving, and had not looked at her once. Quite unable to stop the tears forming in her eyes,

Prudence watched the man she loved shut the kitchen door behind him and with a sob catching in her throat, she sank back into her chair, the spool of burgundy cotton still clutched tight in her hand.

It was only then she realised that she had an audience.

'For pity's sake, Prue,' said Nash, tapping his pencil on the open page of his journal, 'go after him!'

'I can't,' Prudence whispered. 'I am so ashamed.'

'Of what?' asked Katherine, folding her arms in front of her chest like a stern schoolmistress. 'You did nothing wrong. 'Twas only Ralph up to his games.'

'But Mr Hodge does not know that!'

'Because you have not told him.'

'I know,' sniffled Prudence, 'but—'

'But nothing!' called Lowdie from where she stood in the scullery, hands deep in the Belfast sink. 'You go after him, else I will. I don't think I can stand your sulking one day longer. I like you, Prudence B, but you're lucky I've not clobbered you and put us all out of our misery.'

Katherine spun on her heel. 'Loveday,' she scolded, and the footman stifled a snort.

'Well,' the scullery maid shot back, brass as bells, 'don't say I'm the only one to think it. I don't know how poor Mol is coping, sharing a room with you. I'd as lief share it with a wounded ferret as listen to you snivelling away into the early hours.'

'Loveday,' said Katherine again, with rather more force, 'what have we discussed? Manage your words,' to which Lowdie coloured.

'Sorry,' she muttered, and resumed her dishes. Mrs Denby – who was at that moment busying herself with plucking the newly delivered goose – gave Prudence a kindly smile.

'Lowdie does have a point, pet. How can Mr Hodge know how you feel unless you tell him? Look at Miss Partridge and the reverend. It was a misunderstanding that drew *them* apart. If they had only spoken to one another about what happened between them, they would never have wasted so many years. Are you willing to do the same?' When Prudence looked unsure, the cook shook her head. 'As I see it, you have two choices – you either say nothing and suffer, or you go after that young man and tell him how you truly feel. To be sure, you nor none of us shall get any peace until you do.'

Oh, but she was right, of course! They all were. But how – and here Prudence worried her bottom lip with her teeth – might she contrive of a reason to follow Mr Hodge when Mrs Wilson needed her here? With Molly Hart still confined to the lower floors of Wakely Hall on account of that ghastly business with the Duke of Morley (where *was* she, in point of fact? Prudence had not seen her since breakfast), Prudence was required to take on some of the upper housemaid's chores. Why, she still had Lady Falshaw's linens to change, for the woman had insisted on sleeping in that morning on account of having imbibed too much sherry the night before. But as if providence heard Prudence's plight, in rushed the housekeeper, carrying in her arms one of Viscountess Pépin's Christmas boxes.

'Is Mr Hodge still here?' she asked in a huff of expelled air.

Katherine shook her head. 'The cart just left.'

'Drat,' came the reply. 'I forgot to give him this, and I promised the viscountess I would. But perhaps he can still be caught ...'

Nash stood, looked pointedly at Prudence. 'I'm sure he can be.'

'Well, then,' Mrs Wilson said, and though she had appeared to the servants of Wakely less short-tempered of late (she had even spared them a smile or two), remnants of her prior sternness remained. 'Who will take it?'

'I will!' cried Prudence.

Mrs Wilson blinked. 'You? Marmery here would be faster.' 'Tis a heavy box, after all.'

But Prudence was shaking her head.

'I will take it,' she said, a little calmer, 'I can manage perfectly well,' and so with a raise of her eyebrow, Mrs Wilson handed Prudence Nathaniel Hodge's Christmas box.

'Well, then,' she said again. 'Off you go.'

He was halfway up the country lane that bordered Wakely Hall by the time Prudence caught up with him. She had navigated the snow with rather less difficulty than she expected, and when she reached the curving path of the lane found that it had melted there, enabling her to pick up speed. Her afternoon walks on her two days off a month were certainly to her credit; she was only a little out of breath by the time Mr Hodge's cart hove into view, though her arms ached with the weight of the box, and so she was able to call his name without too much exertion.

She was not sure at first if he had heard her, but then little Buck turned about and barked, his short tail wagging furiously, and Prudence cried out with relief when the cart slowed to a halt. Heart in mouth she ran the short distance to where Mr Hodge had stopped, clutching the box to her, tight.

'Oh, Mr Hodge,' she exclaimed, breathless. 'Please. I wish to apologise. I wish to explain.'

The farmer stared straight ahead, soliciting in Prudence a sharp stab of hurt. Did he not see how much he meant to her? Why else would she race to catch him? He knew her nature, knew this wanton behaviour went against it. Surely he should see that, and no matter what Mr Hodge felt in that moment there was no need to be so rude!

'I'm sure there's nothing to explain,' said he, in tones worryingly flat. 'Who you spend your time with in Wakely Forest is no one's business but your own.'

'But you are mistaken!' Prudence cried, and Buck too gave a little indignant *yip*. 'What you saw that day was nothing but Ralph – Mr Hornby that is – being, well . . .'

She paused. How could she explain the valet's behaviour? He flirted with all the female servants at Wakely Hall, always had, but there was nothing to any of it, she found – his flirtations were always in jest.

'Ralph Hornby is an incorrigible flirt,' she settled on saying. 'If he had not danced with me, it would have been Mol. I daresay he would have danced with William Moss too if the notion took him.'

At this, Mr Hodge turned his head slightly. He did not

quite look at her, but Prudence felt that this small motion was a positive sign.

'It was not as if he and I were alone, as you saw. We were collecting garlands for the hall, and enjoying an hour's peace. You know how busy it is this time of year, and Ralph was only being jolly. But I promise, I've never thought of him in any way beyond his being a fellow servant. He . . . he makes me laugh. That is all.'

The farmer hesitated.

'Do you laugh when he says such mean-spirited things to me?'

Prudence sucked in her breath, appalled he should think such a terrible thing of her.

'Of course I do not. I scold him.'

Mr Hodge said nothing to that. Buck uttered a tiny whine and looked between his master and Prudence, as if wondering what the matter was.

'I am sorry he is so beastly sometimes. I do not think he means anything by it. In fact, I often wonder if Mr Hornby knows why he says the things he does at all.'

The farmer shifted in his seat and then, finally, turned to look at her. His cheeks were pink, his brown eyes soft and curious. He looked as nervous as Prudence felt.

'Do you really enjoy dancing?'

'Why yes! I do not have the opportunity to dance often but when I do I enjoy it immensely.'

'I . . . I am not much of a dancer.'

He gestured to his injured leg, but Prudence chose to ignore the implication and smiled brightly.

'Nor I. But I find that one does not have to dance well to dance. One simply has to enjoy the moment. You would enjoy the Twelfth Night Ball, I am sure of it. If you came, we could dance monstrous ill together and laugh at it heartily.'

Mr Hodge bestowed upon her then a small smile of his own, and with relief Prudence stepped closer to the cart.

'Are we friends again? Please do say that we are.'

Nathaniel, in that moment, felt his tentative smile freeze on his face.

He did not want to be friends with Prudence Brown. He wanted far more than that. But even if he had been mistaken about Mr Hornby, had he been mistaken on another matter? Did she only wish *friendship* from him?

The thought was too awful to comprehend, and instead he asked:

'What's that?'

He nodded at the box Miss Brown held in her arms. A look of confusion crossed her face, followed by hurt, before she seemed to shake herself.

'A Christmas box, from Viscountess Pépin. She gave them to all of Wakely's servants the day after Christmas.'

Nathaniel blinked. 'But I am not one of her servants.'

'No,' Miss Brown said, 'but you serve Wakely Hall by providing us with supplies each week.' She hesitated, licked her pretty bud lips, and the sight made Nathaniel's throat constrict. 'I understand your Pa would refuse the box each year – on principle, he said. But we always get such lovely things in our boxes. 'Twould be a shame if you refused yours.'

He did not know what to say. Abraham Hodge had never told Nathaniel of such a gift. Perhaps his father felt that – not being a servant of Wakely Hall – he had no right to accept it. Nor then should Nathaniel. But he was his own man now. The farm was his and his alone. What harm was there in accepting?

Miss Brown shifted in the snow. She was waiting on a reply, he realised, and realised too that he had not spoken for one whole minute.

'Yes,' Nathaniel mumbled – shy, embarrassed, unsure. 'Thank you.'

'Shall I . . . shall I put it on the cart, then?'

She looked up at him so sweetly, her eyes so clear and plead-ing, that Nathaniel knew then he could not leave matters as they were. He wished to know for sure if Miss Brown did indeed think of him only as a friend, and it was not a conversation he felt could be had halfway down a country lane in the bitter cold.

'Please do,' he said, 'but you come up as well. I . . . I want to shew you something. Back at the farm. If you've time?'

Prudence's heart thumped wildly. She did not have time. If she were to come back to Wakely Hall late, Mrs Wilson would be so cross. But in that moment Prudence knew instinctively that to refuse him would somehow harm the progress she had made in repairing the breach, and despite not knowing quite what that progress was (for Mr Hodge had not acceded to her enquiry of friendship), she was not willing to risk the injury.

With a nod she pushed the Christmas box up onto the cart, rounded the other side, and took the farmer's proffered hand to guide her. Buck, excitable again, consented to being moved onto

Prudence's lap, and together the three of them trundled their way towards Hodge Farm.

The journey was completed in nervous silence, and not wishing to make things more awkward than they already were by breaking it, Prudence watched instead the snowy landscape of Merrywake pass them by. Though she had been familiar with the village and its environs all her life, there was something magical about it in winter, when the fields were crisp with snow and the branches of trees adorned with sparkling white clusters. The higher they went, the more the whole of Merrywake was visible – there was the frosted spire of Wakely Church, the Reverend Soppe's rambling parsonage; there too was the bustling marketplace, and the Crown Lodge just off the square. Prudence could even spy Mr Jenkins' toyshop, and just behind it his little cottage, the very same cottage she had once called home. She turned her face and swallowed the lump in her throat, thankful to find Hodge Farm rising before them on the crest of the hill.

She had never been inside the farmhouse. Mr Hodge had always shewn her such courtesy, and understanding that propriety might not extend to their being confined to interiors, was always very careful in not inviting her inside, even though Prudence had expressed an interest. She was curious as to how Mr Hodge lived all alone, and now as she entered the kitchen she discovered the answer – the small, low-eaved room was sparsely decorated but tidy, and Prudence was gratified to find it comfortably cosy. She watched as Mr Hodge set to lighting a fire in the grate with swift and capable hands (strong hands,

Prudence thought), and accepted the small cup of beer from him with a shy word of thanks. Buck – claws tapping away at the stone floor – trotted to a small straw bed in the corner by the range, and settled his wiry head upon his paws.

'Miss Brown—'

'Mr Hodge—'

They both laughed nervously. Nathaniel clutched his cup.

'What did you want to say?'

Miss Brown flushed. 'Only that you wished to shew me something?'

'Yes. Yes.' He put his cup down on the dresser behind him, then gestured to the tablecloth spread upon the kitchen table. 'I wanted to shew you this.'

She looked confused. Nathaniel cleared his throat.

'My ma made it,' he said, shy again. 'It was her way of com-memorating Hodge Farm, my father, me . . .'

He watched as Miss Brown tilted her head, saw how the con-fusion melted away to reveal fascination as she ran a finger over the Ayrshire herd, little Buck, Nathaniel's younger self.

''Tis beautiful,' she said softly, placing her cup upon the table. 'Your ma had skill with the needle.' She paused, her attention drawn then to the milkmaids at the hem. 'And who are these?'

Nathaniel hesitated.

'My sisters.'

She looked up.

'Your sisters?'

'The daughters she lost.'

'Oh . . .'

'Except,' Nathaniel said, stepping forwards to stand closer both to Miss Brown and the cloth. 'This one.'

He shifted the cloth so she could see the unfinished maid. The porridge stain had dried in his absence, and did not appear quite so bad as it had before, but even so, Nathaniel hoped she would not notice.

'Ma did not finish her, and so I never thought of her as one of my sisters.'

Miss Brown squinted at the figure. 'Who did you think of her as?'

Nathaniel hesitated again. Now it came to it, he was shy, frightened. If Miss Brown were to shun his advance then all his hopes would be dashed, and he did not know what he would do in the event of it.

'I call her Prudence-Maid.'

Prudence froze. A feeling of wonderment enveloped her then as she looked closely at the unfinished milkmaid, her pretty pink skirts that matched in shade so perfectly the colour of the spray roses from Miss Juliette's wedding bouquet. Her heart thundered fiercely in her chest, and scarce daring to believe the words she heard, she met Mr Hodge's gaze and sucked in her breath.

He was looking at her with what could only be an expression of hope in his gentle eyes, and Prudence's heart struck a faster beat.

'You named her after me?'

Mr Hodge stepped even closer.

'She *is* you. Or at least I hoped her to be, if you were to finish her.'

Prudence stared. He cleared his throat.

'Prue, I've loved you near since the moment I set eyes on you,' he said, voice uneven with the force of his emotion. 'I hoped you might, in time, feel the same, and these past three years I believed we had grown to understand one another. That we had come to share one thought. But then I saw you in the forest with Ralph Hornby, and I felt so wounded. The pain I experienced on the Peninsula was nothing to how I felt that day.'

'Oh,' breathed Prudence. 'Nathaniel, I—'

'Please,' he said, holding up his hand, 'let me finish,' and so Prudence clamped her mouth.

'I was hurt,' he said, a bitter tone creeping in, 'sick at the thought I had been so mistaken in you, that you should have favoured such an insensitive man. I had not thought you capable. But then I considered – why, after all, would you chuse a cripple like me and the drudgery of farming life when you had such comforts at Wakely Hall?'

He looked at her then with such an expression of misery that Prudence – without a further thought – took his head between her hands, drew him to her, and planted a gentle kiss upon his lips. When they parted, his eyes expressed such shock that a laugh slipped from her, and she gently stroked his freckled cheeks with her thumbs.

'Do you know,' she whispered, 'I have been in such agonies these past few days that you thought me taken with Ralph Hornby. I felt so wretched, knowing you had misunderstood and had been hurt by it. But Nathaniel ... You were *not* mistaken in me!'

The farmer raised his hands and took hers in his.

'Truly? You do not see me as just a friend?'

'I never have!'

For the first time in her memory, Mr Hodge smiled with such unreserve that it lit up his face, and Prudence vowed then and there to make him smile like that for every day ever after.

'But Prue . . . can you really be happy as a lowly farmer's wife?' he asked, and again Prudence laughed.

'A home of my own, animals to care for, with the man I love at my side? I could not want for anything else.'

And as Mr Hodge joyfully took her into his arms, Prudence found herself thinking that the superstition behind wedding bouquets might not be quite so silly, after all.

STAVE IX.

The Wooden Soldier

NINE DRUMMERS DRUMMING

As Miss Prudence Brown observed, the village of Merrywake could be viewed in its entirety from the upper reaches of Hodge Farm. It was a charming prospect as villages go – thatched roofs, yellow bricks, neatly kept gardens and charming shopfronts, all spanning off from a well-maintained square – and if one were to pass by the farmhouse, thence down the north-western field to join the country lane abutting it, they would soon find themself in that bustling square, where the sounds of friendly chatter could be heard amidst the more serious conversation of village trade, for business outside of the vicinity of Wakely Hall in the first week of January continued on just as it ever had.

Indeed, the baker kept his customers in bread, the tailor

worked hard at his needle; the stationers ensured their shelves were full of the finest papers and inks, the basket maker toiled over her weave, and the Crown continued to secure its steady ream of visitors, both local and otherwise. For Barnabus Jenkins, his days passed by in much the same manner as all the rest – he would sit on his tall stool behind his little counter, carving his wooden figures by the hour, always happiest when a parent consented to purchasing for their young boy or girl the fruits of his labour.

As the county's only toymaker for some miles, Barnabus made good trade over the festive period. His shelves had been quite depleted of dolls and whistles and animals and spinning tops, so much so that he found himself somewhat put upon to fill them once more. At that very moment he was carving a cup and ball to add to the others he had made this past week, and once he had done that he would move next on to a new collection of dolls.

His dolls were always popular. Barnabus enjoyed carving their faces and seeing their characters take shape beneath the tip of his paintbrush. Alice would sew them little outfits from leftover scraps of linen donated by the dressmaker across the square, and so when they were complete no one doll was the same, each unique and lovely in her own fashion. Often Barnabus would see his dolls clutched in the arms of little girls when they chanced to pass by his shop window, and the sight always made him proud.

Oh yes, he liked carving dolls. They were a steady source of income, keeping him and Alice in comfort in the small cottage happily situated behind the toyshop, the sales ensuring that food was kept on the table and the woodpile generously stocked. In these winter months, such commodities were of great importance to their well-being, and the quiet course of their lives. But it must still be said that sometimes Barnabus grew bored of his Merrywake Dollies (so did Alice dub them). Many years afore he had made other figurines, even going as far as writing brief histories for them on miniature notecards tied about their necks, so that little boys could imagine them victorious on the high seas or on the battlefields.

But that was before.

Before.

Still, those little boys of Merrywake had other toys with which to amuse themselves – Barnabus was most adept at carving bears or horses or exotic monkeys and, of course, there were the cup and ball sets, the spinning tops, ninepins and ring-toss games. Those he could make without a second thought.

Not that Barnabus *never* thought. He sighed as he pulled his blade over the curve of the ball he held and let the wood shavings drop into the cushion of his lap. Their George would have been seven-and-twenty this past November, and though it had been two years since he was lost to them, not so much time had passed that his death should not still cause pain to his parents.

Absently – as he twisted the knife across the grain – he thought of the girl George had been secretly courting and wondered if the loss of him hurt her, too.

George had always been such a quiet, private fellow, never one for gossip and so very careful in his conduct with others. Such strength of character was commendable, but Barnabus

256

often felt he never truly knew his son because of it, a feeling made even more acute when George's personal effects were returned to Merrywake. It took some months for him and Alice to find strength enough to sort through them, but when they did . . . all those letters! Such neatly written ones they were too, filled with such pretty words of affection. Yet all that Barnabus and Alice could glean from them was that George's sweetheart was a local girl, for she mentioned the village often enough, but never *quite* enough that she could be identified. They did not even know her name. She signed the letters only as *your dearest Heart*. Oh yes, it made Barnabus sad indeed to know that George had kept such a secret from his parents, and sadder still that somewhere out there lived the girl who one day might have been his daughter-in-law. They could, between the three of them, have offered each other comfort.

He could have asked her what George's own letters contained, if he too felt guilt for the manner in which they had parted.

The tiny clock on the counter chimed. A quarter to midday. Soon, Alice would return from her housekeeping duties at the parsonage, and they might partake of the pot pie she had cooked for them that morning. At the thought of it Barnabus' stomach grumbled, and he was just setting the half-carved cup and ball toy down upon the counter to ready the shop for closing when the toyshop door opened, and in walked a tall gentleman in fine yet simply tailored garments, one of the renowned Pépin daughters, and a little girl in an ill-fitting dress with a bandage about her ankle.

'Mr Jenkins, I presume?'

'That I am, sir, yes.'

'Splendid. I am Lord Heysten, and I should like to purchase a doll.'

Lord Heysten! Well now, this was a surprise.

Barnabus had heard of the son's return to Merrywake – it had been the talk of the village for some months – but the toymaker had never had occasion to see the new lord. Lord Heysten kept very much to himself, only coming into the village (so Barnabus heard) to enquire after labouring men or the hiring of new servants (although, on account of Heysten Park's history, there were very few who would consent to accepting a situation there). Sometimes the new lordship partook of the occasional meal at the Crown Lodge, but always alone. That he had with him now a child was perplexing, and accompanied by a Pépin daughter stranger still, for it was no secret that there was little love lost between those two aristocratic families on account of the Pépins assisting Merrywake's vicar after that sorry affair with the maid, Eliza Granville.

All this Barnabus thought but could not express, and so the best the toymaker could venture was a morning greeting and a deep bow befitting the company.

'Good morning,' rejoined Lord Heysten, tipping politely his hat, 'though just barely. The noon hour shall be upon us soon enough and I daresay my young charge here will be begging for sustenance. But first, a present.' He smiled at Barnabus in a manner he considered exceedingly agreeable for a Heysten. 'As I said, I wish to purchase a doll, and I see you have some lovely ones here.'

He gestured to the last of the Merrywake Dollies Barnabus had yet to sell this festive season. They were not so pretty as some of the others he had sold in December – those had worn lovely damasks, floral silks, pretty bombazines and poplins. These that were left wore dresses of poorer materials for the less affluent buyer: checked cottons, dyed linens, barred muslins. None to please a little girl of quality as this child evidently was and Barnabus, feeling humbled, ventured from behind the counter, wood shavings dropping to the floor.

'So I do, my lord,' he said, 'but I confess not as many as usual. I regret that the Christmas season has emptied my shelves.'

'My good man, I should hardly hold it against you. No, no, these dolls are perfectly lovely, exactly what we should want. See, Faith,' said Lord Heysten, pointing to a doll wearing a dress of red-and-green check. 'She has hair just like yours.'

The doll in question had hair made of sheep's wool, gathered from the sheddings of Nathaniel Hodge's flock by Alice whenever she collected the young farmer's laundry. Creating the hair was another task Barnabus left to his good wife – she was particularly adept at cleaning and combing the wool to make it soft, and dying it to mimic the natural hues of human tresses. This particular shade had been treated using the juice of horse chestnuts, and was indeed similar in colour to the child's own mass of curls. So too was the shade similar to Lord Heysten's and dark like Miss Pépin's also, who held the little girl's hand, and it struck Barnabus briefly in that moment what a handsome family the three did make until he remembered only one Pépin daughter was married, and it was not the one that stood before him now. Nor had he heard of the new Lord Heysten having brought a child with him back to Merrywake. To be sure, this really was a curious trio that stood in the middle of Jenkins & Son Toyshop, for Barnabus could not fathom their relation at all.

The child named Faith – having regarded the dolls with curiosity but no apparent enthusiasm – swung her ill-fitting skirts and announced, with a voice so bright and clear as not to be mistaken:

'I do not want a doll.'

There came an awkward pause.

'Sweetheart,' scolded Lord Heysten, looking a little embarrassed, 'do not be rude,' and Miss Pépin, with an apologetic look to Barnabus, bent down to address the child.

'What would you like, then, if not a doll?'

'I'd like one of those.'

The little girl pointed, whereupon Lord Heysten and Miss Pépin looked confuddled, unable to perceive the item at which their charge gestured. It took a moment for Barnabus himself to realise the girl's interest was held by a dusty cabinet in the topmost corner of the toyshop, and he felt a peculiar twisting in the seat of his stomach.

'I'm afraid those are not for sale,' he said.

In fact, Barnabus should have packed them away two years ago. That would have been the easier thing to do and certainly would have cost him less pain, not to be reminded of his son day after day after day. But he had been so very proud of them at the time and Barnabus simply could not bear to let his creations dwindle at the bottom of a storage chest at the mercy of wood-worm. Nor, however, could he bear to have them in the cottage and so – by way of compromise – he had put them in the glass cabinet as a kind of monument, up high and in shadow where no child should chance to see them. And none had, until now. Barnabus blamed his empty shelves, the lack of other more appealing distractions which would have prevented the girl from noticing it.

Lord Heysten in that moment was squinting into that top-most corner, and proceeded to step closer to inspect the cabinet's contents.

'Ah,' he said, his face clearing at last into a more dubious countenance. 'Yes, I see them now. Soldiers.'

Before Barnabus could press upon his lordship that they were for display purposes only, the little girl squared her shoulders and raised her chin.

'Yes,' she answered, 'soldiers. Charles, I should like a soldier!'

In response to the child's claim (who *was* she to him that she should call Lord Heysten by his Christian name?) his lordship's lips thinned as if displeased, and Miss Pépin – if Barnabus was not quite mistaken – bestowed upon him a smirk.

'Did I not tell you?' the lady murmured. 'Not every girl requires a doll.'

Lord Heysten, ignoring this glibly delivered remark, looked to Barnabus with raised brows and opened his mouth to speak, only to be interrupted by the girl tugging at the sleeve of his lordship's greatcoat.

'Please, Charles! Please?'

The child was staring at him so imploringly that Lord Heysten, it seemed, was prevailed upon to at least consider the matter, and so turning back to the toymaker said:

'Why, Mr Jenkins, are they on display if not for sale?'

Barnabus hesitated.

It would be nothing to reveal the reason for it. Those who knew Barnabus Jenkins understood well enough. But to think of it, let alone speak of it, still hurt, and he was just considering how to phrase his next words when Alice entered the shop, a basket filled with Reverend Soppe's weekly linens overflowing from the wicker rim.

'Oh,' his wife exclaimed, at seeing the company her husband kept. 'Good morning to you.'

To which Barnabus said:

'Alice, my dear. This is Lord Heysten.'

Her eyes widened. Lord Heysten, upon her soul!

Now, Mrs Alice Jenkins was no stranger to a Heysten. She had served Witherington Soppe for a good many years, after all, but it was easy enough to forget that the vicar was originally from such an unpleasant family. Certainly, aside from his sometimes terse tongue (which had, Alice must confess, not been near half so bad these past few days on account of his upcoming nuptials), one would not recognise Mr Soppe as being the natural brother of Archibald Heysten. Not that Alice had much experience of the gentleman personally, mind, but she had often heard from the Merrywake women – girls who had once been in his service, or that of the father – that he was a very bad sort. And now to discover this newest Lord

Heysten standing in her husband's shop, with a Miss Pépin and a child in tow ... Well, this was a great shock to her nerves.

Surreptitiously Alice looked at her husband. The flushed expression he wore upon his dear face was one she knew well – it was a look which only appeared when Barnabus felt acute discomfort or was deep in his cups, and since the latter occasion happened but rarely and definitely not on a work day, nor before the hour of noon, Alice was inclined to consider it the former. Which meant Lord Heysten had upset him. And though Alice Jenkins was inferior to his lordship in rank and (so some might say) gender, this was a circumstance she would not tolerate.

'My lord.'

She lowered her basket which then swung against her apron as she dipped her knees in a polite curtsey, a curtsey she then bestowed upon his companion, Miss Pépin, though she knew not which daughter it was. Too old to be Miss Rosalie, Alice thought, and too handsome to be Miss Louisa, yet not pretty enough for Miss Juliette. Was this Miss Maria then? Or Miss Charlotte? In any case it did not matter – though the Pépins had a much more favourable reputation than that of the Heystens, if Barnabus had suffered on account of any of them, then Alice was set to say something most scathing!

'Is everything to your satisfaction?' she asked carefully, to which Lord Heysten replied that it was, and turned to look at the pretty little girl who held Miss Pépin's hand.

'We have just come to select a toy for my Faith here. She ah ... she missed Christmas, you see, and I wanted to purchase something to mark the day. We were just discussing with Mr Jenkins here a sale.'

Alice blinked, somewhat nonplussed, for – aside from a child missing Christmas being a very strange thing – his reply had been exceedingly pleasant, no haughtiness in it at all. In fact, he appeared perfectly agreeable. So why, then, did her poor Barnabus look so out of sorts? At that moment the child named Faith (his daughter, she presumed, for she looked exceedingly like him) released Miss Pépin's hand and stepped forward, clasping her own within her skirts. They were ill-fitting, she saw, as if the dress did not belong to her.

'I was saying that I preferred a soldier to a doll,' the little girl told her now in dejected tones. 'But Mr Jenkins declares they aren't for sale.'

Ah.

Alice looked again to her husband who would not meet her gaze, and sighed quietly with a tiny shake of her bonneted head. She knew his feelings on the matter, of course. But how many countless times had she told Barnabus that letting those toy soldiers moulder away in a dusty cupboard was a shameful waste? By all means, make no more of them if he felt so strongly about the matter ... but to refuse to sell the nine that were left and deprive pleasure from the children who might otherwise enjoy them? 'Twas needless, she always did think it.

'But Faith,' Lord Heysten was saying, his tenor somewhat strained. 'A soldier! A doll is much more in keeping for a ...'

He trailed off for the child pouted and turned her rosy face up to Miss Pépin.

'But I really *would* prefer a soldier to a doll. *You* understand, Charlotte, don't you?'

The third daughter, then. But this fact barely had time to register for the manner in which the child had implored the woman made a peculiar emotion turn within Alice Jenkins' chest.

George had implored her exactly in that manner when he was little. He could ask for anything, and she would have given it. Just as she would give anything to this little girl, now.

'Come, Barnabus,' said Alice, in the gentle cajoling manner in which she always spoke to him when broaching the delicate subject of their son. 'Let the child at least *look* at the soldiers. There can be no harm in that.'

Her husband stared. Alice saw plain the trouble this request cost him, the battle he held within himself . . . but then his face fell under the child's pleading gaze, and Barnabus reached for the small steps set behind the counter which he used to fetch toys from their topmost shelves.

There can be no harm in that.

But oh, there *was* harm, Barnabus thought as he grudgingly climbed the steps and opened the dusty cabinet door. There was harm to him. And as he looked into the cabinet upon those nine wooden soldiers, that harm felt most acute.

There had been twelve at first. Twelve to denote his son's regiment, each holding a painted drum. A drum to represent George's position in the army.

Barnabus had made George a drum once, a glorious bodhrán that hung with gold tassels, which at four years old he had pounded so enthusiastically it near drove his despairing parents mad. But oh, how he loved his music. George even taught the Denby boy to play the tin whistle, and so adept did they both become that the pair were often invited to play at the assemblies held in Merrywake's village hall.

Often, Barnabus wondered what would have happened had he *not* made his son a drum. Would George have stayed and run the toyshop with his father, as Barnabus always imagined he would, or would he have enlisted anyway? He chose the name of the shop with his son in mind, after all – Jenkins & Son. How fine that looked on the sign! How worthless, now.

The toymaker reached in, selected a soldier from the front, rubbed his thumb against the ridges of its red-and-green drum. This batch of wooden figurines had not been the first set he made. In fact, they had been Barnabus' last.

Oh yes. The toy soldiers used to be as popular as the Merrywake Dollies – even more so, perhaps. At the start of the wars, Barnabus had made a rich packet with his drummers and pipers and cavalry figures. It did not occur to him back then that he was glorifying death and making a profit from it – fighting for one's country seemed a thing that Merrywake's men and boys should be proud of. It became something to aspire to, something George aspired to, and naïvely Barnabus did not think there was more to it all than that. But then the letters came. Heartbreaking notifications that those same men and boys had either lost their lives or gone missing in action, and the shine turned to brass, his riches something akin to blood money. And then, *then* . . .

Barnabus sucked in his breath. He would never forget the opening line of that dreadful letter from Sergeant Harrington:

It is with deep regret that I must inform you of the death of your son, George William Jenkins, who died in battle on the eleventh day of April, the year of our Lord . . .

Well. He simply could not bring himself to make more soldiers after that.

'Mr Jenkins?'

It was Miss Pépin who spoke. Barnabus cleared his throat of the bubble that had formed there, and stepped down from the ladder.

'Here you are, young lady,' said he, in a voice brighter than he felt, and watched as the little girl reached for the wooden soldier and took it gently in her arms.

'Oh, look,' the child cried. 'Look how bonny he is!'

She ran her fingers over the soldier's uniform; its tiny buttons, the tasselled epaulettes, its feathered hat. She touched the drum and its finely carved ropes, the little drumsticks and then, finally, she touched the soldier's handsome face.

The face of his poor George.

Alice watched her husband, and was so fully aware of what this moment cost him that her heart fluttered. But so too did it warm at seeing a child once more find joy in his creation, and as Lord Heysten and Miss Pépin admired the artistry of the toy soldier themselves she moved to stand next to Barnabus, took his hand in hers and squeezed.

She need not say anything. She knew he understood what she was telling him.

Let him go, my love. Let him go.

And after some moments, her husband squeezed back.

Alice smiled at Miss Faith. 'Would you like me to wrap him for you, pet?'

Lord Heysten and Miss Pépin raised their eyes to hers.

'But I understood the soldier was not for sale,' his lordship remarked, to which Alice shook her head.

'It had not been, but now it is. Is that not so, Mr Jenkins?'

Beside her, Barnabus took a shallow breath. 'Aye, Mrs Jenkins. 'Tis time.'

Faith – who had clutched the soldier to her at hearing the words – let out a delighted noise of glee.

'I may have it then? Truly?'

Lord Heysten shared a look with Miss Pépin who it must be said, looked, oddly, frightfully smug. After holding her gaze for some seconds, he lifted both hands in a gesture of despair.

'Oh, very well. Though I really do think it strange for a girl to chuse a toy soldier to play with when there are such pretty dolls to be had instead.'

'Just as I said before – not all little girls like dolls, nor should they have to.'

Miss Charlotte's rejoinder was scathing and self-satisfied, and Alice wondered at it. To Lord Heysten (who was shaking his head as he searched his greatcoat for his pocketbook), she said:

'Miss Faith is a very lucky child. We have not sold a soldier these past two years,' to which Lord Heysten nodded almost absently.

'I hope, my dear,' Alice added, addressing now the child, 'you shall take good care of him.'

'Oh, I shall,' she breathed, looking overjoyed by the prospect. 'I shall name him Benoît, after Monsieur de Fortgibu.'

Beside her, Barnabus went very still.

'A French name.'

His whispered words made Miss Pépin frown.

'Are you quite well, sir?' she asked, to which Lord Heysten – having found his pocketbook – regarded Alice's husband with concern.

'I say, Mr Jenkins, you *have* gone rather pale.'

Barnabus turned his back and reached for the grounding comfort of the toyshop counter.

'Forgive me,' he said, then fell silent. He wished to say more – to tell the little girl that such a name was most unsuitable for his wooden soldier – but it was not his place, he knew. Alice, patting his hand and guiding him back onto his stool, sent Lord Heysten an apologetic look.

'Indeed, you must forgive him. 'Tis just there is something of a history with these soldiers.'

'Is that so?' his lordship replied.

'It is. But you need not trouble yourselves about it, my lord.'

Lord Heysten frowned. 'Please, Mrs Jenkins – somehow we have caused you and your good husband distress, and that was not my intention. I should like to rectify the mistake, if I can.'

At such a gracious comment Barnabus found it within himself to offer a smile.

'There is nothing to rectify, my lord. This is my burden.'

'*Our* burden,' his wife corrected. 'My dear, you really do take too much upon yourself.'

Miss Pépin and Lord Heysten looked troubled; however, in the spirit of politeness they accepted the answer without further question. But the child, Faith, had no such compunction.

'Why can't I name my soldier after a Frenchman?'

'Faith!'

'Benoît is a good name,' she insisted, speaking over his lordship. 'Monsieur de Fortgibu is a good man.'

Alice inclined her head. 'I'm sure he is, my dear.'

'Then *why*?'

Lord Heysten offered his sincere apologies; Miss Pépin attempted to hush the child, and in that moment Barnabus hesitated. He had forgotten how insistent children were, and this one was especially tenacious. Just as George had been.

'You may call the soldier any name you like,' Barnabus said quietly, though the words pained him, and so too the next: 'It is only that we lost our son in the Battle of Toulouse.'

Miss Pépin's handsome face flooded with understanding.

'The wooden soldiers,' she said. 'You made them in the image of your son?'

Barnabus gave a small and careful nod.

'And you lost him to a French soldier.'

'We did,' replied Alice.

'I see.' Miss Pépin smiled in sympathy, then turned to address the little girl. 'Faith,' she said, 'do *you* see? It would be in poor taste to name your soldier after the monsieur. Besides,' Miss Pépin added, in more strident tones, 'this soldier has an English uniform. For an *English* soldier. A French name would not suit at all.'

The little girl frowned. 'No,' she said slowly. 'I suppose it would not.' But then her face brightened. 'What was your son's name, Mr Jenkins?'

Barnabus blinked, and though it might seem obvious that such a question should have followed, he was not prepared for it at all. His chest grew tight, his eyes a trifle warm.

'George,' he whispered, and once more Alice squeezed his hand.

'Then I shall call the soldier George,' announced the little girl. 'That would be more fitting, would it not?'

'Yes, Faith,' replied Lord Heysten softly. 'I do believe it would.'

There was silence then, in which Barnabus took up the cup and ball to resume his carving, and Alice dabbed the corners of her eyes with a handkerchief she had just removed from her sleeve. His lordship cleared his throat.

'Well then,' he said, with a cheerfulness that he clearly hoped would disperse the air of melancholy that had befallen the toyshop. 'That settles the matter! Please, Mr and Mrs Jenkins – how much do I owe?'

With Barnabus concentrating so deeply on his carving and with such an air of deliberation that implied he was not truly concentrating at all, it was Alice who opened the purchase ledger and marked the sale.

'We are much obliged to you,' she said once his lordship had paid the soldier's price. 'And I do hope your daughter will treasure our George, though I see my words are not necessary – by the way she clings so tightly to him it is clear she shall.'

Lord Heysten seemed to hesitate. A meaningful look was

shared between him and Miss Pépin, though Alice could not guess at what that meaning could be. The gentleman cleared his throat.

'Faith is not my daughter, Mrs Jenkins.'

'Oh! Oh,' Alice said again for she was not quite sure how to respond. 'Forgive me, my lord. You look so alike. Her colouring, and yours, I assumed . . . Well, what with you being in the Americas so long I wondered if perhaps you had . . .' Alice ducked her head, scolded her strident tongue. 'Forgive me,' she said again. 'It was not my place to comment on the matter, especially in front of the child,' to which his lordship shook his head.

'Pray, do not trouble yourself. We look alike because Faith is my sister.'

Alice started. Lord Heysten returned his pocketbook to the confines of his greatcoat.

'You may well be surprised. Indeed, the circumstances are delicate, but Faith is fully aware of her history for I keep nothing from her. I've only to regret her prolonged absence, which will now be rectified.'

Well, well. It would take a very pious woman not to express some measure of curiosity as to what the aforementioned 'circumstances' might be and Alice was no such woman. Still, this time she held her tongue, and next to her Barnabus intervened, asking in a stronger voice than he had possessed before:

'You plan to stay in Merrywake, then, sir?'

'I do,' Lord Heysten replied. 'Heysten Park is in dire need of improvement – my father neglected it shamefully – but I intend to settle here nonetheless.'

'You are to restore the park, my lord?'

'I am, although I am considering other uses for it.'

Beside him, Miss Charlotte frowned. 'Other uses?'

'On which I am still ruminating,' came the careful reply. 'But either way, I have every intention of renewing its prospects.'

This news gave Alice much pleasure and she told him so.

'Barnabus and I have often passed its gates on the occasions we have left Merrywake and bemoaned its sorry state. The reverend, your uncle, has shewn little interest in the place – quite wiped his hands of it, I do believe, under the circumstances.'

'You know my uncle, Mrs Jenkins?'

'That I do! I keep house for him.' She gestured at the basket she had left by the toyshop door. 'I am just come from the parsonage.'

Lord Heysten frowned. 'I see. Pray, madam. What sort of man is he?'

Alice blinked. 'You . . . you do not know, my lord?'

'I confess I do not. I nearly wrote to him on my return but after the way my father and grandfather treated him, I was not sure of my reception, and so thought it best to leave well enough alone.'

Beside her, Barnabus continued to whittle. Alice cleared her throat.

'Mr Soppe has been, I confess, prone to bad-tempered tendencies. But I have known him these past twelve years, and can attest to the fact that he is a good man of moral principles. Certainly, he would not be a vicar if he were not.' Alice smiled kindly. 'I feel sure that if you were to offer the olive branch it would be readily accepted. I'm certain he would be gratified to know his nephew . . . *and* his niece.'

Lord Heysten glanced down at the little girl, who had been watching the exchange quietly and now gave a small nod of her head.

'Family *is* important,' he murmured. 'Especially at this time of year.'

Barnabus stilled in his carving before continuing once more.

'So it is,' said Alice gently. 'And I suppose with you bringing Heysten Park back to life you shall be filling it with a family of your own in due course. I've no doubt Miss Faith would wish for the company, would you not, my dear?'

The child nodded her head again, and this time more vigorously, but it occurred to Alice then as Lord Heysten went very still that she had once more said the wrong thing – his face shuttered, a muscle in his jaw twitched.

'Alas, madam,' he said, 'I'm afraid my plans for the future allow no room for further children.'

The words were said with such finality that Miss Pépin looked at Lord Heysten sharply. She said nothing, however, and nor did Alice for a moment or two, so mortified was she at having let her tongue again run wild. With a nervous glance at her husband, Alice attempted to divert the conversation by smiling warmly at Lord Heysten's little relation, who was looking between them all with a somewhat bemused expression.

'But your *sister*,' said Alice with a little more bravado than was needed. 'Well, she is a delightful child, and would fill any house

274

with as much laughter as ten children, to be sure. Mr Jenkins and I are very glad to have met you both.'

Lord Heysten inclined his head and proffered a smile that Alice, with relief, perceived to be as friendly as it had been some minutes before her misjudged remarks.

'And we are very glad to have met you,' he returned, with the same bravado that shewed clear the discussion had come to an end. 'I have no doubt that Faith and I will see you again in due course. I am quite determined she shall have a doll at some point, despite Miss Pépin's protests.'

Behind him Miss Pépin rolled her eyes with a slight shake of her head. Alice, not quite knowing what to make of it, dipped her knees in a curtsey.

'Thank you, my lord. Farewell, and a Merry Christmas to you.'

Lord Heysten inclined his head. 'And a Merry Christmas to you as well. Come along, Faith. We've yet to have your new dress adjusted, and Miss Pépin is quite famished. What is it?' he said to his companion in teasing tones. 'Swan for luncheon?'

Miss Pépin's features shifted into one of resigned amusement, and with a shake of her dark head she turned to the door, whereupon Lord Heysten opened it and let in the noisy bustle of Merrywake village. Together gentleman and lady stepped out into the street, but soon paused upon realising their charge did not accompany them.

'Faith?' called Lord Heysten. 'Come along now.'

The little girl – who had not moved one inch from the middle of the toyshop floor – was staring up at Alice and Barnabus with wide button eyes.

'I am sorry about your son,' she said, in so beguiling a manner it made Alice suck in her breath and Barnabus lower his knife. The little girl pressed the wooden soldier to her breast. 'I promise to look after him.'

'Th . . . thank you, miss.'

It was Barnabus who had spoken, and Alice was glad for – unusually for her – she found herself at a loss for words.

'And you should sell the other soldiers,' continued the child, in a voice that belied her age. 'George would like that, I think.'

At such a declaration neither Jenkins quite knew what to say, but no answer it seemed was necessary for the child simply smiled, joined Miss Pépin and Lord Heysten, and reached up to close the shop door behind her. With one last wave through the frosted glass, the little girl followed Lord Heysten and Miss Pépin across the square and disappeared into the Crown, where Alice supposed they might be stopping for one of the proprietor's excellent luncheons, which did not (as far as Alice was aware) include swan.

Having closed the shop to take their own luncheon, Barnabus and Alice sat at their small table in their small kitchen behind Jenkins & Son, quietly partaking of their pot pie and thinking deeply upon the words of little Faith Heysten.

For Alice, the child's suggestion was one which she shared wholeheartedly. She had on many occasions pressed upon her husband the importance of relinquishing the remaining wooden soldiers to any child who might have a wish to give them a home. But, as is often the case, some people do not take the advice solicited so passionately from their loved ones, yet find themselves considering the same advice if offered to them by another party, and such was the situation for Barnabus as he ate a forkful of succulent chicken and pastry, and contemplatively began to chew.

If the girl had simply said she thought he should sell the other soldiers, and left it at that, Barnabus might have ignored her. Leave it at that she did not, however, and her parting words had set Barnabus upon a most torturous course.

George would like that, I think.

After the child left, Barnabus had removed the remaining soldiers from the shop floor. The eight now lay atop the Reverend Soppe's dirty bedsheets in the wicker basket, face down except for one, who stared up at Barnabus from the folds of linen with what he could only describe as judgemental eyes. And thus became the reason for Barnabus' present turmoil:

George's eyes. George's face. George's voice as well, which told him gently, *Yes, Father, I would like that. I should like that very much indeed.*

Barnabus sighed so deeply and so loudly, that Alice laid down her fork.

'My dear,' said she. 'You have lived with your guilt for so long now. You cannot continue to torture yourself.'

''Tis easy for you to say,' Barnabus said, piercing another piece of chicken with his fork. 'Your parting words were not in anger.'

'No,' Alice conceded. 'But it should not serve that you punish yourself and others in the manner that you are.'

'What manner? By not selling the last of the soldiers?'

'Yes! Why, Barnabus – it serves no one but yourself. Toys are supposed to be loved and cherished, not hidden away in the dark.'

In answer Barnabus shook his head, and held so fast to his fork that it shook.

When he first received the letter notifying him of George's death, Barnabus had felt duty bound to cease making the soldiers. He had laboured under the notion that he was somehow profiting from the wars by selling them, and that was as good a reason as any. But there was another reason, one that he had not quite dared put into words, for to say it made it all so painfully real. But say it he must because the truth of it was that Barnabus was weary, and the events of that morning had made him wearier still.

'Alice,' he whispered. 'They are all I have left of him.'

The declaration sat stark between them, as harsh and painful as the day they discovered their son was dead.

'Oh, dearest,' said his wife, pressing a shaking hand to her chest. 'George will always be with us. His death—'

'Was a waste. George did not even die fighting. He stood at the front of that battalion with nothing but a drum and they shot him at point-blank range. He never stood a chance.'

'His role was important,' Alice replied now gently. 'Drummers are essential for delivering instructions on the battlefield, and it took a lot of bravery to do that well. That's what the letter from Sergeant Harrington said, do you not remember? George ...' She stopped, took a steadying breath. 'George died a hero.'

Barnabus shook his head, and realised that the tears which had threatened in the toyshop fell now freely. But Alice – with tears in her own eyes – would not allow him to ignore her.

'He *wanted* to go to war and serve his king and country. There was no stopping him, not when he saw all the other village men go. You know that as well as I.'

Oh, but how could he forget? Barnabus would for ever remember their argument the night before George left. He and George, saying such dreadful things to each other because neither one was willing to relent. All Barnabus could think of was the toyshop and all that he had invested in it, and that if his boy were to die then his dream of Jenkins & Son would die with him too. But George would hear none of it – the shop could wait, said he, but England could not, and so incensed was Barnabus at such stubbornness that he – in his own stubborn will – could not even find it in himself to say goodbye.

He would regret that to his dying day.

'I am proud of our George,' Alice continued, with such passion that only a mother could bestow on her child. 'I am proud, and you should be too.' She glanced at the basket by the hearth, its wooden cargo. 'Hiding those soldiers is no way to honour our boy.'

Shamed, Barnabus ducked his head.

Oh, but he *was* proud of George! Once his son left Merrywake Barnabus realised his error, how unforgivably selfish he had been, and began to carve the wooden soldiers to prove just how proud he was. But some small sense of shame had prevented him from writing to George to confess it, and so his son had died without ever knowing how his father truly felt. It was a guilt Barnabus had suffered under every day since.

'We do not even have a portrait of him,' he whispered. 'These soldiers, they . . .'

'My dear,' said Alice. 'The solution has always been so obvious to me, though you would not hear it. Will you hear it now?'

Barnabus nodded and wiped his eyes.

'The solution,' said she, 'is to keep one of the soldiers. Set one on the mantel of our sitting room, so we might always look upon him of an evening and smile at the happy memories we share. Put the others in the shop window, so Merrywake's young boys might see them and give them a home. They deserve to be loved.'

'I . . . I suppose George *would* like it, wouldn't he?'

'Of course he would.' Alice stood and came about the table so she might put her arms around him. 'Of course he would.'

She kissed him gently on his forehead, just where his hairline had begun to thin, then turned to pick up the basket which she held out to her husband like a gift.

'Which soldier do you chuse?'

Barnabus hesitated before finally selecting one. He chose, of course, the soldier that stared up at him from the folds of linen.

'There now,' said Alice, satisfied. 'Shall I put him on the mantel? And we shall drink a toast to him this evening. To our dearest George.'

He could not speak, only nod, whereupon his wife took the soldier and disappeared into the sitting room. Barnabus stared at the soldiers which remained, and he continued to sit thus until Alice returned.

'Right, then,' she declared, brisk again, like her old self. 'I'll put Mr Soppe's linen in to soak, then head up to Mr Hodge and collect his. Will you be all right?'

'I think so, my dear.'

'Very good.'

She removed the other soldiers from the basket, until they stood tall upon the pitted terrain of the kitchen table, staring up at them with George's gentle eyes. Together husband and wife stared at them in turn, until Barnabus found enough strength to clear his throat.

'I shall put them in the window, Alice, just as you said. But they cannot be displayed without . . .'

Alice frowned. 'Without?'

Barnabus raised himself from the table and kissed his wife's cheek.

'You carry on,' he said. 'You shall soon see.'

And later that afternoon Alice did see, when she returned from Mr Hodge's farm – for in the window of Jenkins & Son Toyshop, front and centre, were seven wooden soldiers, standing atop a bodhrán drum with gold tassels, the very same drum Barnabus had made for George, all those years ago.

STAVE X.

Reunion

Ten Pipers Piping

Phillip Denby had long been absent from the village of Merry-wake, though such an unhappy condition (it must be fervently expressed) had not been his fault.

Circumstances conspired against him, for he did not desert the army willingly. Indeed, he had no notion of the fact that he *had* deserted until he woke up on the battlefield of Toulouse. How Phillip had not bled to death he could not say – the bayonet which pierced his shoulder sliced clean through the other side. He fell in the instant agony of it, his body soon covered by others, and there he spluttered face down in the mud until oblivion mercifully took him. Later, when Phillip found himself at the mercy of French soldiers, he wondered what might have happened to him if he had not been so distracted. If he had not been distracted by the sight of George Jenkins being shot in the chest, he would have seen the bayonet coming. But see George he did, and desperately Phillip had tried to reach him, the man he had looked up to, the man he had followed to war three years before.

When Phillip did wake, he knew not what day it was, only that his fellow troops had departed. He looked for George's body on the field amidst the corpses of soldiers and horses but found it gone, too, and as he staggered about him – bleary-eyed and weak as wet parchment – Phillip wondered why *he* had been left, until he realised the bodies that had covered him were French, their navy uniforms blending seamlessly with his own.

Musicians, after all, also wore blue.

Phillip had sobbed as the truth hit him. George, he remembered, had fallen face up. His uniform would have been more distinctive in such a position, and so the British knew to take him from the field. But Phillip ... he they left. How many other drummers and pipers had found themselves at the mercy of a French bullet or blade? There had been ten pipers in Wellington's army that day – five British, three Portuguese, two Spanish – paired with George's drum and eleven others. He and George were not the only ones to have fallen, Phillip could be sure of that, for musicians faced the front line of enemy fire every day. Had they been missed too, buried under Napoleon's soldiers, as he had? But as Phillip gazed over the battlefield, a sea of bodies and blood, he realised it hardly mattered. The only thing that mattered was that he was somehow alive and had been left all alone in enemy territory, with no notion as to where Sergeant Harrington had taken the troops.

So he walked. There was nothing else for it.

He passed plundered villages, ragged paupers, the bodies of decaying children. If he had not known himself to be in France, Phillip might have blamed the French for such villainy, but he could not ignore the English obscenities that scrawled the walls and realised sickly that all of them – French and British alike – were just as monstrous as each other.

Phillip did his best. He bound his wound with the ripped sleeve of his shirt, survived on water from streams, scavenged the hedgerows for berries, and slept under trees or in abandoned huts that smelt of campfires and urine. But soon it became clear he had travelled in the wrong direction, for how could he possibly lose track of an entire army (however much of it remained)? Miraculously, Phillip had kept hold of his fife when he fell to the bayonet, his hand somehow cushioning the crush. Often he gripped it as a kind of comfort, and when despair began to take him he would play . . . which was, on reflection, the worst decision he could have made, for that was how the enemy discovered him.

Without realising he had done so, Phillip had travelled north-west, stumbling within hearing distance of a French cavalry camp. They mistook him for one of their own at first on account of his navy uniform, but soon discovered their error when Phillip could not understand their questions. They bound him in irons, lashed him until he bled and marched him to the nearest prison, a fortress situated on the coast of a city Phillip later heard called Brest.

How long he remained there Phillip could not rightly say, for the days melted into one another. He could thank God that at least the wretched stone cell which held him was his and his alone, and that he was fed daily, though there could be little to enjoy from the fare – bullock offal, a pound of bread and some pulses, all undercooked and of measly proportions.

Nothing like his mother's cooking. Nothing like it at all.

There had been no window in his cell. Darkness became a part of him, and with the fife confiscated and nothing with which to entertain himself, Phillip often thought of home. He would picture the lush green of Merrywake in summer, the rolling fields of Hodge Farm, the pretty village square, the boisterous assemblies he and George used to play at every month – Phillip with his tin whistle, George with his bodhrán drum. Phillip thought too of Wakely Hall where he had lived since he was a small boy – the cosy servants' hall, its large fireplace where often he would sit and practise his melodies, his mother tapping her foot to its time as she prepared another grand meal for the Pépin family, from which she always reserved a plate, just for him. Dear, *dear* Wakely Hall, where he never wanted for anything, each day just the same and as safe as the one before it . . . and Phillip had had the temerity to be bored. To crave adventure. Following George to war had nothing to do with serving his country. He merely wanted to experience something of the world, to say, *Here now – I have lived!*

How young he had been then. How very naïve.

Too often, when Phillip thought of home, he wondered what

hell his mother was going through. George's parents would have been notified of his death – had Sergeant Harrington written to his mother as well? And if he had, what had he told her? *Missing, presumed dead.* Or, much worse than that:

Deserted.

The days unspooled. The seasons ebbed and flowed. Then at length, finally, word came of the French defeat. Phillip was released into a too-bright world, a great blue sea in front of him and no way to cross it. He found work at the shipyard, scraped enough coin to take him home should the opportunity arise, and it had been providence that some months later a merchant vessel docked at Brest and agreed to take him to Plymouth, the very same port he had departed from five years before. He arrived in England a different man than the boy who left it: humbled, broken. Afraid. But from Plymouth Phillip began the long journey back to Merrywake, with only a knapsack that held a change of clothes and twelve shillings to his name.

He did not waste them by purchasing a seat on the post-chaise. Phillip would walk the distance to Merrywake, buy food and meagre lodgings where he could, and only when he reached the Crown would he use the last of his money to purchase a hot meal and a room so he could tidy himself up before continuing his journey on to Wakely Hall. Certainly, he could not present himself to his mother in such a state – he *looked* like a vagrant, every bit the deserter she must surely think him to be.

Phillip adjusted his knapsack, tightened his woollen scarf about his neck.

Deserter. That *must* be what they took him for, for how can anyone be pronounced dead without a body to prove the fact? He should have written to his mother as soon as he was released, Phillip knew, but the truth of it was that he was too ashamed, too frightened. One overheard terrifying stories, working at the docks. One morning he heard tell of a group of soldiers discovered outside Nantes. They were accused of being deserters and executed when they protested their innocence.

Would Sergeant Harrington believe *him*? Would he believe Phillip if he were to say he encountered no outfit between Toulouse and wherever the French picked him up? Or would he too find himself with a noose about his neck? Phillip shuddered. No, he had not deserted the army willingly yet that meant nothing if he could not prove it. But now, now that the wars were over, he might risk coming home and put his case to the viscount. Surely Viscount Pépin would vouch for him? He had always been, so Phillip remembered, a good and decent man.

Soon he found himself turning onto the long road that led to Merrywake. For some miles he trudged through a slurry of melting snow, made brown from wheels and horses which had churned up mud three inches thick, and he winced as the heel of his boot sank and let it in through the seams. Phillip had experienced worse during his time serving under the sergeant of course, but oh, how thankful he was that he had a change of clothes in his knapsack, a suitable pair of shoes! How wonderful it would be to be warm and dry by the fireplace at Wakely Hall, with one of his mother's delectable mince pies in his hand. Perhaps, too, a slice of her acclaimed plum pudding?

It was these happier and altogether mouth-watering thoughts

that entertained him until Phillip saw in the distance a carriage at a standstill. The sight made him pause, for he did not yet feel ready for company, but even so far away he could see that a problem had occurred, and such was Phillip's sense of chivalry that he picked up pace with the intention to assist.

Phillip saw on his approach that the carriage's back wheels were stuck in the mud. A tall and very beautiful woman with blonde hair wearing a pelisse in a striking shade of crimson stood on the wayside, clutching her skirts so they did not touch the ground, watching as the coachman and three other gentlemen were attempting to push the carriage from its trap.

'For pity's sake, Cordelia!' one of the men puffed. 'Help us, will you? If we can just get a little extra weight there on the right we will be able to—'

'Humphrey, I told you no,' snapped the lady. 'This gown is brand new and I shall not have it ruined. 'Tis bad enough my boots are caked in filth. I *refuse* to dirty myself further.'

There came some ungentlemanlike swearing, some further grunts and a chorus of 'heave-ho's, and reaching them somewhat out of breath Phillip asked:

'Can I be of assistance?'

The men all ceased their struggles and turned to Phillip. The gentlemen – whose faces fell a little as they beheld him – looked him up and down, so too did the coachman with a little less obvious confoundment, but the lady could scarce disguise her disgust, and only then did Phillip remember his nomadic state of dress.

'Forgive my appearance,' said he, clutching his cap. 'I have been travelling a good many days, but I can assure you I'm no vagrant. I can help,' he added, when the gentlemen looked unsure, but the coachman beckoned him.

'You speak well enough like a decent sort,' said he, 'and we should be thankful for help.' The coachman removed a dew-drop from his nose with the pad of his thumb. 'The wheel has jammed on its spike, but I can't free it until the carriage is lifted from the mud.'

Phillip nodded, turned to address the man the lady had called Humphrey.

'Right side you said, sir? Front or back?'

The gentleman nodded, the confoundment clearing from his face to be replaced with an expression of relief.

'Front, if you please.'

The other two gentlemen murmured their agreement, and soon Phillip had positioned himself at the front right of the carriage. It took some strength on all their parts, but the five of them were able to free it, and with a great *squelch* the vehicle's wheels came loose from the ground.

It was just at this moment – in the midst of some rather hearty 'hurrah's uttered by the three gentlemen – that another lady appeared from a narrow country lane to Phillip's left.

This was not a lady of quality such as the one named Cordelia. No indeed, this was a young woman wearing a plain dress of dyed wool and matching spencer jacket, together with a shawl of lace which she clasped now tight to her neck. Truth be told it was not a shawl suitable for winter, but Molly Hart had never owned anything quite so lovely before, and so pleased had the housemaid been to find it in her Christmas box that she had made a point of wearing it at every given opportunity.

Such an opportunity had arisen when Molly – for the third time since Mrs Wilson instructed her *not* to venture upstairs except to the bedroom she shared with Prudence Brown – became frustrated at being kept so confined, and decided to take herself off for a walk. Why, after all, should she be punished for something that was not her fault?

Of course, Molly knew that was not precisely true.

The moment the Duke of Morley had looked at her, Molly knew what he was about. She was conscious of feeling flattered by his admiring stare, of being *seen*, and since Ralph Hornby had only the hour before shunned her in favour of a dance with Prudence in Wakely Forest, Molly was feeling particularly vulnerable to flattery. It had been nothing after that to loiter about the upper rooms of the hall where she might bump into him, nothing at all to agree to meet the duke beneath the mistletoe under the stairs.

What she planned to achieve by such a dalliance, Molly did not quite know. The thrill of it, perhaps. The exhilaration of a good kiss, for it had been so very long since she had experienced one. To feel something. Anything! But she had not accounted for Sir Robert's bruising lips or the rough grip of his hands on her shoulders – Molly did not realise he would be so passionate, nor that he would mistake her moan of distress as encouragement. And as he pushed her dress from her shoulders in the shadowed confines of Wakely's entrance hall, she realised then how foolish she had been to chase the past in arms that were not those of George Jenkins. It had been both relief and torture to be discovered by Viscountess Pépin, to escape the Duke of Morley's clutches and retreat to the safety of her room.

Yet such dread she thus experienced, waiting to be called by Mrs Wilson, or worse, the viscountess herself. Not one wink of sleep did she have that night, listening to Prudence's steady breathing in the bed beside hers, and it was only when it was all over that Molly dared once more to breathe steadily herself.

She would not be dismissed – Viscountess Pépin was adamant on that fact which was terribly kind of her, and the relief Molly felt was acute, for with no family living except an older brother at sea, she had nowhere else to go. But Mrs Wilson ... the scolding she received from the housekeeper served to temper that relief with nausea, for she realised just how close she had been to ruin. *What if you had become with child? What would you have done then? The duke wouldn't have seen you right – men of that ilk never do!* So Molly, humbled, accepted her chores belowstairs with little complaint: tablecloth after tablecloth was pressed, chests of bedlinen checked for moths, rugs beaten in the yard, and down in the cellar used wine bottles cleaned and stored ready for the viscount's batch of honey mead in the summer. But then, as one day began to seep into another and thoughts of George haunted her conscience, Molly could bear it no longer. She had to escape Wakely Hall, the merriment of her fellow servants (especially Prudence, who was positively giddy about finally being engaged to Nathaniel Hodge), and the festive cheer which made her so very, very miserable.

And so she walked. Not for so long that Mrs Wilson should chance to miss her, but long enough that she might gain some respite from her thoughts and renew her chores with vigour on her return. But today . . . today Molly had walked further than she meant and in so doing became quite lost. All those bottles left to wash! Mrs Wilson would surely have discovered her gone by now – she had been absent from the hall for over two hours. What a telling-off the housekeeper would give her! Even if that woman's tongue was not quite so harsh these past few days, there was no excusing Molly's absence for such a long period of time and Mrs Wilson was sure to mark it. Indeed, Molly would deserve the scolding, but equally, she was not altogether sure she could take another one, and for some minutes she wandered the fields in tearful agitation until she heard the distant sounds of men's voices and the distressed whinny of horses. Wiping her eyes the housemaid followed them until she found herself on a dirt track which, she hoped, would take her to the main road leading to Merrywake, and such were Molly Hart's thoughts when she happened upon the scene before her.

'Good heavens,' she exclaimed. 'Has anyone been harmed?'

Phillip turned. Stared. For a moment he was struck dumb, for he would have known her anywhere. One does not forget such striking blue eyes or curls the shade of molasses. Oh yes, Molly Hart had always been a beauty.

No wonder George had adored her.

'Not at all, miss, not at all!'

It was the gentleman named Humphrey who replied. He tipped his hat and turned then to Phillip.

'My name is Sharpe,' said he. 'Bertram Sharpe, and those are my brothers Humphrey and Tarquin –' here the gentleman gestured first at one man, then the other – 'and that lady there who has been abominably unhelpful is our sister, Cordelia.'

Miss Sharpe turned her pointed chin and sniffed.

'I don't see why you are making such a fuss. You managed perfectly well without me.'

'Only because of this man here.' Humphrey Sharpe – wearing an expression of exasperation – shook his head at the lady and turned back to Phillip. 'Pray, to whom is my sister indebted?'

'My name is Denby, sir. Phillip Denby.'

There came then a small gasp from behind him.

'Phillip Denby?' Molly whispered. 'You . . . you are Mrs Denby's son? Bess Denby, of Wakely Hall?'

'That I am,' he said, and Molly (he had never called her Miss Hart) raised a hand to her mouth, looking at Phillip as if she had seen a spirit.

That look could account for many things. His appearance certainly was shocking, for Molly would have remembered a chubby boy of barely sixteen, brought up on Bess Denby's hearty cooking, quiet and painfully shy. Now he was tall and thin, wearing dirty clothes and a month's worth of road dust on his face – no wonder she looked at him so strangely. But . . . she might also look at him in such a way because she did in fact believe he *was* a spirit, and in that moment, Phillip was desperate to ask the maid about his poor mother, what misconception she suffered under. *Did* she think him a deserter? Or did she believe her son to be dead?

'Well!' exclaimed the brother named Tarquin. 'How fortuit-
ous. Wakely Hall, you say? Why, we have been invited there
for the Pépins' Twelfth Night Ball! Not heard the name Denby
though . . .' Mr Sharpe frowned. 'A servant, is she?'

The words were not said in any manner which would be considered superior. Indeed, they had been perfectly cordial, but
Phillip raised himself up all the same.

'She is the cook at Wakely, sir. Has been for many years.'

'Oh, how splendid,' interceded Mr Humphrey Sharpe, who
patted his stomach. 'I've heard great things about Wakely's cook.
Her roast goose dinners are notorious, apparently – I met the
Earl of Starling in Bath last summer, and he waxed lyrical about
them! And to be clear, Mr Denby, the earl is not a man easily
pleased. I look forward to sampling your mother's cooking very
much. I do love a good roast dinner.'

Phillip, feeling somewhat gratified at such praise, ducked his
head, and Bertram Sharpe turned his attention to Molly.

'Are you also from Wakely Hall, Miss . . .?'

'Hart, sir. I'm a housemaid there.'

'You are far from your position, Miss Hart.'

Molly hesitated, a shot of colour appearing in her cheeks.
''Tis my afternoon off, sir.'

'Is it? Then we shall not delay you any longer.' He adjusted the
lip of his top hat. 'You must forgive that we do not offer you both
a ride back to Wakely, but alas . . .'

The gentleman trailed off, his meaning clear – the carriage
was small, fit only to accommodate the Sharpe siblings at close

quarters, and the upper portion of the vehicle had room only for their luggage and the coachman.

And of course, their station would not allow it.

'Even if there were room,' Phillip replied to acknowledge the fact, 'we would have to decline your kind offer.'

'Just so, just so,' Humphrey Sharpe nodded. 'But I hope you do not think us uncharitable. Truly, your help was invaluable, and I shall be sure to tell the viscount of your conduct.'

'That is very kind, sir.'

'Not at all, not at all.'

There came then a loud *tsk* to Phillip's right.

'Pray, let us continue,' said Miss Sharpe, sweeping past him in a shot of crimson velvet. 'My feet ache, and I have no wish to loiter in the cold.'

'Twas uncharitable nerve to say her feet ached when it was clear Phillip and Molly were themselves to walk to Merrywake in such icy conditions, and her brother gave a scolding shake of his head.

'Cordelia, you've no manners. Do you not wish to thank Mr Denby?'

In reply the lady looked down her nose at her rescuer, uttered a very taciturn word of gratitude and proceeded to sidle her gaze to a spot beyond Phillip's shoulder.

'You,' said Miss Sharpe to Molly, in a haughty manner most disagreeable for a woman of quality, 'yes, you,' she added, beckoning the maid who – to her credit – did not move a single inch, at which Miss Sharpe narrowed her eyes.

'You say you are a servant at Wakely Hall?'

'Yes.'

'Yes, *miss*, is the correct answer! Honestly, I declare—'

'Oh, do hush, Cordelia!' snapped Tarquin Sharpe, who too was looking at his sister with barely veiled disgust. 'Honestly, *I* declare that I've never known such shocking manners. Our aunt never raised you to behave thus. She would turn in her grave.' The brother bowed in the face of his sister's look of affront. 'Forgive her, Miss Hart. We've been travelling these past four days from the north in this frightful snow and the delays have put quite a strain on all of us ... though some, it appears, more than others.'

Miss Sharpe sighed with an indifferent air.

'Tarquin, I hardly see why you should declare it to all and sundry, nor why I need be forgiven by a maid! But,' she added, with a smile that was by no means friendly and more than a little condescending, 'in the spirit of the season I shall not hold a grudge. Pray, Miss Hart – you say you're from Wakely Hall. Can you please advise if the Duke of Morley has arrived?'

Curiously, the little patch of colour that had appeared in Molly's cheeks disappeared, to be replaced by a striking paleness. She opened her mouth then closed it again, before managing to visibly compose herself.

'He is, Miss Sharpe. He has been since Christmas Eve.'

'Splendid. And has, per chance, Lord Heysten visited?'

'He is staying at Wakely, miss.'

The lady stared. 'Is that so?'

'But I believe he returns to the park every now and then.'

'I see.' Miss Sharpe's fair eyebrows rose. 'Strange then, Bertram,' she said, turning to him, 'why our letters should have been ignored.'

'Yours have,' returned her other brother. 'And I can hardly blame the man either, not when you make such demands on him. I'd ignore you too if I could.'

'*Bertram!*'

Again Miss Sharpe looked affronted, and taking this as his and Molly's cue to part ways with the strangely matched siblings, Phillip cleared his throat and addressed the waiting coachman:

'If you will not be needing me, I would beg to be excused.' To which the coachman – now seated atop the carriage – expressed his assurances that Phillip had done everything that was needed and the three Sharpe brothers gave their profuse thanks once again. Only Miss Sharpe said not one further word, and looking rather stony-faced ascended the carriage, disappearing into its confines with a flurry of skirts. Her brothers, with polite tips of their hats, joined her, and shortly afterwards the carriage was clattering away, leaving Phillip and Molly quite alone on the open road.

They had watched the carriage depart in silence, but when it curved a bend in the muddy road and disappeared out of sight, Molly turned to the young man who stood so still beside her.

Could this *really* be Phillip Denby? He had been young when he left Merrywake, but the Phillip Denby she looked at now was different. It was not just his physique that had changed; he was taller and leaner than when she saw him last, but there was something about the way he carried himself that could not be hidden by his dirty apparel and uncombed hair. There was a strength, a reserve, a fundamental element of maturity that had not been present before.

He had returned to Merrywake a man.

'Where have you been?' she asked softly, and though Phillip (she could not think of him as Mr Denby) turned to her he did not meet her searching gaze.

'In France.'

'All this time? Your mother. She . . .'

'What does she think?'

His tone was harsh, though she did not think he meant it to be. Molly could tell by the shot of pain that crossed his face, the shuttering of eyes so like the cook's.

'She isn't sure what to think. When word of George came . . .' Molly hesitated. She had not said his name in years and it stuck tightly in her throat. 'When word of George came, everyone presumed the worst. Musicians are always first in the line of fire, so they say. But then a week after that Mrs Denby received word that you were missing, and . . .'

'Missing?' He looked at her then. Straight in the eye, like a bullet. 'Not dead?'

'No, not dead.'

Phillip breathed out. His breath pooled the sky.

'Does she believe me to be a deserter, then?'

Molly hesitated again. It *had* crossed all their minds. But Mrs Denby did not speak one word against her son. In fact, she did not speak of him much at all and Molly told him such.

'I think the subject gives her too much pain.'

Phillip watched her a long moment before giving one single nod. Then he placed his cap back upon his head, and began to walk. She let him take a few steps before she called his name and, reluctant almost, he stopped.

'*Did* you desert?'

At this, he turned about, and Molly saw then he held such an expression of torture in his eyes it made her chest tighten against her stays.

'Not willingly.'

'Not *willingly?*'

Good heaven, what did that even mean? But when he said nothing else Molly felt that tightness clamp about her ribcage and she closed the distance between them, clutching tightly at the lace trellis of her shawl.

'Did you leave before or after George died?'

'George?' Phillip echoed, as if he had not followed him about like a besotted dog all those years before, and Molly – whose emotions had been so lately in turmoil – began to give in to her agitation.

'You were in the same regiment! Played together, side by side! You'd have seen him, wouldn't you? Seen him die. Unless you left before then.'

Though Phillip's skin was dark with dirt, Molly saw him pale nonetheless. He swallowed – hard – and for one moment she thought he might admit to it. But then he shook his head.

'Yes, I saw him die.'

Molly sucked in her breath. 'Was . . . was it quick?'

Phillip nodded.

'How?'

'A bullet,' he said quietly. 'To the chest. It was instant, I promise you.'

She shut her eyes, as much in relief as in pain. Molly had tortured herself over George's death – she knew no details beyond that he fell at the Battle of Toulouse, for gossip spread from the Jenkins' toyshop to the dressmaker, thence to the baker and the Crown Lodge where Richard Marmery had heard it and brought the unhappy news back to Wakely Hall, where Molly learned the awful truth at supper that very evening. The footman delivered it without preamble, not realising such unhappy communication should be imparted gently, and it took all of Molly's strength not to sob into her mutton then and there. Instead she had excused herself on the pretence she had a headache, and taken to her bed where she cried herself to sleep.

They had met in the village square. She was on her way to hand in a letter to her brother at the Receiving House, and George was on his way back from collecting a loaf of bread from the baker. Molly had dropped her letter, he had retrieved it, and when their eyes met he later claimed hers were the loveliest blue he ever did see.

They kept their courtship private. It had been a decision they had both come to; at seventeen and still only a scullery maid, Molly did not want to risk her position, and George already had aspirations to take the king's shilling. Only one person knew that Molly spent her days off in the company of George Jenkins, the toymaker's son, for he had caught them once, kissing passionately behind Wakely Hall's woodshed. But instead of shooing Phillip Denby away as she might have done, George had been kind. Offered him a tin whistle his father had made. Taught him how to play. Two years later he went to war, taking Bess Denby's boy with him, and three years after that, George was dead.

Molly never knew how or why. Nor could she mourn him or share her pain. The letters she received from George were always presumed to be from her merchant sailor brother and therefore never questioned. She grieved alone, and the loss of him – of the life that would have been hers if he had lived, the torture of it – changed her. She felt her resentment grow, day after day, transforming her into someone George would not have recognised or loved. But oh, how Molly *wished* to be loved! She craved it, wanted so desperately to feel again. Why else did she flirt outrageously with Mr Hornby and any other man who took the trouble to flatter her? Why else did she throw herself into the arms of the Duke of Morley?

But now ... now she knew how George had died. And though it hurt, she felt a sort of peace come over her, and Molly did something then she had not done since that fateful night two years ago. She began to cry.

Phillip watched her, watched the way she clung to the lace with white knuckles as tears ran down her face, and did not know what to say.

George had been like a brother to him. He had worshipped

him, looked up to him – the moment Phillip saw that bullet hit George clean in the chest, time seemed to stop, and as Molly began to wrap her arms about herself Phillip felt tears of his own warm his eyes. No, he did not know what to say, but he did know what to *do*, and so Phillip took her in his arms. Molly pressed into him, and now being much taller than her he pressed his chin on the crown of her head. She did not wear a bonnet – her dark curls tickled his skin, and suddenly Phillip realised she smelt of cooking, his mother's cooking, and moved by this as much as by Molly's sobs he held her closer, and let the tears come.

How long they stood thus, absorbed in their sorrow on the turnpike road that led to Merrywake, neither of them could be quite sure. But at length they parted, shared a small smile of understanding, and began to walk the three remaining miles to Merrywake. They spoke little – there was no need, it seemed – and soon they reached the turnpike, passed the rusting gates of Heysten Park, and found themselves in view of Wakely Church. A small graveyard was situated a little way away from the Reverend Soppe's orchard, and this was where Phillip slowed and gestured to the frosty lychgate.

'I suppose they put up a marker for him?'

Molly hesitated. 'They did. But I never go there. I . . . I cannot bear to.'

Phillip nodded. He could understand that.

'Did they put a marker up for me?'

'It was suggested to Mrs Denby,' she replied after a moment. 'Viscount Pépin even offered to pay for it, but she declined.'

Molly looked at him. 'I suppose she hoped you would still come home . . .'

There was a question in her eyes. It was direct, no softening of it with either a smile or a touch, and Phillip realised that somewhere between his leaving and return she had grown hard, like him. But Phillip did not want her to think badly of him, to have his honour doubted, and so as they resumed their walk deeper into the village, he told her the truth.

Molly listened, not with shock or horror, but a numb sort of acknowledgement. The tears she shed for George had drained her, and hearing Phillip's ordeal now, Molly found herself unable to voice a single coherent thought. Yet she sensed in him a gratification for that – he needed not sympathy, nor her words, but simply someone to listen. To understand.

'I'm sorry,' was all she said once he was done, and Phillip gave one single nod.

They had reached the square. As it always was, the village was a bustle of activity, and Molly watched as Phillip took it all in – Merrywake alive and thriving, its shops all the same as they had been before he left: the baker, the basket weaver, the stationer, the . . .

She knew without needing to know where his gaze had caught. Molly had always been careful to never look in its direction but she could always picture the toyshop in her mind, the faded sign that had stated once so proudly the words Jenkins & Son but was now an unhappy reminder of George's absence. She had no intention of looking at it now, except Phillip touched her hand gently and whispered, '*Look*'.

His face had upon it such a queer expression that Molly consented to turn, and when she did a lump formed in her chest, just where her heart was situated, for in the toyshop window there was a display: seven toy soldiers, standing upon an old bodhrán drum. George's drum. And the soldiers' faces, Molly realised, were all the likeness of him.

The sight of them made her feel weak. She barely registered that Phillip was leading her forwards until they stood before the glass, where together they stared down at the display. There he was, George Jenkins in miniature. The man who meant so very much to them both.

'You should buy one.'

It was Phillip who said it, and Molly took in a shuddering breath.

'I couldn't,' she whispered. 'I would have to speak to his parents, then, and I do not think I could bear it.'

'Would speaking to them be so very bad? *I* must face them, at some point.'

''Tis different for you.'

'Yes, it is. I saw their son die.'

Molly shook her head. 'They knew you, Phillip. They'd be grateful to hear you speak of him. It might bring them peace. But they never even knew I existed. What could I possibly tell them?'

'The truth,' Phillip said simply.

'But—'

'Do you still have his letters?'

'Of course I do,' she whispered, and Phillip lifted his

shoulder in a half-shrug as if that solved the matter. Which, Molly acknowledged, it rather did.

The church clocktower struck four then, and beside her Phillip sighed.

'I'd best be getting on to the Crown.'

Molly turned to him. 'You aren't coming back to Wakely Hall?'

Phillip made a gesture indicating his attire. 'Like this?' he asked, and Molly did concede he had a point. 'I shall freshen myself, have a nap. A meal, too, though it will be nothing to Mother's. But I cannot present myself to her like this.'

'I understand.'

He nodded. Then, shyly almost, he took her hand.

'Don't say anything to her,' Phillip said. 'I want it to be a surprise.'

Molly nodded, squeezed his cold fingers. 'I shan't say a word.'

'Thank you,' he said, and released her hand.

'What ... what will you do, Phillip? If Sergeant Harrington does think you a deserter, then ...'

She trailed off. Something like fear crossed his features, and Molly knew why.

At best, deserters were imprisoned. At worst, they were hanged.

'I must speak with Viscount Pépin,' Phillip said quietly. 'Ask his advice. I know not what else to do.'

He left her then. She watched him cross the square. At the Crown's threshold, Phillip turned to give her a small wave, and it was only when he had disappeared into the lodge's bustling confines that Molly turned back to the toy soldiers.

One day, she thought, looking down into the eyes of the soldier nearest to her, the eyes of her dear George. *One day I shall tell them who I am.*

Phillip found himself in the grounds of Wakely Hall some hours later – finally clean and rested in a fresh set of clothes and shoes, with a hearty meal of venison in his stomach. The sun had long set, and in the star-kissed dark the way to his childhood home would have been near impossible if he had not already known it blindfolded. How often had he ventured back there after a Merrywake assembly, high in both spirits and liquor? Of course, at such a young age Phillip should not have partaken of the punch, but George would sneak him a cupful every now and then. Still, he always arrived back at Wakely unscathed, and so had Phillip done now, albeit in less high spirits than he had before.

He was frightened.

Walking the turnpike road with Molly and sharing their grief at George's loss, Phillip had been able to quench his fears of what lay ahead. Even in the square he had stamped it down, did not think of it once at the Crown, but as he stood now on the gravel drive looking up at Wakely Hall – lit from within in candlelit shades of gold – he felt fear. What would his mother think of him? *Would* she be happy? Or ashamed? Molly had not indicated either way, only that his mother found speaking of him painful, and so Phillip had no notion as to how he would be received. And then, *then*, he would have to face the viscount. He would have to beg.

It was not a habit Phillip was accustomed to. Even when the French caught him, he had not begged.

He had too much pride.

With a deep breath he rounded the back of Wakely Hall to seek the tradesmen's entrance, but in the yard he lingered for some time, listening to the bustle of the servants' hall, smelling the scent of cooked meat and sugared spices on the cold night-time air. Phillip closed his eyes, pretended he was a youth again where he had nothing to concern himself over except helping the stable boy muck out the horses and what wonderful meal his mother would prepare for that evening. He might have lingered thus for some time had it not been for the kitchen door swinging open, and a great gush of steaming water being thrown out upon the icy step.

Phillip could not make her out at first. He saw the person was a woman for she wore skirts, but her features were obscured by the light behind her. It was only when she stepped back to spread the water about the step with a broom, that he realised to his relief that it was Molly.

'Mol,' he whispered.

She did not hear. The *scritch* of the broom was too loud. Phillip sucked in his breath, and moved into the beam of light that shone from the doorway onto the cobbles.

'*Mol!*'

Molly paused, looked up. Then, quickly turning her head

to ascertain if anyone was watching, she brought the door to behind her.

'I wondered when you'd come,' she whispered, and Phillip realised she looked tired.

'Are you all right?'

She looked surprised at this, as if nobody had asked her such a question before. 'Yes, 'tis just ... Mrs Wilson was not best pleased I'd abandoned my work. But at least it is done now. I've not long finished.'

He winced – Phillip remembered well what the housekeeper could be like, though her sharp tongue had never been directed at him. His mother had not allowed it.

'Did she punish you?'

'No,' Molly said, though the word was drawn out. 'She seems to have mellowed these past few days. 'Tis Christmas, after all. But she had been worried. Thought I might have absconded.'

'Absconded?'

'Deserted, I suppose. In my own fashion.'

Phillip reeled slightly, but then he saw she was smiling and had, it seemed, attempted a jest. It was not amusing, but it served somehow to relax him, and so Phillip said:

'Is my mother still busy?'

She shook her head. 'Not now. We were just clearing up.' Molly paused. 'How long have you been out here in the cold?'

'A while.'

Molly sighed. 'Come in. No good will come from delaying this further.'

It was just as she was gently taking Phillip's arm that the

kitchen door opened wide once more, and a tall woman was silhouetted on the threshold. Both Molly and Phillip were flooded with golden light, and both had to shield their eyes from it.

'Molly Hart! *What* are you about?'

'Mrs Wilson, I . . .'

The housekeeper folded her bony arms, and though neither one of them could see her expression, it could well be imagined.

'I have tried to be accommodating these past couple of days,' the housekeeper said in weary tones, 'but this is too much.'

'Mrs Wilson—'

'Skulking about the yard with another man! It is not to be borne! For shame, have you not learnt your lesson? I—'

'Mrs Wilson?'

Phillip stepped forwards then. He had no notion what it was the housekeeper spoke of, what ill Molly had done to warrant such words, nor did he wish to know their implications, but here at least she was wrong, and he could not let Mrs Wilson say such things when they were not deserved.

The moment he spoke, the housekeeper brought herself up short. Her eyes widened, she stepped closer – unsteady, almost – and as she did her expression could finally be seen. It was not one of anger but wonderment, and Phillip knew she knew him then, and felt a lump form in his throat.

'Phillip Denby,' she breathed. 'Is that really you?'

He could only nod. Mrs Wilson looked between him and Molly.

'By heaven, come inside. Come inside, for pity's sake, before you both catch cold!'

Whatever doubts he had about his return, they could not now be entertained, for Mrs Wilson was steering him across the flagstones, and through the door into the servants' hall.

It was bright. Warm. Just as Phillip remembered it, though there were some faces he did not recognise, all who looked at him with unabashed curiosity. But he did recognise Nash and Kate (whose hand had flown to her mouth), and the valet, Ralph. And, of course, he recognised his own dear mother, who stood with a tray of mince pies in her hands and was staring at him now just as Molly had earlier that day in the lane.

Phillip could barely contain himself, and nor could the cook. The tray of mince pies began to wobble precariously, and like a gull a maid with a round face and dimpled chin swooped in to rescue them, just in time for Mrs Denby's face to collapse into a great and almighty sob.

'Oh! *Oh!*'

She rushed to him, a bundle of aprons and skirts, and Phillip fell into her arms as if he were not a grown man of one-and-twenty, but a boy of barely sixteen once again.

His mother's embrace was everything he had dreamt of those long months in his prison cell – it enveloped him like a blanket, strong yet tender. She smelt of goose fat and cinnamon, and Phillip cried hard into the cushion of her shoulder.

'Where have you been?' she asked him over and over again, though there was no opportunity for him to answer; she kissed his hair (how relieved Phillip was that he was clean), his cheeks, his forehead, his hands. 'Look at you! Look how you've grown! Oh,' she exclaimed again, joyful now, her red face jolly and wet. 'You're alive! My darling boy, I knew you were, deep down. I knew it!'

'I didn't desert,' Phillip said, muffled still in the cambric of her dress. 'I swear I didn't.'

At this the cook stilled. Phillip became conscious once again of the other servants, some watching on with tears in their eyes but all of them smiling. Molly and Mrs Wilson stood side by side, arms about each other's waists, smiling widest of all.

'I never, *ever*,' said his mother, looking at him fiercely, 'thought for one moment that you did. Not my boy. Not my Phillip.'

Phillip let out a breath, and upon doing so realised just how much he had feared her answer. To know she did not believe him an enemy of the king, to know she did not feel shame at his disappearance, was a great balm to his conscience.

Aside from George, hers had been the only opinion that ever mattered to him.

'Oh, Mother,' he said now, meeting her gaze. 'I cannot tell you how relieved I am to hear you say those words. To know you do not think the worst of me. But . . .'

'But what?' Mrs Denby asked gently.

'But you might be the only one who believes it. Sergeant Harrington . . . The viscount . . . If they think I deserted, I'm done for. And what of you and your position at Wakely? You would lose it. I don't think I could bear—'

His mother pressed a finger to his lips to silence him. Then, without a care of their audience, she drew out a chair from the table and beckoned Phillip to sit. When he had, she joined him.

'Tell me what happened,' she said. 'Tell me it all.'

And so he did. For the second time that day Phillip explained what happened at the Battle of Toulouse and its aftermath; how he came to wake up amid a mass of bodies, that the only choice open to him was to simply walk; how he was captured by the French and found himself at the prison in Brest; how long he had stayed there, how he survived upon his release. All this Mrs Denby listened to with a quiet, comforting acceptance, and Phillip felt the years of guilt and fear slip from him like warm melted butter.

When Phillip had finished, Mrs Denby drew him to her and simply held him. They stayed thus for some minutes, in which Phillip became vaguely conscious that the servants' hall was busying itself again, that Mrs Wilson had orchestrated a measure of privacy. Phillip closed his eyes, found himself awash with the familiarity of it – the cordial chatterings of the housemaids and the footman amid the clatter of dishes, the sweep of brooms, the wiping of tables. The sounds of his childhood that had, always, though Phillip had not known it then, given him such contentment.

'Come, my boy,' said Mrs Denby after a while, and she pushed him away to firmly clasp his shoulders. 'Let us seek out the viscount. He shall see you right, mark my words.'

And though it was clear his mother believed this assurance,

Phillip still could not. He had lived with the fear of it too long. But in that moment, as Mrs Denby led him from the room, Phillip realised he must face whatever might come and took strength in knowing that no matter what happened now, his mother knew the truth. And that was enough.

STAVE XI.

$C\sharp$

Eleven Ladies Dancing

It was a custom upheld every year, that on the day preceding the Twelfth Night Ball, Merrywake's dancing master, Mr Thorpe, would teach the guests of Wakely Hall a new country dance. This year he had decided upon 'The Midnight Ramble' – an old but lively piece to be performed at midnight – which Maria Pépin thought an excellent idea, for she did so enjoy a spirited set at the peak hour of a ball.

Maria enjoyed any and all dances, whether they be a country, a cotillion or a reel, and endeavoured to participate in every single one of them, no matter how much her feet might hurt by the end of the night. Indeed, she never tired of the London season and its many balls, nor the summers she spent in Bath where she attended each assembly listed on that city's social calendar, and could be depended upon to make a jolly time of it. Unfortunately, as had so often been the case, Maria had perhaps been a little *too* jolly on such occasions, and would frequently be required to leave early in the carriage, which meant that as a consequence her feet never hurt *quite* as much as she hoped they would.

Thankfully, no carriage would be called upon tomorrow evening for Maria would already be home, and so she was determined to have as much fun as possible, no matter what her mother might say, with blissfully aching feet to match!

Of course, such gaieties were somewhat diminished when the likes of Miss Cordelia Sharpe were in the vicinity. Maria glared at the said Miss Sharpe from across the ballroom, where she was speaking with Sir Robert by the garlanded fireplace commandeering all that gentleman's time (though the duke did not appear to mind one bit). How *dare* her mother invite Cordelia Sharpe to stay at Wakely, especially after Maria told her what the little witch had done to Louisa at Lady Warwick's Midsummer Soirée. And Cordelia *was* a witch, Maria thought – vain, conceited, unapologetically mean – and a fortune hunter to boot. The Sharpes were, after all, the poorer relations of Charles Heysten by way of his maternal grandmother, Georgiana Soppe, whose sister had scandalously married a man by the surname of Sharpe who came from new money rather than old. (Maria found their whole family tree ridiculously complicated, made even more so by the arrival of the child, Faith, who – imagine! – was none other than Charles Heysten's illegitimate half-sister by a maid, if you please.) Cordelia was clearly intent on finding some way of gaining at least a portion of her cousin's wealth ever since the old Lord Heysten died.

Certainly, that awful witch wasted no time prevaricating about the matter – only a few hours after the Sharpes arrived late yesterday afternoon, Cordelia had asked his lordship in a wounded manner as she won a trick at Whist why he had ignored her letters regarding an allowance. That Cordelia should say such a thing so publicly was clearly a ploy to force Lord Heysten's hand, and Maria had been gleeful when the ruse backfired – his lordship had sternly informed his cousin she had already benefited from a handsome settlement in a shew of goodwill, and if she were to continue in her harassments he would withdraw it forthwith.

This greatly esteemed him in Maria's eyes. When she told her sisters and mother of the exchange (for she had been one fourth of the Whist party, the other being the Earl of Starling, who had been staring at Cordelia all night in an embarrassingly besotted fashion), Louisa had been prevailed upon to confess that Lord Charles Heysten was not quite so boorish after all, to which even Charlotte agreed, much to the delighted shock of the viscountess.

Maria tweaked the puffed sleeves of her gown as she waited for Mr Thorpe to finish ruminating with the piper, the lately returned son of Wakely Hall's cook, Mrs Denby.

It seemed to her the Sharpe brothers were cut from a different cloth than their sister. *They* were deeply embarrassed to hear the exchange (for they had been in earshot at the next table) and apologised to their cousin profusely. Maria glanced at Bertram Sharpe where he stood conversing with his two brothers, and her two younger sisters. The viscountess had placed Mr Sharpe next to her at dinner that night (a ruse which Maria saw straight through, for it had been abundantly clear what her mother was about from the hopeful expression on her face), and the gentleman revealed in tones most sincere that he, Tarquin and Humphrey merely wished to strengthen the Sharpe–Heysten familial connections now that the barrier of old Lord Heysten and his objections had been removed, nothing more. Indeed, said Mr Sharpe, he should be gratified Maria did not tar him with the same metaphorical brush as his shameful sister, and hoped some gentleman would take Cordelia off their hands as soon as possible.

At the memory Maria frowned. She glanced once again at Cordelia, standing close to Sir Robert in a manner a little too familiar. It was clear to anybody who looked at them that Miss Sharpe had set her designs upon Sir Robert. Five days ago Maria might have felt deeply resentful at such a prospect, but since the duke had maintained a coolly civil demeanour whenever they had by chance been thrown together of an evening, Maria did not now mind so very much. Rudeness, after all, can serve to dampen one's ardour. There was a littleness to the man she had not seen before then, and though she herself once had designs on him, Maria had been thinking only of the prudence of the match. Yes, she had been flattered by his (then) flirtatious manners and imagined herself to feel some glimmerings of affection for him, but after a few days of his shunning her Maria could safely say that while the Duke of Morley had imposed upon her, she was not injured. Not like poor Rosalie, who had taken his spurning to heart. Maria soon came to the conclusion he was *just* the sort of lout and cove Charlotte always said she despised, and if that were the case then Miss Sharpe and the duke appeared a perfectly suited match.

'Come,' the dancing master called, clapping his hands together. 'Come, ladies and gentlemen – chuse your partners, and form your lines, if you please!'

There was much chatter and creaking of the floorboards as those gathered in the ballroom did as Mr Thorpe bade. Eleven ladies there were including herself, together with eleven gentlemen which meant no man or woman should be without a partner. Maria was glad of the fact, for it was always so awkward when a person should be forced to observe from the periphery of the dance floor like a wallflower, as Charlotte often did. How frustrating it was, to always see her sister standing on the sidelines, though 'twas true it was of her own doing. At least she could not do the same now – Charlotte had chosen to accompany Lord Heysten, Miss Faith Heysten, Nicolas, Juliette and their father to Wakely Church, where at that precise moment a rehearsal ceremony between Miss Partridge and Reverend Soppe was being performed, which Charlotte declared was a much better use of her time than spending the afternoon getting her feet stepped upon.

Maria on the other hand *never* thought dancing a waste of time, nor was she ever (as one can easily suppose) in want of a partner to dance with, and Bertram Sharpe made no hesitation in approaching her now. With a smile and bow he asked if she might take to the floor, for his brothers had already partnered her sisters, a request Maria graciously accepted.

As they formed their lines, Maria looked at Humphrey Sharpe and Louisa, and Tarquin Sharpe and Rosalie. These gentlemen, too, she thought, suited her sisters admirably well. Louisa had already been impressed by her dancing partner's enthusiasm for last night's goose dinner, even going so far as to challenge the gentlemen to a competition to see how many mince pies one could consume in the space of a minute (the answer was ten, and Humphrey Sharpe the victor), and Rosalie – though still in somewhat mournful spirits – did not object when Mr Tarquin read aloud from his own dog-eared copy of the *Romance of the Forest* (she was, by the end of Chapter 3, looking rather moved). And while not one of the Sharpe brothers could be deemed particularly handsome (Cordelia alone, it seemed, had taken all the Sharpe good looks for herself), all three were blessed with good manners, breeding, sense and principles, which – quite frankly – there was a lot to be said for. Adequate money, too (though not near as much as the Duke of Morley, which was a shame). If the Sharpe brothers were willing to offer for their hands and overlook each of their faults so bemoaned by their mother, then Maria supposed she and her sisters could not do better. She sidled a glance at the viscountess on the arm of Monsieur Benoît. Perhaps their *Maman* had not been *completely* erroneous in her well-meaning machinations . . . not that Maria would allow her to know it.

One must maintain at least a modicum of pride.

'Now then,' announced Mr Thorpe, interrupting her musings. '"The Midnight Ramble" is a Duple Minor dance – the minor set lasts thirty-two bars and is played in the key of D major. The dance contains the following movements: hand turn, lead, half figure eight, rights and lefts, cross go below. Mrs Thorpe and I shall demonstrate the first steps.'

Mrs Cecily Thorpe, the Pépin sisters' former governess, took her husband's proffered hand.

'You shall each,' intoned he, 'as is typical for a country dance, be allocated Ones and Twos. Mrs Thorpe and I shall in this instance be Ones and, ah, your grace,' bowed Mr Thorpe, 'would you permit yourself and your lovely partner to act as our first Twos?'

Cordelia Sharpe fair simpered in her gown of burgundy bombazine as Sir Robert consented, and Maria barely refrained from rolling her eyes. Next to her, Rosalie sucked in her breath.

'Ah, very good, very good. See then,' continued Mr Thorpe, 'there shall first be two notes from our piper, and we begin on the third. Ones clap –' here the dancing master and his wife clapped – 'we cross go below –' here the couple demonstrated – 'and Twos lead up. Your grace, if you would?'

Here the duke took Miss Sharpe's hand and did as instructed, and watching the couple Maria narrowed her eyes. Did not Miss Sharpe gaze at her partner in a manner far too intimate and did Sir Robert not then, in turn, surreptitiously *wink* at her? She glanced at Rosalie to see if her sister had chanced to see the display, and by the expression writ upon her features it was clear she had. Rosalie then looked questioningly down the line at their mother, who was watching the handsome couple, but with an aspect of such deep contemplation that Maria wondered at it. The other couples were not paying the slightest bit of attention, however, for Mr Thorpe was already announcing his next instructions.

'Ones perform a two-hand turn once and a half, then Twos clap, and cross go below as Ones lead up. Miss Falshaw, Mr Busgrove, if you will join the line so we might . . .?'

There was much kerfuffle then, for Nigel Busgrove was profuse in his agreements and so bumbled to the front, dragging poor Lucy inelegantly with him, who gave Louisa such a look of pained chagrin that Maria was put upon not to snort, and Bertram Sharpe – catching her eye – seemed ready to do the same.

'That's it, that's it!' cried Mr Thorpe. 'Now we have our Twos two-hand turn one and a half, then Ones cross . . . Come, Sir Victor, Lady Marshchild, won't you oblige? Excellent! Then go below as Twos lead up—'

It was clear that as each instruction was imparted a new couple should join the line, and this they did until all eleven pairs were joined in the dance. In such a vast ballroom, the footsteps of two-and-twenty people created an echoing din, and Maria longed for Mr Denby to play so that the whole business did not seem quite so inelegant.

'And to finish,' said Mr Thorpe, looking pleased with the progress, 'ones half figure eight up, then all face partners and perform four changes of rights and lefts.'

The entire party of twenty-two obliged (though some better than others), and satisfied, Mr Thorpe announced that it was time – at last – for the music to be introduced. 'And remember,' he said with a smile, 'two notes from the tin whistle first, and our Ones clap on the third.'

Oh, did those first two notes bring such a thrill to Maria's heart! It had been, after all, some time since she had danced. Indeed, Maria could not recall dancing after returning from Bath in the summer – the last opportunity she had had was at Lady Warwick's soirée – and so (being assigned the number of One) Maria gave a hearty clap, and proceeded to cross below with Mr Sharpe.

The notes of Mr Denby's tin whistle trilled light and clear, resulting in a charming melody. How much easier it was to dance, with music to give one's feet flight! And while such intricate steps and turns might have seemed complicated to a novice dancer – certainly, Mr and Mrs Busgrove (being no less blundering than their son) appeared to take to it with some difficulty, though Sir Gregory Warwick and his wife (being such stalwarts of London society) accomplished the movements with ease – Maria found them no problem at all, and was pleasantly surprised to find Bertram Sharpe, too, a natural at the amusement, and she smiled at him widely.

'You are an accomplished dancer, Mr Sharpe.'

'I am happy you think so, Miss Maria – I do so love to dance.'

'Then why is it,' remarked she, 'we did not see you at the assemblies in Bath, as your sister was this summer past?'

Mr Bertram Sharpe inclined his head. 'Cordelia accompanied my elderly aunt there to take the waters, whilst my brothers and I were otherwise engaged at home. If I had known you were there, however, I might have been prevailed upon to make the journey.'

Maria smiled at the compliment as Lady Falshaw and the Earl of Starling crossed below.

'And where is home, sir? Lord Heysten mentioned something about the north?'

'Just so,' came the jovial reply. 'The Humber. My grandfather built up his fortune in land ownership across the region, and it has required careful supervision to sustain the profits. Though I enjoy society, as the eldest brother it is up to me to ensure our investments are managed wisely. And often that means forfeiting visits to Bath.'

'It sounds awfully boring,' Maria remarked, to which Mr Sharpe shouted out a laugh, and Maria thought then what a nice smile he had. Lovely straight teeth.

'So it is, so it is! Which was why I was so gratified to be extended an invitation to your parents' Twelfth Night Ball.'

'And I am in turn gratified by your gratification! But what of your aunt? I hope you did not leave her all alone for Twelfth Night?'

'Ah,' said Mr Sharpe, his features dropping with a sorry sigh. 'I'm afraid our dear aunt passed away the week after Michaelmas. Alas, the waters did nothing for her.'

'Oh, Mr Sharpe. I am sorry.'

'Please, do not concern yourself. She was happy to go, I dare say, being so very unwell. Most fed up with it all she was. 'Tis only a pity that Cordelia has been left without engagement.'

'Sir?'

'Well, Cordelia was our aunt's companion. My brothers and I – being men of business and so rarely from home – were unable to offer our sister a London season, or any of the fashionable entertainments that befitted her station. It was our aunt, you see, who provided all that. Indeed, Cordelia has been wholly spoilt.'

'What of your parents?'

'Died some years ago. A carriage accident.' Mr Sharpe waved Maria's commiserations away. 'But now our aunt has gone too and, well, Cordelia is quite determined to leave what she calls "the dreary north" and marry someone who can provide her with every luxury to which she has become accustomed. You see, I suppose, who she has her eye on?'

Maria glanced at Cordelia and Sir Robert. 'I suspect your sister might be disappointed.'

'Oh?'

'Well, considering the duke has been flirting outrageously with me and my sisters, especially poor Rosalie –' who was still mulishly looking at Miss Sharpe and Sir Robert, to the obvious confusion of her dancing partner – 'I should warn her to be on her guard.'

Mr Sharpe looked surprised.

'Is that so? Cordelia said that she and Morley had been thrown together quite a bit in Bath. In fact, she gave me the impression that her affections were reciprocated.'

At that moment Maria's mother crossed below, and upon catching Bertram Sharpe's words sucked in her breath.

'*Maman?*' asked Maria as the viscountess slipped into line beside her. 'Is anything the matter?'

Viscountess Pépin took a moment to reply, before saying on a clap, 'No, dearest. I have just realised something, that is all.'

'Oh?'

But her mother was already passing by. Mr Sharpe cleared his throat.

'Miss Maria, might I ask what, exactly, you meant by the term "flirting"?'

Maria coloured. She could not deny that Sir Robert had been perhaps too revealing of his time in Europe, his many escapades during the Grand Tour, and being a girl disinclined to be offended by anything Maria had greedily absorbed the duke's wild stories. Italian opera singers, Dutch models, French concubines! Mayhap it *had* been inappropriate of her to listen to Sir Robert, to beg him to continue when he appeared to linger over details he professed were not for her delicate ears ... But that was truly the extent of it, and as Mr Sharpe led her upon a half figure eight up, Maria assured him as much. Still, her dancing partner looked displeased.

'And what of Miss Louisa? Miss Rosalie? Did the duke treat your sisters as he treated you?'

Mr Sharpe had lowered his voice, leant across the space of the line in a clear bid to keep the particulars unheard by the other dancers, and while one might consider such a frank conversation unwise when there were so many who might overhear them, Maria had never held any qualms about such things. Since she and her sisters had been so misused by the duke, Maria found no reason to protect him, and so she replied without altering the tenor of her voice:

'Louisa and I have discussed the matter, and come to the conclusion that Sir Robert treated us in much the same way. As for Rosalie ... well, she will not speak to us about it at all, being so very upset by his shunning her these past few days.'

'He shunned her?'

'Indeed, he has shunned us all. He was amiable the one day, then cold the next. Neither one of us could understand it. But, returning to Rosalie,' added Maria with a reassuring smile, 'she is a romantic, that is all, and easily hurt. I do not believe anything more occurred between them than occurred between the duke and ourselves, and I do believe the matter will soon be entirely forgotten. Especially if your brother keeps reciting the Gothick melancholy of Mrs Radcliffe!'

To this answer, Bertram Sharpe appeared – if not entirely satisfied – then at least somewhat mollified. Still, it was clear Maria's words had set upon him a particular train of thought in regards to the suitability of a match between his sister and the Duke of Morley, and Maria felt then a spiteful surge of satisfaction that Cordelia Sharpe might be thwarted in her plans and Sir Robert shamed for treating the Pépin sisters so monstrously ill.

They both deserved it, after all.

'Excellent!' announced Mr Thorpe as the dance came to an end and Mr Denby's lips lifted from the mouthpiece of his pipe. 'I should like, if you do not mind, to run through the dance once more now the steps have been perfected. And then as our well-deserved reward we can partake of Mrs Denby's excellent bowl of wassail, which I believe she has made available to us in the dining room?'

To this the cook's son nodded, and murmurs of appreciation were heard from the party, not least from Nigel Busgrove who hooked his thumbs over the lapels of his damask waistcoat of eye-watering mustard silk.

'How splendid,' said he, rosy-cheeked, evidently already chirping merry. 'I do so like a decent spiced punch. It so perfectly encapsulates the festive spirit, do you not agree, Miss Falshaw?'

Maria caught Louisa's eye across the line, and the sisters shared a look of half-amusement, half-relief. Ever since the Busgroves had arrived at Wakely Hall, it had been clear to everyone that the son favoured Charlotte, and made more than a nuisance of himself in his pursuit. But since Lord Heysten had arrived and appeared to take an interest in their elder sister (and it truly was astonishing that Charlotte had not *entirely* denounced him), the buffoonish young man transferred his attentions to that of poor Lucy, and though she was Louisa's dearest friend, it could not be denied the relief on the Pépins' part was most acute. To be sure, the idea of Nigel Busgrove of all people becoming their brother-in-law . . . well, it really was too much to be borne.

Lucy shyly murmured her agreement; the younger Mr Busgrove gave a simpering laugh, a laugh which was mercifully lost amid the claps of Mr Thorpe who turned once more to Mr Denby.

'After the count of three, my good fellow. One, two . . .'

And so began the music once more, and the eleven ladies

and eleven gentlemen their dancing. This time, however, rather than gossip with her partner, Maria concentrated instead on her steps, and found so much pleasure in being guided about the ballroom floor by Bertram Sharpe that she let herself be lulled into the merry notes of Thompson's 'Ramble'. The polite conversation that so often accompanied such country dances flittered and fizzed about Maria's ears, and she closed her eyes with the enjoyment of it. Oh, how wonderful it would all be, tomorrow evening, with thrice the number of couples bounding about Wakely's ballroom floor! Maria could imagine no felicity better than the excitable chatter, the lively orchestra, the swirls of heavy silks and fine muslins; the ballroom filled with candlelight, the atmosphere enlightened with the scent of fir and pine, and she and all of them having a high old time of it. Truly, if Maria were put upon to chuse, she would say that her parents' annual Twelfth Night Ball was her favourite ball of the entire year.

She sighed happily at all of these wondrous thoughts, only to then be pulled from her contented reverie by a snippet of conversation from the couple to her right as they passed below:

—*You cheated? But how?*

—*Why, I paid the footman for the answers.*

—*For shame, sir!*

—*Do not think badly of me. I only wished to make a good impression!*

Incensed, Maria turned her head to address the speaker of this last.

'Why, Mr Busgrove,' she fair hissed. 'You should be ashamed of yourself.'

Upon such a fierce reprimand – standing so squat in the line – the man blinked rather owlishly.

'Perhaps I should, Miss Pépin, but I assure you it was all in good spirits.'

'Hardly! Our annual treasure hunt is a matter of pride in this household. You do not deserve the crown. In fact, I have a mind to declare so and it shall be taken from you, upon my word!'

At this Mr Busgrove pouted. 'Would you be so very cruel as to shew me up, Miss Maria? Truly, I meant no harm. I only wished to impress—'

Here he cut himself off, and Maria knew precisely whose name he meant to say.

'Believe me when I tell you, sir, that it takes an awful lot to impress my sister Charlotte. And cheating would have got you nowhere at all.'

Sir Victor Marshchild and his wife passed below then, Mr Sharpe reached to take her hand, and all eleven of the couples were obliged to perform the four changes of rights and lefts, after which Maria would have spoken more on the matter (after all, *she* would have won the golden egg hunt if it had not been for Nigel Busgrove's deception), were it not for a cry of *Oh!* and an almighty thump that echoed about the ballroom and caused Mr Denby to cease playing and thus the other couples to stop dancing.

There was a gasp, a sob; Maria turned to see her sister Rosalie collapsed upon the floor, clasping her knee.

'Whatever happened?' cried Viscountess Pépin, rushing to crouch beside Tarquin Sharpe who was attending Rosalie, while

Rosalie, with tears running down her face, glared up at Cordelia Sharpe.

'She tripped me, *Maman!*' she cried, to which Miss Sharpe pressed an offended hand to her throat.

'Me, Miss Rosalie?' came the reply, all innocence, and Rosalie unsteadily drew herself up to point a shaking finger.

'You did! She did! She did it deliberately!'

At this Cordelia trilled a laugh and looked at the Duke of Morley with such an air of camaraderie that Maria rather felt she would slap the condescending smile off her beautiful face there and then.

'Why, I did no such thing,' insisted Miss Sharpe. 'I would not be so clumsy, would I, Sir Robert?'

'Of course not,' the duke demurred, a quirk about his lips. 'You are the finest partner one might hope for. Perhaps it was you, Miss Rosalie, who tripped upon your skirts?'

Miss Sharpe openly smirked. Viscountess Pépin narrowed her eyes. Her daughter, bottom lip wobbling, stared up at the Duke of Morley, and though it must be said the youngest Pépin girl was as good-natured as the eldest, the expression on her face in that moment was one of pure hatred.

'You cad,' she declared. 'You *oaf!*'

The ballroom filled with scandalised gasps. Rosalie, not appearing to care one bit of it, looked about the dancers and shook her head, her brown curls bobbing at her spotted chin.

'I mean it, I swear I do! Sir Robert has treated me cruelly, and two weeks ago I never thought him capable of it. I thought,' said she, her voice catching as she addressed the party, 'when he would not speak to me these past few days that I must have done something to upset him, but now –' and here she turned to the duke who looked thoroughly bored – 'to accuse *me* of being clumsy, when it was so obviously Miss Sharpe at fault ... Well, 'tis clear I was mistaken in you, Sir Robert.' Rosalie gulped. '*Maman* was right!'

At this, Louisa frowned.

'Right?' she asked, and all eyes then went to Viscountess Pépin.

'*Maman* warned me,' cried Rosalie. 'She said Sir Robert was dishonourable and I did not believe her!'

The viscountess coloured. 'My dear, now is not the time, nor the place.'

The Duke of Morley scoffed. 'Well now, viscountess, I fear that was most uncharitable of you, blackening my character in such a way.'

'I have the proof of my own eyes, your grace,' the viscountess shot back, 'as you well know. Would you care to explain to the company how, only the other day, I discovered you beneath the grand staircase with one of my maids?'

Again, there were scandalised murmurs, and Monsieur de Fortgibu – clearly more discreet than the rest – made a gentlemanly retreat from the room, upon which the Thorpes and Mr Denby (looking very thoughtful indeed) swiftly followed.

'By Jove,' interceded then Sir Gregory, wide-eyed. 'Is this true, Morley?'

The duke looked stymied, as if he had not anticipated the

rejoinder that so damned his character, as did poor Rosalie who whispered:

'But *Maman*! You said you observed a dalliance in Bath, not here.'

Viscountess Pépin sent her daughter a pitying look. 'So I did, my dear, but it was only moments after you ran from the drawing room that I happened upon them.'

At this, Cordelia Sharpe laughed in disbelieving tones.

'Come now, viscountess. A maid? Why, Sir Robert would not lower himself.'

Sir Victor Marshchild cleared his throat.

'Are you calling Viscountess Pépin a liar, Miss Sharpe?'

'I . . .' She coloured. 'Well, not a liar per se . . . more that she has clearly been mistaken.'

'*Cordelia!*' Mr Humphrey Sharpe hissed, and it must be said that all three of her brothers looked dreadfully embarrassed.

The viscountess shook her head at Miss Sharpe in admonishment.

'I suppose you might believe such a thing. It seems the duke has filled your head with lies. I would feel sorry for you, Miss Cordelia, that you should be so deceived in him, if you had not treated my daughters with such cruelty.'

There was a pause in which Miss Sharpe laughed again, her gaze flitting nervously about the others, but this time her laugh was decidedly less strident, and its echoes fell flat and dull in the vast ballroom.

'Why, my lady. I cannot understand what you mean.'

'Oh, I rather think that you do,' said Viscountess Pépin. 'You *did* trip Rosalie. I might not have seen it, but like myself my daughter is no liar, and I trust her words over yours. I also understand that you were deliberately spiteful to my Louisa at Lady Warwick's Midsummer Soirée. In fact, you set about humiliating her and rejoiced in doing so! Believe me, Miss Sharpe, if there had been a way to exclude you from the invitation extended to your brothers, I would have done it. Still,' she added in a more calculating tone, 'I am glad you're here, for if you had not been, I would never have made the connection.'

Miss Sharpe paled. 'I beg your pardon?'

'The Pump Room in Bath, last summer. I saw there, in a darkened corner, the duke taking liberties with another lady. Tall and blonde she was, but I did not realise the lady was you until I overhead Mr Sharpe's words to my Maria.'

At this revelation, the Falshaws departed, but Maria – who had observed the whole exchange in silent rapture – could not move a muscle. Never had she seen her mother speak thus to another human being! Never had any of the sisters seen her so angry! Always they considered their mother such a kind and gentle woman, with not one bad word to say about anybody, but here she was giving Cordelia Sharpe and the Duke of Morley what-for, and Maria could barely conceal her glee.

'Viscountess,' said the Earl of Starling, with an apologetic half-bow. 'The incident with your maid can be verified, I assume, but I must say that there are many ladies of Miss Sharpe's colouring and stature in Bath. To accuse her of such grievous conduct . . . Well, her reputation is at stake. This is a very serious accusation. Are you *quite* sure it was her?'

'I am,' said the viscountess. 'That lady wore the same comb in her hair. Tortoiseshell, adorned with a shooting star of cut steel. I should know it anywhere.'

'But,' flustered Miss Sharpe. 'This comb belonged to my mother. It is one of a kind!'

Viscountess Pépin smiled.

'Precisely.'

There was a shocked silence, and in the face of it Miss Sharpe appeared to realise what she had done. Both she and the Duke of Morley froze, and there followed murmurs of such an appalled and scandalised nature that Bertram Sharpe – having recovered now from the shock of it all – was forced to address the matter.

'Cordelia,' he said, looking to Maria most authoritative, '*has* this man been taking liberties with you?' to which his sister trilled a shocked laugh.

'Honestly, brother, this is very unfair.'

'*Has* he?'

Tarquin Sharpe, this, at which Miss Sharpe tweaked the cuff of her dress.

'Really, I do object! How can you accuse me of such a thing?'

Humphrey Sharpe folded his arms. 'Cordelia!'

Miss Sharpe stared at her brothers for a long moment. Then, to the astoundment of everybody in the room, most notably the Duke of Morley himself, she linked her arm possessively through his.

'Yes,' she said boldly. 'He has.'

Such shouts of outrage that followed! The Sharpe brothers

spoke furiously between themselves, the Busgroves looked positively delighted at being witness to such a delicious scandal, while the Marshchilds and the Earl of Starling attempted to maintain order as Maria, Rosalie and Louisa gathered about their mother, who held them close.

'Well, Morley,' said Bertram Sharpe when the ballroom had quietened once more. 'You shall marry my sister.'

'I shall not.'

The duke's answer came like a shot, and held no hesitation whatsoever, to which Cordelia Sharpe released his arm.

'What?'

Her voice was so sharp she fare sang the word, but he did not even flinch.

'I will not marry you,' said the Duke of Morley, in such firm tones that one could not mistake his resolve.

Maria stared at Sir Robert. However could she or any of her sisters have considered him a gentleman? How had they been so easily taken in?

'By God, you have a nerve, Morley!' Tarquin Sharpe cried. 'Do you dare stand there and refuse to marry my sister?'

''Twas a kiss, nothing more.'

'So says you! But from the sounds of it you have not acted honourably to any woman, so we can hardly be expected to believe you in this case. *Was* it just a kiss, Cordelia?'

'No, it was not,' swore the sister, looking at the duke accusingly. 'It was far more besides. You must understand, brother. He made promises.'

The last was said innocently, but Maria did not miss the sly

335

glint in Miss Sharpe's fine eyes, nor the tweak of a muscle in Sir Robert's jaw.

'Why, you money-grabbing—'

'Watch yourself, Morley,' warned Bertram Sharpe, at which the duke turned on him.

'Your sister lies,' Sir Robert spat, his face growing red as puce. 'I shall not deny the maid, nor shall I deny that I engaged in flirtations with the Pépin sisters, or with *your* sister. But nothing else happened, and certainly nothing she did not beg for.'

Cordelia Sharpe's green eyes filled with tears, but to Maria they shone like a crocodile's.

'Bertram,' she cried. 'The duke is lying!'

'I am not!'

'Then,' declared Humphrey Sharpe, stepping forwards most forcefully, 'I call you out. Swords at dawn! There is nothing else for it – it's the only honourable way.'

'On no, it isn't,' interceded Sir Victor. 'I am ——shire's magistrate, so unless you both wish to spend Twelfth Night in gaol, I suggest you think of another solution.'

'What on earth is going on?'

The commanding voice made her jump; Maria turned, and so too did the others in the room.

At the threshold of the ballroom stood her sister Juliette on the arm of Nicolas Toussaint, together with Lord Heysten, his little sister, Faith (who held in her hand three leads to which were attached Monsieur Benoît's clucking hens), and Charlotte, on the arm of their father, Viscount Pépin. All six of them looked upon the scene before them with expressions of complete bemusement.

'I ask again,' said Nicolas. 'What is going on?'

It was rare for Juliette's new husband to speak forcefully. He was always so soft in his addresses, so courteous and polite. It was why, Maria knew, her elder sister liked him so very much.

'Nic, old boy,' exclaimed the Duke of Morley in tones of deep relief. 'Do help out a friend – I have been unfairly maligned. If you had only heard—'

'I did hear,' came Nicolas' reply. 'At least, a part of it. What is it you lie about? Why is there talk of a duel?'

There was much chatter then from all sides, in which the whole situation was explained, and Lord Heysten cleared his throat.

'Though I am inclined to agree my cousin is no angel, it seems there can be no doubt upon the matter, Morley. This is a lady's word against yours.'

Sir Robert sniffed. 'Which counts for nothing, I assume? I am a duke after all.'

'I couldn't give a damn if you were the Archbishop of Canterbury. If you have compromised Cordelia, then it is your duty to marry her.'

Beside him, Nicolas sighed.

'He cannot marry her.'

Lord Heysten frowned. 'Why not?' asked he, and as if in answer one of the hens clucked at his feet.

'Because,' said Nicolas, with a reproachful look at the duke, 'Sir Robert is already married.'

What loud silence followed! Shock was writ clearly upon the faces of everyone in the room but for Nicolas Toussaint and the Duke of Morley, and Cordelia Sharpe turned on the latter like a whip.

'*What?*'

'To an actress. In London.'

'An *actress?*'

'Nicolas,' breathed Juliette, 'you didn't tell me,' and Sir Robert cleared his throat.

'You must not blame your husband, seigneuresse. I swore him to secrecy, and being such a soft cull, he agreed. I was in my altitudes you see when I married her, and if *my* father found out . . .'

'You fiend, Morley,' the Earl of Starling spluttered. 'How could you abuse poor Miss Sharpe's honour? How could you promise her marriage when you already had a wife?'

'But I *didn't* promise her marriage,' the Duke of Morley glowered. 'Besides, I was rather hoping I could get my marriage annulled before anyone discovered it. But now that's all for naught, for the secret is out. What a grave disappointment you are to me, Toussaint.'

Oh, Maria thought, this was all too glorious! It was as if she were witnessing a Covent Garden play. Indeed, she was not the only one to think it either for the three Busgroves had long since taken seats upon the chairs set about the periphery of the ballroom floor, and little Faith Heysten sat cross-legged on the polished hardwood with the three hens collected about her, all of them watching the back and forth as if it were a game of shuttlecock. If it had not been for the look of mortification set upon each of the Sharpe brothers' faces, and the clear upset shewn by her brother-in-law, Maria would have laughed heartily. Viscountess Pépin, however, was not the least bit amused.

'Your grace,' said she, in such a dangerously low cadence that even the viscount looked surprised. 'You are a worse scoundrel than I thought. I am glad I was able to warn you away from my daughters before you could do further damage.'

'*Maman?*'

This came from Rosalie, and was echoed in turn by Louisa and Maria herself. Was their mother, then, responsible for Sir Robert avoiding them these past few days? But then, before Maria could broach the question, Viscount Pépin at last made himself heard.

'It seems,' said he, in a voice most grave, 'there is much that has been kept from me. Pray, dearest, would you care to explain?'

So it was that Viscountess Pépin divulged to her husband (and a very rapt audience) all that had occurred since the duke arrived in Merrywake, after which the viscount stared aghast.

'*Dieu nous en préserve!*' he said once he had recovered. 'I am appalled,' and drawing himself tall, Maria's father bestowed upon the Duke of Morley a stern look. 'Your grace. I would have you remove yourself from my home immediately. You are no longer welcome at Wakely Hall.'

Sir Robert smiled tightly. 'It would be my pleasure, my lord. I cannot imagine spending one more moment in such vulgar company.' He turned a disdainful gaze upon Nicolas. 'Farewell, old boy. Enjoy Paris, won't you?'

And with not one further word or single bow, the Duke of Morley departed the room, leaving the rest of the party staring after him. That is, except for Miss Cordelia Sharpe, who looked ready to fall into a bout of hysterics.

'Oh!' she cried. '*Oh!* Whatever shall I do!' to which Tarquin Sharpe pursed his lips.

'You shall return home,' said he, 'that's what you shall do, until we can think of a way to manage the scandal.'

At this Cordelia's beautiful face collapsed into tears, tears which Maria supposed now were genuine, since her ruse had failed so spectacularly.

'He deceived me, brother! He offered me marriage! He said he loved me! Pity me, please!'

She looked about wildly, and upon seeing who stood closely at her elbow with a look of deep concern about his lined face, Miss Cordelia Sharpe promptly collapsed into a faint, right into the Earl of Starling's waiting arms.

This then, appeared to be the end of it. All attention was now on Miss Sharpe, and Viscount Pépin announced that it was time to depart for the drawing room, where they might all be revived by the wassail bowl.

'Well,' Bertram Sharpe said, watching his sister carried out of the ballroom in the ageing earl's arms, her burgundy skirts trailing upon the shining hardwood floor. 'I be.'

Maria turned, and when she saw the troubled expression on Mr Sharpe's face she felt – if not sympathy, since Cordelia deserved none – then a sense of obligation to shew it for her brother's sake. None of it, after all, was his fault.

'I am sorry it has come to this,' she said. 'I cannot imagine what you must be feeling,' to which Mr Sharpe shook his head.

'It is I who should apologise on Cordelia's behalf. She has always been so troublesome, so headstrong. She was given too much free rein, I see that now, a terrible oversight on my part. I should have taken greater care of her.'

'You could not have known of her deception,' Maria murmured as the party departed the ballroom in search of Mrs Denby's spiced punch.

'But I should have,' came the dejected reply. 'It was my duty to mind her.'

Maria reached out to gently press his arm.

'Mr Sharpe, you are not to blame for your sister's behaviour. She was in perfect command of everything she said and did. That was clear enough in Bath.'

At this Mr Sharpe regarded her.

'What was it Cordelia did there? Your mother implied . . .'

'Ah,' Maria said, colouring a little, and as she regaled the unhappy incident at Lady Warwick's Midsummer Soirée, Mr Sharpe's frown grew ever deeper. 'And I confess I'm not the least bit sorry for spilling my wine over her,' Maria admitted. 'I'm afraid my temper rises exponentially if anyone dares treat any of my sisters ill.'

'A commendable trait, to be sure. I just wish Cordelia possessed the same caring spirit. Alas, she has shewn herself to be a spiteful creature, and dishonest, too, and see where this has got us. Whatever am I to do?'

So troubled did Mr Sharpe sound, that Maria felt inclined to lift his spirits in the only way she knew how, and that was to say something outrageous.

'Well, you can look on the bright side of things.'

Mr Sharpe drew his brows. 'The bright side?'

'Why yes,' she said, a smile lurking about her lips. 'I hear the Earl of Starling is in want of a wife, and since an earl is only two ranks down from a duke, I scarce think Cordelia will complain. I wonder if we can contrive an engagement between the two of them before the night is out? It would save us all a great deal of bother.'

To this Bertram Sharpe stared, before his face creased into a laugh. 'You certainly are blunt, Miss Maria.'

'I speak as I find.'

'So I see.' He looked at her admiringly, before his face settled once more into a serious mien. 'But let us consider the alternative. If the earl does *not* offer for my sister, and society hears word of what happened here today, the prospects of my entire family will be ruined. No one will wish to marry Cordelia, and –' here Mr Sharpe flushed a little – 'myself and my brothers will not be looked upon favourably either. You . . . forgive my own bluntness, Miss Maria, but a gentleman such as your father would not wish any of his daughters connected to a family tarnished by scandal.'

Maria stilled. Her chest grew warm. His implication was clear, and only then did she realise the true import of what had happened. What was it she had thought earlier?

She and her sisters could not do better.

Well, they certainly could if the Sharpe family were disgraced. But then, since when had Maria cared about such things? If she wanted to marry Bertram Sharpe (and the prospect was growing ever more favourable in her mind) then she would, no matter what her father thought about it.

'Do you know what I find, Mr Sharpe?' said Maria in musing tones. 'I find that the older I become, the more I think one cannot be led by the expectations of the *haut ton*. I couldn't give two figs what society thinks.'

It occurred to her then that she sounded exactly like Charlotte did whenever she launched into one of her lectures. The notion made her laugh, and Mr Sharpe bestowed on Maria a hesitant smile.

'You are a singular creature, Miss Maria. No matter what happens. I hope you can accept my sincerest apologies for my sister's behaviour. What a way to repay the hospitality of your esteemed parents, and yourself.'

Maria, still in high humour, regarded him with a dazzling smile. 'There is nothing to forgive. Think no more of it, Mr Sharpe.'

The gentleman looked at her thoughtfully. 'A truly singular creature. I don't suppose that you would consent to call me Bertram? I should like it above all things.'

To which Maria *did* consent, and most heartily indeed.

343

STAVE XII.

Twelfth Night
TWELVE LORDS A LEAPING

So it is that a tale such as this did *indeed* finish with a wedding, and one that brought great joy to all, especially those who understood that the event was long overdue. Wakely Church – though not as full as it had been twelve days afore, for the couple wished only a quiet and intimate ceremony – had still found within itself a very merry congregation, to witness the happy marriage of one Frances Partridge to that of Merrywake's esteemed reverend, Witherington Soppe.

The lady was given away by Lord Charles Heysten and, at the insistence of his little sister, Faith (who had been given the honour of acting as the couple's flower girl), the ring bearer was none other than the child's favourite hen, Foi (much to the amusement of everybody in attendance, particularly Monsieur de Fortgibu who watched on with pride). It was widely agreed at the reception held in Wakely Hall's parlour earlier that morning that the newlyweds' nuptials had been a triumph, and that there could have been no better way to begin the household's annual Twelfth Night celebrations.

For Fernand Pépin, however, the happy occasion was marred by two things – first, that he would lose his dearest daughter Juliette to his native France on the morrow, together with a son-in-law of whom he had become extremely fond, as well as his oldest friend Benoît who would escort them; second, by way of the unfortunate events of the day before, the knowledge that his wife felt unable to speak to him about what had been happening under his roof, and that – worse – Fernand had been so wrapt up in the festivities of the Christmas season, he had not even noticed that something was amiss.

Truly, it was something the viscount was thoroughly ashamed of. Fernand had always prided himself on being attentive to everyone under his care but somehow he had neglected his own family, those who were closest to him of all.

He had not meant to be so remiss in his attentions. Fernand had troubled over the matter at the dinner table last evening, and should at least be admired for keeping his countenance when, later that night and in front of the whole company which had gathered together for charades in the drawing room, the Earl of Starling offered his hand in marriage to Miss Cordelia Sharpe, averting what would surely have been a terrible scandal (if, of course, the Busgroves could be prevailed upon not to wag their tongues). But while such an event should have instilled in him a relief most profound it left the viscount feeling only a sense of disgrace, for the whole sorry business might have been prevented if he had only noticed the Duke of Morley's behaviour towards his dear daughters. To be sure, if Fernand *had* known, the duke would have been put out on his dastardly heels.

Nicolas had professed himself deeply apologetic for the part he had inadvertently played. If he had been aware of his friend's unscrupulous behaviour at Wakely he would never have kept silent about that man's clandestine marriage, and while his son-in-law had been forgiven by all, the whole business for Fernand had rather put a dampener on the excitement that usually preluded his annual Twelfth Night Ball.

And he had nobody to blame for it but himself.

Had not Ambrosia tried to discuss her concerns with him? Fernand frowned as he attempted to remember her exact words and his response to them:

—*Sir Robert is far too attentive, my dear. He is turning their heads!*

—*Now, now, whatever is wrong with a little bit of harmless flirting?*

—*But it is not harmless! You know how impressionable the girls can be. Especially our Rosalie.*

—*Oh, I am quite convinced the duke has no designs upon them. 'Tis all perfectly innocent, as I said, and nothing untoward will come of it.*

—*He is a cad, Fernand, I am sure of it. Why, in Bath I saw—*

—*Dearest, you imagine things. A man of Morley's rank would*

346

not be so foolish as to behave in an inappropriate manner. Truly, there is nothing to worry about, and I would rather you did not upset Juliette and Nicolas about the matter, not so soon after the wedding.

At least, that is what Fernand remembered of the conversation. What with it being the night of his eldest daughter's marriage and Christmas Day to boot, he had perhaps imbibed too much of Mrs Denby's good punch to pay much attention to a curtain lecture, but now Fernand was unhappily conscious of not taking his wife's apprehensions to heart.

The fact of the matter was, he had not taken them seriously. His daughters were young and flighty – especially dear Rosalie – and did not everyone become a little too excitable during the Christmas season? But seeing his wife so overwrought yesterday, so very unlike herself, had made Fernand realise just how wrong he had been. Unusually for him, he was avoiding company – instead of joining the reception of the newlyweds where the guests were currently involved in a spirited game of snap-dragon (he could hear the *whoops!* and *huzzahs!* that resounded from three rooms down the corridor quite clearly), the viscount had removed to the privacy of his study, where he was at that moment writing out a character for Mrs Denby's son by means of a distraction.

He had already written to Sergeant Harrington inviting him to Wakely Hall that evening, for what with Phillip Denby's predicament being such a delicate one, the viscount felt a discussion face to face might be best. But since the snow had begun again in earnest Fernand had doubts as to whether the sergeant would arrive from London in time. As it was, the services of a scraper had been secured to clear Wakely Hall's drive, and he was only thankful many of his guests had already arrived and settled themselves at the Crown Lodge in the village, so their own journey that evening would not be too perilous. In any case, in the event that Sergeant Harrington should *not* arrive, Fernand had determined to put into place certain measures; he had already tasked the boy to write a deposition outlining all that occurred after he woke upon the battlefield at Toulouse, and sent a letter across to the French prison at Brest to see if they might provide a record of Mr Denby's confinement. The only matter remaining was Fernand's character reference, but being so very low of spirits . . .

Viscount Pépin sighed heavily and laid his swan-feather quill upon the leather-topped desk. Oh, whatever could he do to make up for his negligence!

There came then a knock upon the door to which he bade entry, and Fernand managed a weary smile when his third daughter, Charlotte, entered the room.

'*Père*,' said she, closing the study door behind her. 'Might I ask something of you?'

'*Bien sûr, ma chère.*'

Charlotte sat at the seat across from his desk. She looked most chagrined, and with concern her father asked what the matter was.

'I am vexed to ask you at all,' said she, a scowl upon her handsome face.

'Whyever so?'

'Because,' his daughter replied stoutly, 'I am dependent on your saying yes.'

'To?'

Charlotte pressed her lips. 'Lord Heysten has finally – after some days of teasing, I might add – consented to allow me to teach Faith.'

'Why, that is splendid!' And the viscount, despite his melancholy, *was* pleased, for he often bemoaned his daughter's lack of diversions. Juliette had always happily given her time in assisting the viscountess with the running of the household whilst Maria, when she was not enjoying (perhaps a little too much) the delights of the Bath and London seasons, might be found at her needle. Louisa and Rosalie were too young (and lacking any particular talent) to engage in entertainments beyond those of reading novels and attending the odd ball, but Charlotte – having no interest in any of these things – had always found herself somewhat at a loss. Fernand recognised her frustration; there were, after all, only so many books one could read about abolition and women's rights, and whilst his wife was quite correct in stating that the daughter of a viscount could not become a governess, Fernand knew that denying his daughter the pleasure of being useful would do more harm than good.

It would not be for ever, after all. Viscount Pépin felt sure of it.

'Splendid, yes,' said Charlotte now with a roll of her dark eyes, 'but having spoken to Mrs Thorpe, she has made me aware that I will be in need of a few more items other than the books already at my disposal.'

She then proceeded to provide a list of items conducive to

the teaching of a seven-year-old girl, and when she was done, she tossed her head.

'If you gave me my dowry, *Père*, I would not have to ask you, but as it is . . .'

Fernand did not commit to an answer. He knew, of course, how she felt, for Charlotte lamented the matter all too often. However, the viscount was a man of tradition, and he could not possibly allow his headstrong daughter full rein of her finances. Why, she would likely attempt some reformative enterprise and bankrupt herself in the process.

'I shall send for the items you require,' her father advised, making a note of each one. 'If we allow for the snow –' and here both Fernand and Charlotte looked out the window onto Wakely's white-covered lawns, where fresh flakes fell softly past the panes – 'you can expect them to arrive next week.'

Charlotte thanked him and moved to stand, but then, upon looking more intently at his face, sank back into the seat.

'Are you quite all right, *Père*? You look aggrieved, and that is not like you – especially not on the day of a Twelfth Night Ball.'

Fernand hesitated, touched that she should have noticed, and because she *had* noticed, the viscount felt obliged to be honest.

'In truth, I am not.'

Charlotte took her father's hand. The viscount sighed.

'Oh, but I am most ashamed of myself, Charlotte. I should have been more attentive to you all, instead of letting the spirit of the season cloud my judgement.'

'*Père* . . .'

'Truly, if I were your mother I should not wish to see or speak to me at all,' he said, and his daughter gently shook her head.

'You know that is not *Maman*'s way.'

'But mayhap it should be. I cannot fathom why she is not angrier with me.'

'*Père*, you are too hard on yourself. Besides, all has come well in the end, has it not?'

Fernand sighed. 'Be that as it may, it does not excuse my being so blind. Did *you* know of Morley's carryings-on?'

Charlotte hesitated. 'I confess I scarce paid the matter much attention. I knew Louisa, Maria and Rosalie – *especially* Rosalie – were somewhat smitten with him. Such fancies she had! Only a few days ago she was convinced she was to marry him, all because she *almost* caught Juliette's wedding bouquet, and became extremely defensive when I scolded her for it.' She shook her head despairingly. 'Why, oh why, must all my sisters be obsessed with marriage?'

A smile tugged at the viscount's lips. His dear girl, stubborn as a mule!

'Perhaps, *ma chère*, your sisters do not have the strength of character you possess. But Charlotte – marriage need not be a prison. Not if the couple love one another.'

She scoffed. 'You sound like *Maman*. Love is a myth, a fantasy.'

'Is it, when I love her and she loves me?'

He felt a tug at his heart then, for no matter what Ambrosia thought of his mistake regarding the Duke of Morley, he did not doubt his wife's affections, and at this remembrance Fernand's

351

spirits lifted a little. But Charlotte was frowning at her father's words.

'Your marriage, *Père*, is the exception not the rule.'

'But that does not mean ours is the only one. Look at Juliette and Nicolas. Our newly married friends, the Reverend and Mrs Soppe!' The frown between his daughter's eyebrows grew deeper. The viscount squeezed her fingers. 'I would have you happy, Charlotte, and books – no matter how much knowledge they contain, no matter how many adventures you might find therein – are not a substitute for happiness.'

'But a man is?'

Fernand (being a romantic at heart, and thus warming to the subject) smiled at his daughter.

'*Non*. But a marriage, a *true* marriage, is. Your sisters do not see matrimony as a prison, as you do. Maria considers matters in a more material sense, whilst Louisa wishes to be looked after and Rosalie adored. But you, Charlotte ... You need only find a gentleman to match your spirit, your humour, your beliefs.' Fernand squeezed her fingers. 'You need a partner who would challenge you, someone who you can respect, and then the rest of it, well, the rest of it will all fall into place. Do you really wish to spend your life alone?'

Charlotte was not looking at him, had instead directed her pensive gaze back to the snow-covered lawns where, at that moment, the two Wakely swans were ambling by the window.

'I wish for freedom, *Père*,' she murmured, watching the swans groom their feathers. 'To be independent. For my life to have meaning. No man can give me that, especially not a husband. He would wish me to be docile and bear his children year upon year, and that is simply not for me. Why is that so very hard for you and *Maman* to understand?'

'But *ma chère*,' he replied gently. 'Why must you think in absolutes? What you wish for is not impossible. You merely think it is.'

Charlotte said nothing. Again, Fernand pressed her fingers and then, an idea forming in his mind, patted Charlotte's hand as he released them.

'Come now,' he said, deliberately brisk – and his daughter's eyes swung back to his – 'let us speak no more of such matters. I shall send Marmery into the village with your order tomorrow. No point taking it today, when the snow prevents the post being collected. Is there anything you wish to add?'

'No,' she said faintly. 'No, thank you.'

'I do wonder, though,' the viscount added as Charlotte rose from the chair, 'at the price of the items you have listed here. A globe, a large one, will be costly. How much might little Faith need the subject of Geography, after all?'

'*Père*, of course she shall need Geography! She might wish to travel, after all, and—'

'Still,' Fernand continued, cutting her off, 'I suppose it can always be donated to Lord Heysten, when work on the park has been completed to accommodate his new enterprise. I daresay he shall appreciate it, given the expense of such a restoration. The estate has long been neglected, after all.'

Charlotte's brows knit in confusion.

'Enterprise? What do you mean?'

The viscount dipped his quill in the inkwell. 'Oh,' he replied, not a little sly, 'I spoke with him about it the other day – his lordship asked my opinion in regards to turning Heysten Park into a charitable establishment for the poor and destitute. Indeed, he even applied for the advice of the Thorpes, since he considered including a finishing school in the plans.'

'A finishing school,' Charlotte echoed, to which Fernand – for he heard how this news affected her – hid a smile.

'Y-e-s,' he replied idly as he wrote out the relevant directions at the top of Charlotte's list. 'Something about giving those less fortunate an opportunity to learn new skills to aid them in finding suitable employment.'

His daughter stared.

'But where would he and Faith live?'

'There is a sizeable dowager's cottage on the estate he thinks would suit them admirably, rather than residing at the main house.'

'Oh,' Charlotte said after a lengthy pause. 'He ... he did not say.'

Fernand, having composed himself, met her gaze once more, and was thrilled to see that his daughter appeared every bit as intrigued as he had hoped she might.

'Did he not? Well, perhaps he wished to settle on his plans before revealing them. 'Tis an awful lot to manage on his own, and there will be much to deliberate. Still, it is early days yet, so you need not fear – you shall have plenty of time in which to teach Faith everything you desire before she removes there to live with him.'

'Yes.'

Her reply was faint, but not so faint that her father could not hear the confusion under which she was now suffering . . . which was precisely what Fernand had hoped to achieve.

'Now, my dear,' he said, 'I simply must finish writing this character for Mr Denby before I get ready for the evening. Would you mind very much if . . .?'

His daughter inclined her dark head. 'Of course, *Père*. I shall . . .' and here Charlotte trailed off, and in turn departed the viscount's study, closing the door very quietly but firmly behind her.

Fernand chuckled. Lord Heysten – so he had suspected almost from the first moment he met the man – was a perfect match for his headstrong daughter. Though the gentleman was nearer in age to Ambrosia than Charlotte, the fortune he had inherited from his father – together with the one he amassed by his own means (though unfortunate in its origins) – was more than ample, and his ambition to bestow his wealth on those less fortunate ampler still. Now that the viscount had sown the seed he felt sure that, in time, his dear Charlotte might find it in herself to recognise that no other man than Charles Heysten could match her so perfectly in both temperament and manner of feeling.

She was, after all, a creature to be guided gently and never, ever forced.

Outside, the swans ambled out of sight. The snow continued to fall. The viscount's chuckle ceased, and his expression fell into a frown.

If his meddling were successful, there would be another wedding in Merrywake by the time the first daffodil sprouted in spring. Two daughters married – how delighted the viscountess would be! Nonetheless that still left Maria, Louisa and Rosalie. Ambrosia had professed two nights before that the Sharpe brothers would suit their daughters *very* well, and while they were not so dashing nor as rich as Sir Robert, they were decent, affable gentlemen. A pity about their sister. But at least scandal had been averted, and so there could now be no impediment that prevented a union. Fernand liked them, too, for Bertram, Humphrey and Tarquin Sharpe were men of his own ilk – no one, whether they be servant, shopkeeper or squire, was beneath or above their notice, a fact they made abundantly clear by their generous praise of Mrs Denby's son who had assisted them on the roadside, and it was this train of thought that prompted the viscount to reach for the piece of paper he had set aside when Charlotte entered his study.

Indeed, Fernand thought as he set the nib of his quill to the page, though he had remarked to his wife some days afore that she had wedding bells ringing in her ears, he also wished to see his daughters settled.

Wakely Hall was a buzz of activity. The snow had stopped two hours before, and the scraper had succeeded (under the observation of Mr Moss) in clearing the driveway so that the guests staying at the Crown would experience no difficulty arriving in their carriages. The guests already in residence chattered excitably at the prospect of a wonderful evening and marvelled at the abundant spread of food the servants had diligently been arranging upon the dining room table this past hour (some of which Miss Louisa Pépin and Mr Humphrey Sharpe had already pilfered when no one was looking). The musicians came promptly at seven, and having set themselves up upon the raised platform at the far end of the ballroom could be heard tuning their instruments even from the viscount's dressing room two floors up, where at that very moment his valet, Ralph Hornby, was brushing lint from his tail coat, and Mr Palamedes was circling their legs with loud contented purrs.

In previous years, with the ball being a whisper away from starting, Viscount Pépin would have been beside himself with excitement. Like his daughter Maria, the Twelfth Night Ball was his favourite social event of the year, but it was troubling to him that – though some hours had passed – he *still* felt that deep-seated melancholy from earlier. It was a damn nuisance, and as he regarded his valet in the mirror he was unpleasantly reminded that his daughters had not been the Duke of Morley's only victims.

'Hornby,' said Fernand, having cleared his throat and made Mr Palamedes jump, 'might I enquire as to how the housemaid Miss Hart does?'

Mr Hornby hesitated, then resumed his brushing.

'She has been kept busy by Mrs Wilson, my lord, but I understand she is in rather downhearted spirits.'

'Oh dear. Oh dear, dear, dear,' Fernand murmured, his guilt growing ever stronger.

One might be surprised to find that a man of his elevated status should care about the well-being of one of his maids, but the truth of it was, he did. In truth, he genuinely *liked* his servants, and wished to know they were happy. The fact that Miss Hart was not bothered him greatly, and anxiously the viscount tweaked his cravat.

'Do please advise Miss Hart that Sir Robert is no longer in residence at Wakely, if she does not know it already, and that I hope she will still come to the ball. She is very welcome, and I can only hope she will be able to put this whole sorry business behind her.'

His valet inclined his head. 'The news had reached us belowstairs, my lord, but I shall let Miss Hart know the invitation is still open to her, rest assured.'

'Thank you, Hornby,' he said, as the valet returned the lint brush to its case. 'I assume you will be attending?'

'Oh yes.'

'Very good! And the others, too, I trust? I should, ah, like to congratulate Marmery for his excellent riddles, though we were all mightily disappointed the Busgrove boy got to the answers before the rest of us.' Mr Hornby's lip twitched – Fernand saw it do so in the gilt mirror. 'My daughter explained what happened. Most put out she is, and I too, I must confess. The spirit of the game was quite ruined.'

'My lord,' said Mr Hornby quietly after a moment. 'I wish to apologise on Mr Marmery's behalf and assure you that none of us would take advantage of you, or any one of the family. We are all very aware how well we're treated here at Wakely. I was gratified to receive my Christmas box this year. I have never owned such a fine set of oil paints. And a gold colour, too! The goose eggs came out beautifully when I used it on them.'

Fernand was mollified at this and acknowledged the valet's words with a nod. With a small bow in turn Mr Hornby set about retrieving his master's dancing shoes from the wardrobe.

'How much,' Fernand asked, pushing his stockinged feet into the soft black pumps, 'did Busgrove pay Marmery, do you know?'

'A pound, my lord,' came the guarded reply.

'Hmm. A pretty sum.'

His valet ducked his head. 'I understand Mr Marmery is saving so that he and Miss Allen can marry. Since Miss Brown has become engaged to Mr Hodge, Mr Marmery has been rather keen to speed things along. However, I'm sure, my lord, if you were to ask for the money to be returned it would be willingly given. I know Mr Marmery would be horrified to have caused offence.'

But Fernand waved Mr Hornby off. 'No, no. The deed is done, and no real harm has come of it, in the end. I suppose it probably did Maria good to lose for once. She has been crowned queen one too many times over the years.'

Neither man spoke for a moment, and Mr Palamedes took the opportunity to curl up in the brush case, which had not yet been shut.

'So, our footman wishes to marry Miss Allen, does he? And Miss Brown is betrothed to young Mr Hodge?'

'Yes, my lord,' answered his valet, and the viscount found it in himself to smile wistfully.

'Merrywake does not seem short of lovers, does it?' Fernand turned and looked at the younger man appraisingly. 'Do you have a sweetheart, Hornby? Some pretty miss?'

The valet shifted upon the Indian rug.

'No, sir, I do not.'

'Well!' exclaimed Fernand, for he was much surprised. Mr Hornby was a handsome fellow, make no mistake. 'A fine man like you will find a girl at some point, I expect. But who shall you dance with tonight?'

'Oh,' said Mr Hornby, a spot of colour appearing on his cheeks. 'I expect I shall dance with someone, my lord.'

'My dear?'

Fernand turned at the voice of his wife, who was at that moment poking her head from behind the dressing room door, and he instantly forgot everything else.

Ambrosia Pépin – a beautiful woman when young, grown lovelier still upon passing into her middle years – was dressed in a shimmering gown of white silk embellished with silver embroidery, and looked to Fernand a picture, worthy of the Dutch masters themselves, which he told her with pride.

The viscountess trilled a laugh. 'Nonsense! It is only the dress. The dressmaker did a splendid job. Mr Hornby,' said she then, 'would you excuse us? You will need to get ready yourself, after all.'

'Yes, my lady.'

The valet bowed deeply, and left Viscount and Viscountess Pépin quite alone, except for Mr Palamedes who snored softly in the brush box, ginger tail curled about his body, touching his fine pink nose.

'I spoke with Charlotte earlier,' Ambrosia said once the bedroom door had shut. 'She says you are still ruminating.'

Fernand turned away from her, tweaking the cuffs of his tail coat in the mirror. 'Can you blame me? *Do* you blame me? If I had only listened—'

His wife raised her hand to indicate he should cease speaking.

'Was I a little vexed that you dismissed my concerns so readily?' She inclined her head, and the white crystals adorning her hair bobbed on their silver wires. 'Yes, I was. Do I hope that from this whole sorry affair you might learn something? Of course. And judging from the guilt you are so clearly suffering under, I can see that you already have.' Ambrosia smiled at his reflection, then proceeded to wrap her arms about his waist and laid her cheek upon his shoulder. 'But all is well. Our girls have not been permanently injured, Miss Hart shall keep her place. The duke has gone, and the Earl of Starling has saved us from any scandal that might have come from it. Most of our guests can be counted upon not to whisper a word, although . . .'

She trailed off, and Fernand knew instinctively of whom his wife was thinking.

'The Busgroves?'

Ambrosia *tsked*. 'They are not bad sorts. 'Tis the son, Nigel, who worries me. Such a prattling buffoon he is, and when in his cups far worse. I am sure he had already imbibed from the wassail bowl before our dancing lesson yesterday. If he had not, I'm certain he would never have told Miss Falshaw about his cheating at the riddles.'

But Fernand was nodding. 'I believe I have already come upon the solution.'

Viscountess Pépin turned so that husband and wife stood face to face.

'Oh? And what is that?'

'Well, you know I have been considering an investment in pineapples and rely upon the Busgroves to manage my money wisely. This afternoon I intimated that if Mr Busgrove and his family did not hold their tongues about the whole sorry matter, I might be forced to take our finances elsewhere.'

Ambrosia laughed, and such a lovely sound it was that Fernand took great pleasure in it.

'Oh, what a canny ploy! Mr Busgrove would be horrified to think you might leave him on account of gossipmongering and will be sure to instruct his son to keep his silence.'

They both chuckled together a moment, but then Fernand's smile faded, and Ambrosia wrapt her arms about his neck.

'*Je suis désolé, très chère*,' the viscount said to her. 'I promise never to be so blind again.'

'All is well,' the viscountess said once more, and echoing too the earlier words of their daughter. 'Think no more on it. Tomorrow is Twelfth Day, and marks for us all the beginning of a brand-new year. Mistakes shall be made, as mistakes inevitably are, but they will be *new* ones, Fernand, and we have no room to accommodate the old. So let us greet our guests – I hear the first carriages arrive, don't you?'

Fernand *could* hear the rumble of wheels upon the driveway below, the snort of horses, the merry chatter as lords and ladies entered the doors of Wakely Hall, and for the first time that day felt his excitement grow.

'I think,' said he, 'that is a perfectly splendid idea,' and to confirm the fact he planted a very tender kiss upon his wife's smiling mouth.

For some, allowing one's servants to intermingle with members of the higher social classes might be frowned upon, but for the Pépin family it was a tradition they had upheld from the very first year they settled in Merrywake, and neither one of them cared a whit if others should object to it. When asked why they allowed the servants' ball to become part of their Twelfth Night festivities, the viscount and viscountess explained that it was a mediaeval tradition, and everyone should be thankful they had foregone the convention of allowing the servants to become the masters. Their guests would certainly find much to complain of then! Besides, the Twelfth Night Ball was the perfect opportunity for the Pépins to let their servants know how grateful they were for all that they did, and should not everybody do the same?

There were certain people who would vehemently deny such a suggestion (one might suppose Miss Cordelia Sharpe, soon to be the new Countess of Starling, to be one of them) but more often than not Fernand's guests found the idea enterprising, and over the years they had perfected a list of guests who – if they did not agree with Fernand's more romantic sensibilities – would happily overlook them in the spirit of the occasion. As he descended the garlanded staircase (such delightful scents of bay and pine!), his elegant wife on his arm, the viscount was gratified to find footmen conversing with lords and maids with ladies, the divide already successfully breached, and upon seeing Wakely's cook and her son speaking quietly together in a candle-lit alcove, Fernand excused himself from Ambrosia's clasp and approached them.

'Mrs Denby,' said he with a bow, to which she offered up a curtsey and greeting. 'I saw the dining room table earlier, and cannot be more pleased. You have positively outdone yourself.'

Indeed, the great table had been extended and was filled with a delectable spread of breads, cold plates and sweets – little butter cows could be found dotted between dishes of seeded rolls, poached eggs, and a generous offering of Stilton, Wiltshire and cream cheeses (it had taken all of Fernand's self-control not to demolish the latter there and then). So too were upon the large table slices of roast chicken and ham, boiled round, pick-led salmon, and mackerel topped with fennel and mint, together with biscuits infused with ginger and orange, glistening jellies and syllabubs, honeyed dates and sugared plums, little savoury pies of cranberry and pork, and a large platter of mince pies, while the silver wassail bowl stood directly in the middle, its sides shimmering with the dancing flames of candlelight.

'I cannot wait to see what hot culinary delights shall be served when we break for supper! There will be goose and ven-ison, I presume?'

'Oh, never fear, my lord,' assured the cook, with a note of pride in her voice. 'Myself and Miss Allen have been hard at work – you shall not be disappointed.'

'I declare, madam, I never could be.'

The cook thanked him, and once again dipped her knees.

'But,' remarked Fernand, 'I did not see your delicious Twelfth Night cake at the table as it usually is? You *have* made one, have you not?'

'Forgive me, my lord, I have made a cake but …' The cook hesitated. 'I'm afraid I've already caught one or two of the, ah, guests, stealing rather a few of the mince pies, and felt it best to bring the cake up at the appointed hour as to prevent anyone else from helping themselves to a slice.'

Fernand could not help but smile. He could tell by Mrs Denby's hesitation that the culprit must have been none other than his daughter Louisa, no doubt aided by one of the Sharpe brothers. Like himself, Louisa always did have a long stomach, but of late she had become rather more gluttonous, and since Twelfth Night Cake was his favourite festive dish in all the world, he too did not want to risk its ruin before midnight.

Once he had assured the cook she had done the right thing, the viscount turned to Mrs Denby's son, who stood quietly at her side.

'I wished to tell you that I have written your character,' advised Fernand, 'and feel sure it will commend you to Sergeant Harrington. I hope you can forget about it all for this evening at least – I should hate for your enjoyment of the ball to be lessened.'

'Yes, my lord,' replied Phillip Denby, though he did not look at ease at all. 'I cannot tell you how grateful I am for your support.'

'Think nothing of it, my good man. But I see you hold your whistle. Are you not to dance this evening?'

The piper shook his head. 'I am not much for dancing, Viscount Pépin, and so would prefer to play with the musicians. I used to play at the assemblies held in the village, if you recall?'

'Quite so! And with young George Jenkins, I understand. A great shame. There is a drummer here tonight, I think?'

Mr Denby nodded. 'He and I are to be seated beside one another. It will be strange not to have George next to me, but pleasant to hear a bodhrán drum again.'

'Well,' said Fernand, keen to remove the sadness that had appeared on the young man's face, 'if you feel inclined to rest between sets, please do – I am sure there are many ladies here in want of a partner. See there, for instance,' he added, with a twinge of his earlier guilt. 'Miss Hart stands quite alone.'

And so the housemaid did in a pretty frock of simple blue cotton, clutching a lace shawl as she lingered beside the garlanded staircase, looking distinctly uncomfortable, and when he marked her Mr Denby coloured.

'I think Molly is still feeling a little out of sorts, my lord.'

'I truly am sorry for it. Oh, but look,' he said as his valet, Mr Hornby, approached the housemaid and offered his hand, which Miss Hart took with a small and grateful smile. 'That's better. Much better!'

There came then winding through the bustling chatter of the entrance hall, the plucking of violin strings.

'Ah,' said Mr Denby. 'I believe the dancing is about to begin

366

and so I must join my fellow musicians. Mother, my lord – if you will excuse me?'

At which he was excused, and the viscount and cook parted ways, whereupon Ambrosia was soon beside him.

'Are you well, my love?'

'Extremely,' Fernand replied, clasping her hand in the crook of his arm. 'Now that we are to begin, I feel much more at ease.'

And he did feel more at ease; as the viscount and viscountess entered the grandly furnished ballroom, decorated so beautifully with pear-crowned festive garlands, gilded mirrors and candles that made the room glow serenely in a soft golden light, and seeing so many pleasant faces – *haut ton* and domestic alike – it all gave Fernand a feeling of great joy, a joy which was heightened by seeing his daughters being led into the ballroom. There were Juliette and Nicolas, Maria and Bertram Sharpe, followed closely behind by his brothers Humphrey, who accompanied Louisa, and Tarquin with a blushing Rosalie on his arm ... Fernand frowned as he searched for Charlotte amidst the crowd but could not see her. Was she with Lord Heysten perhaps? But alas, he was already standing in line for Paine's 'First Set of Quadrilles', partnered by a positively awestruck Loveday Lucas.

The dancing commenced. The violins and cellos sang across their strings, the horn resounded deeply, Mr Denby's tin whistle flew, and the drummer beat a hearty tempo on his drum. As was always the case at the very beginning of Viscount Pépin's Twelfth Night Ball, the servants struggled somewhat with the steps, but soon found the intricacies of them did not matter and there was much laughing to be had by all, particularly Miss Allen, Mr Marmery, Mr Hornby and Miss Hart, who together made a most jovial crew as they danced together in their squares. 'Mr Beveridge's Maggot' was performed next (led by a very sour-faced Miss Cordelia Sharpe and the Earl of Starling), then a livelier and less formal country dance during which Mr Hodge (wearing a lovely new waistcoat) was convinced to laugh at his missteps by his newly betrothed Miss Brown, after which a reel followed, and then another country dance.

All this the viscount observed with great pleasure. So too did he observe that little Faith (who had been allowed a few hours to attend the ball, for she had never experienced one before and was extremely excitable at the prospect) had been taken in hand by Monsieur de Fortgibu, leading his pet hens on their leads during the dance of 'Grimstock' (which Mrs Denby and the gardener, Mr Cobb – having now recovered from his cold – appeared to enjoy immensely), and many others found amusement by steadily depleting the dining room of food and conversing together upon the chairs that lined the walls. All manner of topics might have been spoken of, but Fernand – dancing a jig with a surprisingly high-spirited Mrs Wilson – marked with keen interest the Busgroves in an intimate tête-à-tête, and sincerely hoped they were behaving themselves. By the time the Warwicks and Marshchilds requested an allemande, Fernand deemed it time to retreat to the dining room where the table had been generously replenished with hot dishes.

White soup! Dishes of brawn and sturgeon! Warden

pie, beef and mutton, a medley of winter vegetables and of course, a crisp golden goose, succulent venison, and beautifully spiced plum puddings! No felicity could ever be greater than a festive banquet, thought Fernand, closing his eyes in delight over a forkful of rosemary-infused potatoes, and though many similar dishes had been served at Wakely since St Nicholas Day, the viscount could not remember when he had enjoyed a meal more.

Between the savoury and sweet dishes, a lively game of rounds was played using the rhyme 'The Twelve Days of Christmas' which Miss Falshaw was gratified to win, and after supper the dancing resumed, whereupon 'The Midnight Ramble' was performed by all who knew it, but Fernand – somewhat weary from consuming too much of Mrs Denby's excellent food – decided to take a turn about the garden. The night air was sharp with cold, but the sky was clear and filled with twinkling stars. He was pleased to find the snow had stopped completely, and that a path had been cleared down towards the pond.

He was about to turn upon it when from the corner of his eye he saw two figures in dance. A minuet was at that point being played by the musicians, and being a slower dance conducted in triple metre it was conducive to more intimate steps, so it was a surprise indeed that he saw the two figures were none other than his valet and the gardener's assistant, William Moss!

'My lord,' the latter stuttered as the two men broke apart. 'We were . . . it is not . . .'

'Whatever are you two fellows doing, dancing together outside in this cold?'

Mr Hornby – looking almost strangely afraid – pressed his hands together in a plea.

'My lord,' he said in hushed tones, ''tis just ... that is to say we ...'

Fernand's face cleared, for then he realised what the two must be about.

'Ah! You are teaching Moss to dance, are you not, Hornby? I wondered where you'd got to as I have not seen you since you took Miss Hart to the floor. I hope you have both eaten?'

It took a moment to receive an answer, and it was Mr Moss who managed it.

'Thank you, my lord, yes. We ate in the servants' hall. Found it all a little overwhelming, you see, what with—'

The viscount nodded sagely. 'I quite understand. But I am glad you wish to participate, nonetheless. Do not worry too much of the footwork, though, Hornby – on the livelier jigs no one is paying the slightest bit of attention.'

Mr Hornby hesitated before breathing out a sigh of relief, which Fernand thought a little odd, for whatever should he be relieved about?

'Well then,' said he with an encouraging clap. 'Carry on, carry on!'

And so they did.

Fernand left the men there in the shadows of the portico (what good friends they must be!) and continued down the path, flanked by his lovely yew trees, silvered with thick frost, humming a festive tune. But he fell silent as he realised on his approach to the pond, where his poor little Edmond lay in eternal rest, that, sitting at the edge of the pond with their backs to him, were Lord Heysten and his own dear Charlotte.

'You understand, don't you?' the gentleman was murmuring, the breath from his lips clouding in the cold night air. 'I cannot have children. I am not even sure I wanted them to begin with.'

Charlotte said nothing. Oh, how her father wished to see the expression on her face!

'But I have no objection to children as a rule. Why else would I have taken to Faith's care?'

'Guilt, I assume,' came Charlotte's wry answer, and Fernand resisted the urge to shake her. But Lord Heysten uttered a small laugh without humour, and in the moonlit dark the viscount saw his lordship nod.

'You're perfectly right. I do feel guilt. I am ashamed of all my father, and his father, did over the years, of how so many people suffered because of them. But it all ends with me, Charlotte, I promise you that. I shall make Heysten Park prosperous again, and use it to do some good in the world. I . . .' The man paused. 'I'd be honoured if you would help me make that possible.'

Viscount Pépin shut his eyes, prayed that his daughter would acquiesce, and nervously waited for her reply.

'You would have my dowry,' said Charlotte cautiously. 'You'd take it and smother me.'

'Fudge. I do not give one damn about your dowry. I have plenty of money at my disposal without the need of yours. If you married me, you could do with it whatever you wish. Of course, if you wished to help financially with my endeavours that would be a grand thing, but I've no expectations on that score.'

'But—'

'Good God, you're an obstinate creature. Do you like me at all?'

Fernand heard his daughter's intake of breath and then, her whispered answer:

'I do.'

Charles Heysten hesitated. 'And do you think that liking of me might one day grow into love? Enough that you would consider marriage?'

For endless moments Charlotte did not speak. But then, finally, she replied in the only way Viscount Pépin's strong-willed daughter could. She said, 'Perhaps.'

Perhaps.

Perhaps was not a yes. But it was as good *as* a yes, and Fernand, smiling widely, retreated as silently as his feet might carry him, thankful that the snow had been cleared from the path so he might make his escape unheard. Up he went, through the avenue of yew trees, onto the portico where Misters Hornby and Moss danced still, and back into the gleaming warmth of the ballroom.

A country dance was in full swing, and so crowded was the room Fernand almost did not see Sergeant Harrington standing at the fireplace, where at that very moment he was shaking Phillip Denby's hand. When the older man released him, Bess Denby took both the sergeant's hands and kissed them in turn. Fernand would have endeavoured to brave the hot press of the dancing crowd in that moment to join the three of them, but the viscount felt a gentle hand on his elbow, and turned to see his darling Ambrosia, pink-faced and merry, at his side.

'Sergeant Harrington arrived a quarter of an hour ago,' she told him with a smile. 'I hope you do not mind but I retrieved the character you wrote for Mr Denby and, well, you can see the result.'

'So I can, my love, so I can. Ah, *ma chérie*,' he breathed, linking his arm about her shoulders to hold the viscountess close. 'How well it has all turned out. What a wonderful night it is proving to be!'

'I do agree. And see, Fernand, the Twelfth Night Cake has been brought up, a fresh wassail bowl too –' and here Ambrosia gestured to the large console table next to the French doors, where a steaming silver punch bowl rested beside the largest fruit cake the viscount had ever beheld. It was twice the size of last year's, and Fernand's mouth positively watered at the sight of its elaborately decorated ornaments of royal icing, its pink and white top near groaning under the weight of sugar figures of swans and crowns and pears. Oh, thought Fernand, what complete and utter joy!

It was then that the dance came to an end, and feeling now in such delightfully high spirits, he called the musicians to a halt.

'Dear friends and family,' called Fernand, and his guests turned their attention wholly to him. 'Our Twelfth Night festivities are almost at an end, and so I urge you all to claim a glass, and avail yourselves of this marvellous wassail bowl, so we might raise a toast.'

373

It was some minutes before this task could be achieved, during which Mr Hornby and Mr Moss, together with Lord Heysten and Charlotte, surreptitiously rejoined the clamouring party. But soon Fernand held reign once more, and looking upon the smiling faces in Wakely Hall's grand candlelit ballroom, he drew breath to speak.

'These past few years of conflict have been a trial. We have lost many good men, and there can be no greater sorrow to be had at such an unhappy truth.' The room grew sombre. Nods of heads abounded. 'But this festive season, we might find it in ourselves to look to the future – to seek happiness and peace in the years to come. That will shape itself in different ways for all of us, I realise. We stand together this evening as equals but I know that, in rank at least, we are not.' Fernand saw the furtive looks between maids and counts, of footmen and noblewomen alike. 'We can, however, be equal in spirit, and learn to appreciate our fellow men. We can learn to be humble, to be kind. I ask that, now we have begun a new year, we remember the joy we have each experienced by joining together this night. I ask you to recognise that each of us – no matter our station – has the capability to love and be loved, and not to forget that each of us is deserving of it.'

There were murmurs of assent, a melody of agreements. Fernand paused, looked then at his wife, his daughters, and smiled.

'I have learnt a precious lesson this past week. I am ashamed to say that I have been guilty of blindness – I became so enthralled by the excitement of Christmastime that I forgot to pay attention to that which was under my very nose. I have realised now the error of my ways and implore you all to recognise that the greatest gift any of us can give, is the gift of your care and attention. Do not forget to whom we owe our happiness. Do not forget to honour them.'

The viscount raised his glass and caught the tantalising scent of apples, brandy and spice.

'The only thing that remains is to thank you all for coming tonight, and say to you all, as is the custom on Twelfth Night, good health! Be well!'

'Drink well!' came the traditional chorused reply, at which the party drank deeply, and – feeling now overcome with perfect happiness – Viscount Pépin put his arm about Viscountess Pépin's shoulders and raised his glass once more.

'Merry Christmas,' he cried. 'Merry Christmas and a Happy New Year, one and all!'

FINIS.

THE
TWELVE DAYS
OF
CHRISTMAS.

THE first day of Chriftmas,
My true love fent to me
A partridge in a pear tree.

The fecond day of Chriftmas,
My true love fent to me,
Two turtle doves, and
A partridge in a pear tree.

The third day of Chriftmas,
My true love fent to me
Three French hens,
Two turtle doves, and
A partridge in a pear tree.

The fourth day of Chriftmas,
My true love fent to me
Four colly birds,
Three French hens,
Two turtle doves, and
A partridge in a pear tree.

The fifth day of Chriftmas,
My true love fent to me
Five gold rings,
Four colly birds,
Three French hens,
Two turtle doves, and
A partridge in a pear tree.

The fixth day of Chriftmas,
My true love fent to me
Six geefe a laying,
Five gold rings,
Four colly birds,
Three French hens,
Two turtle doves, and
A partridge in a pear tree.

The feventh day of Chriftmas,
My true love fent to me
Seven fwans a fwimming,
Six geefe a laying,
Five gold rings,
Four colly birds,
Three French hens,
Two turtle doves, and
A partridge in a pear tree.

The eight day of Chriftmas,
My true love fent to me
Eight maids a milking,
Seven fwans a fwimming,
Six geefe a laying,
Five gold rings,
Four colly birds,

Three French hens,
Two turtle doves, and
A partridge in a pear tree.

The ninth day of Chriftmas,
My true love fent to me
Nine drummers drumming,
Eight maids a milking,
Seven fwans a fwimming,
Six geefe a laying,
Five gold rings,
Four colly birds,
Three French hens,
Two turtle doves, and
A partridge in a pear tree.

The tenth day of Chriftmas,
My true love fent to me
Ten pipers piping,
Nine drummers drumming,
Eight maids a milking,
Seven fwans a fwimming,
Six geefe a laying,
Five gold rings,
Four colly birds,
Three French hens,
Two turtle doves, and
A partridge in a pear tree.

The eleventh day of Chriftmas,
My true love fent to me
Eleven ladies dancing,
Ten pipers piping,
Nine drummers drumming,
Eight maids a milking,
Seven fwans a fwimming,
Six geefe a laying,
Five gold rings,
Four colly birds,
Three French hens,
Two turtle doves, and
A partridge in a pear tree.

The twelfth day of Chriftmas,
My true love fent to me
Twelve lords a leaping,
Eleven ladies dancing,
Ten pipers piping,
Nine drummers drumming,
Eight maids a milking,
Seven fwans a fwimming,
Six geefe a laying,
Five gold rings,
Four colly birds,
Three French hens,
Two turtle doves, and
A partridge in a pear tree.

Angus, Printer.

AUTHOR'S NOTE & ACKNOWLEDGEMENTS

The earliest known publication of 'The Twelve Days of Christmas' appeared in a children's book titled *Mirth Without Mischief* which was published in London in 1780 (its illustrations have been used here as chapter headers), alongside a broadsheet published in Newcastle about the same time. It was claimed the carol had been sung at 'King Pepin's Ball' and, having discovered all this during one of my many stints down a Google rabbit hole, I knew that I had to write a book about it. Considering that the last day of the festive period culminated in the Georgian tradition of throwing a Twelfth Night Ball, this gave me the perfect springboard to work from, enabling me to consider what Christmastime might have been like at a country estate such as Wakely Hall.

I had a lot of fun writing these stories, and aside from it being a pure pleasure project, *The Twelve Days of Christmas* is also my homage to Jane Austen and Georgette Heyer, two authors who have been incredibly influential to me over the years as both a writer and a reader of historical fiction. (Their works were where it started for me, after all – *Pride and Prejudice* and *Regency Buck* have a lot to answer for.) As such, the construction of the narrative is deliberately formal to emulate the longer sentence structures of Austen, and while *A Pocket Dictionary of the Vulgar Tongue* by Captain Francis Grose – originally published in 1785 – provided some era-specific etymological humdingers to add some extra flavour, generally I attempted to maintain a style that was readable and accessible in a way similar to that of Heyer, yet still undeniably 'me', a statement with which I hope my readers will agree.

In that vein, I have never been one to ignore the darker aspects of Georgian Britain, and though the temptation to completely romanticise these stories in the spirit of the season was very great, I couldn't help adding in some harsh realities. I certainly could not write anything set in the Regency period without acknowledging the devastation of the Napoleonic Wars, nor could I ignore the truths of childbirth, the sometimes bleak elements of domestic life for servants, nor the often-corrupt behaviour of the aristocracy. Still, I've tried to keep the overall theme light-hearted, and I think that cheerful spirit is obvious in each of these stories. Aside from being somewhat tongue-in-cheek in terms of how some of the twelve gifts are portrayed, I really wanted to have fun with them and found little ways to do that by borrowing from historic sources.

For instance, Monsieur de Fortgibu was inspired by a genuine early nineteenth-century account I read in a *Reader's Digest* volume titled *Mysteries of the Unexplained*, about that gentleman's encounters with French poet Émile Deschamps and their shared love of plum pudding, which made me smile so much I just had to add de Fortgibu into one of the stories, and the idea of him having three hens as pets was so delightfully silly I simply couldn't resist! My use of the surname Pépin came, as you may have guessed, from *Mirth Without Mischief*, mentioned above. The poem that preludes the stories themselves was taken from a pamphlet originally published in 1730 titled *Round about our Coal Fire: OR, Christmas Entertainments*, and I chose to use references to it within the story arc wherever possible, whether they were actions, foodstuffs or people; Prue, Ralph and Molly et al. all found their way in, but I wonder if you can spot the coded name of Dick Merryman too? As a side, 'Heysten' is also a little Easter egg that I couldn't resist adding in, although the solution to that one is a little more obvious.

One other name holds special meaning for me. When I was fourteen and first decided I wanted to write historical fiction, I took to reading eighteenth-century-set 'corset rippers' where many of the character names were, well, rather ridiculous. As a joke my parents kept providing equally ridiculous names for my own stories, over which we had many a laugh. I still have a list of them which my mother keeps adding to when the mood takes her, but one name in particular always stuck. I knew one day it would appear in *something* I wrote, and it's a constant source of delight for me to be able to use the name in this collection – the Reverend Witherington Soppe was the creation of my mother, and because of that this collection is dedicated to her. Thank you, Mum (and Dad), for providing endless amusement during those name-making sessions, and supporting my lofty dreams of authorship, even then.

Of course, *The Twelve Days of Christmas* could not have become a reality at all if not for the continued support of a wonderful team of people working fiercely behind the scenes. Thanks as always to my agent, Juliet Mushens, and everyone at Mushens Entertainment; my editor, Liz Foley, and all at Harvill and Vintage; my publishers in the US and in translation; cover designer extraordinaire Micaela Alcaino; passionate booksellers, enthusiastic readers, fellow authors, trusted friends and family (you all know who you are) – everything is possible because of you.

CREDITS

Vintage would like to thank everyone who worked on the
publication of *THE TWELVE DAYS OF CHRISTMAS*

Agent
Juliet Mushens

Editor
Liz Foley

Editorial
Chris Sturtivant

Copy-editor
Mary Chamberlain

Proofreaders
Gabbie Chant
Carolyn McAndrew

**Managing
Editorial**
Lucy Chaudhuri

Contracts
Amy Green

Design
Lucy Thorne
Micaela Alcaino

Digital
Anna Baggaley

Claire Dolan
Brydie Scott
Charlotte Ridsdale
Zaheerah Khalik

Inventory
Rebecca Evans

Publicity
Jessie Spivey

Finance
Ed Grande
Aya Daghem

Marketing
Sam Rees-Williams

Production
Konrad Kirkham
Polly Dorner

Sales
Nathaniel
Breakwell
Malissa Mistry
Justin Ward-Turner
Ben Taplan
Lewis Cain

Nick Cordingly
Kate Gunn
Sophie Dwyer
Maiya Grant
Danielle Appleton
Phoebe Edwards
Amber Blundell
Rachel Cram
David Atkinson
Amanda Dean
Andy Taylor
Dan Higgins

Rights
Lucy
Beresford-Knox
Celia Long
Beth Wood
Annamika Singh
Agnes Watters
Lucie Deacon
Liv Diomedes
Jake Dickson

Audio
Nile Faure-Bryan
Hannah Cawse

Thank you to our group companies and our sales teams
around the world

385